LUNATIC

The Kensington Killers
(Book One)

MIRA GIBSON

Prologue

THE DARKENED SIDEWALK smelled of exhaust fumes and dank trash, which the brutal downpour seemed to magnify, kicking up all kinds of odors.

Vehicles rushed down the avenue in both directions, headlights blazing, tires bouncing over potholes and splashing puddles. The swishing sound of never ending traffic in concert with the dull hum of the city.

Danielle Foster angled her umbrella against the stiff wind, its nylon canopy taking a beating, as she shuffled along Caton Avenue, galoshes sloshing through puddles, the plastic bag of diapers in her left hand slick with rain. The front of her jeans were uncomfortably damp, but stealing twenty minutes to herself made it worthwhile.

She fought the urge to hunch her shoulders and instead embraced the bad weather, as a sixteen wheeler growled by, the sound of its engine diluting the usual street noises—intermittent honks, shouted disagreements billowing out from the bodegas and five-and-dimes that kept their doors propped open despite the thrashing downpour. The truck driver seemed anxious to find the interstate. He was miles off course.

Though she felt pathetically grateful for the walk, the sinister weather tugged on her mood.

The neighborhood of Kensington, Brooklyn, was a gritty, residential grid comprised of rowhouses, pre-war brick apartment buildings, and detached one-family Victorians, the latter of which seemed eerily out of place. Convenience stores, Chinese take-out joints, and the occasional bar added to the hodgepodge personality of nearly every intersection, though Danny had come to appreciate the aesthetic. It wasn't pretty, but neither was she.

As she came to the curb, stopping at the crosswalk signal, asphalt rumbled beneath her feet. The F train was barreling through a tunnel underground, a familiar sensation.

Trotting up beside her, a pair of teenagers—sopping wet, hiding under hoodies, cackling at the sting of chilly rain assaulting them—took turns pushing the crosswalk button, an act of good faith they couldn't live up to. When they darted into the street, eyeing oncoming cars and jogging in-between, Danny held her breath until they had safely reached the other side.

No sooner than they had, the crosswalk signal changed.

Danny leapt and cleared the street gutter where grimy water rushed towards a storm drain. Hurrying through the intersection, she came to another stream, but hopped onto the curb.

As long as the wind didn't change directions and snap her umbrella inside out she wouldn't complain. At least she was stretching her legs, getting some air, no longer cooped up in her apartment where her son's cries—the ear splitting screams of a tantruming infant—had a way of blaring through the baby monitor moments after she had put him down.

At the next corner the wooden sign for O'Toole's was swaying in the wind, rain spitting off it.

Guardedly, she slowed her pace, nearing the cloudy windows and spying the off-duty cops inside. They huddled around their favorite tables, pounding pints as though they were one drink away from forgetting how rough it could be—serving and protecting a city that considered them the enemy.

Danny felt naked without her gun at her hip, an outsider in her own world.

Offering one another feigned smiles, a consoling shoulder squeeze here, an arm jab there, the bar patrons exchanged monosyllabic remarks, but Danny looked past them to the bartender behind the bar, while rain streaked down the glass, obscuring her view.

Without realizing it, she wriggled her hand through the plastic bag's handle, the diapers inside banging against her raincoat, and touched her stomach, as she watched the bartender—the one who had gotten away.

He threw a dishrag over his broad shoulder, delivering another damp stain to his gray tee-shirt, and plowed his fingers through his salt-and-pepper hair, his gaze down, face in profile as though he couldn't quite commit to the tale that one of his buddies was telling him from across the counter. His deep-set eyes narrowed—the story was getting interesting —and when he glimpsed his friend, his eyebrows shot up to his hairline and his lip curled into a wry smile.

Danny knew that look. A booming laugh would come next, then his slate-gray eyes would liven. Maybe he'd straighten his spine and fold his arms skeptically, making the most of his six-foot height as if to challenge—*you serious?*

He had the build of a firefighter, because he used to be one. He had the busted nose of a bar owner who had broken up his fair share of fights. The burn mark running down the side of his neck was among her favorite battle scars. His body was a playground of old cuts, bones that had healed badly, injuries that acted up when the air turned damp and nasty like tonight. But that was as much as she knew about him—physical intimacy. Had there ever been an emotional connection between them?

Of course, Danny had learned a few details over the months about Tommy. He was divorced. No children. Born and raised in Brooklyn, and hardened because of it, which summed up the extent of what she knew about him.

It hadn't been enough.

She had missed the signal more than once so when it flipped, she started through the crosswalk, cutting up Ocean Parkway where brick rowhouses lined the block, hers among them.

Rain bounced off the stoop steps, as she lumbered up to the entrance door, her sopping jeans giving very little at the knees.

With stiff fingers, she fit her key into the lock and just as she pushed into the dingy entryway of her building, a sharp gust of wind snapped her umbrella inside out.

A sheet of rain sliced down the back of her neck.

She set the wet plastic bag of diapers on the tiles in favor of collapsing her umbrella, as the door slapped shut behind her.

On the opposite side of the cramped lobby, the building super, Camil Usov—a cranky old Russian with a thick accent—loosened his hold on the mop he was gripping as if the water she'd brought in with her had defeated him. He swore in Russian under his breath.

He shuffled over, carrying a yellow 'wet floor' sign, and set it beside her, as if she wasn't aware of the puddle she had made.

"Nasty out," he commented.

As she picked up her plastic bag, having wrestled her mangled umbrella into shape, she commiserated, mentioning, "It's not going to let up until May."

"Good for the baby, eh?" he said, mopping at her heels as she made her way to the stairwell door. "Rain lulls baby right to sleep."

Whipping the steel door open, she smiled companionably and said, "Wouldn't that be nice?"

Camil scratched his jowls, the pricks of stubble on his sunken cheeks, and asked her to be careful on the stairs.

The door slammed shut behind her, sending an echo through the stairwell. She clamped her umbrella under her armpit and heeded his advice, holding the railing as she climbed to the second floor where he had laid out mats so the tenants wouldn't slip and break their necks.

When she entered her threadbare apartment—weathered hardwood floors, peeling wall paint, sooty window sills, and tarnished appliances, though she cleaned regularly and kept the place homey—her ears perked up, but by some miracle her baby, Gregory, wasn't crying.

Her mother, Nora wasted no time setting the baby monitor on the end table, springing off the couch, and making herself useful, all the while her dainty features pinched with marked concern.

"You didn't take any detours, did you?" she asked as she took the plastic bag from Danny.

It was a loaded question, but she said, "No, Ma," knowing that the truth would only incite an argument.

Danny started towards the living room. Her galoshes snicked over the wooden floor, which reminded her to kick them off.

"You went to Kumar's on Ditmas, right?" Nora went on, helping Danny out of her raincoat once she'd rounded back. Gingerly, she shook the coat free of rain, holding it away from herself so she wouldn't sprinkle her cardigan or corduroys—Nora liked to keep her clothes nice since, in her words, she didn't have much. "Diapers are fifteen cents less there, I told you that."

"Yes, Ma, I went to Kumar's," she lied.

After hanging the raincoat on a rack, she straightened Danny's galoshes against the wall like a knowing chambermaid, and trailed after her into the living room, her every criticism veiled in tender, loving care. "Your hair is damp. You should've let me go out. Look at your jeans. They're sopping wet."

"I needed to stretch my legs," she reminded her, scrunching her mop of graying-brown hair where it had grown out on top. She kept the sides short rather than covering the worst of the gray.

Nora padded around the islet and into the kitchen, set the wet plastic bag on the counter, and began filling a teakettle, angling the spout under the sink faucet.

"I didn't tell you," she said, shutting the water off and placing the kettle on the front burner. She turned the dial and after the stove clicked, a flare of fire puffed out and she went on, "Nance is free tomorrow night."

"My hair looks fine," she bristled softly. Bickering would wake the baby not that she wasn't overdue for a trim.

"I want to treat you," she pressed, facing Danny with her most convincing smile. "What's wrong with getting the color done? She'll give you a blow out and do your nails as well."

Same old song and dance.

Danny's appearance caused Nora almost physical pangs of remorse. She nagged constantly about her daughter's lack of personal preening, a deficiency that Danny attributed to, quite frankly, not giving a crap about her looks, at least not since Tommy had walked out of her life.

Nora, by contrast, poured every last penny she earned into sprucing up and maintaining her modest style, which came as a strange sacrifice considering her babysitting wages.

"You deserve it," she went on. "And Nance will come here so you don't have to leave Gregory."

"I'll think about it."

"I'd like to see you grow out your hair, get some long layers framing those big eyes of yours. You're such a pretty girl, but no one would know it the way you carry yourself like a tomboy."

"Thanks, Ma," she said dryly, as she pulled the diapers from the plastic bag. She liked her hair short so perps couldn't grab it, but that logic had never worked on her mother.

"And you could dress a little nicer, too," Nora added. "Your stomach will go down. You can't hide your figure under floppy sweaters forever. There's a big Spring sale happening at K-Mart."

Danny wasn't in the habit of wearing sweaters because of her stomach, but because she had been lactating at the most inopportune times and was tired of changing her shirt.

Feeling boxed in to agreeing, she conceded, "Then let's hit the sale," and offered her mother a tired smile.

It was worth it just to see Nora brighten. She clapped her hands together then touched her blonde, wavy hair, which was also in need of a trim since it brushed her frail shoulders.

The kettle whistled so she plucked it off the burner, asking, "Chamomile or..." She was hunting through the cabinets now, her expression drooping at the slim options. "Well, chamomile is all you've got. Lipton or Stash?"

Danny clamped the diapers under her armpit, joined her mother at the counter, and hooked her free arm around Nora's bird-brittle shoulders, teasing: "These options are terrible."

At 5'10" Danny had a solid five inches on her mother so she nuzzled the top of her head, as Nora elbowed her, letting out a little laugh. "Oh, stop."

"What would I do without you, Ma?" she said, starting for the baby's room.

"You know I love helping out," she called after her.

The room was dim and quiet except for the sound of rain ticking against the window. As cars drove along the street outside, the flare from their headlights crept across the green walls. She stepped softly so she wouldn't wake her son and placed the diapers on the changing table then neared his crib.

He looked so small swaddled under his fleece blanket. His closed eyes were as puffy as the day he'd been born and in the three weeks since his birth he had lost the full head of dark hair that he'd come into the world with. It was hard to imagine this tiny creature would one day be a grown man, would one day tower over her, challenge her and love her and drive her crazy at times.

At the risk of stirring him, she gently caressed his bald head.

He felt cool.

It gave her pause.

Angling over him, she cupped his cheek.

He didn't move.

His narrow mouth looked slack and as her heart rate spiked she placed her finger under his button nose.

He wasn't breathing.

Her mind whirled, launching into sudden panic. She threw the blanket off and pressed her palm against his chest. She couldn't feel his heart thump.

"Mom!" she yelled, scooping her son's limp body out of the crib. He flopped against her chest, as Nora rushed into the room.

"What?"

"Call an ambulance!"

"What?" she asked, the urgency in Danny's tone disorienting her. She groped for the light switch.

"Get the phone," she ordered. "Call 911."

As Nora rocketed down the hallway and into the living room, Danny began patting Gregory's back and gently bouncing him. Her mind felt paralyzed. A sob stuttered out of her. This couldn't be happening.

Her mother appeared in the doorway, phone pressed to her ear, a look of stunned dismay on her aged face, and in a confused frenzy she recited the address.

Danny shouted over her, "He's not breathing!"

"He's a newborn," Nora relayed to the 911 operator then asked Danny, "Is he blue?"

"I can't feel his heart! What happened? When did you last check on him?"

Nora began stammering, "He was quiet. I... I don't know, not since before you went out." Into the receiver she demanded, "Send help!"

"What do I do?" she pleaded, tone shrill and cracking, but when she locked eyes with her mother, Nora had no suggestions.

Nora's mouth drifted open. The phone slipped out of her hand and hit the floor, busting apart.

As Danny held her infant tightly, sirens blaring in the distance, she knew it was too late.

Chapter One

PROSPECT PARK WAS cloaked in fog on this rainy day.

Situated in the middle of Brooklyn, the park was a 585-acre diamond of leafy trees, rolling hills, ballparks, and jogging trails.

Fat raindrops plopped down against treetops, soggy grass, and the asphalt path where Danny was walking. She held her umbrella high over her head so the brim wouldn't block her view of the lake in the distance. The gun at her hip jostled under her raincoat, which she unbuttoned single-handedly in order to make her badge visible.

A crowd had gathered, pressing into yellow police tape that ran parallel to the shore. These onlookers obstructed Danny's view of the crime scene where her lieutenant, Martin Franco, stood.

Franco angled his way through the residents and when he finally cleared the thick cluster, he walked briskly through the rain towards her.

No umbrella, his trench coat flapping in the wind, he glanced at her through his eyebrows.

Danny was surprised at how good it felt to see his face—those paternal dark eyes, his clenched jaw that suggested the Vic had left a bitter impression, his gelled black hair, olive skin tone, and prominent cheekbones that defied aging though he was pushing sixty.

A descendant of Cuban immigrants, Franco spoke with a faint, Latino lilt that to Danny had always sounded melodic compared to the clunky Brooklyn accent she had been cursed with.

As he neared her, slowing his step, he took a long, hard look at her and said, "I was hoping your first day back would be quiet."

"When is it ever quiet?" she said amicably.

Skepticism was written all over his face. She hadn't allowed a full week to lapse since the death of her son before calling Franco about returning to her position at the Special Victims Unit. Mourning at home had done nothing but fill her with multiplying anxieties. There was no point in riding out the remainder of her maternity leave. Tragically, she wasn't a mother anymore, and if she wasn't on the job, she would only wallow in bone-aching despair. She had to work, period.

He studied her, but knew better than to ask if she was okay. Instead he mentioned, "I've got a cousin down in Florida. Her baby died of SIDS as well."

Deflecting, she glanced down at her sneakers and said, "I'm sorry to hear that."

"There's no making sense of it."

She stared out at the crowd, the lake, the crime scene in-between, twisting her mouth to the side, then agreed, "No, there is not."

When she met his gaze again, Franco afforded her the benefit of the doubt. His eyes told her that he was impressed with her resolve. Then he began leading her down the walking path towards the lake.

One minute Gregory had been alive and well. A healthy, albeit colicky baby boy. The next he had left this world. Sudden Infant Death Syndrome. He'd stopped breathing. When she'd heard the explanation, it had been so simple that it had boggled her mind. Sometimes babies stopped breathing. They died for no reason. She was supposed to accept it and go on living, move on, but she didn't have it in her. It would be far easier to throw herself headlong into a world of other people's tragedies—rape and homicide, *special victims*. She wanted to submerge herself in a brand new case. There was no greater distraction from her own misery than focusing on the hell that someone else hadn't survived.

With authority, Franco parted the crowd, making room for Danny to cross through. A uniformed officer lifted the police tape and they ducked under it, stepping off asphalt and into mud.

Fifteen yards ahead, crime scene investigators worked in tandem with forensic specialists, taking photographs, setting out evidence identification markers, and keeping their distance from the Vic.

As Franco veered off to meet with one of the forensic analysts, Danny folded her umbrella, taking short strides over the slick mud so she wouldn't slip.

When she reached the body, she took in an overall impression of the scene. The victim appeared to be middle-aged in the ballpark of fifty-five, female, naked, Nordic-looking with blonde wispy hair and pale skin. She was beautiful with a wide mouth, but there was something stern in the dead woman's expression.

Lying face up, her head was sunken in the mud up to her ears, her legs splayed, the right stretching into the lake, the left bent to the side, exposing her genitals. She had a sturdy figure—thick limbs, round middle, legs like tree trunks—though she wasn't overweight. In fact she was tall and if Danny had to guess, the woman might have been of German descent.

The cause of death wasn't immediately obvious. She had no wounds—gunshot or otherwise.

Near her left hand and embedded in the mud were a handful of 5x8" photographs, fanned out. Raindrops ticked at their glossy surfaces. Danny didn't eye them, not yet. She was too engrossed in wondering about the dead woman, her stories and secrets, and how this grisly end might have come to pass. She examined her bone structure and the attitude it implied—judgment, perhaps to an Old Testament extent.

"Hey, Jill?" she called out, garnering the chief medical examiner's attention.

Jill was squatting next to what could have been a shoeprint. The spritely forty-year old—the more gruesome the crime, the more pep in Jill's step—lifted her head and wasted no time joining Danny.

Shielding her eyes from the rain, Jill gave Danny a little smile, then raked her fingernails through her sandy-blonde hair, which was pulled back in a low ponytail and two shades darker than usual thanks to the drizzle.

"Raped?" Danny asked, as she stood.

"The rain washed away any fluids," said Jill regretfully as she squinted up at Danny who had a knack for towering over most women. "But there's trauma consistent with forced penetration. I'll know more when I examine her at the morgue."

After staring down at the Vic for a pondering beat, she asked, "Cause of death?"

Jill crouched and pulled on a fresh pair of latex gloves then slipped her hands under the Vic's shoulders. With a grunt she made an honest attempt at rolling the body over, but it was too heavy.

Danny wriggled on a pair of gloves as well, which she kept in her raincoat pocket, and wedged her hands under the Vic's torso. Together they muscled the body over and the dead woman fell to her stomach with a squishy thud.

Shouting, "Let's photograph this," over her shoulder to no particular investigator, Danny kept her eyes on the back of the woman's head—a casserole of skull fragments and blood. The sight made her feel queasy, which was a testament to the vulgar nature of the crime since she historically had an iron stomach for such images.

"Blunt force trauma," said Jill, pointing to the bloody gash in the skull. As muddy as it was, Jill had to examine the wound for a long moment, delicately parting the Vic's hair to get a clearer look. Then she noted, "Probably struck more than once."

As a forensic photographer angled over the body and snapped photos, Danny glanced around the immediate area and let out a balking groan. If it hadn't been raining—weeks on end for that matter—they might have gotten lucky with a clear shoe print, a struggle pattern, something that would tell them the story of how this murder went down.

But as she scanned the shore, the muddy alcove, the drenched grass, nothing jumped out at her, not even a murder weapon. Regardless, she instructed the unis to bag and tag all fist-sized rocks they could find.

Complicating matters was the fact that there were no clothes in sight, which told her that the perp had taken the victim's garments with him, or...

Her gaze landed on the wet photographs embedded in the mud beside Jill.

Danny made her way over to Jill, and as an afterthought, she asked, "No ID?"

A faint, derisive smile crept sideways across Jill's face, her version of an answer—*wouldn't I tell you if I found her ID?*

"Just being optimistic," she said, as she crouched near the photographs. Danny called out to one of the unis that was collecting rocks as she had instructed, "Hey, can I get a few evidence bags?"

He was quick to fulfill the request, rain sliding down his blue poncho as he handed Danny a thin stack of plastic bags, after which he resumed trailing along the shore in search of possible weapons.

Danny peeled the first photograph out of the mud and, getting a good hard look at it, she hissed, "Damn" under her breath.

The photo was of a naked little boy.

Stripped of all clothing except for a pair of ratty socks, the little boy in the photo couldn't have been a day older than four. He seemed to cower, looking up at the camera, as he tried to cover his private parts with his hands.

She shook an evidence bag open and slipped the photograph inside then moved on to the next one, which depicted the same boy—blonde, bedraggled hair, pale green and almost vacant eyes, gangly limbs, ribs poking through porcelain skin—this time lying naked on his back, a stained tile floor beneath him, *a bathroom?*

Each photo was more disturbing than the last, as she reviewed and bagged them one after the next.

A strange feeling came over her, but it wasn't inspired by the vile images.

"Same perp," said a man hovering behind her.

Without looking at him, she shot back, "I'm not interested in your guesses."

"You sure about that?" he challenged, tone deep and confident.

She squinted up through the rain and found an African-American man with dark-black skin and a shaved head angling over her. His hands were planted on his knees, but he straightened up in what appeared to be a confrontational manner when Danny stood, coming into her full height.

He was stacked—a mountain of muscle—though dressed sharply in a crisp suit, his black parka open down the front. As she feared, there was a badge clipped to his belt, but she didn't see a gun. The bulge under his left arm explained it, however. He must have been one of the few detectives left who still wore a shoulder holster, preferring a slow and sloppy cross-draw to the concise pull of whipping a weapon off his hip like the rest of the cops in this city.

When she hadn't replied to his comment, he asked, "You think the killer caught her naked and getting off to some kiddie porn in the rain?"

Danny didn't appreciate his sarcasm.

"You think women can't be sex offenders?" she challenged.

"Offender? She's the Vic," he pointed out bluntly.

"You don't think the two are related?"

Before he could answer, she stalked off through the rain, making a beeline for Franco who was waving in an ambulance, as a set of unis urged the crowd away from the police tape to make room.

"Tell me that's not my new partner," she said hotly, coming up behind her lieutenant.

Franco touched eyes with her briefly, as he held his hands up for the ambulance to stop.

"You knew this day was coming," he told her. "Connolly timed his transfer with your maternity leave. You can't say I sprung this on you."

Something in Franco's tone made her proceed warily so she pressed her mouth into a hard line, holding her tongue and wondering if she shouldn't be more pissed at her old partner, Mick Connolly, for having concluded that *enough is enough*. Mick had reached a breaking point with the Special Victims Unit a few months back when they'd failed to locate a kidnapped girl. Danny had done everything in her power to get through to Mick and pull him out of the deep hole he'd sunken into. But it hadn't worked. The girl had been assaulted and killed. It didn't matter that they had caught the guy a moment later or that he would spend the rest of his life behind bars. Nothing could erase the loss.

"Carter Dobbs is a good detective," he went on. "He put in ten years with Vice. Most cops want out after five, you know how rough it gets. He worked sex trafficking. You couldn't ask for a better fit."

"You're selling this too hard," she pointed out, stealing a glance at Carter who was taking an intrigued lap around the body—huge hands on his hips, barrel chest rising and falling, jaw clenched, *put me in, coach!*

Carter wasn't a jock, but he certainly seemed at the athletic end of the spectrum, an imposing, strong, and stubborn creature who reminded her of a once-glorified yet washed up football hero that had every intention of resurrecting his heyday. Yet everything about his demeanor seemed to work against him, implying he had already failed. Regardless, she wondered who might be doting on him behind closed doors. He had that glimmer about him. The confidence of knowing he could attract any woman he wanted.

"Does he get how things work around here?" she asked, not liking her tone.

Franco's brows knit together, as he said, "Make him get it. I've got my eye on him as well."

She would have to be satisfied with that if for no other reason than Franco was starting off towards the unis and shouting, "I want this neighborhood canvassed. Someone had to have seen something. Start with Prospect Park Southwest and work your way east around the park. Every building, every apartment, every bodega and business."

Near the shore, a pair of medics zipped up a black body bag, having set the victim inside. After hoisting the body onto a collapsed gurney, they lifted the rickety legs and began rolling it with slips and starts towards the back of the ambulance.

Danny called out, "Hey, Jill!"

Anticipating the question, the medical examiner said, "At least two hours."

"You want me to call ahead?"

"No need. I should know enough by then. I'll be ready for you."

Thunder clapped overhead and the rain thickened, coming down in sheets. Danny pushed her umbrella open and rested the pole on her shoulder as she watched the forensic team scurry about, gathering up the evidence identification markers before they could wash away in a mudslide.

An eerie sense of peace came over her. No one would abuse or exploit her baby Gregory. No one would violate him. He would never be the victim of a crime. She would never find him scared and cowering in a photograph stained with mud, because he was already dead.

This was a small consolation that just might keep Danny from falling apart.

Carter hiked over and asked, "Do you go by Foster?"

Her monotone response was, "We're on a first name basis at SVU," and she didn't look at him when she said it, as if the ambulance puttering away required her watchful eye.

"So Danielle?"

"Danny." After a beat, she added, "Sex trafficking doesn't hold the same weight as working with an individual victim. You're lucky your first one's dead. Living victims aren't nearly as easy."

"I'm not here to step on your toes," he stated, hunching his shoulders against the downpour that had him drenched.

Suspending hostilities, she sighed and angled her umbrella over him.

"I'm sorry about your son," he said.

If he was trying to thank her for sharing her umbrella or apologizing for their prior friction, she couldn't tell.

She pressed her lips together. It was as much of a smile as she could muster.

"I have kids myself," he offered.

Absently, Danny stared at where the body had been. "Whoever did this wanted to humiliate her," she said, struck by a sudden thought.

Carter glanced in the same direction, adding, "I want to find that boy."

Chapter Two

HOLDING HER CELL phone to her ear and listening to her mother blather on about all the ways in which Danny was sabotaging her own health and sanity by having the audacity to work so soon after Gregory's passing, Danny distractedly paced the corridor, her sneakers tapping the blue linoleum floor outside of the chief medical examiner's office in Kings County Hospital.

Even though Danny was early for Jill Andover, she told her mother, "I can't be on the phone right now."

"Have you set time aside for lunch?" asked Nora, her questions always loaded.

Clamping her cell between her ear and shoulder, she pulled her raincoat sleeve up her wrist and checked her watch. "I can't think about that right now."

"It's your first day back and I don't want you to push yourself too hard," she pleaded.

Irked, Danny rolled her eyes up at the fluorescent lights so she wouldn't get short with her mother then returned her gaze to the cracked linoleum.

"You don't have to work the *whole* day," Nora argued.

"You know it doesn't work like that."

"Franco put you on a case?" she asked as if alarmed because Danny wasn't. "That's too much too soon. What in God's name is he thinking?"

"That I'm a detective," she supplied dryly as she peeked through the narrow window of the exam room door.

Inside, Jill was speaking softly into a microphone that was hanging from the ceiling, as she circled a stainless steel table where the victim was lying under a white sheet.

"I'll bring dinner over," Nora offered.

"I'm not sure when I'll be home, Ma."

"It's no bother," she said, uneasiness bubbling up in her otherwise determined tone. "I'll wait."

Danny let out a discouraging sigh and told her, "Tonight's no good."

"Please." She sounded distraught and for the life of her Danny couldn't understand why her mother was getting so bent out of shape. "I'll pop a casserole in the oven and tidy up. It doesn't matter when you get home. I just need to know that you're eating."

"You already tidied my place up yesterday," she pointed out. "And the day before, if I recall."

"I can do your laundry," she countered, the conversation becoming something of a negotiation in which Danny simply wasn't invested.

When Carter rounded the corner, trailing towards her through the corridor with two paper cups of coffee in his meaty hands, she told her mother, "I have to go."

"So I'll see you later?"

"I have to go now, Ma-"

"Will I see you later?"

Again she sighed at Nora's incessant coddling, turning her back to Carter to spare herself embarrassment, and used a firm tone as she asserted, "I really don't know. Talk later, alright?"

Danny pocketed her cell phone, eyes widening in delayed reaction to her mother's persistence, and once the wave of astonishment had passed, she faced her new partner.

"Husband nagging you?" he asked casually, offering her one of the coffees he'd bought in the cafeteria vending machine.

"No," she said, taking the cup and peeling the lip back. "Thanks."

"I didn't know how you take it," he mentioned, referring to the coffee.

It was black she noticed, which wasn't how she liked her coffee, but it didn't matter. As soon as she stepped into the ME's office, she would lose her appetite.

As she brought the cup to her mouth, steam burned her upper lip. She took a sip anyway, demonstrating her appreciation for his thoughtfulness, though she'd learned from experience that the hospital's dark roast was notoriously terrible—watery and stale and scalding hot as though temperature could mask its many shortcomings. Carter would catch on eventually.

"Yeah, it took me more years than I care to admit to get down to it and tie the knot," he ruminated from out of nowhere as though making small talk was an integral part of waiting for Jill to invite them inside.

"My dead baby's father isn't in the picture," she said bluntly.

Carter looked horrified.

"Bartender. No big loss there," she added, though her tone betrayed her. The loss was felt deeply and suspended only by swells of grief when she thought about her son, their child.

But Danny wasn't interested in bonding with her new SVU partner.

As she fell silent, hit by one of those swells, Carter narrowed his eyes as if sensing there was much more to the story.

She hoped he wouldn't ask her if Gregory's sudden death had anything to do with her split from the man who should've only been a fling in the first place.

He looked like he might comment at the very least so she told him, "That was my mother on the phone. It's not enough that she lives in the building next to mine. She has to make sure I eat and breathe and remember to check if my head's attached to my body every time I step out the door."

Finding that relatable or perhaps funny, he smiled, which lifted his whole face—revealing gleaming white teeth, the apples of his cheeks popping, his almond eyes brightening. He was a good-looking man and it wasn't hard to imagine him charming his way through ten years worth of Vice assignments. Perhaps this was how he had lasted for so long working one of the toughest divisions in the city.

His expression relaxed until he tasted his coffee, breaking then returning eye contact. He grimaced down at the cup in his hand and didn't dare sip from it again.

She noticed a wedding band on his finger.

Curious, she asked, "How does your wife handle it, you working as a detective?"

"Kathy is her name." He shrugged, letting out a long breath. "She hated me working at Vice. That's why I transferred. My way of caving to her ultimatum."

"She ever ask you to retire?" she wondered, curious how real couples handled this life.

Danny had never had a real relationship thanks to the grueling hours she worked.

"She wanted me to," he allowed. "That's why I transferred to SVU. Unlike Vice, the Special Victims Unit isn't going to send me out on long undercover assignments," he explained, adding another little shrug that accentuated his Herculean build—massive shoulders tensing then broadening with his conclusion. "If that doesn't fix it, I don't know what will."

Beside them, the steel door clicked open and Jill popped her head out, saying, "Hey, kids."

After chucking their coffee cups into a trash bin on the far side of the door, they followed Jill into the exam room, Danny at her heels and Carter trailing tightly behind.

Blue linoleum floors. A grid of fluorescent lights on high ceilings. The room was lofty and sterile with a row of stainless steel tables in the back. The table in the center of the room was where their Vic was lying.

Jill had removed the white sheet.

She'd also cleaned up the body. No longer streaked with mud, the woman now appeared manicured. In the park, Danny hadn't noticed the dead woman's pale pink manicure or that her hair had been dyed recently. The Vic's blonde curls revealed only a breath of dark roots at her scalp. Her lashes were dusted with smudged eyeliner and brown powder, which indicated she had likely been far more 'done-up' before the rain had gotten to her. She looked like someone who had cared about her appearance.

Jill neared a computer monitor at the head of the table and explained, "I made a dental impression." She tapped the mouse and an X-ray of the Vic's teeth filled the screen. "I was hoping for an implant, but only found a few fillings."

Damn, thought Danny. A dental implant would have a branded serial number they could use to identify the woman.

"Her teeth did allow me to approximate her age," she went on. "Mid-fifties. The time of death was between eight and ten last night according to rigor."

Danny thumbed at a notepad—her 2x4" spiral bound sidekick—in her raincoat pocket, but felt awkward about jotting down details in front of her new partner, though she didn't know why.

"Prospect Park wasn't the crime scene," Jill stated, which caused Carter to cock his head with interest. "She was killed somewhere else. Her clothes were removed then she was dumped at the lake."

Carter's confrontational tone returned as he asked, "How do you know?"

But challenges only fired Jill up. "I examined the blows on the back of her head. There would've been a hell of a lot more blood in the mud if she'd been killed there."

"It was pouring," he countered, stubborn as a mule as far as Danny was concerned. She generally didn't waste her time challenging the ME.

"Even still," Jill said, a flirtatious smile forming at the corners of her mouth—sparring with Carter was probably as much sex as she'd had in the past six months, an uncomfortable tidbit Danny wished hadn't come to mind right now. "She wasn't killed there. If she was, we would've found her face down. I found the position of her body far too neat for her to have been bludgeoned at that site."

"What was she hit with?" asked Danny, accepting the latex gloves that Jill was offering.

As she pulled them on, she neared the head of the table and waited for Carter to wriggle his big hands into his own pair of gloves, also provided by Jill.

The medical examiner lifted the Vic's head so that the detectives could have a closer look.

"A blunt, hard object," Jill answered, cradling the head with her left hand and using her free one to point to the gash. "I'd guess some sort of decorative sculpture, maybe marble or stone. It was strong enough not to break off and get embedded in her skull. And she was struck more than once, though the first blow probably killed her."

Danny leaned in even closer and studied the fractured layers. "Someone wanted to make sure she was dead."

"Also you'll note how the blows were nearly at the crown of her head," she went on, gently setting the Vic's head down on the steel table. "This woman is just shy of 5'11"."

"So she was seated," Carter guessed, as he accompanied Jill to the middle of the table.

"That's the most likely scenario," she agreed, offering the new detective a gentle smile, which he refused to acknowledge, preferring instead to stalk around the table.

When he stilled, Danny touched eyes with him and said, "We have to find the original crime scene."

Jill gave them a moment to silently confer then she explained, "As I mentioned in the park, there are clear signs of vaginal and anal trauma consistent with rape, but I found no fluids or condom residue after a thorough examination."

Carter screwed his face up and asked, "Meaning?"

Lifting her brows and turning serious—flirting during this portion of the meeting would be in exceptionally poor taste—she clarified, "It wasn't a penis. Splinter shards indicate a wooden object was used, but it was done post-mortem."

"Mud in the cavities?" asked Danny, who couldn't look at the Vic a moment longer. She fixed her gaze on Jill.

"No," she said before again insisting, "the attack didn't occur in the park."

"Why dump her there?" Carter said, but only to himself.

Thinking out loud, Danny began walking through the story that the blows and trauma told. "He was impulsive. Saw an opportunity and took it. But then spent time with the body, defiling her with an object as soon as she was dead. Then he moves her, dumps her in the park. Why risk bringing her to such a public place? Any way to tell what time she was dumped?"

Jill knew the second question was meant for her so she said, "Unfortunately no, but pruning on her toes indicates she was in the water for at least an hour."

Carter sucked his lips in, pressing his mouth into a grimace that Danny had never seen on another human being before. When finally he commented, "This is one sick bastard," she couldn't agree more.

"As you can see," Jill continued, indicating the Vic's hands and forearms. "There are absolutely no signs of a struggle, no defensive wounds, no bruises or cuts or abrasions. No skin under the fingernails."

"So we've got nothing on this guy," Danny concluded.

Barreling ahead, Jill mentioned, "I ran her prints through the system and she didn't come up."

Carter took a moment to do the math on that then supplied, "Ruling out the possibility that she was a parolee or worked for the city in some capacity."

"Correct," she said, nearing her computer and once again perking up. "I did find fibers in her hair, however."

Intrigued, Danny quickly asked, "What kind of fibers?" as Jill opened an image on the computer screen.

Though it was highly magnified, all Danny could tell was that the single fiber was short and black. "Thread?"

"Synthetic, but I couldn't tell you where it came from."

"Great," she grumbled.

"I'll know more once I run a series of tests."

"Venture a guess?" asked Carter, finally shining some of that sports hero charm.

Jill lingered, drinking it in before meeting him halfway. "I'll call you when I narrow it down."

Danny snapped the latex gloves off her hands and stuffed them into a medical waste bin, prompting Carter to do the same, then thanked Jill, and pushed the steel door open on her way out.

Carter hurried up beside her as they walked along the corridor, which led directly to the side exit of the building. He was quick to push the door open for her when they reached it, but neither was eager to venture out into the drizzling rain.

Winthrop Avenue was quiet. Lining the cement sidewalk was a row of poplar trees softly undulating in the wind. Beyond the line of trees was the parking lot. Danny scanned for their vehicle, having forgotten where they'd parked. Though Franco considered her a brilliant investigator, she didn't exactly have a mind like a steel trap.

After starting into the dreary atmosphere, she slowed her pace, allowing Carter to go ahead of her towards their Crown Victoria—an unmarked Ford sedan as brown as wet wood. She pulled her notepad out of her raincoat along with a pen and quickly scribbled down the few facts she'd learned from Jill as well as her own observations, as raindrops dampened the paper.

When she reached the sedan, she was equally discrete about hiding her notepad before she opened the passenger side door.

As soon as she'd climbed in, she shut the door and fastened her seatbelt, listening to rain piddle against the roof, and then shook her short hair free of water, her mother's well-intentioned yet overbearing reminder to stay dry nagging her from the back of her mind.

After settling behind the steering wheel and turning the engine, Carter flipped the windshield wipers to their highest setting and drove off through the parking lot and onto Winthrop, heading west deeper into Kensington.

"With all the rain last night," Danny began thinking through the timeline as she wedged her fingers into the vent, angling the cool breeze at her neck. "The park wouldn't have been populated, but I still don't see our guy risking it until the middle of the night, after midnight."

"So the perp kills her at eight or ten at the latest then spends at least two hours violating the body, maybe more. He probably thought he had all the time in the world," he commented as if the thought disturbed him.

The windshield was fogging up so Danny adjusted the dials, freeing Carter to concentrate on changing lanes.

"Not if she was killed in her own home," she countered. "He'd want to get out of there."

"So he kills her at her own home, takes her someplace else, then moves her again to the park? That's way too risky."

"If they were close, she could've gone to his place willingly. If he lives alone, then..."

"Or he knew *she* lived alone," he theorized.

Danny realized she liked her new partner.

"Do you often start with this kind of hurdle?" he asked, stealing a glance at her.

"What do you mean?"

"An unknown identity?"

She angled the vent off of her, having gotten enough fresh air, and said, "No, most of my Vics are alive. Rape survivors. The dead ones have had IDs if not some clear cut indication of who they were."

Carter popped the turn signal and cut a left onto 16th Avenue where the buildings resembled one another—brick, boxy structures of pre-war design.

"Why do I get the feeling this guy knew what he was doing?" he pondered. "He strips her down after killing her. He has his sick way with her body, but doesn't leave a trace of himself behind. He attacks during the rainiest month that Brooklyn has. If he's not smart, he's God damn lucky."

"He might be both," she suggested just as another possibility occurred to her. "Or impotent."

Carter stared at her for a beat, and as his eyes snapped back to the road, he said, "This work doesn't bother you?"

Danny smiled, an inside joke she'd once shared with her old partner, Connolly coming to mind. "I've learned to curb my emotions, but trust me every single case bothers me and that's an understatement."

Carter squeezed the brakes, pulling in front of the 66th Precinct—a two-story brick building with narrow windows and an American flag angled and flapping over the entrance door.

Her folded umbrella was resting at her feet, but after a moment's consideration Danny decided it would be a short jog into the building so she left her umbrella, pushed her door open, and stepped out into the light rain. With any luck it would turn into a fine mist by tonight, she thought.

She kept her head down as they walked briskly to the entrance where a few uniformed officers were getting a bit of fresh air, though they stood with their backs pressed to the brick siding so that the awning overhead would block the rain.

Danny held the glass door open for Carter and as she crossed through the lobby, her partner at her heels, and rounded into the Special Victims Unit at the back of the floor, she peeled off her raincoat and slung it over her arm.

From out of nowhere, Nora blindsided her, rushing up from behind and whisper-shouting, "Danielle!"

"Ma?" she said, alarmed to find her mother at the precinct. "What are you doing here?"

Nora's answer was to thrust a soft-sided cooler bag at her daughter, after which she began listing, "A turkey sandwich and lentil soup. It's still hot." She tapped her finger against the nylon cooler, as Danny held it. "And a soda, plus a few cookies."

Danny stared at her in abject horror, as a wave of embarrassment flared hot in her chest. She felt eyes on her, but when she glanced at Carter, he did her the courtesy of diverting his gaze and crossing to his desk, though something in the tilt of his head told her he had an ear out, curious about the personal mother-daughter exchange.

"I know I'm being over the top," Nora went on, a preemptive confession bubbling out of her. "I'll lighten up. I will. I just want to make sure you're eating and taking care of yourself." She leaned in close, but glanced over her shoulder, scanning the bullpen for Franco, Danny presumed. "He's not working you too hard, is he?"

Danny sometimes suspected that her mother lamented the long detective hours Danny worked, mainly because it had robbed Nora of quality time with her daughter. Nora was good at making Danny feel guilty for not being around. The irony, however, was that when Danny 'wasn't around' it was usually because she had been at O'Toole's with Tommy. Or at least this had been the case back when Danny and Tommy had been involved.

Deep down, Danny wondered and even suspected that Nora had known all along that Danny had been lying whenever she had claimed to 'work late.' Nora had obviously known about O'Toole's and Tommy. Danny's baby had come from *somewhere*, after all.

And yet whatever fears her mother was wrestling with at this moment were completely unfounded. Danny wasn't seeing Tommy and she was clearly on the job.

So why did Danny now feel guilty?

Firm in her intention, sheepish in the execution, she took her mother by the arm and began ushering her towards the lobby. "Thanks for lunch. I have to get back to work now."

"I promise not to bother you again," said Nora, which was her version of an apology not that it swayed her daughter.

Clearly, Nora saw nothing wrong with dropping by and demonstrating for all of the precinct to see how oppressively close their dynamic had become. Thank God Danny hadn't been pouring over crime scene photos. Her mother would've had a heart attack and made an even worse scene.

"Really, I mean it. I'm respecting your schedule."

"Well, I appreciate that," said Danny, who remained entirely unconvinced.

"But when will you be home?"

"We talked about this," she said in a stern whisper once they'd reached the glass door. "I really can't say." When it suddenly dawned on her, she asked, "Don't you babysit Monday nights?"

"No families tonight," said Nora with an optimistic smile. Regrettably, she had rearranged her schedule in order to nurse Danny into losing her mind. "Oh!" she exclaimed, eyeing the top of Danny's head. "Your hair's wet." As she reached out to touch her hair, Danny gently caught her hand and returned it to her mother's side. "I've got the Walsh's first thing tomorrow so if you need extra help tonight-"

"Goodbye, Ma," she said, urging her through the door. "Thanks for lunch!"

Nora seemed hesitant about starting off for her car and because of it Danny was tempted to escort her if for no other reason than to make certain her mother was in fact going home. But instead she waved at Nora, beaming a big thumbs up to show she was A-Okay. It did the trick.

As she turned from the glass door, her mother having climbed into her Volvo, a uniformed officer entered from outside, sniffed, and after a bright glance at Danny's lunch cooler said, "Smells good."

She feigned agreement and scurried off through the bullpen. When she reached her desk, which faced Carter's, she tucked the soft-sided cooler in the bottom drawer and avoided eye contact.

"Photos of the Vic came through," he said, clicking his mouse and engaging in a silent war with his chair, which was teetering precariously to the left. Budget cuts.

She opened her laptop as well and scrolled through her emails so that she could look at the same images.

"I sent a shot of the Vic to Missing Persons," he added, glancing at her over the top of his screen.

She hoped her cheeks weren't red. She certainly felt flush thanks to her mother's coddling display.

"I'm putting her through facial recognition as well," he went on. "Doubt we'll get lucky, though."

She touched eyes with him.

Carter leaned towards her, his tone filled with discretion as he said, "A few years ago I got shot on the job. It was nowhere near fatal and I was assigned to desk duty when I got back. Didn't matter. Kathy would show up three or four times a day to check on me."

She shielded her eyes with her hand and laughed. When she looked up again, she muttered, "I'm embarrassed."

"Don't worry about it," he said easily. A shrug came next as though they both might brush over how strangely Nora had behaved. "Really. Happens to the best of us."

"Thanks."

The lieutenant's office was directly behind Danny's desk and when Carter's gaze locked on it, she turned in her swivel chair to find Franco filling the doorway.

"Foster, Dobbs," he barked, summoning the detectives before disappearing inside again.

The detectives reported to his office and after Carter had closed the door, they each settled onto the chairs across from Franco's desk, though he hadn't sat.

Instead, he planted his fists on his hips and stared at the photographs of the four year-old boy they had found in the park, which were fanned out across his desk.

"I reached out to the Cyber Crimes Exploitation Unit," he began, then took a moment to scrape his teeth over his bottom lip, wincing. "They're hunting through their databases to see if they have any record of the same child, but it's going to take awhile. Days. Weeks. There's no telling so I don't want you to count on them." Finally, he sat at his desk and clasped his hands together. "We've got two Vics and we don't know the identities of either," he summarized, which landed like a fist to Danny's gut. Franco pressed his forefinger against one of the photos, locking eyes with her. "I want to know everything about these people and I want to know it yesterday."

Chapter Three

THE CONVENIENCE store looked dreary. The tiles were slick with rainwater, the aisles cramped, too narrow for customers to comfortably pass one another. Items lining the shelves—boxed and canned food, generic brands, their labels colorful—seemed in cheerful contrast to the otherwise drab bodega.

The clerk behind the counter, whose unfortunate resemblance to a basset hound reminded Carter Dobbs of the seedier pimps he'd booked over the years, was stuffing cigarette packs into a display rack overhead, filling the compartments brand-by-brand.

Carter tossed a tissue-pack on the counter and asked for a scratch ticket, neither of which he cared about.

The clerk was in no rush to accommodate, having caught sight of the badge at Carter's hip. Warily, he grumbled, raked his dirty nails through his greasy comb-over, and pointed to the options.

Clarifying, Carter told him, "The Gold Rush lotto," as he worked a few bills out of his wallet.

The man flicked the scratch ticket onto the counter, punched his thick knuckle against the cash register keys, and mentioned the total, as the drawer popped open with a ding.

Carter didn't pay, not immediately. "How late is this place open?"

The clerk hesitated, sizing Carter up for a tense moment. It had been a friendly question, but the guy was smart enough to know he was in the throes of being roped into something he'd rather avoid.

"Is this about the police this morning?" he asked, planting his fists on the counter and jutting his chin towards the storefront windows, indicating the park across the street. "That crowd?"

"Did you see anything go down last night?"

"What happened over there?" he said, taking a clumsy stab at turning the tables. "I heard some woman was found dead."

Carter was tempted to insist that the clerk answer the question, but he tempered his response instead. "How late were you working?"

"Until midnight," he belched out, stuffing a pack of Marlboro Lights into the display rack.

"You stick around? Work late?"

"I didn't see nothing," he shot back before glancing at the cash in Carter's hand.

"You didn't see anyone go into the park?" he pressed, reluctant to pay the man, which would only end the conversation.

"I don't stare out the window all night."

"Look, man. I'm just trying to find out what happened," he told him, not liking the timbre of his own tone, which implied both aggravation and contempt. "If you saw a car idling near the entrance or someone carrying a heavy load into the park, it would really help me out."

The details seemed to spark the clerk's recollection, which would have been promising if the clerk had been willing to share his account no matter how trivial. But when he said, "Cars slow down across the street all the time. They idle at the entrance. People go in and out. I don't think nothing of it," Carter knew the man was evading.

He set the cash down and assured him, "I don't have to take your name. I'm not going to bring you down to the station. Are you sure you didn't see anything?"

Taking the money and making slow work of counting it, he said, "I didn't notice anything out of the ordinary."

Carter told him to keep the change. A surveillance camera had caught his eye, but as he assessed its line of sight—the lens was angled at the door and couldn't have covered the park entrance across the street—he reasoned that he was wasting his time.

Annoyed, he pocketed the tissues along with the scratch ticket. He didn't have business cards with his new SVU numbers so he found an old one in his wallet. There was a pen chained to the counter, which he used to cross out the old Vice information before jotting down his new desk and cell numbers.

"If you remember something," he said, sliding the card across the counter. "Have a nice day."

The rain had tapered off into a fine mist, but the sky was swollen with the threat of another downpour.

Carter stepped out onto the sidewalk and moved away from the door, but kept under the awning where raindrops were beading up and falling from its hem.

Vehicles passed along the street. He stared through them, his gaze fixed on Prospect Park, the wrought-iron fence that marked its perimeter, the sparse poplars on the other side—dismal scenery.

Beyond the tree line was Danny, who paced slowly, scanning the area. He could almost hear the thoughts in her fast-working mind. Which route had the killer taken? Why had he chosen this side of the park, the lake in particular? Would he have come from the sidewalk outside of the park or perhaps used a different entrance?

It wasn't lost on Carter that he was undoubtedly rusty at this type of police work. He had spent the last decade infiltrating one criminal organization after the next. His chief had provided him with files of the criminal targets. Carter had always known who the bad guys were. Working undercover, he had befriended them, collected information, and reported to his superiors, as his team had built each case.

He wasn't used to investigating with no leads. This case was daunting to say the least. It already infuriated him.

Complicating matters was the strange feeling he'd gotten from Franco. The man hadn't yet warmed to him, and Carter had a hunch that his new lieutenant wouldn't easily warm up to him, if at all.

Franco didn't think Carter would last. It had been written all over his unemotional face. Every order, every glance in fact had been heavily weighted with skepticism. Not that Carter wasn't used to friction, he could handle it. But he didn't like having to prove himself, not in this case, not when he knew he was at high risk of failing.

Though Carter was fluent in the language of undercover work and the gumption and deception it required, he had lost the edge that hardboiled cops exude—that distinctly domineering tone and intimidating presence.

For Carter, the innate muscle that compelled witnesses to talk was sorely out of shape. The clerk hadn't feared him, hadn't sweated the consequences of keeping his mouth shut, and that was a major problem.

If he was unsure of himself and whether or not he would 'fit in' with the SVU department, his new partner's personality didn't help. She struck him as a loner. Brassy. Masculine, though he considered that particular detail to be a redeeming quality. Her big, puppy dog eyes—downward sloping, muddy blue, and cunningly innocent—seemed to contradict the asymmetrical slant of her mouth, which made her look like she was in a constant state of smirking wickedly.

Tough as hell.

That's how the lieutenant had described her when they'd first sat down in his office at the 66th. Danny was tall for a woman, lean yet wiry, and because of it she came across as ten times her size. But according to Franco she had delivered far fewer blows than she'd received.

The way Franco told it, five years ago when Danny had been working as a cop in the Burglary & Theft Division, she had tracked down a perp who had broken into a townhouse in Kensington. The perp had knocked Danny out in an effort to escape. But incapacitating her had also given the guy an idea. He had tried to sexually assault her. Bleeding and dizzy, she'd fought like hell, and the guy fled.

Danny had then proceeded to hunt him.

She had been smart, calculating, patient, and most importantly, ruthless, and it had worked.

If she hadn't set her mind to nailing the guy's ass to the wall and if she hadn't succeeded at doing precisely that, Franco wouldn't have thought twice about passing her application over in favor of the next seasoned cop. Instead, he had recruited her, her tenacity having been the defining factor, and her spunk hadn't faded since.

From where Carter was standing, it was a lot to live up to. He just hoped she would let him in. And he hoped that she would help Carter to quickly get on top of his game.

Cases moved in Vice. This one had been at a standstill straight out of the gate and it was giving him a bad feeling.

Glancing up the street, he neared the curb and waited for a line of traffic to pass then jogged across at the first opportunity.

His face was damp with mist so he wiped his forehead with the sleeve of his parka, as he hooked around the wrought-iron fence, entering Prospect Park.

Danny was waiting on a walking path that ran beside a bare-bones playground where preschoolers were tottering about, exploring the seesaws and jungle gym. Their parents watched nearby while casually chatting.

Joining his partner, he said, "No luck at the store."

She shot him an amicable frown as if to say, *I'm not surprised.*

They headed down the path, trailing deeper into the park towards the lake.

As a stiff breeze blew through, jangling spotty rain from the leafy trees, he snuck a glance at her.

Danny's eyes were fixed on the fog billowing over the lake, the peaceful yet eerie landscape. "Any reason the 78th didn't pick this one up?"

Guessing his implication, she asked, "Are you asking because this location is technically a block north of Kensington?"

"Territory is territory."

"Our clearance rate is better," she said, as they came to the muddy shore. She turned, facing the street they'd come from, and scanned the buildings through the trees in the distance. She touched eyes with him, flashing that wicked smile that brought out the dimples in her cheeks. "I think Franco wants to see what you can do."

"Ha," he said, staring off in the direction that Danny was looking.

Past the playground, trees shimmied in the breeze, but in terms of the line of sight, they weren't taller than the buildings along Prospect Park Southwest.

His gaze snapped to one of the walking paths where outdoor lamp posts were standing about ten yards apart from one another. The path that spanned the south side of the lake had park lamps as well, all of which would've been on from dusk to sunrise. There was a chance the body had been bathed in dim light, which meant there was a chance that someone in the second floor apartments across the way might have seen something.

"Unis canvassed and got nothing?" he asked her.

"You think they went into every building? Knocked on every door?"

As they walked towards the street, he exercised his sense of humor, commenting, "I thought working a beat was behind me."

"Get used to it, my friend."

Thunder clapped overhead and the sky darkened, turning the landscape gray. As Carter glanced up, anticipating another downpour, he felt eyes on him and then noticed a man lurking near the south side of the lake not twenty yards from where they'd been standing.

He was staring through his eyebrows at Carter—his head tipped down, his shoulders hunched, the denim jacket he wore so wet it looked black. His jeans were stained with mud.

If he hadn't held Carter's gaze for so long, the detective wouldn't have noticed the long, jagged scar—raised and discolored—across his forehead that arched downward at a slant into his eyebrow.

In an instant, Carter headed towards him with long, authoritative strides, pulling his badge from his waist and presenting it. "Excuse me!"

As the man lingered, Carter got a really good look at him—hovering between 6' and 6'2", Caucasian, in his early or mid thirties, lean build though on the muscular side, deep-set eyes of indeterminate color.

Frankly, the guy had a predatory look, like he was hungry.

The overall impression he gave off—a deviant rubbernecker—was enough to send Carter's spleen leaping up his throat.

He sensed the man would bolt a split second before he did.

"Hey!" he shouted, tearing after the guy, who was sprinting through the mud that hooked around the lake. "Stop!"

Why would the guy run if he wasn't guilty of *something?*

Carter started gaining on him. Determined, he pumped his arms, pounding his sneakers into the slick mud that was giving way too much under his feet to be trusted.

He sensed more than saw Danny at his heels, but when he picked up his pace, closing in on the man—ten yards away then eight then five, squinting through the mist that stung his eyes and using his last shred of breath to shout, *stop!*—his partner fell behind.

Just as Carter reached out, close enough to grab the man's jacket, the guy sprang to the right, employing dexterity that Carter couldn't match. He tore up through the soggy grass, dodging away from Carter.

When Carter shifted after him, his sneaker hit the slick grass at a bad angle and the next thing he knew he was sliding sideways. His feet flew out from under him.

He landed squarely in the mud, his elbow slamming hard against the ground. His pant leg pushed up his calf. A second later, he felt water seep through his slacks and he cursed, as Danny ran like hellfire, cutting up the grass to catch the guy before he could reach Parkside Avenue.

Hoisting himself off the ground, his hand pressing against soft, wet earth, his blood pressure skyrocketed from embarrassment rather than exertion.

Carter remembered the lousy pack of tissues he had bought and when he straightened up to his feet, he made a futile attempt at cleaning himself up—tearing the plastic packaging, shaking out a few tissues, blotting his soaking pant leg.

It was comical.

He heard heavy breathing and realized Danny was back, empty-handed.

"You okay?" she asked breathlessly, planting her fists on her hips to give her lungs some room.

"I had him," he said hotly.

Though not unpleasantly, she told him, "You don't know what you had," implying that people ran for all kinds of reasons besides guilt.

Carter's square jaw tightened. He didn't agree.

"Let's knock on some doors," she suggested.

"Great," he said with a pronounced lack of enthusiasm, as he glanced at the muddy wad of tissues balled in his hand. He muttered something even he didn't understand and they started off around the lake towards Prospect Park Southwest.

Talk about a miserable first day. He was covered in mud and about to slosh around Kensington, knocking on doors. His new lieutenant was itching for a reason to get rid of him.

It finally hit Carter.

He hadn't let himself admit it until now.

This case cut too damn close to home.

It should have felt like a lifetime ago, but it didn't.

Carter knew all too well what it meant to be the boy in the photograph.

Chapter Four

HAVING FORGOTTEN her umbrella in the sedan before heading out, Danny squinted through the mist as she shuffled along Caton Avenue where pedestrians from all walks of life were hurrying in both directions, eager to get home.

Light shafting from the storefront windows bounced off wet cars parked along the street, casting the block in an eerie twinkle, though it failed to distract her from the long, arduous day she'd survived at the 66th.

After the painstaking hours she and Carter had spent pounding on doors and ringing buzzers, she knew no more about the Vic than she had when she'd first laid eyes on the body in the park.

Carter had grown increasingly impatient, though he'd done a soldierly job of masking his frustration. Every time he had sucked his lips in and forced himself to breathe through the sting of yet another resident slamming their door in his face, Danny had done him the courtesy of pushing onward to the next apartment instead of prying into the specific reason behind his souring mood.

He had seemed to take each dead-end personally, and as the afternoon had progressed, her curiosity had mounted to agitating levels.

Carter was new to the division, but not to Brooklyn. The fact that all the residents they had tried to talk to had refused to cooperate couldn't have surprised him. On the whole, New Yorkers minded their own and avoided the police as a general rule. Her partner must have known, and yet he had approached one door after the next with the kind of urgency she would expect if it had been his own son in those photos.

Or maybe he was simply an urgent guy and she was reading too much into it.

Her old partner, Mick Connolly had operated with quiet confidence. He had been methodical, scrutinizing every detail in silent, careful observation. When Franco had brought Danny into the fold, Connolly had a solid eight years at SVU under his belt, and because of it he had been cool and steadfast while teaching her the ropes.

Carter would benefit from the same guidance and if Danny wanted a tight partnership—which was the only way to tackle case after case and maintain her stellar clearance rate—she would have to afford him the same favor, she reasoned as she came upon O'Toole's.

Nothing lifted her out of deep thought like sensing Tommy was near.

She crept up to the edge of the glass pane and peered inside the bar. As always, Tommy was behind the counter, his back to the windows, his broad shoulders causing the tee shirt he wore to pull taut. By the looks of it, he was mixing a drink, but she couldn't be sure unless he turned around.

The regulars were seated in their usual spots, assembled drinkers nursing lagers and pilsners and IPAs in frosted glasses. Familiar faces. Cops she used to know for no other reason than they secretly admired Tommy as much as she did. They frequented this pub and no other, overspending what little spare cash they had because a few hours at O'Toole's had the power to make them feel like they weren't alone.

It had started as a fling and should've stayed that way. Tommy had taken an interest in her, thought she was being funny one night when she had lingered sloppily after the last call. Really she had been sincere about not wanting to go home—*my mother's always there, comes and goes freely, can I live at the bar, please?*

All mothers are like that, he had assured her, but by then she'd decided on a new objective—going home with the bartender instead of going home.

Tommy lived in an apartment above the bar, and as they'd tripped their way up the stairs, tearing each other's clothes off and kissing roughly—booze on her breath, cigarettes mingling with whiskey on his—Danny had never felt freer in her whole life.

They had kept it a secret—those late nights spent at his hole-in-the-wall apartment above O'Toole's.

It had been simple and invigorating and perfect.

And it had ended…

Badly.

A car honked, its sharp bleat shattering her time warp, but she thought nothing of it until the driver leaned on the horn.

Glancing over her shoulder, Danny recognized the vehicle—a clunky, early model Volvo. It had rolled to a stop, its passenger side window down.

Nora was inside, leaning over the seat and eyeing her. Her mother hollered for her to get in.

As Danny crossed the sidewalk and stepped off the curb in-between two parked cars, her mother shouted, "Honey, I would've picked you up!"

"The train was fine," she said, pulling the car door open and hopping in, as the drivers behind them began punching their horns.

Nora eased on the gas, giving Danny just enough time to yank her door shut. They merged into the steady flow of traffic, which didn't last long. Nora flicked the blinker, squeezing the brakes and preparing to turn up Ocean Parkway if only the oncoming traffic weren't so dense.

In the interim, Danny caught sight of her mother glimpsing the rearview mirror—the bar, no doubt.

"You have to stop doing that to yourself," said Nora crossly, returning her eyes to the road.

"I'm not doing anything to myself. What did you do today?" she asked, trying to change the topic so it wouldn't be her ex. The subject of Tommy was a festering wound that might never heal.

Nora let some time pass before complaining, "Tommy was no good."

At first, Danny said nothing as she stared at the windshield, the tinkling rain, its long streaky drops, and the way the wipers slid across the glass, clearing the rain every few seconds with a squeaky pulse.

A moment later, Danny said in a small voice, "You don't know him like I do."

"I know he got the hell out of dodge when he found out he was going to be a father," she pointed out as though the entire concept of Tommy O'Toole disgusted her.

Danny didn't have it in her to defend him, but Nora's statement hadn't been accurate. "He didn't walk away when he found out," she reminded her mom. "It was six months in."

"Same thing," she grumbled, having lost steam as well.

Finally, the line of oncoming cars cleared and she hit the gas, turning up Ocean Parkway and nearing the rowhouses. "You're better off without him," she added in a noncommittal tone. "It does you no good to stroll by that bar. Hey," she said, perking up as she shifted into Park and killed the engine, having angled the Volvo along the curb. "We should get out of town one of these weekends. Nance is getting her cabin in order. You had fun in the Catskills last year, remember?"

The last thing Danny wanted was to spend another long weekend cooped up in a cabin with that chatterbox. Nance literally never shut up—*let me see your eyebrows, do you pluck or wax? Seeing anyone special? Another cookie and you'll get fat!* Her every comment was an act of intrusion.

But Danny knew that if she objected to Nora's Catskills idea it would only incite an argument so she changed the subject, jutting her thumb at the backseat. "Is that all the groceries?"

"There are a few more bags in the trunk," she said, pulling the lever at her feet.

The trunk popped open and as Danny climbed out and began collecting grocery bags from the backseat, Nora padded to the rear of the Volvo and grabbed the rest.

But she didn't pass Danny's stoop to continue walking to her own building.

"You didn't buy all this for me, did you?"

Nora paused on the second step, fishing her keys out of her coat pocket, and told her, "I already have everything I need."

"You shouldn't have, Ma," she said, joining Nora at the entrance door.

"I had to do *something* today," she said earnestly. "You were right. You had hardly any laundry."

Danny had to laugh.

That was the thing about her mother. Her kindness far outweighed her nitpicking and tendency to blur or rather ignore personal boundaries, and because of it Danny, at the end of the day, deeply appreciated their relationship.

She pulled the door open once her mother had unlocked it, and together they trailed through the lobby where the building super, Camil Usov, was balancing on a ladder in a precarious effort to change a light bulb.

As Nora whipped the stairwell door open, she asked Danny, "Did you like the lunch I brought you?" without acknowledging Camil, who had grunted 'hello' in Russian.

Danny greeted Camil before replying, "Yes, Ma."

As Camil continued twisting in the light bulb, it blew, cracking the glass in his hand.

"You okay?" Danny asked him.

She didn't have to look at her mother to know Nora was annoyed.

"Fine, I'm fine," he said, sucking his finger as he climbed off the ladder. He glared at the socket as though it had bit him on purpose and then waved them off.

As they lumbered up the stairs, Danny whispered, "You could be nicer to Camil."

"I'm plenty nice considering he's raised your rent time and again."

"Ma, he just drops the notices off. He's not the one in charge of the rent increases. You know that."

The look Nora shot her spoke volumes—*that's what you think?* or *you're so naïve* commingling with *good grief!*—as she yanked the stairwell door open and spilled out into the second floor corridor.

Shuffling with three grocery bags in each hand, Danny led the way to her apartment, but it was Nora who opened the door.

"Hey," said Danny, "did my Netflix movie come?"

"I put it on the islet," she said, disinterested.

She held the door for her daughter and as soon as Danny had set her bags down in the foyer and relieved Nora of the others, Nora locked up.

"I want to watch that documentary tonight. Did you check it out?"

"I read the jacket," she allowed, wasting no time carrying the bags into the kitchen. "You really want to watch that cop stuff? Don't you get enough of it at work?"

Danny wriggled out of her raincoat, hung it on the rack, and said, "You'd think so." She was still overheating so she pulled her sweater up and over her head and tossed it on the couch as she made her way to the islet where Nora was pulling grocery items from the bags.

Nora did a double-take, her eyes bouncing to Danny's chest.

At first, Danny assumed it was because of the ratty, gray tee shirt she was wearing.

Nora's expression twisted with sympathy, as she said, "Oh, honey."

Danny looked down at her chest. There were two damp stains around her nipples. "Shoot," she muttered.

As she made her way into her bedroom, listening to Nora chattering about cop documentaries and how she hoped Danny hadn't suffered too much her first day back at work, Danny wondered when this would end—the swollen breasts, leaking milk, hormones rushing through her veins. It was as though her body didn't know that her baby, Gregory, had passed away.

It struck a nerve.

She pulled open one of the dresser drawers, but as she began hunting for another tee shirt, tears welled up in her eyes, blurring her vision.

Leaning against the open drawer for support, she let the emotions out as quietly as she could. Face flexing, air pushing past her vocal chords, eyes pinching shut, she cried without making a sound. Every part of her screaming inwardly as she slowly keeled over.

She felt robbed.

He shouldn't have died.

There was just no moving on.

And the man who she had fallen in love with; the man whose baby she had loved, still didn't know their child had died.

After three minutes of solid, soundless weeping, she sobered up, opened her eyes, and let out a soft moan, forcing herself to get it together.

But Danny was standing on the edge of a very dark place.

She wiped her wet face with the heels of her hands then picked out a tee shirt. She changed quickly, threw her stained tee into the hamper, and returned to the kitchen where Nora was waiting for her with a glass of red wine, having tucked the groceries into the cabinets.

Her mother's face said it all. She hadn't heard Danny crying in there, but she *knew*. Whenever Danny grew too quiet in her room, Nora knew.

Yet they had never addressed it.

Though it contradicted the worry on her face, Nora used a chipper tone to suggest, "Your documentary sounds fascinating." Her voice had cracked badly, but she brushed over their mutual grief and offered her daughter the wine glass. "I've got a casserole heating up. Let's recharge that battery of yours."

If her mother said one more nice thing, Danny would have broken down all over again, so she pulled Nora in for a long hug to shut her up.

Her voice came muffled from Danny's shoulder as she said, "You are so strong." After a beat she added, "Don't you spill that wine now."

But Danny was bringing the wine glass to her mouth anyway. She stole a sip, as her mother squeezed her.

When finally they released one another, Nora busied herself in the kitchen, while Danny curled up on the couch with her glass of wine.

Steering her thoughts away from Gregory, she wrapped her mind around the one subject that had always had the power to make her forget herself.

The killer's logic.

Bludgeoned, raped, left naked in a public place, outside no less where the elements could degrade her even further, the victim had been positioned next to damning evidence—child pornography. The scene had been saturated in 'shame,' but whose? Had this murder been the ultimate act of exposure? Had the victim harmed the boy? Did those photos belong to her? Had dumping her body in the park been a symbol of exposing her demented secret life? Was that what using a wooden object to defile her body had been about, giving her a taste of her own medicine?

Or was Carter's instinct correct? Had the boy in the photographs and the dead woman been victimized by the same perp?

Either way one thing was clear, though she was light years away from proving it—the killer must have known both victims intimately. And Danny's gut was telling her that the desperate measure he'd taken—murdering the woman—could have been a twisted effort to right a wrong.

Perverse justice.

Nora had been blathering on from the kitchen, but it wasn't until she mentioned, "...clear out the room, paint the walls white or maybe beige, put the crib on Craigslist" that Danny snapped back into herself.

"What?" she said, staring at her mother who was pulling the casserole out of the oven.

Regretfully, Nora said, "I don't think the reminder is doing you any good, Danny," as she set the steaming pan on the burner.

"Do not touch his room," she warned.

"I don't want to see you living in the past."

"It's not the past," she shot back, talking over her mother. "It was less than two weeks ago."

"Which is why it's not healthy for you to be back at work," she argued, convoluting her point with another as if it was of equal importance. She studied Danny and a silent negotiation ensued. "I just want you to be happy."

The complete disconnect between mourning and happiness pitched Danny into sudden stammering. Words flew from her mouth without her consent. She couldn't believe her mother would suggest such a thing! Clean out Gregory's room? Remove all traces of her son from her home? How the hell would that help? But just as Danny was about to voice the final word on the subject, her cell phone vibrated in the front pocket of her jeans.

She grabbed her cell, and when she glanced at the screen, she saw the precinct's number.

"Ma," she barked, silencing her mother, who had been trying to apologize without sounding wrong. Danny swiped her thumb across the screen, accepting the call. "Foster."

"This is Cruz from Missing Persons," said the man on the other end.

Danny hopped off the couch and made a beeline for the foyer. "What have you got for me?"

Nora called out, "Danny?"

"There's a guy here who wants to file a report for a missing fifty-five year old woman," he explained in a low, whispering tone. "He brought a photo of her and I'm looking at it right now. I think it's your Vic."

Urgently, she asked, "Can you hold him there?"

"I can try."

"I'm on my way." She shoved her cell into her pocket, circling back to the couch where she'd left her sweater. After yanking it on, she blindly slid her feet into her sneakers as she threw on her raincoat.

"Was that work?" asked Nora, rushing over and wringing her hands in a fretful manner.

She dropped to her knees to tie one sneaker then the next, saying, "I have to go." When she popped up again, she patted her pockets to be sure she had her keys.

"When will you be home?" asked Nora, her tone implying she didn't want to sound like a nag. "When will you eat?"

But Danny was already closing the door behind her and calling out, "Lock up when you go, thanks!"

Chapter Five

THE MISSING PERSONS Unit was located on the second floor of the 66th Precinct.

Jogging up the stairs, Danny took the treads two at a time.

As soon as she reached the landing, she saw Carter through the narrow window on the stairwell door. He was standing in front of the counter and gesticulating at the officer on the other side in what looked like a heated debate.

Throwing the door open, she entered the bullpen, which bore an unfortunate resemblance to her own on the first floor. Beyond the counter were clustered desks overwrought with case files. The room had bad lighting.

As she briskly approached, Carter glanced over his shoulder and locked eyes with her—his jaw clenching, brow furrowed, anger rolling off him like steam from an engine.

Officer Cruz on the other hand looked bewildered, one palm pressed to the countertop, the other balled in a fist and planted on his hip. Though she had never met him before face-to-face, he had the demeanor of every rookie cop she'd ever encountered—a fit figure, alert eyes, but an overall look of insecurity.

The plastic chairs directly across from the counter were empty, she noted, which told her why her partner seemed furious.

"You couldn't hold him?" she asked, nearing Cruz, who looked relieved that Danny had arrived.

Carter wouldn't be able to rake Cruz over the coals anymore.

Irritably, Carter paced away, running his hand over his shaved head, as Cruz offered her the report he'd taken not twenty minutes ago.

"The guy said he was in a big hurry," he explained, his gaze darting to Carter as though he expected the quarterback to tackle him for making excuses. But Carter had reeled in his emotions, or so it seemed.

Skimming the form, Danny noticed the lower half that should have contained contact information had been left blank. "He didn't leave his phone number?"

Cruz shook his head, 'no.'

Danny screwed her face up. "He reported the woman missing, but doesn't want the cops to let him know if and when the woman is found?"

She touched eyes with Carter.

"If you ask me," said Officer Cruz, who by this point seemed afraid to say anything in front of Carter, "he was concerned but didn't want to get involved."

Carter turned to Danny. He didn't agree with Cruz's rookie impression. Quietly, he said, "Who anonymously reports someone missing?" After a beat, he provided the answer, "No one."

As her partner paced away for the second time, she studied the photograph that was stapled to the upper left hand corner of the form.

The woman in the photo was Nordic-looking as ever with blonde, wavy curls spilling around her austere face. Sharp green eyes, a wide mouth, thin lips straight as a pin, distinct seriousness in her expression—this was definitely their Vic. But the photo was cropped too tightly around her head for Danny to get any sense of the setting.

"Agatha Bauer?" she read before glancing at Cruz.

"Lives in Kensington," he confirmed, tensely glimpsing Carter and adding, "on Cortelyou."

"I see," she said softly, skimming the other details, which included her place of employment. Without lifting her eyes from the report, she told her partner, "Let's have Jill confirm the identity using our Vic's dental impression."

"I've already called her," Carter said.

Impressed, Danny asked, "How late was I?"

"You weren't."

She set the form on the counter and asked Cruz, "Can I get a copy?" As Cruz marched off to do just that—there was an industrial printer at the back of the bullpen—she turned to Carter. "I say we check out 112 Cortelyou Road."

He summarized, "This guy knows where she lives, where she works. He had a photo of her." His undertone was crystal clear.

"And he didn't leave any personal information," she added, feeling his frustration. "One step at a time."

"He did this," Carter insisted. "He's one of those sickos who gets off on meddling in his own investigation."

There was a wry twist to her mouth as she said, "Then lucky for us. It means he'll make a mistake." She let that hang for a beat before daring to suggest, "It's also possible he didn't kill her and was legitimately concerned."

"Yeah," Carter snorted, sarcastic in his agreement. "He's so concerned, he doesn't want to be contacted if and when she's found."

Officer Cruz returned with a photocopy of the report and as Danny reviewed it, Carter asked him, "What did the guy look like?"

Immediately, Cruz lifted the desk phone to his ear, mentioning, "I'll have the surveillance footage from downstairs pulled."

Carter pressed his finger on the telephone switch hook before the officer could dial. "Just tell me what the guy looked like so I have something to investigate while you take hours to obtain that footage."

"Six feet tall or so, white," he said, rattling off the guy's characteristics. "Thirties."

Urgently, he asked, "Denim jacket, scar across his forehead?" Anticipating Danny's question, he spat out, "From the park."

"Neither," said Cruz bluntly, who was by now equally annoyed as Carter. "He was wearing a black windbreaker and a skullcap."

"Down to his eyebrows?" he asked, but it sounded more like an assertion. "Covering his forehead?"

"A picture's worth a thousand words," he told him, once again lifting the phone to his ear.

Unsatisfied, Carter eyed the officer, as he dialed security downstairs. Danny could almost see her partner's mind racing with theories—Cruz's description hadn't ruled out the man from Prospect Park.

"Let's get forensics on this," she said, nudging Carter away from the counter. As they headed towards the stairwell door, she added, "I'll call Franco and see if we can get a warrant."

Carter's attitude was extremely difficult to read, so she said, "Hey."

He looked consumed in deep thought and didn't respond.

"Carter?"

"Yeah?" he said absently, but with his eyes fixed on the row of plastic chairs where their perp should've been.

Turning just shy of the stairwell door, she stood in his path so he would be forced to listen. "You can't talk to the other officers like that."

"Like what?" he challenged, staring dead at her.

"Accusingly," she shot back. "That's not how we operate." When he shifted his stance, looking off, she again said, "Hey," and his gaze drifted back in a way that reminded her of a brooding teenager. "Is there something you want to tell me?"

"It won't happen again," he conceded.

"That's not what I meant."

Evading the question, he stated, "Something's off about this case."

She swiftly assured him, "We'll talk to Bauer's neighbors, coworkers, friends, and family. This is a huge break."

"Yeah, hand delivered to us by the man who did it."

"You don't know that-"

"I know," he insisted. "I might not 'know,' but I *know*." He opened the door for her, adding, "I don't like being toyed with."

Chapter Six

DRIZZLING RAIN pissed over the 66th Precinct as well as the police cruisers lining the block.

Lewis Sauter stood in-between parked cars on the other side of the darkened street.

He watched the entrance door, or more specifically, the two detectives inside the precinct who were engaged in what appeared to be a tired disagreement.

Rain tapped against his skullcap. Beneath it, his scalp felt itchy. His forehead was damp wool pressed into his skin. But his curiosity far outweighed his desire to escape the miserable weather.

The Black detective was built like a tank—athletic and stiff in his movements—his skin tone so dark that from this distance Lewis couldn't make out the man's expression. Given the present company, he figured the guy was oscillating between hope and exasperation...

Because of the woman—the female detective.

Lewis felt it too—instantaneous intrigue, obsession, a compulsion to take her to his secret place and never let her go.

The female detective hadn't been Lewis' initial reason for loitering, but she was now.

As soon as she'd neared the glass door, a floating sense of calm had washed over him. He liked her face—sad doe-eyes, her slanted mouth, the skepticism it implied as if she was almost pleased to be arguing. He found her raincoat endearing, likewise her little feet, those soggy sneakers, her no-nonsense haircut. Few women could pull off the look.

He should have let her catch him in the park that day. Should've let her wrestle him to the grass. Would she have mounted him, pinned his hands above his head if only for a moment before flipping him onto his stomach and cuffing him? He wondered what she smelled like and if he'd ever get close enough to find out.

As the detectives streamed out of the precinct, the African-American all-star holding the door for his porcelain doll partner, Lewis lowered his head, sensing more than seeing that he was still bathed in a pool of shadows, light from the two lamp posts at either end of the block unable to reach him.

Staring through his eyebrows at the detectives as they lingered under the precinct awning to further debate, Lewis hooked his finger under the brim of his skullcap and itched the eyebrow-end of his scar.

Touching the scar sent him to places he didn't want to go mentally.

Seized by a slideshow of images flashing through his mind—broken bones, bruised arms, cracked ribs—he winced, buried his hands in his pockets, and reminded himself that the object of his sudden obsession (the female detective) would be nothing like the woman who had raised him. *That* woman couldn't hurt him anymore. She was long since dead, and yet the memories buzzed in his head like a hornet's nest.

The detectives started off down the sidewalk through the drizzling rain, passing a line of police cruisers and jarring Lewis from a dirty swell of recollection.

He studied the woman's gait, visualizing her figure beneath the bulky raincoat she wore. Legs long yet shapely, hips wide and shoulders wider—a mouthwatering hourglass he'd like to drink. She seemed just maternal enough to quench his thirst...

Infatuation at first sight was a powerful motivator.

When the detectives reached a brown sedan and climbed in—the football player behind the steering wheel, the woman in the passenger seat—he darted across the street, coming to the cruisers for a closer look, but he didn't catch sight of her pretty face in the side-view mirror.

The rain thickened into a downpour, as he watched their vehicle pull away from the curb—tail lights glowing, water flowing down the rear windshield. The detective driving rolled down his window and snapped a cherry siren onto the roof before the vehicle banked around the corner.

"Ford, Crown Victoria, 2007, license plate number XVF9878," he murmured, memorizing its make and model, as he stared at the intersection though the car had disappeared.

He pulled the skullcap off his head, letting the cold rain saturate his hair, run down his face and neck, drip off the tip of his nose, bringing him into sharp focus.

He began walking north then east then north again, zigzagging his way home.

When he turned onto Ditmas Avenue, he was soaking yet he felt more alive than ever. Vehicles streamed in both directions along the street, tires kicking up water and spraying the sidewalk, headlights glaring in his eyes, as he waited on the curb for traffic to thin out.

He jogged across at the first opportunity, pausing briefly on the double yellow for a lone truck to growl by.

Lewis lived in a pre-war, brick building that seemed as old as the city itself. Looming over the avenue, his apartment building was four stories taller than the other structures lining the block, which was the only thing about it that gave him a sense of pride.

After keying into the dimly lit lobby, he ran his hand down his face, wiping off rainwater, and hurried to the elevator, eager to get up to the sixth floor. He flung the outer door open and its inner twin slid lazily into the wall, allowing him entry.

It was a shaky crawl to the top floor and as soon as the inner door rattled aside, he pushed the outer door open and barreled into the corridor, mentally willing his erection not to pop before he could fully enjoy it. The female detective, that impish mouth of hers, was burning into the forefront of his mind.

The slum he'd called home for the past twelve months was just as he'd left it, he noted, as he stepped inside his dilapidated studio apartment. The place looked as though it hadn't undergone a renovation since the Second World War.

Plaster peeling from the walls, ceiling bowed, the oblong room smelled of mildew.

On the floor was a bare mattress angled against the wall where rain tapped the windows. His desk, though child-sized, was kitty-cornered and the only piece of furniture he owned.

He locked the door and edged into the kitchen area where he tossed his keys on the laminate countertop, scaring away a pair of roaches that slithered into the sink. The tin can he'd placed in the far corner of the room was full, he realized having neared it, so he dumped the water out in the sink, once again giving the roaches a new reason to scurry off. And then he crouched, returning the empty can to the floor.

He stared at the ceiling.

As he waited for the next drip to fall, a draft seeping through the window panes chilled his bones. When finally the leak beaded into a fat drop and plunked against the scuffed-wood floor, he adjusted the tin can an inch to the left then neared the miniature desk.

The neighbors below were having a fight, which made him shrivel slightly in his jeans.

After forcefully peeling off his black windbreaker along with the denim jacket underneath and chucking both onto the sunken mattress, he sat down on the small chair and flipped on the lamp.

A soft, tungsten glow brightened a bulletin board that was propped against the wall.

Photographs of Agatha Bauer were pinned across the cork surface of the bulletin board. In one photo, the sinister woman was laughing in front of a glass shelving unit filled with trinkets, as she held her meaty arms around a little girl, who looked disturbed. The girl wore an *I heart NYC* tee shirt.

Another photo depicted Agatha in a supermarket angrily squeezing peaches to find a ripe one. There were a smattering of other photos, all images of her private life, such as bathing and dressing and nursing steaming cups of tea inside her house. As far as Lewis was concerned, none of the photos conveyed her true personality.

The woman had been a monster.

Lewis grabbed a bottle of whiskey, which he kept tucked between the leg of the desk and a trash bin. He unscrewed the top and took a swig, welcoming the familiar sting.

His gaze fell to the sketchpad on his desk, those drawings of the German woman who had deceived him for so long. He'd managed remarkable realism capturing Agatha's likeness. His skill was almost photographic.

After pounding a few more swigs, he slapped the bottle onto his desk and flipped to a blank page. As he crudely shoved his hand down the front of his damp jeans, exploring his arousal, he began drawing the female detective with the slanted mouth and boyish hair.

"They're not all the same," he reminded himself, pushing his mother's wicked smirk from his mind as he dug his pencil into the paper, using angry strokes to draw Detective Danielle Foster. "But when they are, they get what they deserve."

Chapter Seven

ALL THE HOUSES lining Cortelyou Road looked identical, perhaps because it was night but Danny didn't think so.

Detached one-family Victorians made of ticky-tacky. Three stories. Narrow. Chipped clapboards and accents built with other shoddy materials that hadn't held up over the years.

Each cookie-cutter house had a stoop of six steps leading up to the front door. The steps were lined with shrubs so wide, they blocked the living room windows.

There were barely five feet separating the Vic's home from the neighboring ones, Danny noted.

She squinted through the misting rain. The second floor of Agatha Bauer's house had three windows that were hooded under a long clipped-gable roof. No lights were on inside, she observed as she thumbed her notepad in her raincoat pocket.

Restlessly, Carter paced behind her on the sidewalk, clutching his cell phone. They were expecting a call. Danny's phone hadn't rung either.

The judge was taking his sweet time signing the warrant, that was for damn sure, and the uniformed officers assembled on the sidewalk were getting impatient because of it.

Danny pushed her raincoat sleeve up her wrist and checked the time before touching eyes with Jill Andover, who was huddled under a giant black umbrella with a few other forensic investigators. She seemed more interested in Carter's simmering disposition than the holdup.

Everyone was getting antsy so Danny decided to put a few officers to work despite her uncertainty as to whether or not she would find a crime scene within the morose-looking house.

Raising her voice, she called out, "Martinez, Wong," and the officers promptly stepped forward, straightening their spines. "Go knock on some doors." She indicated the homes on either side of Agatha's. "See if anyone saw or heard something the night of the 10th. Time of death was between eight and ten," she reminded them.

When she turned to Carter, having given the cops their assignments, she realized he was now on the phone. His cell was clamped tightly to his ear.

A moment later, he waved two officers over. The cops were holding a tactical ram—a four-foot metal cylinder meant to smash through locked doors.

Carter yelled, "Let's go!"

Danny breathed, "Finally," and stepped aside, as the men jogged the ram up the stoop, swung it back, and bashed the front door open, breaking into the house.

Drawing her weapon, she joined Carter. Together they padded up the steps, a flutter of excitement between them where nerves had once been. They charged past the officers who were standing in the dimly lit foyer of the house, awaiting orders.

But Danny didn't give any. Instead she edged deeper into the house, her partner was at her heels with his gun drawn.

The living room was bathed in shadows. Light from the neighboring house spilled through the curtained windows on the west wall, creating hazy pools around a Bridgewater couch, rustic coffee table, bookshelves packed to the gills with hardcovers. Danny could hear the neighbor's television as well, muffled laugh tracks, chattering dialogue, more laughs, as she slowly crept deeper into the room.

The overhead lights flipped on, surprising her, and when she glanced over her shoulder, she found Carter near the switch.

A quick sweep of the room, and she noticed a profound lack of noises overhead. This told her that the house was empty.

She holstered her gun.

"No signs of forced entry," he commented, eyeing the doorframe. "Aside from us."

"Ha, ha," she said with a smile before scanning the living room more carefully.

The wooden coffee table sat squarely on top of an area rug. The floor was otherwise hardwood, the couch—cracked brown leather with an afghan blanket resting over its back—was in front of the kitchen by a good eight feet. Every surface—the table, the bookshelves, the kitchen counter beyond the way—was covered with trinkets and tchotchkes, framed photos of Agatha, catalogs and magazines running the full gamut, from fly fishing to knitting to crafting the perfect Halloween costume.

Danny took a slow lap around the room.

"I think we found our crime scene," she said when she noticed the far side of the area rug, or more specifically the floor beside it where a pool of blood had congealed.

"Hey, Jill?"

The medical examiner approached, thrilled to have Carter in tow. She snuck a self-conscious glance at him and he bristled without returning her gaze.

Then he noticed the blood. He got a quick impression of the crime scene and asked Danny, "You got this?"

Jill frowned, but pretended she was responding to the blood.

Danny nodded at Carter, excusing him—why was he so sensitive about a little harmless crush?

She crouched near the pool of blood next to Jill.

Carter called a few unis over and told them to come with him upstairs. Before he left, he said to Danny, "Something tells me the post-mortem offenses happened in the bedroom."

Deflated, Jill watched him follow the officers up to the second floor, then she let out a ragged sigh, shifting gears before closely eyeing the couch, its dimpled leather, and the afghan blanket, looking for blood splatter.

Danny guessed, "Bauer was sitting on the couch and someone struck her from behind? She fell forward onto the floor?"

Jill used what appeared to be a massive Q-tip to swab the blood on the floor as she said, "I'd say so."

With her partner out of sight, Danny freely scrawled on her notepad, recording the ME's observations as well as her own.

Rising to her feet again, she scanned the room, looking for a stone or marble object, but there was no obvious murder weapon in sight. She walked around to the back of the couch, as Jill called her forensic analysts over. They immediately began assisting her, swabbing blood and taking photographs, bagging and tagging.

Danny spotted scuff marks on the floor behind the couch and said, "Let's figure out what caused these," even though the marks could have been inconsequential and have nothing to do with the murder.

Jill was on it none-the-less, joining her and looking at the wooden floor.

"Why isn't there a trail of blood leading away from the pool?" Danny asked, addressing no one in particular, though the unis knew what to do.

They began swarming the area, hunting for trace evidence. "Bauer lived alone," Danny went on, having gleaned the details earlier at the precinct. "I want every inch of this place dusted for prints. Our killer spent hours here. He had to have left something behind."

She found a pair of latex gloves in her raincoat pocket and pulled them on, as she crossed deeper into the house, passing the tawdry kitchen on her left. She trailed through a truncated hallway and came to the rear entrance.

At first she carefully eyed the door—beige, 6-panel texture, no window—noting that it sat flush in the frame, the deadbolt turned, which meant it was locked. She studied the doorknob. No blood, but with any luck there would be a print or two, touch DNA if they were lucky.

The killer had locked up on his way out.

Why?

From the second floor, Carter shouted, "Danny?"

"Yeah?" she called out, starting through the house and pocketing her notepad before rounding to the foot of the stairs just off the foyer.

Carter was gripping the banister with his gloved hand and stooping to make eye contact from the top of the stairs. "You're going to want to see this. Jill, too."

As the medical examiner sang, "Give me a minute!" Danny padded up the treads, passing a grid of framed photos covering the walls—Agatha beaming a breezy smile, head thrown back, eyes bright; Agatha in profile, squinting into the blazing summer sun; Agatha flaunting all ten manicured fingernails, her expression one of smug satisfaction. The woman was in every photo and alone at that.

It struck Danny as odd.

Why so many photos of herself all over the house?

It didn't seem like innocent vanity, but rather akin to narcissism.

Danny thought of her own apartment. The walls weren't bare, but at the same time they weren't covered with pictures of herself. It seemed Agatha had celebrated her looks.

When she reached the landing, Carter explained, "You've got to see her bedroom."

They stampeded down a narrow hallway where the walls were peppered with more photos of Agatha posing or otherwise boasting her distinguished, handsome looks, and came into a small, airless room.

A four-poster bed filled the bedroom. An antique dresser with a brass mirror on top was nearby.

Danny detected the faint scent of potpourri and saw a dish of decorative hand soaps—hearts and seashells—on the nightstand.

Quaint and cute, yet unlike the shabby downstairs, Agatha's bedroom looked like it had never made it out of 1940's Germany.

It was remarkably well preserved.

But it was slightly disarranged.

The duvet was bunched at the foot of the bed and spilling onto the floor. The pillows were pushed out of place as well, exposing a paisley fitted sheet.

Curious, Danny neared Carter at the side of the bed where a disheveled garbage bag lay on the tufted carpet beside what appeared to be a modest heap of laundry.

Carter pointed to the fitted sheet and when Danny inspected the pattern, smeared blood droplets jumped out at her.

"The killer might have wrapped her head in this after killing her downstairs," he theorized, picking up the garbage bag. "Then carried her up here. It wasn't a perfect system," he went on, "given the blood that seeped out onto the sheet."

Danny noticed duct tape stuck to the garbage bag, which gave her a clearer picture of the killer's strategy.

Next, Carter lifted an article of clothing from the floor. It was a long-sleeved sweater. When he opened it, she saw that the killer had cut the garment clean down the front.

"Unis bagged and tagged the scissors," he explained, showing her a pair of jeans that had also been cut off the body. "I'll get these bagged and tagged."

Danny's gaze landed on the dish of hand soap and the dust it had collected. Then she glanced at the other nightstand where another framed photo of Agatha sat under cloudy glass. Unlike the other photos, this one was black and white. But when Danny took the framed photo in her hands, she realized it wasn't a photograph at all.

It was a drawing.

Sketched in pencil.

The pencil drawing was extremely impressive.

Carter watched her with interest so she held the drawing up for him and asked, "Am I the only one who finds this strange?"

"What?" he said, not quite getting it.

Demonstratively, she gestured to the bedroom walls, all of which contained photos of Agatha and no one else.

"Why so many photos of herself?" she wondered, and honesty compelled her to add, "It's creepy."

"Unless it ties into the killer's motive..." he trailed off, shaking his head as if the sketch didn't matter, and shrugged.

"Maybe it's related," she pushed. "The Vic was obsessed with herself and her looks, evidently. The killer put a garbage bag over her head before he violated her post-mortem."

"So he didn't have to look at her?" he played along but used a skeptical tone. "I think the guy just didn't want to get blood on the sheets."

"Why would he care? It's not like he cleaned up downstairs."

Carter glanced around the room, considering her point, but when he replied, he addressed a different element, one she was also curious about.

"There are a hell of a lot of collectables. Look at this," he said, pointing to a brass tchotchke that resembled a tiny mallard duck. As he plucked it off the nightstand, it rattled. "You can't buy stuff like this anymore." He returned the item, his interest having ebbed away, and added, "Is it a baby's toy? I wouldn't let my kids play with that. It's cold, heartless. The whole room is heartless. It looks like post-war Europe in here."

She smiled, testing him with, "Do you recognize the decor?"

"German," he said easily then teased, "I know you think I'm just a pretty face."

"No," she teased. "That's what Jill thinks."

Of course Jill would fill the doorway at that precise moment with three forensic investigators in tow. Danny hadn't even heard them clatter up the stairs.

Indignantly, the medical examiner held her head high, refusing Carter eye contact and marching towards the four-poster bed, ready to examine whatever evidence they'd found.

They worked all night. Danny suppressed frustrations as she scribbled through her entire notepad, cluttering each page with questions and observations. Carter grew increasingly miffed as well but was far less graceful about hiding it.

Morale sank as reality gradually set in—the killer had left no trace of himself behind.

By dawn the unis had diligently bagged and tagged every single item—photographs and tchotchkes alike. The forensic team had dusted every last inch of surface space for fingerprints, of which they'd found none, not even a partial print. And worse, the unis that had canvased the neighboring houses had returned with no leads.

The sun crept up the sky, rising between the buildings lining Cortelyou, as Danny and Carter left Agatha Bauer's townhouse and descended the stoop.

As the sunshine brightened the fragile sky and turned the misty atmosphere to fog, the detectives soldiered onward into the next leg of their investigation.

Danny's eyes felt scratchy and dry, her legs felt like rubber, and it didn't help that her stomach had been rumbling for hours.

Carter on the other hand seemed keyed up. He'd gotten knocked around, the lack of evidence having landed like a bare-knuckle punch to his jaw. But now he was ready for round two, determined to win the fight. And he looked it. Eyes flaring. Breathing hard through his mouth. His necktie was loose and cockeyed, and the back of his shirt was hanging out. It made Danny wonder how unkempt she herself had become. If Carter had gotten a second-wind around dawn, at least that made one of them, she thought.

"The Statue of Liberty Museum Gift Shop opens in an hour," she mentioned, noting the time on her cell phone. She was hugely distracted by all the missed call notifications. They were from her mother. She could almost feel Nora's anxiety blazing through the LCD screen.

"Just enough time for coffee and bagels," he said optimistically.

Lumbering sluggishly along the sidewalk, she echoed, "Coffee..."

"As long as it's better than the hospital cafeteria's coffee," he warned with a sense of humor, elbowing her companionably before stepping off the curb and rounding to the driver's side of their unmarked sedan.

He unlocked the car and as they settled inside the vehicle—Carter bringing the engine to life and Danny mustering the motivation to find her seatbelt—he mentally shifted into an analytic gear, asking, "Premeditated or impulsive?"

Danny muscled her seatbelt across her chest, her grip feeling feeble, and agonized, "If the DA doesn't go for murder one..." Trailing off, Danny was momentarily crippled by the possibility that this case would deteriorate if the defense cut a deal for murder in the second or third degree. Or, God forbid, the killer pleaded guilty to manslaughter.

"He'll go for murder in the first," he assured her, focusing fully on Danny as he blindly groped for the headlight switch, the morning too balmy to drive without.

She corrected him, saying, "The DA is a she, and you never know."

Absorbing the detail, he steered the sedan into the street, heading northwest towards Red Hook where they would grab breakfast before taking a ferry across Upper Bay to Ellis Island. After a comfortable silence, he asked, "Is there a lot of head butting?"

"With the district attorney? I don't butt heads with her directly, no," she told him, closing her eyes in the vain hope that she might grab ten minutes of sleep. "Franco's gotten into it with her more than a few times, though."

But resting wasn't in the cards for Danny. Her cell phone vibrated. She opened her eyes only to make sure it wasn't Nora and seeing the precinct's prefix she swiped her thumb across the LCD screen and pressed her cell to her ear.

"Foster."

The man on the other end wasted no time delivering bad news. "There's no clear shot of the guy on the footage."

"Cruz?"

Once the officer had confirmed, he went on to elaborate. "I watched all the footage twice over. The guy who reported Agatha Bauer missing kept his head down the entire time he was here. His hand shielded his face too at times. Must have known where the cameras were. I'm emailing you the best shot anyway, but it isn't good."

She had the urge to curse, but thanked him instead before hanging up.

"No luck on the video?" Carter asked, the strained encounter with Cruz the night prior darkening his mood. When she shook her head, confirming the dead end, he pushed, "I want Cruz to sit down with a composite artist. I want that guy's face on paper."

"The department doesn't have it."

"A sketch artist?"

"The funds to pay for one," she clarified, apologizing with her eyes not that he noticed. He was glowering through the windshield, his fists wrapping the steering wheel in a white-knuckle grip.

"They won't front the funds based on a hunch anyway."

He fell silent, wrestling with recycled suspicions that the man who had reported Agatha missing had also taken her life.

She watched the windshield wipers hypnotically pulse across the glass and hoped that the tension rising between them wouldn't last.

Whether or not Carter's hunch about the guy from Missing Persons was accurate, one thing was glaringly evident.

They were being toyed with.

And yet that wasn't what consumed Danny as she stared lazily out of the passenger side window at the mist that was thickening over the neighborhood.

Agatha Bauer didn't strike her as an innocent pawn. Danny rarely contemplated a victim's culpability, but in this case she couldn't avoid it.

The child pornography photos. The narcissism that saturated every inch of Agatha's ticky-tacky house.

Danny had to wonder—*Agatha Bauer, what have you done?*

Why had Agatha been caught dead with those photos?

Did this case hinge on all that the boy from the photographs had endured?

How had the child exploitation motivated the murder, if at all?

As they drove through the neighborhood of Red Hook, apartment buildings soon gave way to warehouses—meat packing plants and manufacturing companies housed in one-story structures that reminded her of Lego blocks.

Buildings of any kind soon became few and far between as the piers came into view.

Upper Bay was balmy. Mist thickened over the water, gray swollen clouds covered a heavy sky.

Carter pulled the sedan into a parking spot in front of a diner at Pier 6, home of the NYC Water Taxi.

After ordering coffees and bagels inside where the scent of cleaning products overpowered that of food, an indication they were among the first customers that morning, the detectives left the diner and claimed one of the concrete picnic tables—circular, damp, and a far cry from comfortable—that overlooked the bay.

Having privately mulled over her own ideas, Danny started to wonder about her partner's. She was curious. What was he thinking? She decided to ask, "Any theories?"

He swallowed the bagel bite he had been chewing, sucked a morsel of cream cheese off his index finger, and said, "I think the jackass from the park killed her."

"Still?" she said, lifting her coffee cup to her mouth. "What's his motive? Don't look at me like that. I'm genuinely interested in knowing what you're thinking."

Danny chugged her coffee to flood her system with caffeine, as Carter took his time, pulling his thoughts together.

A pair of gulls swooped over the water. A few others squawked around a trash bin, too preoccupied with fighting with each other to actually eat.

Carter returned his gaze to her. His eyes seemed to darken, and when a faraway look came over him, Danny wondered if her new partner might have *personal* insights about this case.

"Let's just say if we find out that Bauer had a son she used to beat everyday, I wouldn't be surprised."

"Huh," she murmured, slipping into deep thought before hypothesizing. "Agatha moves from Germany to Brooklyn. Her son can't function as an adult, because the psychological effects of the abuse finally catch up with him. So he flies over to New York. Hunts her down."

"Gives her a taste of her own medicine," he supplied, as he balled his bagel wrapper, having lost his appetite.

"Mom abuses son. Son retaliates."

Carter frowned, perhaps not liking her cut-and-dry summary. "It's too neat and tidy for that to be the case, but I think the murder was deeply personal, an act of revenge. Whether the guy snapped one night or planned the whole thing..." he trailed off and shrugged. "Time will tell."

"According to Franco, Agatha didn't have any kids," she reminded him, referring to one of many phone calls they'd had with their lieutenant throughout the long night of investigating at the house. "But I think you're onto something."

He cracked a smile, and she realized her compliment held far more weight than she'd intended.

Rising from the table, they collected their trash and stuffed it in a garbage bin. The gulls hopped around excitedly, and the detectives made their way to their parked sedan. They climbed in and drove down to the parking area next to the water taxi stand.

After flashing their badges at the booth attendant to skip the fare, Danny accompanied Carter up a rickety metal ramp and onto the sea-level deck of the water taxi—an ugly yellow tugboat with a checkered strip on the side.

There was an indoor seating area on the deck level, but after one look at the steamy plexiglass, the moist-looking passengers crowding one another inside, they opted to walk around to the front of the boat where they found stairs to the roof deck.

The roof deck was equally crowded but far less miserable. A number of tourists were already snapping photographs of the cityscape, their cameras pressed to their faces, wowed by the charm and history of New York City's Hudson River and Brooklyn Bridge.

Carter leaned his elbows on the slick railing, which Danny also gripped, as the boat puttered out into brackish waters. When it cleared the buoys, the motors kicked up and the boat began sailing over the choppy bay, heading straight for Ellis Island.

The Statue of Liberty lurked like a ghostly apparition through the fog.

"I've never been to Lady Liberty," Carter commented.

"Ah," she mused, staring out at the dark water. "I guess when you immigrate from Germany, that's who you want to work for."

The damp air was thickening with misting rain, the wind stiff at this speed. Soon Danny's face felt clammy, her cheeks cold. She glanced at Carter who was no longer casually gripping the railing but holding it with two fists and looking a bit green. Clearly, the open water didn't agree with him.

Twelve nauseating minutes later, the balmy haze cleared, as the boat slowed to a putter and angled towards a dock at Ellis Island, the Statue of Liberty towering over the briny bay.

Woozy, Carter seemed in no rush to release the railing, perhaps fearing that if he did, he'd lose his lunch. The deck beneath his feet was still rising and falling with the swells of lapping waves.

"You okay?" she asked, watching as tourists filtered down the steps.

"Yeah," he lied.

"Not a fan of boats?"

"Something like that," he told her.

He ventured a few rocky steps towards the stairs where a lovey-dovey couple was blocking their way and smooching, unaware the boat had docked. Danny cleared her throat, inviting them back to planet Earth. Though they were still obnoxious when they arrived, angling their cameras up at the statue and snapping off a few shots, they kept it moving, flirting their way down the stairs so Carter and Danny could get off the boat.

It had been just the breather Carter needed to get his bearings, his nausea having ebbed away, and soon Danny was leading him down the stairs, along the sea-level deck, and off the back of the boat where they trailed across another rickety ramp, metal clanking with their every step.

After breaking away from the tourist group, which had been moving like a herd of cattle, the detectives finally entered the Statue of Liberty's museum and gift shop.

On the ground floor of the museum there was pink marble everywhere. Their footsteps echoed and they came into the gift shop.

Souvenirs and memorabilia lined the shelves. The gift shop seemed to twinkle, glass and mirrored trinkets everywhere Danny turned. There were racks stuffed with postcards, and others holding calendars, as well as stands filled with tee shirts, all boasting New York pride.

Behind the glass-top counter was a young sales girl—frizzy blonde hair piled high on her head in a messy bun, big owl eyes rimmed with black liner, her pillowy figure dwarfed in an oversized *I heart NYC* sweatshirt.

The sales girl chatted with a family of tourists, welcoming them to New York and encouraging them to purchase coffee mugs and other items.

Danny scanned the remaining tourists that were milling through the gleaming aisles in hopes that she might find the manager.

Carter wasn't nearly as patient. He barreled up to the counter, having pulled his badge from his waist, and wasted no time introducing himself.

Thrown by the interruption, the sales girl looked immediately worried.

The tourists, however, were thrilled that a New York City detective was about to *do something.*

A teenager pressed his camera to his eye and began photographing Carter.

Carter didn't like that.

Luckily, the teen's mother ushered him away along with the rest of her family.

"I'll be with you in a minute," the sales girl sang after them as they vanished behind a glass-shelving unit filled with ritzy paperweights.

"Agatha Bauer," he began, as Danny joined him at the counter. "She worked here, correct?"

"What about Agatha?" asked the sales girl, suddenly worried. "She didn't make it to work this morning. I called her several times. Is she okay?"

"Did you know her well?" he pressed. Carter didn't have time to dance around the matter.

"I knew her well enough. Did something happen?"

The sales girl glanced nervously from Carter to Danny, who was thumbing through her notepad, annoyed there wasn't a single blank sheet left. Giving up, she pocketed the thing, and broke the news to the girl. "Agatha was killed two nights ago."

The young woman's reaction was almost imperceptible. Her lips parted ever so slightly. Her breathing quickened, as a faraway look came over her.

Danny had been on the job long enough to recognize the signs of shock.

"She was killed?" she repeated as if to herself.

Danny waited for the shock that had overcome the girl to subside then asked, "Was she working on the 10th?"

"Um," she stammered, unable to think straight all over again. "That was Sunday? No, she doesn't usually work weekends."

Aiming to nail down their Vic's timeline, Carter asked, "So Friday was her last day here?"

"I think so," said the girl, whose name was *Jocelyn* according to the nametag clipped at a lazy angle to her shirt. "Let me get the schedule," she murmured. It took her a moment to get her bearings. She came out from behind the counter. "It's in the back."

Danny watched her trail through the gift shop. The girl pushed through a door marked *Private* and disappeared on the other side.

"Doesn't help our timeline," said Carter in a low, irritable tone. "Two full days? Agatha could've been anywhere doing anything."

Danny agreed it wasn't ideal.

When Jocelyn returned, a mousy-looking man who could only be the manager was at her heels. Thin wisps of sandy brown hair were dusted over the crown of his head. His mustache lifted as he offered the detectives a good-natured smile.

"Can I help you?" he asked, nervously. The young sales girl must have gotten him up to speed. He flipped open the binder in his hands, and after skimming one of the sheets inside, he told them, "You wanted to know when Agatha was last in? That was Friday. She left at six as always."

He asked Jocelyn to help a group of customers that had just walked in.

Wringing her hands, the sales girl made her reluctant way to the front of the gift shop.

"Agatha Bauer was killed Sunday night," Danny explained in a discrete tone. "This is Detective Dobbs and I'm Foster."

"Bill Muller," he said, a confused smile coming over him. "I can't believe anyone would kill her."

"And why's that?" asked Carter.

He frowned, as a look of concern washed over him. "Because I can't believe anyone would kill anyone. It's surreal. I'm beside myself."

Danny assumed that Bill Muller lived in a fantasyland where murder was inconceivable, and tried not to roll her eyes. "Did she contact you at all over the weekend?"

After a brief moment to think, he said, "She called me Sunday."

"What time?" asked Carter.

"Ah, around six or seven. She said she wasn't feeling well and needed to take Monday off. I granted her the day without thinking twice."

Carter told Danny, "She expected the confrontation."

"With her attacker," she quietly agreed. "Knew it would take a lot out of her and she would need a personal day."

"Does she do that often?" she asked Bill. "Call you?"

He let out a breathy sigh and mentioned, "We didn't have a personal relationship, no."

Carter studied the manager's demeanor for a beat. Was he nervous because he was hiding something? Or was this conversation so unusual that Bill Muller was starting to lose it a little? He seemed dissociative.

"Did she have a personal relationship with any of your employees?" Carter asked.

"We were happy to have Agatha and she pulled her weight," he began, neutralizing his emotions as he went on. "But most of my employees are young, in their twenties. As you might imagine working at a gift shop doesn't pay much," he said, implying that the age difference between Agatha and her coworkers would have prevented her from socializing outside of work.

Danny asked, "Was she dating anyone?" but was met with the same response—a frown, a shake of the head, Bill appearing generally lost.

A strange *hanging on by a thread* attitude filled him.

She neared Bill and tried to come across as sensitively as possible as she asked "Was Agatha *especially* fond of children?"

"Oh, yes," he said brightly. "She loved kids, made a point to ask them how they liked New York, and recommended fun things to do. If a child came through those doors, Agatha was on them."

Danny was tempted to consider this a red flag, but unfortunately Bill's response couldn't be trusted since he wasn't quite picking up what she was putting down, so she tried again. "Did her interest in children ever seem... inappropriate?"

Her point gradually dawned on Bill, which was lucky for Danny. She didn't want to have to mention that Agatha had been found dead with a stack of child pornography.

"For God's sake, no," he insisted, horrified. "Agatha? Never. No."

Appalled, he was at a loss for words after that. He stammered, checked his wristwatch, and then folded his arms. He obviously wanted this conversation to be over.

As Carter rephrased the question and asked him others, Danny felt eyes on her and found Jocelyn staring at her from behind the counter.

She recognized the look on the girl's face. Jocelyn had overheard them and was itching to add her two cents.

Excusing herself, Danny slipped away from her partner and neared the clerk. "Jocelyn? You okay?"

"Agatha wasn't... like that," she managed to say, choosing her words carefully. "Why? Do you think she was?"

"There's some evidence that incriminates Agatha," she disclosed. "It's something we have to ask about."

"You mean, whoever killed her was... *funny* like that?"

The girl's question was strange. Danny leaned over the counter a bit.

"It's possible," Danny said, studying the young woman, whose face was all screwed up—teenaged squeamishness trapped inside a twenty-two year-old. "Do you know something about that?"

Jocelyn held her breath as if debating whether or not to mention what was on her mind. After what felt like a long moment, she said, "We have a janitor. He only works nights, but I mean... *that's* why."

"What's why?"

"He's...*funny* like that."

Bingo.

Rather than jump on top of the girl, Danny simply asked the girl to elaborate.

"We just *know*," she went on, embarrassed to have to come out with it. "You know... all the kids that come in here... they just *know*."

For a frustrated moment, she stared at Danny and prayed the detective understood. She didn't want to explain the situation in plain terms.

"What gave it away?" Danny needed a statement from Jocelyn, if this was heading in the direction she suspected it was.

"Look, when I got hired here, they gave me a notice about him."

"You received a notice about the janitor? What's his name?"

"Lewis Sauter," she said, an easy answer for an easy question. She took a moment to collect her thoughts. "He's a really weird guy. Creeps me out, not that he ever did anything to me."

Sensing her partner approaching, Danny glanced over her shoulder and touched eyes with Carter. She then returned her attention to Jocelyn and asked, "Do you know if Sauter was working Sunday night?"

"He wasn't," she said definitively. Next she shuddered and her face screwed up. "I know because he always gets here like an hour early for his shift and lurks around the back even though he's not supposed to."

Lurks? Danny thought, as in *keeping his eye on people he shouldn't?*

"It makes getting my purse out of my locker at the end of the day a real chore," she complained, slumping her shoulders before deciding to restyle her messy bun. "He wasn't here."

Getting Carter up to speed, Danny summarized, "One of the janitors is a registered sex offender who wasn't working the night in question. Lewis Sauter."

Pleased as all hell, he said, "Let's bring him in."

Chapter Eight

FROM THE LIEUTENANT'S office, Carter watched Lewis Sauter through a one-way mirror. Seated inside an interrogation room—an 8x10' windowless box—the guy looked seedy yet patient.

From the business side of his desk, Franco walked Danny through the suspect's mile high rap sheet, as she paced with her fists planted on her hips, elbows out, her bulky sweater swallowing her thin frame yet making her appear ten times her size.

Though he was standing with his back to them and seething, Carter caught bits and pieces of the conversation—*indecent exposure* and *stalking* and *statutory rape* and *drunken disorderly conduct* and *illegal possession of an unregistered weapon* and *possession of narcotics*, the list of offenses was never ending. Sauter had been in and out of Attica and Sing Sing so many times it was a wonder the judge hadn't locked him up for good and thrown away the key.

Carter's bones itched with certainty. Lewis Sauter had gotten into Agatha's house that night and bludgeoned her to death. He could feel it. He could smell it, see it in the man's idle posture, in the way his deep-set eyes were resting on his own reflection in the mirrored glass. Evil poured through those dark eyes. Sauter knew exactly why he was here.

And Carter's gut was telling him that the slippery son-of-a-bitch had *planned* this police interview. It was all part of his twisted plans, or so Carter thought.

The only thing keeping Carter from sharing his gut feeling about Lewis Sauter was Franco. The lieutenant had been on the fence about Carter, skeptical. Carter wasn't being paranoid either. Whenever Franco addressed his newest detective, a criticism usually followed. The guy didn't like him.

It set Carter's teeth on edge.

He couldn't afford to be wrong about Sauter. He would have to tread carefully and not tip his hand until he secured hard evidence against the parolee. Since there was none at the moment, tripping the guy up and getting him to implicate himself would be his only option.

And it would be one hell of a long shot. The satisfied smirk on Sauter's face, the confidence it implied—he was already enjoying this—told Carter that the man in the interrogation room might have more than a few tricks up his sleeve.

And because of it Carter was the one who felt anxious.

Danny joined him at the one-way mirror and studied Sauter who was now searching the glass, perhaps interested in who might be on the other side.

"We've got nothing on him," the lieutenant reminded them. "Which means that unless he says something to incriminate himself-"

"Innocent until proven otherwise," he supplied, aiming to escape a lecture.

"Dobbs?"

"Yeah?"

When Franco had his attention, he ordered, "I want Foster taking the lead on this. Sauter is here voluntarily."

"You got it," he replied, tempering his anger.

He took one last look at Sauter—those deep-set eyes, the flat eyebrows, the left of which was sliced in two thanks to the nasty scar slanting across his forehead. He'd taken his denim jacket off, draped it over the back of his chair like he owned the place. The old tee shirt he wore was black and tight, and accentuated his muscular build. In the park, Carter had pegged him as lean and wiry, but it had only been an optical illusion based on his height. All told, Sauter looked dangerous, but the impression he gave off would hardly be enough to convict him.

Danny skimmed the contents of a manila-filing folder, which Franco had armed her with, indicating they ought to head in.

It piqued Carter's interest. She needed to review Sauter's rap sheet even though the lieutenant had just outlined the long list of offenses?

Her Achilles heel, he decided, as they strode out of Franco's office and rounded into the interrogation room.

Sauter's eyes locked on Danny as soon as she opened the door, and his mouth curled into a crooked, little smile that he couldn't suppress.

"I'm Detective Foster and this is Dobbs," she mentioned, settling into one of the chairs across from him.

Carter closed the door and hung back against the wall.

Ordinarily, Carter wouldn't mind his superior observing him from the other side of the mirror, but this time the stakes felt high.

"Foster," Sauter said in a raspy tone. "What's your first name?"

"You can call me Foster," she said curtly, as she placed the folder on the table.

Sauter still hadn't acknowledged Carter. Danny was all he cared about. He seemed mesmerized by her.

It gave Carter a bad feeling and he didn't like the fact that the only thing separating the suspect from his partner was a flimsy aluminum table.

Sauter planted his elbows on the table, closing the gap between himself and Danny.

Carter bristled.

The guy seemed to be drinking in the sight of Danny. He clasped his hands together in front of his mouth, pressing his thumbs against his lips as though it was all he could do to contain his excitement.

Lowering his fists, Sauter finally replied, "You can call me Lewis. Why be formal when I'm here to help?"

Though it was true that Sauter hadn't been arrested, referring to this interview as 'helping the police' was ludicrous.

As Carter stalked around the perimeter of the room, coming behind Sauter, Danny feigned an agreeable smile and said, "Very well, you can call me Danny."

"Danny," he repeated, the vowels softly pouring out of him like an aroused moan. "Is that short for Danica or Daniella?"

"Danielle," she said, shooting Carter a quick glance that spoke volumes—Sauter had taken an interest in her?

He pushed against the table, leaning back in his chair and tilting his head. Easy gazing. He liked what he saw.

"You worked with Agatha Bauer?" she asked, using a friendly, conversational tone.

Air seeped out between his lips, a hint of exasperation, which soon twisted into a strange groan. He corrected her, "I didn't work *with* her. Agatha and I just work at the same place."

"But you know her personally?" she stated point blank, studying his reaction from across the table. But Sauter didn't have one. She pushed, "Did you socialize outside of the gift shop?"

The smirk slipped off of his face, as he said, "Don't you want to ask me if I killed her?"

"Did you?" she asked unemotionally.

Rather than answering her question, he had one of his own. "What makes you think I did?"

As Sauter held her gaze, tension rising between them, Carter clenched his jaw. The guy wasn't just toying with her. The undercurrent of their exchange was a one-way flirtation that turned Carter's stomach.

"Why did you run away from my partner in Prospect Park yesterday?"

Sauter laughed, a deep and booming sound that landed like a fist to Carter's solar plexus. "I'm sure you know about my record?"

Carter couldn't hang back a second longer. Angling over the suspect, he barked, "That's why you ran?"

"You don't believe me?"

He hadn't even looked at Carter.

Carter took a slow lap around the table, cooling off.

Danny barreled ahead, asking, "Why were you there?"

"I saw the news. Didn't believe it."

"You believed it enough to file a Missing Persons report," she pointed out.

"I was concerned when Agatha didn't show up to work on Monday," he said easily.

"But you aren't that close," she challenged, cornering him in his own lie, as a wry twist formed at the corner of her mouth.

It wasn't a question so he didn't answer. He leered at her instead, stared at her chest, and flashed Carter a slimy smile as if the detective might agree that Danny's figure was a real treat.

Instead of slamming the guy against the wall, which would've been his first choice, Carter dryly asked, "Are you wasting our time on purpose?"

"Let's try this again," said Danny, who seemed unmoved by both her partner and the suspect's incessant ogling. "Why did you file a Missing Persons report last night?"

"Because I thought she was missing," he said smugly.

She fired back, "What led you to believe that?"

He let out a frustrated sigh and leaned back in his chair as though this was a day at the beach but his cocktail waitress had brought him the wrong drink.

"I've often wondered," he said, glancing at the one-way mirror for a moment, "if maybe I'm psychic." When he returned his attention to Danny, he leaned forward across the table so abruptly that she flinched. "I think children have that ability."

Thrown, Danny's brows knit together and she proceeded warily.

"You're not a child, Sauter," she reminded him.

"But when I was..." he said, trailing off.

"When you were," she prodded. "What?"

"I developed a sixth sense."

Carter felt the urge to smack him upside the head.

Exercising patience, she asked, "So your sixth sense alerted you to the possibility that Agatha had gone missing?"

"I'm the biggest lead you have right now, aren't I?" he said, pleased with himself.

She smiled, letting him feel flattered, but didn't hold his gaze. She placed her hand on the manila folder and upped the ante.

"Unfortunately, you aren't."

His smug expression drooped and a slight frown crept across his face.

"I had high hopes for you," she went on in a tone strained with mock regret. "I thought you knew her well. I thought you could really aid us in our investigation."

"I *can* aid you," he offered almost nervously.

He didn't want to go. He preferred Danny's company to whatever depraved life he was leading.

"So in addition to you sensing that something had happened to Agatha, what made you come into the precinct?" she asked, taking another stab at cracking him.

"People think Brooklyn's a big city, and it *is* geographically speaking. But I'm sure I don't have to explain to you that it's really just a bunch of little neighborhoods. You learn the rhythm. You see the same faces. You know when something's out of place, when someone doesn't belong, when someone who does belong doesn't show up. I take the same train every evening followed by the same water taxi. I see the same faces on the platform, the same people getting to their destinations on the same timetable every day. When something changes, it sticks out."

Agitated, Carter angled over him, bracing the table and the back of his chair, and hissed, "You were stalking her."

"I'm *observant*," he replied, unruffled. "And if I hadn't filed that report, you'd be nowhere, would you?"

Playing along, Danny indulged him. "What makes you so observant?"

Carter paced away and stood against the wall, forcing his anger to subside.

"Is it your psychic abilities?" she guessed.

"You can mock me all you want, Detective," he said in a cool tone. "I'll take it as a thank you."

Danny studied him for a long moment and allowed a keen smile to gradually shine through her hardened expression. Sauter seemed to like her shifting mood, but he didn't know she was preparing to reel him in.

"I've worked a lot of homicides," she began.

"I'm sure you have," he said, impressed.

"I've also investigated less straightforward crimes. You know you're in the Special Victims Unit."

"I'm aware."

"I've worked with abused children," she gently explained, searching his eyes and boldly assuming he had been one of them. "I'm not mocking you. Kids have an uncanny ability to disappear into their minds when they can't mentally or emotionally process what's happening to them. They can flee their bodies. Hide on the ceiling, if you will. Dissociate."

As Carter slowly paced the perimeter of the room, he noticed Lewis' eyes brightening, the thick hood of his brow rising, a distinct vulnerability shining through his otherwise dangerous features.

"Abused children develop an *awareness*," she went on. "They don't simply read the moods of their abusers in a conventional sense. They intuitively *feel* them."

She let that hang for a moment before asking, "What happened to you?"

When he didn't respond but rather darkened, the light behind his deep-set eyes dimming, she speculated, "Was it your father?"

No shift in his expression to indicate she had been right so she guessed, "Your mom?"

Sauter seemed to harden, not only clamming up, but nearly quaking as if the molten core of his psyche was about to erupt. He wasn't so much looking at Danny as glaring through her, her question having sucked him into some dark abyss.

"Lewis?" she asked in an effort to bring him back. "Who made you psychic? Who did you have to 'psychically read' so that you could save yourself from getting hurt?" She was leaning over the table now, closely studying him. "Was it the same person who gave you that scar?"

She had gotten through to him, but it had only worked against her. When she glanced back at

Carter, indicating he could take a run at their suspect, Sauter began scraping his teeth over his lower lip, dazed.

Following Danny's lead, Carter opened the manila-filing folder, revealing a face shot of the four-year old boy, which their forensic analyst had prepared, cropping out all nudity and signs of abuse. He slid the photo across the table for Sauter to look at.

"You don't want any children to suffer," he told him. "Can you tell me who this boy is?"

Gradually, Sauter seemed to come back into himself. He glanced briefly at the photo and asked, "What does this have to do with Agatha?"

"You want to help Agatha, don't you?" He pushed the photo even closer. "Help us."

Again, Sauter looked at the photo and though recognition flashed behind his eyes, he frowned and shook his head. "I don't know him."

"You don't know who he is?" he pressed.

"No."

"You've never seen him before?"

"I don't know who he is," he insisted.

"But have you seen him before?" When he didn't answer, Carter demanded, "Have you seen pictures like this before? Photos of this child?"

"No," he said firmly.

"Did Agatha ever tell you about a boy? Did she ever talk about a kid she knew? Someone in her life?"

He was pushing too hard and because of it Sauter kept repeating, "No, no, no!"

"Okay," said Danny, diffusing the tension. "Let's focus on Sunday. What did you do that day?"

"I was home," he responded, but Carter could tell Lewis had completely checked out. He wasn't even leering at Danny anymore.

"Ah, but you couldn't have been," she countered, a *checkmate* smirk formed at the corners of her asymmetrical mouth. "You were out and about. That's how you knew Agatha wasn't where she was supposed to be."

Like a switch being flipped, Sauter abruptly beamed a strange smile at her and leaned across the table.

"Where were you when you realized Agatha wasn't where she belonged?"

His gaze fell to the bulky sweater, her chest underneath. When his eyes locked with hers, he pouted sympathetically, "Do they ache? Swollen, right?"

Carter advanced on him and shoved him against the back of his chair, hard, so he couldn't lean towards Danny.

"Answer the question," he shouted and Sauter's hands flew up in surrender.

"She had a baby, didn't she? Didn't you? I told you, I'm psychic." As Carter released him, Sauter offered, "I could suck the-"

Carter smacked him upside the head, surprising both Danny and himself. But no one was more stunned than Sauter.

Carter took a lap around the interview room to cool off, but kept his attention on the one-way mirror.

Well, it was worth it, he thought, even if Franco would have no choice but to rip him a new one.

As Sauter rubbed the back of his head, gaping at Carter, Danny asked, "Lewis, where were you that day?"

"This conversation is over," he said, vacating his chair, but Carter wasn't having it.

Advancing on him in an instant, Carter grabbed his shoulders, shoved him down onto the chair, and after roughly snatching a crime scene photo of Agatha from the manila folder, slapped it against the table in front of Sauter.

"You killed her," he shouted in his ear. "You raped her and dumped her in the park, and you came back the next day to get off on your work."

"I'd like to go now," he said in a small voice.

"You'll go when you've answered my questions," he shot back, breathing down his neck, his fists balling the scruff of Sauter's tee shirt in a white-knuckle grip. "You knew Agatha. She let you into her house and you killed her."

"I don't hear a question, Detective," he said in a brittle tone that was meant to sound calm, but Carter's ear detected clear signs he would crack.

However, the look on Danny's face told him he would have to release the guy so he did, stepping backwards until he reached the brick wall.

Swallowing hard, Sauter smoothed the front of his tee shirt then told Danny, "I'm disappointed in you," as if the company she kept—her partner—reflected badly on her.

"What were you and Agatha involved in, hmm?" asked Danny, lifting the photo of the boy out from under Agatha's. "Did you share the same interest? Maybe she wasn't gentle like you? It infuriated you."

Sauter pushed the photos away, insisting, "I like women."

"You raped a minor," she pointed out.

"I didn't rape anyone. That charge was trumped up, you can look into it. I don't go for kids."

"Is that why you killed Agatha?" she pressed as instinct took hold and she began speculating with remarkable intuition. "Because she was molesting this boy and you couldn't stomach it? Maybe she threatened you? You found out about her secret and to prevent you from exposing her she threatened to send you back to prison so you had no choice but to silence her, eliminate the risk. Is that why you killed her?"

Sauter was back to leaning across the table, leering at Danny, a slick smile on his face. "Oh, the things I'd like to do to you," he mused. "Plow into you, listen to you scream."

Enraged, Carter kicked the chair out from under him and Sauter spilled to the floor then popped up, rattled and alert.

Knocking him down a peg had felt too good and he couldn't help himself. Carter fisted Sauter's shirt and slammed him against the wall.

But it only made the guy laugh—booming, raspy laughter that swelled into hysterics as if being roughed up had freed his wild side.

"You don't know what you're talking about," he finally managed to say, though Carter braced him hard against the wall and didn't let go. "You've got some story you're trying to cram full of facts, except that you can't."

Without thinking twice, Carter slammed him against the wall again, vaguely aware of Danny leaping out of her chair and starting after him—*Carter!* He could feel Franco's eyes on him through the one-way mirror as well, and knew he was pushing his luck, but releasing Sauter would require a specific strength he didn't have.

Someone had tortured that little boy and because the lines between Carter and that young victim were blurring more and more with each passing second, he was losing himself, losing control. Sauter had to have done it. Robbed that little boy of his innocence. Robbed him of knowing what it meant to be a child.

"You're good for this," Carter sneered, nose-to-nose with the guy. Sauter coughed and struggled to breathe. "It's only a matter of time."

Danny warned, "Carter."

Gradually, he loosened his fists and, breathing heavily, edged away from Sauter, who immediately gasped for air, adjusting his tee shirt, the heated flush cooling from his cheeks.

When he recovered, he told Danny, "I'm going to do you a favor, because I like your pretty little mouth so much."

Carter was itching to take a swing at him, but when his partner held her hand up, warding him off and nearing Sauter, he tempered the impulse.

"And what's that?" she asked, folding her arms, as she closed the gap between them.

He stared at her for a creepy moment then suggested, "Why don't you talk to her sister?"

Danny and Carter touched eyes.

Agatha had a sister?

"Wilhelmina," he added almost arrogantly. He was still getting off on doling out crumbs of information. He smirked at Danny and whispered, "I'm already looking forward to cashing in that favor."

She snorted a laugh. "You wouldn't know what to do with me."

"Oh no?"

Sauter actually thought they were flirting, and Carter almost felt sorry for the guy because of it, but when Danny added, "Your mother must have done a number on you," he knew the tables were about to turn.

And they did.

Sauter threw a mean right-hook in response, blindsiding her, his fist making hard contact with her jaw. The blow sent her flying sideways, addling her brain, but Carter caught her before she could spill across the floor.

In the seconds it took Danny to shake it off—bracing the wall with one hand, holding her jaw with the other; Sauter glaring at her, his face a slideshow of contradictory emotions: hatred and shock and regret and a bizarre glimmer of admiration—Carter's blood thickened in his veins and his heart rate spiked to what felt like fatal levels.

He lunged, seizing the guy, and slammed him face down against the table.

Franco pounded against the one-way mirror, but Carter was deaf to it.

Sauter laughed—wet, chortled cries—his cheek pressed to the table, but Carter only heard the sound of his own pulse thumping in his ears.

When he looked at Danny, she was walking it off, all ten fingers forked in her short mop of hair, as she opened and closed her mouth, working the sting out of her jaw.

More pounding and Danny finally snapped out of it. She threw the door open and left.

Carter began handcuffing Sauter to the table, jerking his hands behind his back while flipping open a metal ring on the edge of the table, in which he clamped the handcuff chain, finally apprehending Sauter like he had wanted to all along.

Sauter had assaulted a police officer. He had the inside of a jail to look forward to.

"Shut up," Carter hissed, though Sauter's laughter had been dying down.

As Carter stormed out, leaving Sauter behind in the interrogation room, he couldn't leave behind the bad feeling that lingered in his gut.

He made his way into the lieutenant's office, knowing that Franco was going to chew him out. He should've never let Danny get that close. He should've seen it coming—the punch—and stopped it.

When he entered the office, Franco didn't have to ask him to shut the door.

Danny was inside, holding her head high. She stood stoically with her fists on her hips and her back to the one-way mirror.

Franco stared intensely at her, but everything about her attitude insisted she was fine. When he angled his dark eyes on Carter, he didn't immediately tear into him like Carter thought he would.

"I can hold him for assaulting a police officer," he barked. "But nothing else."

"We need a warrant," said Danny, who was back to nursing her jaw.

"For Sauter's home?" asked Franco, stunned. Had that punch knocked the good sense out of her head? "You didn't establish probable cause." Next he stared Carter down as he berated, "He hit her in retaliation. You were roughing him up."

"He was egging us on," he shot back.

"It doesn't work like that!" yelled Franco even louder. "Look, he creeps me out, too, but that's not something I can bring to the DA for the purposes of getting a search warrant. Sauter knew Agatha. And he knows this Wilhelmina character. Find her. She might give us the probable cause we need."

Chapter Nine

DEPLETED AND EXHAUSTED. Running on no sleep, her jaw sore and bruised where Lewis Sauter had sucker punched her, and a dull headache blossoming behind her eyes because of it, Danny felt as though she would like to sleep through the rest of her life.

But sleep would have to wait.

She entered a photography studio called Vital, located in the heart of Manhattan. Soho to be precise. Vital was where high-fashion magazine photo-editorials and major fashion campaigns were shot.

As Carter walked closely beside Danny, they edged through a dimly lit, lofty studio. Loud music played, the bass heavy. The photoshoot was in progress on the far side of the studio.

Danny hoped her partner wouldn't apologize to her for the millionth time.

If she had found fault with Carter for any reason, it wouldn't have been because her partner had failed to prevent the altercation with Sauter, but rather due to the fact that Sauter had brought out the ugly in him.

Beating confessions out of suspects wasn't how the 66th conducted investigations.

At the moment, Danny felt too drained to broach the topic. Her reservations with his behavior would have to wait.

They came to the photoshoot, and slowed their step when they reached a wall of stylists, makeup artists, and other production assistants who were watching the photographer and model.

The photographer shouted, "More! Arch your back! Liven those eyes!"

A fashionable-looking woman, one of the producers, glimpsed the detectives over her shoulder. Everything about her looked immaculate. She wore black-framed glasses and a snobby expression on her face. She whispered something to a man beside her, and he glanced at the detectives.

After a moment of whispering, the pair marched off towards a table where a handful of assistants were working on laptops—to point the detectives out, Danny assumed.

Danny squeezed through the wall of people to get a better look at the model being photographed. She didn't like what she saw.

Lying on a white settee was a young girl, fifteen years old at best. She was slender, nearly emaciated. Worse, she was topless, and covering herself with her bony arm that was draped across her chest. The black skinny jeans she wore were unzipped, exposing lacy panties. Posed on her back, her blonde hair spilled onto the floor.

This was way too sexy for a young girl.

If that wasn't alarming enough, the photographer who was angling over her had planted his knee on the settee between the girls legs. He was so close to the young, vulnerable model that the hanging nylon strap of his camera brushed her bare stomach.

When the model turned her head towards the crowd, her eyes caught the light, giving Danny the clear impression the girl was distressed. She appeared to be cringing, anxious to get away from the photographer.

A moment later, Danny noticed a large monitor that was set back from the photoshoot. Every photograph the photographer took of the young model appeared on the monitor, faster than a slideshow.

Sexy. Sultry. Aroused. *Nervous*—the young model's face said it all.

Danny had seen enough.

She pushed through the wall of production assistants and yanked the photographer off the girl.

"What the hell's going on here?" she demanded, thrusting her badge in his face. "She's a child."

As he gaped at her, astonished, the snobby woman with black-framed glasses advanced on Danny and said hotly, "This is a closed set! You'll have to leave."

"Are you in charge?" she demanded. "Minors cannot consent to nude photoshoots."

"I'm the creative director. You can't be here," she informed Danny with a deluded sense of self-confidence before attempting to get the detective off the set.

Carter neared the girl, who was seated upright now, mildly bored if not confused by the interruption. Quickly, he wrapped his parka around the model's frail shoulders, covering her up.

"How old is she?" Danny asked, her tone sounding as horrified as she felt.

"That's none of your business," said the woman indignantly. "Now would you please leave?"

When Carter shouted, "Wilhelmina Bauer!"

The young girl shrank from where she was sitting on the settee.

"We need to speak with Wilhelmina Bauer!" he repeated.

Every assistant in the studio was on their cell phone, calling for reinforcements, while the creative director assured the photographer that the shoot would resume in a moment. She showered him with compliments and offered him an espresso.

Carter stalked through the crowd, shouting for Agatha's sister.

Danny approached the girl. She looked up at the detective with confusion in her eyes. Her pale lips parted, and Danny was instantly struck by her youthful beauty—high cheekbones, a wide crisp jawline, and naturally rosy cheeks. She resembled a porcelain doll, and she didn't have the good sense to clasp Carter's parka closed in front.

"Are you okay?" Danny asked her, as commotion ensued from the other side of the studio. The girl said nothing, only stared at her, so she asked, "Where's your guardian?"

The creative director complained to Carter, "You can't just barge in here! We're on a very tight schedule! *Mirabelle is fine!*"

Carter insisted, "We need to speak with Wilhelmina Bauer. She's an agent. She's supposed to be here."

A Nordic-looking woman breezed into the lofty studio. She looked expensive, wearing a sleek, designer pantsuit that restricted her movements. She also looked like Agatha Bauer.

"I'm Wilhelmina," she announced, as a confident smile spread across her middle-aged face.

Ignoring the detectives, she turned on her very high heels and clicked her way over to the young model, Mirabelle.

The girl refused to look at her.

"We can talk outside. I won't have you ruining her flow of this photoshoot," said Wilhelmina, as she stroked the girl's long hair.

Great, thought Danny. The woman was giving her the creeps.

Wilhelmina tossed her hair off her shoulder, lifted her tight mouth into a smile, and started walking towards the entrance of the studio, her designer heels clicking as she went.

Again, Danny asked the girl if she was alright.

"I'm fine," she responded in a smoky voice as she stood, slipping out of the parka with no sense of modesty, as if she was used to being topless in a room full of adults.

"For God's sake!" Danny rushed and covered the girl up again.

"What do you need my mom for?"

Wilhelmina was the girl's mother?

What kind of mother allows their daughter to model topless?

"We have to ask her a few questions about your aunt."

The last thing Danny wanted to do was leave the young girl with the photographer, but Carter had escorted Wilhelmina out of the studio and into the brightly lit corridor.

Danny moved swiftly through the studio and found Carter and Wilhelmina, as the photoshoot got underway.

Wilhelmina asked the detectives, "What is this about?"

"Your sister," said Carter.

Wilhelmina relaxed and rolled her green eyes. "Agatha, Agatha," she sang. "What about her?"

Danny informed her, "She was found murdered a few nights ago."

Wilhelmina gasped, genuinely shocked. She clutched her heart.

"Murdered? When?"

"Sunday night," Danny said, as she closely analyzed her reaction.

Was that genuine shock? Or was Wilhelmina faking it?

"Good Lord," she murmured, taking a few rocky steps down the corridor before turning on her heel to stare at them. "Killed? My God." Collecting herself, Wilhelmina took a moment to smooth her hands down the front of her sleek blazer. "When? Why?" she asked, rattling off impossible questions. "Who killed her?"

"That's what we're trying to determine," Danny said before giving her another moment to process the news.

"I just saw her," she breathed, a dazed look coming over her plastic features.

You did?" Carter questioned.

Danny was interested as well.

"Yes, um, last week," she recalled. "You don't know anything?"

Danny assured her, "We're piecing it together. When you saw her last week, where were you? What did you do?"

"Well, let's see," she said, thinking out loud, which seemed to calm her. "We had tea, did a little shopping."

"Did you stop by her house?" Carter interrupted.

"Ah, I'm not sure I did *that* day, but I have. Why?" she bristled.

"And what day was that?" Danny was angling in on her, though the woman towered over her. In high heels, Wilhelmina must have been 6'3".

"Thursday or Friday evening, I believe." A strange glimmer filled her eyes, as she added, "It's all a blur managing my daughter's schedule."

Danny tried not to sound dry when she commented, "I can imagine."

"Mirabelle," she sang proudly, floating into her happy place. "A true beauty, isn't she?"

It would seem Wilhelmina loved her daughter, but to Danny, the woman's treatment of Mirabelle was grotesque and offensive.

Carter stepped in and asked, "What about Sunday night?"

"What about it?"

Danny explained, "These are routine questions."

"Was that when Agatha was killed?" she realized, her mood darkening all over again. Danny nodded. "Let's see," she said, pulling a slim Blackberry from her blazer pocket and scrolling through her calendar. "Ah," she said, having located the evening. "I was at the office prepping Mirabelle."

"Can anyone confirm that?" Carter asked.

"Mirabelle can, of course," she innocently offered.

Danny made note, scratching her pen against the cardboard cover of her notepad, and when their eyes met—Wilhelmina seemed both pathetically hopeful and disturbed—she said, "And how late were you at the office?"

But Carter was already asking, "Where is this office?"

For a bewildered moment, Wilhelmina glanced from one detective to the next as if unsure about whom to answer. "Until about two in the morning, I believe."

"That's pretty late for a teenager to be up, wouldn't you say?" she commented frankly.

A knowing grin spread across the woman's face. "This is a tough business and Mirabelle's a big girl, just three years shy of being an adult." She shifted her gaze onto Carter and drank in the sight of him, as she oozed into her hip, accentuating her feminine curves. "And my office is in Brooklyn, in Kensington."

"Is that right?" he asked, unmoved.

"Where do you *live*?" Danny asked. "We'd love addresses."

Danny knew the line that Carter was blurring, and by the looks of it, so did Wilhelmina, though she didn't act on it further.

"As Mirabelle's manager and agent and *mother*, my office is the same address as my home." Wilhelmina looked slightly embarrassed. "We pinch pennies where we can," she added. "We were both home that night."

Danny asked, "Did Agatha ever mention a man named Lewis Sauter?"

"Lewis," she repeated to herself.

Danny got the feeling that the name was ringing a bell.

"I don't believe so, no," said Wilhelmina.

"Ever visit her at the Statue of Liberty Museum Gift Shop?" she asked.

With a little laugh she told them, "I'm a very busy lady. Mirabelle has me running all over the city for go-sees and shoots and fashion shows. If I have a spare moment to myself, I wouldn't waste it on Ellis Island. Now, if you'll excuse me, I really must get back to-"

"One more question," said Carter, catching her by the upper arm, as she motioned for the door.

Hardly minding, she heaved in a sensual breath and melted against him as she exhaled.

"I'm dying to hear this question of yours, Detective," she cooed in a sultry tone.

Danny thought she might puke.

Carter released her and asked, "Did Agatha spend any time around children?" When her expression softened with what appeared to be confusion—*I don't follow*—he clarified, "Did she babysit? Was she friends with anyone who has young children?"

Wilhelmina said, "I don't think so."

Danny took it from there, explaining, "Your sister may have had a... questionable relationship with a young boy." Gauging the woman's reaction, though she didn't exactly have one, Danny added, "You're her sister. You might have noticed an... *inclination?*"

Offended, Wilhelmina's eyebrows shot up to her hairline, as she hissed, "Excuse me?"

"Your sister may have had an inappropriate relationship with a child-"

"And you think I would know something about that?"

Wilhelmina tugged the hem of her blazer and straightened her spine, pulling herself together. She stared down her nose at Danny, unable to regain her composure.

"She was ten years older than me! We hardly had a relationship! We reconnected when she moved to Brooklyn, but I never had time for that woman!."

"You reconnected after she moved her from Germany?" asked Carter.

"That's right."

"You don't have an accent," he pointed out.

"I moved when I was a very young girl. It faded," she said, her sharp tone softening. "If you really must know, our reunion didn't go smoothly." She let that hang for a moment, making a point to lock eyes with each of them. "Agatha had a very hard life," she said charitably before her point grew dark. "I couldn't begin to understand why she did the things she did. I only knew it would be best if she stayed away from my Mirabelle." She let out a heavy sigh before concluding, "If you suspect Agatha of something, well then... I suppose my instinct to protect my daughter was justified."

"And yet you continued to have tea with your sister," he questioned.

"Like I said, Detective, she had a very hard life," she asserted with distinct caginess in her voice that slightly unnerved Danny.

No one at the museum gift shop had mentioned Wilhelmina. When Danny had combed through the house on Cortelyou, she'd found no evidence of a sister, only clear and present narcissism in every direction she'd turned. Which was why she asked, "What was she like?"

Wilhelmina spent a thoughtful moment considering the question until it seemed to pain her. "She was secretive. Absent. I never felt close to her even when I was sitting across a table from her. She was bitter and she resented me, my easy life." She got mad. "My life is not easy. I work very hard, but I suppose I make it look easy. I have nice things. I work in glamorous settings," she said with an airy smile, waving her hand towards the studio door, its flashy logo—*Vital!*

"Can anyone," Carter began, "anyone besides your daughter verify that you were home the entire evening of the 10th?"

In a steely tone, deep and guttural, she stated, "I didn't kill my sister."

With that she whipped the studio door open and marched inside, leaving Danny and Carter to make sense of all the ground they'd failed to cover.

Running his big hand down his face, he groaned, "She doesn't know Sauter."

Danny was equally frustrated so she highlighted the silver lining. "Wilhemina implied that Agatha could very well have been a pedophile."

"She didn't deny it," he countered. Before heading down the corridor, he added, "But that's not enough."

Out of exhaustion, Danny pinched her eyes shut and saw Lewis Sauter's dangerous face burning into the forefront of her mind. At this very moment, he was sitting in a jail cell in the basement of the 66th. Was he laughing? Was he getting off on knowing he had sent them to chase a red herring? If he wanted them to *know* that *he* had killed Agatha, that he'd masterfully orchestrated the entire crime, why throw suspicion on the sister?

She was getting the feeling that this was Sauter's way of bringing her to her knees, crippling her, compelling her to crawl back to him and beg for another crumb, and it made her want to punch a wall.

Having collected herself as much as possible, she trailed down the corridor and slapped the exit door open.

Outside, Carter was standing under an awning and watching the tinkling rain tap against the slick cobblestone street, as traffic swished by.

She joined him, taking a deep breath, damp air filling her lungs.

When she glanced up at the gray sky, a billboard looming over the intersection caught her eye.

It was Mirabelle.

On the billboard, the young girl was standing with her bony fists planted on her pointy hips, her skinny jeans riding low. The lace blouse she wore was way too thin. It left nothing to the imagination. In the billboard photo, Mirabelle was glaring right at Danny, her chin tipped down to her chest, blonde hair a wild mess framing her chiseled features. The wry curl of her lip was unnerving.

It was an advertisement for Juicy James, a clothing company notorious for portraying underage girls as sex objects.

"Christ," said Carter, realizing what Danny had been staring at. "My daughter's almost her age. If she ever asked me if she could model..." he trailed off, shaking his head. "Over my dead body."

"How that isn't child exploitation I'll never understand," she said before padding down the cobblestone sidewalk.

Carter followed.

She kept her head down, walking briskly through the drizzle, her partner hurrying beside her. When they reached their sedan, her cell phone began vibrating in her raincoat pocket.

"It's Franco," she said, glancing at the screen and dreading the conversation to come. She had nothing worthwhile to update the lieutenant with. Regardless, she accepted the call and pressed her cell to her ear. "Yeah?"

"How'd it go?" he asked, his timing impeccable.

"Nothing concrete. It looks like Bauer may have led a dark life. Nothing we can prove, though."

"Things just got darker," said the lieutenant.

Danny glanced at Carter, who was angling over her in order to hear Franco's voice through the receiver.

"Meet me at Cyber Crimes," he said with a heavy sigh. "I've got a lead regarding the boy."

Chapter Ten

THE CYBER CRIMES Unit, located on the second floor of the 66th Precinct, was confined to a dismal, windowless room. Cramped, overwrought with hard drives lining the shelves and tables alike, there was barely enough room for Danny, Carter, and Franco to crowd around the investigator's workstation, which was replete with three computer monitors and an ergonomic keyboard.

The images on each monitor were tragic.

And because of it, the investigator, Vince Tenenbaum, wore a grimace on his ruddy face. He angled his bloodshot eyes up at Danny to be certain she could see just as well as her partner and the lieutenant.

When he returned his gaze to the grid of photographs on the screen directly in front of him, he began scrolling his cursor over one disturbing image then the next and the next, magnifying each as he grimly stated, "I found him in the database as 'John Unknown'."

Danny leaned in, her chest tightening, as she examined every shot.

The same pale green eyes, fearfully round and containing a world of sadness dominated the bedraggled boy's expression from where he stood naked in a corner of a room, at age two.

The following photo depicted him shivering in a bathtub, soaking wet and trying to cover himself, age three; cowering on a stained mattress, his knees to his chin, huddled in a terrified ball, but obeying his abuser by looking into the camera lens, age four.

Each image was grainy, some out of focus, others under or over exposed, but one thing was certain, each was more heartbreaking than the last.

There must have been hundreds of photos.

"We tracked the abuse online for years," Vince said, breaking the heavy silence. "But we never discovered the IP address or physical location. To this day, more images continue to surface, but when we realized the boy's age never progressed past about eight years old, we had to assume the worst."

"That he'd been killed," Carter supplied after taking an unsteady breath.

"A body hasn't turned up as far as we know," Vince continued. "The fact of the matter is, this is the internet. These photos could've been taken anywhere in the country or the world for that matter. Without knowing where he was being abused, we were at a loss."

It was definitely the same child as the one featured in the photographs that had been found with the body, Danny thought. The background—that bathroom—was undeniably identical, though there was nothing particularly distinguishing about it. Peeling walls, tarnished grout, and cracked tiles described every rundown urban bathroom in the country. The main room was no better with weathered wooden floors, a bare, sunken mattress, no windows, no view of the outside that might help pinpoint a location.

She began thinking out loud, directing her observation to Franco. "So the photos we found with Agatha in the park were old."

As Franco mulled that over, Vince responded, "They were printed from the internet, likely by using a home printer. We know it was with an Epson PictureMate, but we're not certain about the exact model."

She briefly touched eyes with Carter and was struck by a sudden thought.

"We didn't find a printer at Bauer's house," she told Franco. "Has forensics searched her computer, the one we recovered from her home?"

"They're going through it now," he allowed, though not optimistically. "So far nothing, but that doesn't mean she didn't keep the images hidden somewhere on the hard drive."

"She didn't print them out," said Carter, agreeing with her. He tried to take a step back, perhaps to get some air, but his massive shoulders collided with a shelving unit, causing the equipment it contained to rattle.

When he hissed, "Crap" under his breath, Danny knew it had more to do with this emotionally trying investigation than because he felt like a bull in a China shop.

Reading his mind, she proposed, "We have to get into Sauter's apartment."

"The district attorney's never going to go for it," said Franco in a low and puzzled tone. "I talked to her. Without probable cause it's not going to happen." He mentally debated with himself for a beat then instructed, "Forget the boy."

"Forget him?" Danny blurted out, as her partner grew outraged.

"He could be anywhere in the world. He could be dead," Franco said unemotionally. "I don't want you wasting your time. Focus on finding Bauer's killer. That's an order."

Vince had been watching them with mild interest, having swiveled around in his chair, and when their argument lulled thanks to Danny's speechlessness and Carter's jaw-clenching astonishment, he mentioned, "I found the actual photos that you recovered from the park." Quickly, he turned and pulled the exact images up on one of the monitors. "So, if and when you find the guy who planted them with the body, you can nail him for all the child porn that was produced over the years."

Well, at least that's something.

Danny offered Vince a grateful smile, feeling a bit encouraged. Then she and Carter left the room.

When they reached the stairs, she paused, as an idea came over her.

Carter recognized the look on her face, and asked, "What's our next move?"

The lieutenant joined them, having wrapped things up with Vince, and she said, "Sauter doesn't know what Wilhelmina Bauer told us."

Franco considered the significance, which caused his dark brow to furrow. "You want to take another run at him?"

She did, but with one condition. "I'd like to speak with him alone."

"Danny..." he groaned, highly reluctant. "He assaulted you."

"He's also interested in me," she argued. "Until Carter started leaning on him, he was opening up to me." She glanced at her partner, who didn't appreciate the implication, and added, "No offense."

"He might have been inclined to drop hints about his difficult upbringing," said Franco, countering her request. "But as far as I could tell he wasn't about to admit he had anything to do with Bauer's murder."

"One would've caused the other," she insisted, her face brightening excitedly as she explained, "his mother probably abused him, therefore he has volatile relationships with women. Agatha might have struck a nerve, causing him to snap. It's a real possibility, Franco, and if I can get him talking, he might just feel the need to get me to understand why he did what he did."

"*If* he did it," Franco corrected her before sizing up the two detectives. "I'm not convinced he did."

Defensive on his partner's behalf, Carter blurted out, "You can't be serious!"

"You have your hunches, I have my facts. And the fact of the matter is that we've got nothing on Sauter."

"Lieutenant," she pleaded, growing vulnerable. "I'm not done digging. Let me see this through."

For the first time ever, Franco looked moved. "Fine." He exhaled, letting the tension go. "What am I going to do with you?" he asked, shaking his head.

"I want to talk to him in his cell," she added, knowing she was pushing her luck. The lieutenant was about to object, so she explained, "He knew you were listening from the other side of the mirror. The formality caused his guard to go up. I can appeal to him if we're alone and he knows he isn't being watched." Again, she firmly pointed out, "He doesn't know what Wilhelmina told us. He has no way of knowing how close Agatha was to her sister. I can use that. At the very least, I know I can get enough to warrant probable cause."

Franco's cantankerous expression waned, but he didn't agree outright.

Carter suggested, "Put him in handcuffs, leg-cuffs, shackle him up, so he can't assault Danny again."

Franco mulled the suggestion over and slowly came around. "I want a guard outside the cell at all times."

"Out of view," she negotiated. "Otherwise he's not going to talk."

"Fine," Franco finally agreed, not that he sounded pleased. He slapped the stairwell door open and started through, adding, "You're getting some sleep afterwards! You'll go home and take a solid eight hours off! You look like crap, Foster!"

"Thanks."

The detectives followed Franco down the stairs.

When they reached the ground floor, Carter locked eyes with her for an anxious moment—they were on the same side, pursuing the same hunch, but that didn't mean he wanted her alone with Sauter.

"I'll be fine," she promised him.

Carter didn't look so sure about that, but he veered off towards his desk anyway.

Franco rested his hand on her shoulder and reminded her not to do anything stupid. After mentioning he would call the guards desk in the basement to let them know she was heading down to talk to Sauter, he barreled through the bullpen, leaving Danny.

Admittedly, she felt lost in terms of how to proceed. She only knew she had to. Sauter was enthralled with no one else. So she made her gradual way to another stairwell that led to the basement level.

Sauter was sensitive about his mother, that much had been clear.

In her mind, she replayed the prior interview, as she padded down the echoing stairwell.

Those eyes of his had darkened as soon as she'd said the word *Mom*. He'd also leered at her, shamelessly aroused. He'd made inappropriate comments about Danny's own motherhood, her lactating specifically. Maybe there was something there that she could explore. He wanted to engage and he also wanted to lead her around by the nose. He had pointed a finger at Wilhelmina, which meant he was confident that not a single shred of concrete evidence against him could've turned up as a result of the detectives questioning Wilhelmina.

So how could she convince Sauter that Wilhelmina had implicated *him* in the murder of her sister?

And if she managed to successfully execute that strategy, would he buy it? Or had he known the German sisters so well that he would be able to sort fact from fiction?

The bottom line was that Sauter was connected to the Bauers. And to the murder. Somehow.

Finding out precisely *why* would be the only way to link Sauter to the murder and draw out a confession.

She came to the guard who was standing post in front of the jail door.

Franco must have been quick with that phone call.

The guard immediately punched a code into the alarm pad and hoisted the steel door open for Danny.

There was another guard standing on the other side, and as she cleared that second doorway, he told her, "Sauter's ready for you." He led her down into the precinct jail.

There were jail cells on either side of the aisle she was walking down. The cells contained sloppy drunks and prostitutes—men on the right, women on the left. Some stood, gripping the bars in the hope their public defender had arrived.

The guard stopped at the last cell on the right. As he unlocked the door and pulled it sideways, metal bars rattling, Lewis Sauter—alone and shackled—lifted his head from where he was seated on an aluminum bench.

He tilted his head, angling his deep-set eyes up at her as though his lover had just returned from a long trip. As he drank in the sight of her, he grinned.

Heart rate quickening, she swallowed but it didn't change the fact that her mouth had gone dry. She inched into the cell and when she crossed the threshold, the guard slid the bars across. She flinched when metal slammed against metal behind her. The jail cell was closed.

She was locked inside with a dangerous man.

There were a few windows along the upper wall of the cell, positioned at street level. Outside, rain bounced against asphalt, the sound of which was strangely soothing.

Sauter let out a long sigh at his handcuffs, the long chains of which were connected to the cuffs around his ankles. "So I won't hit you again?" he guessed. "You look fine to me."

"I've had worse," she allowed.

"And you just take it on the chin, go your merry way, unaffected," he elaborated, impressed with her.

"You get used to it," she said as though getting knocked around from time to time was of no consequence.

Yet an uneasy feeling came over her.

There was a second bench perpendicular to Sauter's so she sat, keeping her distance from him and reminding herself to watch her tone and temper her emotions. She wasn't here for a confrontation. If he felt she could identify with him, he would talk. If not, she would be back to a game of cat and mouse she couldn't win.

"Do you know why I'm here?" she asked, as she studied his expression and posture, both of which indicated that he probably felt at ease and wasn't at all concerned about being sent back to prison.

"Because you feel it, too?" he guessed optimistically.

"Feel what?"

He hesitated, holding his answer back.

It seemed like he would rather study her than talk. His lingering stares were unnerving.

"There's something between us," he insisted in a deep, almost smooth tone of voice that she hadn't noticed before. "Mutual attraction."

"Is that what you think?" she challenged.

His dark eyes widened ever so slightly. He knew she was scared.

Tilting his head to the other side, he chose not to address her fear and instead corrected her. "It's what I feel."

She suddenly wondered, had he flirted with Agatha in the same manner? He wasn't terrible looking. Had he tried to seduce the woman?

"That's not why I'm here, Lewis."

His gaze drifted to the holster on her right hip, the gun inside, the way her sweater was bunched up around it. He was getting ideas so she slid away by a few inches, but doing so only made him chuckle, as if he was pleased to have such an effect on her.

"You asked me to talk to Wilhelmina and I did," she mentioned, closely analyzing his reaction.

His crooked grin waned, mouth straightening, as he leaned forward and planted his elbows on his knees, glimpsing her through his eyebrows.

His entire face looked threatening.

"She told me all about you, Lewis," she lied, trying to control her pounding heart, her wavering tone. "She was close with Agatha. Agatha told her that she was being stalked."

As if none of what she was saying mattered, he asked, "How's your jaw?"

He was back to tilting his head and leering at her.

She intentionally provoked him by asking, "What was it about Agatha that reminded you of your mother? What did she say or do to you that made you snap?"

His big hands curled into fists, indicating she had struck a nerve. She became instantly concerned he might take another swing at her.

But he was shackled. He would fail if he tried.

The tension that had overcome his entire body ebbed away, so shifting gears Danny prepared for the tactic she intuitively knew would work—showing Sauter that she was on his side.

Offhandedly, she mentioned, "I've wanted to kill my mother so many times."

He was immediately interested.

"She smothers me. It's not enough that she lives in the neighboring building and is constantly at my apartment. She wants to live inside my head. She wants to control the words that come out of my mouth. She would feed me my own thoughts if she could. She's not a person, she's a parasite."

She held his gaze. His dark eyes were white all around. He identified with her, and Danny felt a strange mix of emotions because of it.

Two seconds later, she realized that not only did Sauter identify with her.

But she identified with Sauter.

Her mother *was* smothering.

What if he was right? What if they *did* share a connection?

"But I don't care," she said, having scared herself. "I love her and I just don't care." That was true, she thought. Or so, she hoped. Convincing herself, she went on, "I feel off when my mom doesn't check in with me. It doesn't feel right when I'm alone at home. And the conflict I feel, the terrible internal war inside me, these clashing feelings... they build and build and build... The pressure is incredible."

She let that hang, as she studied him.

"But she never did wrong by me," Danny continued when Sauter hadn't chimed in. "Never did a thing to me. She's only guilty of loving me too much."

It was at this point, while Danny wrestled with the shame of having disclosed her darkest secret to a complete stranger—a possible killer no less—that she really needed Sauter to start talking.

She needed him to come clean about the night of April 10th.

"Loved you too much," he echoed, and though it seemed he might say more, he fell silent.

Attempting to steer the conversation away from herself, she asked, "Was Agatha like a mother to you?" as soon as the notion occurred to her. Maybe she'd gotten him all wrong. "Was she the mother you should've had?"

"I didn't kill her," he said in a low tone.

"You did something, Lewis," she pressed, keeping her voice soft and sympathetic. She leaned forward, their faces coming very close. "You did something and you want to tell me about it. I know you do."

But he wasn't budging. In fact, he leaned against the bricks again, claiming some distance between them.

"We have a warrant to search your apartment," she lied. "What are we going to find?"

He looked worried.

After a tense silence, she offered, "If you tell me now, I can help you. I can put in a good word with the DA, tell her you cooperated, that you showed sincere remorse. But if you wait, there won't be anything I can do for you. The DA will run with whatever we find out about you."

A disturbing smirk spread across his face.

It shook Danny's resolve.

"Now is the time, Lewis," she went on.

He drew in a deep breath. He was back to leering at her.

"Why did you send me to Wilhelmina?" she asked, rounding the same bend. "You want me, Lewis," she began, supplying his answer. "You want me and you want me to know what you did, and yet you know that I'm never going to forgive you once I learn what you're guilty of. Isn't that right? There's a terrible war brewing inside you because of that, isn't there?"

Interrupting, he confidently said, "I have something for you."

"You do," she agreed, her heart rate elevating—*this is it, he's going to confess!* "What do you have for me?"

A strange smirk came over him, as he said, "It's in my pants."

"I'm not going to touch your penis, Lewis."

He burst out laughing.

She wasn't amused.

Sauter looked strangely innocent, however.

"That's not what I meant, but it's nice to hear that you're not that kind of girl."

He tried to wedge his hand into the front pocket of his jeans, but the handcuffs were restricting him.

"Front right pocket," he told her.

"What's in your pocket?"

"See for yourself."

"You can take it out," she told him.

"Not with these chains."

"Yes, you can," she insisted.

As it turned out, he could. Though he seemed put-off because she wouldn't play along, he wriggled his handcuffs, manipulating the connecting chain and creating some room to reach inside his pocket. After wedging his hand down and fishing around, he pulled out a folded piece of paper and offered it to her.

Cautiously, she snatched it and backed away.

The paper was thick, unlike regular copy paper. She could see the fibers in the grain. She carefully unfolded it and found a drawing of herself—round puppy dog eyes, downward sloping at the outer edges, her slanted mouth, lower lip thicker than the upper, her mop of dark hair, the sides short, her ears sticking out.

It was as detailed as a photograph and to her amazement it captured the pain she had felt with each passing day since Gregory's tragic death.

Once her astonishment at his talent had subsided, she realized the drawing also resembled the one of Agatha she'd discovered framed on the bedside table in the dead woman's house.

She locked eyes with him and said, "You gave a similar one to Bauer."

He didn't deny it.

"When did you draw this?" she asked in an unsteady voice.

But she already knew. Somewhere between reporting Agatha missing and coming into the station, he had become infatuated with her, which meant he'd seen her... Had he been stalking her?

Just like he had been stalking Agatha?

She felt threatened, and yet, the fact that he had taken the time to draw her was bizarrely touching.

In an instant, she understood how easy it might have been for the victim to unlock her door that night.

"She let you in that night," she said. "You killed her after she let you in."

But that was the problem—his brilliance. He hadn't confessed.

And even though she now knew he had been close with Agatha, the two drawings would amount to circumstantial evidence at best.

Sauter took a step towards her, chains rattling between his feet, then another, which compelled her to edge backwards—*don't panic!*—until her shoulders clanked against the iron bars.

"She had so many stories," he whispered. He was too close, she could feel heat rolling off of him. "Such sad stories, and I listened to every one."

"So you put her out of her misery," she guessed, her voice hitching in her throat.

"I want to hear your sad stories, Danny. I want to see you let out the hard emotions." He stepped in even closer and whispered, "Who ruined you?"

"No one," she said in a small voice, as he pressed his hips against hers, the firm wall of his chest pushing into her tender one, pinning her to the bars.

"You're a prisoner," he informed her. "You're locked up, bottled up. You're hiding. You run away to secret places, secret people in order to finally be yourself, but I can see it in your eyes. You're trapped. I'm psychic, remember?"

"Guard!" she yelled, desperate to get out of there.

She tried to squirm out from under him, but he was too strong, blocking her too tightly, overpowering her.

"There's no escape," he breathed into her ear, and she cringed. "You're out of options."

"Guard!" she screamed, terror cloying up her throat, choking her.

"You need me."

As the guard barreled up the aisle, keys jingling in hand, Sauter shuffled away, leaving Danny trembling and turning for the bars.

She grasped the bars tightly in an effort to pull herself together.

"We're done here," she told the guard, testing the strength in her tone, of which there was very little.

Once the guard had slid the door aside, she spilled out into the aisle and didn't stop until she reached the ground floor.

She took a moment to overcome her emotions. Tears stung her eyes but she blinked them away.

Vaguely aware of her colossal failure—she hadn't gotten a damn thing out of him—she clutched the eerie drawing in her hand and made a beeline for her desk. She kept her head down and avoided eye contact with anyone. She grabbed her raincoat without giving Carter so much as a glance.

"I'm heading home, Franco's orders," she said, throwing her coat on before starting for the lobby.

Confused, Carter called after her, "How'd it go?" But when she didn't respond or even slow down, he shouted, "Keep your phone on. I'll let you know as soon as we get something!"

She waved in acknowledgement then rounded the corner, walking briskly towards the glass entrance door, which she slammed open, coming into a downpour.

Exhausted, her thoughts turned muddy. Sauter's strangely inviting smile burned into the forefront of her mind, as her stomach twisted with knots.

Danny just kept going—walking and walking, veering around pedestrians that hurried through the rain, the canopies of their umbrellas flinging rainwater in her face.

Her feet knew the route, *make this left, turn that corner.* She wove her way northeast for nearly a mile, heading home in a torrential downpour without so much as a garbage bag over her head.

Why had she told Sauter about her mother?

She didn't really feel that way—*smothered.*

Did she?

Sure, she had been guilty of a little tongue-and-cheek venting, but it didn't mean she actually resented her mother.

But when she had disclosed to Sauter that she found her mother's love oppressive, it hadn't been in the spirit of innocent venting.

Did she truly feel that way, and if so, where had it all come from?

She cringed at her lack of judgment. Disclosure worked, but she should've thought long and hard before using it on Sauter.

That's what it had been, right? Disclosure. An investigative strategy?

Then it hit her.

It had been real, and that's what was so perplexing about it.

She had told him the truth.

As Danny came to the corner of Caton Avenue and Ocean Parkway, she realized why there had been a pit growing in her stomach ever since her son had died unexpectedly.

She blamed Nora.

She hated feeling this way, which was why she'd been pushing it down into her spleen and ignoring it. She hated carrying it around with her. She knew that 'blame' was only a desperate attempt to make sense of something that was senseless.

It was no one's fault Gregory had died. If her mother had been holding him, feeding him, he still would have slipped away. If Danny had been home alone that night, the result would have been just as tragic.

Waiting for the walk signal to flash as the downpour assaulted her, drenching her every inch, she challenged herself not to glance at O'Toole's, but soon she caved.

Rain cascaded down the window panes of the bar. The wooden sign swung in the wind.

Inside, Tommy was righting chairs, which rested upside down on the tabletops. Setting them on the floor one at a time, he seemed agitated. And as Danny neared the rippling glass, she realized why.

Nora was at his heels, pointing her finger at him in the throes of what looked like a heated confrontation. Tommy seemed to be doing a soldierly job of focusing on opening the bar.

What the hell was her mother doing?

Soon the argument escalated—Tommy turned, spitting words through his teeth that Danny couldn't hear with rain pounding all around her.

Nora angled her bony finger in his face, her cheeks red, her eyes furious, as she yelled at him.

When he pointed his finger at the door—*get out, now!*—Nora huffed and marched off.

Thinking fast, Danny scurried down the avenue, away from the bar. She couldn't begin to imagine the meaning of what she'd just witnessed. And though part of her was itching to confront her mother right then and there, she didn't have the mental faculties to follow through. Not now. Not when her legs were rubber and her mind was soup, coming off of fifty straight hours of investigating.

Glancing over her shoulder, she caught sight of Nora crossing the intersection and walking briskly towards the row-houses along Ocean Avenue.

When her mother rounded up the stoop of her own building, Danny let out a relieved breath.

Why would Nora stop by Tommy's bar?

What could she have possibly said to him?

She realized how disturbed she was when she felt her breasts begin to secrete milk.

Holy hell, she needed to sleep.

Chapter Eleven

WHILE PRODUCTION hands dismantled the photography lights and assistants flitted around the studio, cleaning up, Wilhelmina hovered near the curtained changing area where her daughter was fumbling around inside.

"Put your pants on," she hissed, reminding Mirabelle to accomplish the obvious, because the girl, often dazed after a long photoshoot, tended to forget these things. "Are you dressed yet?"

A thin groan was the girl's only reply.

The creative director swooped through the bustling studio and peeled her black glasses off her face when she reached the changing area.

Wilhelmina stepped in front of the woman, preventing her from barging in on her daughter.

"She's not decent yet," said Wilhelmina, though not impolitely.

The creative director had been like this all day—pushy and entitled.

Wilhelmina flashed the woman a breezy smile to lighten the mood.

"We're all girls," said the woman, as she tried to get around Wilhelmina.

"She needs her privacy," she insisted. "It's one thing to expect her to expose herself while modeling, but it's quite another to barge in on a young girl when she's changing."

The creative director didn't happen to agree.

"We had quite the interruption earlier," she reminded Wilhelmina, implying it was her fault.

Wilhelmina shrank, but couldn't apologize or get a word in.

The creative director complained, "The way the police treated Jean Pierre was unacceptable. Offensive, in fact. He's the most important fashion photographer in the world. Nevertheless, Jean Pierre loved working with Mirabelle, and he hopes to work with her again."

She handed Wilhemina an envelope full of cash.

Wilhelmina smiled, thanked the woman for the payment, and asked, "He loved working with my Mirabelle?"

"Of course he did. I'm sure he'll use Mirabelle in future shoots. But Jean Pierre is *very* important. If he wants a model to take her top off, then that's what she'll do. Hell, if he wants her completely nude, that's what he'll get! Any model that won't comply will be replaced. He's an *artist* for God's sake!"

"I understand."

Wilhelmina watched the creative director join the production crew. She hugged the photographer and showered him with compliments.

Eagerly, Wilhelmina tore open the envelope and counted the cash. It was the correct amount. As she tucked it into her designer purse, otherwise known as how she had spent the Juicy James income, she barked at Mirabelle to get the hell out of the changing room already.

Her daughter remained inside, so Wilhelmina decided to exercise her patience.

She thought about what she could buy with the cash.

She only owned one designer pantsuit and one pair of fashionable high heels though they were scuffed badly. She needed more than one outfit if she was going to fit in with this crowd… Her Prada purse was still in excellent condition, but only because she'd recently purchased it.

Wilhelmina had been gradually improving her image. She had poured every last penny into her daughter's career, too, and despite the citywide Juicy James ad, her bank account was in constant danger of bouncing.

The costs of comp cards, test shoots, and commuting around the city had been bleeding her dry. Each modeling job only earned a few hundred bucks, sometimes a thousand, but it was never enough.

But if Jean Pierre booked Mirabelle again, if he turned her into his muse, then that would be their big break.

Wilhelmina could very well become the woman she had been pretending to be all along!

"Did you hear what the creative director said?" she asked her daughter through the slit in the curtain. "They loved you! Jean Pierre's going to book you again." She was met with silence so she peeked her head in.

Mirabelle was seated on a stool. Her pointy elbows were planted on her knees, and her legs were splayed. Wispy hair hung in her eyes.

She looked like she didn't have the energy to go on living.

Unbelievable.

At least the girl had managed to get her pants on, but that was about it.

Wilhelmina slipped inside and closed the curtains then neared her daughter who was making an honest effort to lift her face.

"My beautiful baby," she gently cooed. "What the hell is taking you so long?"

"I feel sick," she groaned, the smoky timbre of her voice sounding faint.

Stooping, she lifted her daughter's chin with her big hand and brushed the blonde wisps off her face. The girl felt clammy to the touch and her cheeks were pale, but Wilhelmina reasoned that her daughter was just being dramatic.

"Stand up," she instructed. They needed to stay on schedule. "Let's get you dressed, shall we?"

"Can I have something to eat?" she asked, as she stared vacantly up at her mother.

Sighing, Wilhelmina checked the time on her wristwatch.

"We both know I shouldn't give in," she said, suspicious that her daughter was trying to pull one over on her. "We have three go-sees and if you're bloated..."

"Water then?"

"Of course," she allowed—water was calorie free.

She snapped her Prada purse open and found a 6 oz bottle of water. She unscrewed the cap before handing it to Mirabelle.

As the girl guzzled it down, Wilhelmina walked slowly around the dressing room floor and collected her daughter's clothes that were on the floor. When she found a crumpled bra underneath the stool, she didn't recognize it, but shoved it into her purse anyway. It was La Perla for God's sake.

Mirabelle complained about being hungry.

"Don't be insane," she said dryly. "Your stomach is full of water."

Mirabelle finally stood up.

"Remember what we talked about?"

"Don't change in front of anyone," the girl answered.

Wilhelmina stooped. "Sweetheart, modeling is based on contracts. Sometimes you're topless. That's fashion. But no one, and I mean absolutely no one has the right to spy on you while you're changing your outfits. There are a lot of perverts in this industry. You understand that, right?"

Mirabelle looked up at her with tired eyes and nodded.

Despite the girl's fatigue, all her mother could see was Mirabelle's incredible beauty—those hollow cheeks, a jawline that could cut glass, her perfect nose, and pouty lips.

In her heart, she knew Mirabelle was destined to be a star. She was no Cindy Crawford or Kate Moss, but femininity hadn't been in vogue since the early 2000s. Androgyny was in—tiny boobs, narrow hips, unusual facial features. And Mirabelle's look—an anorexic porcelain doll—was so *en vogue* right now! This coupled with the girl's height made her perfect for the fashion industry.

And perfect for making Wilhelmina a ton of money.

"Come," she said, as she began to dress her daughter.

"It pains me that you don't feel well," she went on, helping Mirabelle into her shirt and sweater.

"Isn't there a bite left?" she pleaded, referring to the protein bar that Wilhelmina had been rationing out to her all afternoon.

The mother rolled her eyes in an exasperated manner and popped her purse open once again.

"If ever you doubt my love for you," she said, reaching into her purse and finally offering her daughter the last morsel of a protein bar. "Think thin thoughts, please."

Mirabelle scarfed it down then gulped what was left of the water.

"We have to get going," she said, eyeing her wristwatch and calculating the commute uptown they were facing. "We can't afford to be late."

As her daughter wriggled her feet into high-heeled boots, Wilhelmina peered through the crack between the curtains, spying the dark and empty studio.

She was lucky. Damn lucky, if she was being honest with herself. It didn't bode well that Mirabelle's first shoot with Jean Pierre Johansan had included an impromptu visit from the police. It could've been the kiss of death, an interruption like that.

Once again Agatha was ruining her life and from beyond the grave no less.

She thought those days were behind her.

Once her daughter was fully dressed in a sleek bomber jacket, she ushered her through the studio and down the corridor.

"Damn," she muttered, eyeing the rainfall clattering over the street the moment they stepped outside.

She wrestled open her dime-store umbrella. The flimsy thing was on its last leg. Like a bird with a broken wing, it was limp on one side, spokes bent and poking through nylon on the other.

With an arm around her daughter to spare her from getting wet, they scurried along the cobblestone sidewalk, as the chilly rain nipped at their backs.

Cautiously optimistic, Mirabelle asked, "Can we take a cab?"

"One day, sweetheart," she said, giving Mirabelle a companionable pat before squeezing her closely again. "One day."

They turned up the avenue where traffic was swishing in both directions. The sidewalk was thick with pedestrians hustling to their destinations to escape the cranky weather.

As they pressed through the rain, heading towards the uptown C train, she mentioned, "You'll have to model a few different outfits at the go-see, but it shouldn't take longer than three hours if we factor in the waiting time before the designer sees you."

"It's okay," she said weakly. "I don't feel sick anymore."

"The rainy air is bringing you back to life," she observed, catching her daughter's eye.

They waded into a thick cluster of pedestrians approaching the C train. It was miserable how these people pushed and shouldered each other with no sense of common courtesy, she thought before shoving through the cluster herself, swearing and yanking her daughter along.

When finally they began descending the subway steps amidst a sea of New Yorkers, Mirabelle asked, "Who were those people at the shoot? Detectives?"

Instead of answering, Wilhelmina hurried her daughter along, as she folded the umbrella. There was congestion in front of the turnstiles, dozens of people bottlenecking into lines. It took a moment for her to fish their MetroCards out of her purse, but not long enough for her daughter to stop staring at her expectantly for an answer.

Refusing to be moved by Mirabelle's curiosity, she swiped the first card through the turnstile and shoved her daughter forward. As she ran the second card through, paying for herself and following after, she said, "Soon we won't have to set foot in this filthy subway."

"Mom?"

"Oh, they were no one," she said, deeply worried that the scandal surrounding her sister's murder would eventually bite her daughter's modeling career in the ass.

She clenched her jaw at the thought, as the C train barreled through the station and screeched to a deafening stop.

When the doors opened and people began streaming out, she clutched her daughter by the shoulders, anchoring her against the side of the car so that the stampede wouldn't whisk her away.

With a ding the doors began sliding together, and the train took off, lurching through the tunnel. Soon the ride became smooth.

She didn't like how her daughter was looking at her—as hungry to learn about the detectives as she was for a proper meal—so she turned her attention to her own reflection in the plexiglass window.

But all she saw was self-doubt and resentment, a crude expression permanently fixed on her aging face.

Agatha came to mind.

Her sister's murder had caused such bad anxiety that Wilhelmina's stomach burned like acid.

Suddenly, the train car's lights began flickering. Wilhelmina's eyes played tricks on her, Agatha's face interchanging with her own in the plexiglass. Then a tidal wave of memories crashed over her.

That horrible trip.

Flying to New York City.

Wilhelmina had been a young girl of eight dressed conservatively in a petticoat and knit tights. Her older sister, Agatha, had barely been an adult.

Agatha had explained nothing to Wilhelmina after snatching Wilhelmina in the middle of the night from their home in Germany.

Agatha had smuggled her out of bed, brought her over to the United States, and deposited her with relatives—*so he can't find you.*

She had promised to come back...

As the years had rolled on, however, Agatha's motive gradually became all too clear. She had abandoned Wilhelmina in New York.

And decades later, when Agatha had eventually returned, it was far too late.

Wilhelmina pushed the thought from her mind, focusing only on the sway of the train car as it careened to a stop at the next subway station.

"Two more," she whispered to Mirabelle. "Mind your purse," she advised, stealing sly glances at the other passengers.

Heeding the warning, her daughter gathered her bag against her chest.

"No one looks like you. You're a diamond, and I want you to act like it," she said to encourage her daughter.

Hardly agreeing, Mirabelle's gaze went slack.

"You *are* striking," she insisted. "You're our ticket out. We won't always have to share a broken umbrella and suffer this sardine can of a subway," she promised. "I love you."

Her daughter stared blankly at her and just when she thought it was safe to once again spy her own reflection, Mirabelle asked in a smoky voice, "But who *were* they?"

Irritated, she stated, "Our enemies."

The train pulled into the 14th Street station. The doors opened, and Wilhelmina steered her daughter through the crowd, as they headed towards the exit. Grasping her by the wrist, she walked briskly, moving with the flow of pedestrians.

When finally they emerged onto the street, the rain was coming down in sheets.

Wilhelmina cursed, but it wasn't directed at the nasty weather.

She had to do something about those detectives. She had to prevent them from sniffing around. Her life and her daughter's career were none of their business. If she could divert their investigation, she might be able to go on as though nothing had happened to Agatha.

Her cheeks flushed hotly at the notion, her blood pressure rising. She could not afford to lose control. Not now.

She jerked Mirabelle to a standstill on the sidewalk, having cleared the dispersing crowd, and fished her cell phone out of her purse.

Grady Willis was the crumbling rock on which she had built her life, though recently their relationship had been tinged with mutual animosity and long, drunken nights. Even so, he was trustworthy to play a role when necessary.

Stealing a glance at her daughter, she shivered in the damp wind, rain pounding against their bent umbrella.

She dialed the apartment and prayed he wouldn't be passed out on the couch.

When she heard his familiar voice grunt into the receiver, she said, "I need you to do something. It's very important."

Chapter Twelve

SEATED AT HER DESK in the 66th, her eyes glued to her computer monitor, Danny diligently scrolled through the forensic photographs of Agatha Bauer lying face up in the mud, as well as the ones that had been recovered from the house on Cortelyou Road.

Balmy sunlight shafted through the windows, brightening the quiet station and marking a brand new day.

She had arrived early with the aim of avoiding her mother as well as thoughts of Gregory. She was sharper in the morning, and stealing a few hours before the other detectives arrived would hopefully provide the time she would need to make connections in the case that hadn't yet occurred to her.

A bludgeoned German woman, an estranged sister, a mysterious boy, and a dangerous man meddling in the investigation—each was a piece of the puzzle, but nothing fit together.

Though she studied every photograph filling the screen, she knew she wasn't seeing the full picture. She couldn't concentrate. It was like she had goggles on her face, and the plastic was fogging up. She felt a world away.

Nora had been weighing heavily on her mind, that argument she'd had with Tommy in the bar, Tommy's furious reaction—*get out!*

What had their argument been about?

Danny hadn't spoken to Tommy since he had walked out. She hadn't told him about Gregory's shocking death, that he'd died of SIDS. He had a right to know, but she hadn't been able to bring herself to explain. She couldn't face him, and it was eating her up inside—the guilt and shame of withholding the truth.

Or…

Did he know?

Had Nora told him in an effort to keep him away from Danny?

That's how it had seemed. The sense she had gotten having watched her mother verbally attack Tommy inside O'Toole's. But Nora had no reason to keep him away from Danny. Tommy had been staying out of Danny's life all on his own. So why would Nora have gone to such lengths? Unless...

Danny surged out of deep thought, as detectives and police officers began filtering into the precinct, setting their belongings on their desks, scraping their chairs out, and booting up their computers, greeting one another all the while.

Soon telephones were blaring, and the hum of the bullpen swelled all around her.

She focused on analyzing the crime scene photos. She leaned towards her computer and examined a photograph of Agatha lying in the mud. She studied the particular placement of the child pornography beside the dead woman. How were these two individuals connected?

The answer refused to jump out at her.

Yet Lewis Sauter kept springing to mind.

But had he known Agatha personally? Danny had assumed that the sketch he'd drawn of Agatha with photographic realism was evidence of their personal relationship. However, Danny now had a sketch of herself. Sauter had drawn her and given her the drawing. She obviously didn't have a personal relationship with him.

Did Sauter know the boy? Would it matter if he did? Or was the lieutenant right? Did that angle not matter?

Was Sauter telling the truth?

Could he be innocent?

Franco was still holding Sauter in jail for assaulting her. There would be a hearing in a few hours, which would likely result in the judge sentencing Sauter to a month or two in Attica.

This would do her no good, she realized. Sauter would be far more useful if he were released and free to roam the city. If he were free, then she could follow him. Where might he go if he didn't know he was being tracked? What might he do?

Franco entered the precinct and walked with purpose through the station, shaking out his wet umbrella as he headed straight for his office.

The rain must have picked up again, she thought, rising to her feet.

She followed after him, not entirely confident about the request she was about to make.

In his office, Franco pulled his trench coat off and hung it on a rack. When he rounded to the business side of his desk, she quietly knocked on the doorframe and peeked in.

"Can I ask you about something?"

Franco glanced at her through his eyebrows as he straightened a stack of reports on his desk. "Yeah, Danny?" He eased into his chair, but seemed distracted.

Inching towards him, she smoothed her hands down the gray sweater she was wearing. It fit her tightly and she felt slightly awkward because of it, her stomach still puffed and protruding.

"What about letting Sauter go?"

He leaned back in his chair and stared at her like she might have lost her damn mind

She went on, "Just hear me out. We're spinning our wheels. The person who seems to know the most is Sauter, but we've got nothing on him."

"And you think he'll incriminate himself if he's free to do as he pleases?"

"We can stake him out, keep a close watch," she suggested. "He knew Agatha, but catching him in a lie isn't enough for a search warrant. I think if he's left to his own devices, he could lead us to hard proof."

"Or lead you straight back to his apartment, which we can't get into without a warrant," he countered, playing devil's advocate.

The steely look on his face—eyes darkening, mouth tugging downward at the corners—indicated he wasn't pleased with her tenacity, not this time.

Regardless, she argued, "If he's out, he'll mess up and that'll give us a shot. He can't mess up if he's in Attica."

Franco held his breath, drumming his thumb on the edge of his desk, while he considered the strategy.

"For what it's worth," she added. "I didn't press charges."

"No, you didn't," he shot back in agreement. "The department did, on your behalf. Assaulting an officer is a felony."

"We don't need him locked up," she pressed, hoping like hell the disagreement between them wouldn't cause her to lactate. Her sweater was much too thin and she'd never survive the embarrassment. "We need him out on the streets so we can catch him."

The lieutenant studied her for a moment.

She hadn't told him about the drawing Sauter had given her, but the look in his eyes indicated that he didn't trust her judgment when it came to this particular suspect, nor this specific case, so mentioning the sketch probably wouldn't benefit her.

"I'll think about it," he compromised, just as Carter filled the doorway, stealing his attention. "Yeah?"

Danny glanced over her shoulder at Carter and he informed them, "A man named Grady Willis is here. Says he wants to talk to us about Agatha Bauer."

"Did he work with her?" she asked.

"No," he said as though the man's connection to the victim was far more interesting. "He's Wilhelmina Bauer's boyfriend."

Surprised in the best possible way—a break in the case might have just fallen into their laps—Danny shot her lieutenant a smile. Franco was just as excited.

"Take him into One," he suggested, rising from his chair and nearing the one-way mirror that looked into the first interview room.

The blinds were down so he yanked the cord, lifting them out of the way.

Without further discussion, Danny accompanied Carter into the bullpen where a middle-aged man with a slicked-back ducktail mullet and sunken cheeks was shifting awkwardly near the wall, nervous to be so far out of his element.

Recalling Wilhelmina's polished appearance—the designer clothes, coiffed hair, and thoroughly manicured facade—Danny was surprised by the man who claimed to be the modeling manager's boyfriend.

He had to be at least eight years younger than her, which put him in the ballpark of thirty-eight, but that wasn't what was so bizarre about him. Compared to Wilhelmina, he looked washed up. His chiseled jaw, prominent bone structure, and thick dusting of facial hair, however, suggested a once-handsome face. But he hadn't aged well. Perhaps he was a former model who had been drinking himself into the ground for the last decade as some form of punishment for not making it big during his prime.

Dressed in faded blue jeans and a heavy Carhartt jacket, a stained tee shirt peeking out where his coat failed to meet in front, he seemed better suited to fix a leaky pipe than share a snobby German woman's bed.

As she shook his hand, she noticed dirt under the fingernails and booze on his breath.

"I'm Detective Foster," she said. "And you met Dobbs."

"That's right," he answered.

She pegged him as a chain smoker based on the tone of his voice. He seemed rattled, his beady eyes scanned the busy police station, the countless detectives throughout the room.

"I know about Agatha," he informed them.

His tone was just confident enough to lead Danny to believe he might actually have something worthwhile.

"How did you know Agatha?" she asked casually, as she walked Grady into the interview room.

He circled to the far side of the table. His eyes were glued to the chair as though he was unsure about all this.

Good-naturedly, Carter closed the door and invited him to have a seat.

As he did, Grady finally answered, "She's my girlfriend's sister. I live with Wilhelmina."

"I see," she said, producing a fresh notepad from the back pocket of her jeans before sitting down on one of the chairs across from him.

She uncapped her pen, as Carter joined her, taking the seat next to her.

As if having answered a single, straightforward question had drained him, Grady ran his hand down his face and began fidgeting with the hem of his jacket.

"Wilhelmina can't handle this," he said, sounding defeated.

"Does she know you're here?" asked Danny

Snorting a laugh that caused his boozy breath to waft across the table, he said, "Yeah, she knows." He stiffened uncomfortably.

She gave him a moment to collect himself. Carter wasn't nearly as patient or so it seemed. His amicable manner had expired and irritation was now rolling off of him.

"You know about Mirabelle, right?" he began. "Her *career*?"

His eyes widened and he let out another little snort as though he hardly agreed that a fifteen year old should be given so much credit.

"Yes, we spoke with them," she allowed.

"I've been with Wilhelmina for the past, oh what is it now?" he asked himself, recollecting how long he'd been with the woman. "Twelve, fourteen years. I raised that little girl. I know everything there is to know about both of them."

"Okay…?" she encouraged. She could already tell Grady wasn't fond of Mirabelle.

"Wilhelmina doesn't want the whole Agatha thing to impact her daughter's *modeling* opportunities."

He used air quotes as he said the word *modeling*, and it took awhile for his hands to find the table again. Apparently, letting the implication hang meant something to him, but Danny wasn't impressed.

She eagerly waited for him to give her something she could actually use.

"You asked her about Lewis Sauter?" he went on, screwing his face up as though he didn't like the guy.

"We did," Carter confirmed.

"Yeah, she can't get roped into this," he stated, pressing his palms flat against the table and glancing around the room until his eyes landed on the one-way mirror.

There was something about his demeanor. He wasn't authentic. Grady reminded Danny of a poorly trained actor.

"Mr. Willis," she said, quickly losing patience. "You came here for a reason, and I'd like to know what it is."

"My girlfriend knows Sauter, okay? Or knows *of* him," he explained. "She had three go-sees with Mirabelle yesterday, and that's why she was a little unfriendly with you guys the other day."

"Did she ask you to come here and tell us that?" said Danny curtly.

He frowned and asked, "Is she in trouble?"

Danny and Carter glanced at one another.

"I mean, can she get arrested for that?" he asked, concerned.

Carter told him, "No, she can't get in trouble for not answering questions."

"What about obstruction of justice, or whatever it's called?"

Again, Danny and Carter exchanged a look.

"*Did* she obstruct justice?" Danny asked.

"I don't know," said Grady.

"We're only interested in catching whoever killed Agatha," she assured him.

Relieved, Grady relaxed a bit. "Look, Agatha came back into the picture a year ago. It turned Wilhelmina's world upside down. At first they fought, then they were friends. I couldn't keep up. All I knew was that she wasn't okay."

She jotted *sisters reconnected a year ago* onto her notepad, then asked, "*Wilhelmina* wasn't okay?"

"How would you feel?" he asked defensively. "Her older sister dumped her in a foreign city when she was a child. Wilhelmina didn't know the language. Agatha left Wilhelmina with their aunt and uncle, but to Wilhelmina they were strangers. Then almost forty years later she comes back, demands to be in Wilhelmina's life, brings this whole cast of characters along with her. My girlfriend didn't know those people."

"What people?" asked Carter, highly interested.

"Doesn't matter," said Grady, waving the question off with his big hand. "The only one who set her teeth on edge was Lewis Sauter. I'm telling you that man took one look at Mirabelle, and Wilhelmina knew..."

"Knew what?" asked Danny when he had trailed off into what appeared to be deep, disturbed thoughts.

"Knew that Agatha and Sauter were up to something. Something dark." He shook his head for a moment. "Wilhelmina wanted to see the good in her sister, you know? Love is blind? So she trusted Agatha, but she *never* trusted Sauter. She knew that the only way to keep Sauter away from her daughter was to put distance between herself and Agatha."

"Agatha and Sauter were up to 'something dark'?" asked Carter, quickly touching eyes with Danny. "Can you be more specific?"

Danny could read his face, no question, and both detectives were dying to hear that Grady knew for a fact Lewis Sauter had child pornography in his possession.

"A fifty-five year old woman hanging around with a thirty something year old man?" he bristled as though the statement itself implied all that was wrong with it. "And Sauter's over there pushing into Agatha's business? Come on."

He raised his eyebrows like, *case closed.*

But it wasn't.

"So, Sauter's interest in Agatha wasn't genuine," Danny surmised, filling in the gaps though she wasn't entirely convinced. Sauter had taken the time to sketch Agatha. Why direct his infatuation towards the older woman if Mirabelle had been his target? "He was using Agatha to get close to the girl?"

"I told Wilhelmina," he replied, emotion flooding his tone. "I told her not to let Mirabelle do that damned advertisement. That Juicy James bullcrap. I told her, 'you put your daughter up there for all of New York City to see, wearing a dang see-through shirt, you're going to have all kinds of perverts and weirdos crawling out of the woodwork'."

Danny happened to agree.

Allowing a fifteen year old to model in a citywide campaign would have invited predators.

"And it's not just the billboard in Manhattan," he pointed out. "There's another one near the BQE, and a third one over in Jersey."

The theory that Sauter was just another run-of-the-mill pervert who had successfully weaseled his way into Agatha's life for the purpose of molesting Mirabelle was plausible, but not concrete.

Danny was feeling sick to her stomach. The longer she investigated, the more fluff she found. She needed hard evidence, and hearsay wasn't going to cut it.

She looked Grady dead in the eye and asked, "Mr. Willis, are you telling me that Lewis Sauter killed Agatha?"

His mood darkened. He began jabbing his finger at them to emphasize each word. "Wilhelmina confronted Agatha about him. She-"

Slowing him down, she said. "What was the context of the confrontation?"

"Agatha had been taking Mirabelle out, you know, taking her off Wilhelmina's hands here and there. Aunt-niece quality time or what have you. But then Mirabelle would come home all shaken up and withdrawn and like… You could just tell something bad had happened to her. Next thing we know, we learn that Agatha had this guy in the mix all along. We asked Mirabelle about the guy, Sauter, but she doesn't want to talk about it. Then you've got Agatha saying how Sauter is no one and he's not around Mirabelle, which was a *lie*. You know, like she's lying to her sister's face about it. It was dark, man, I'm telling you."

It sounded like there could have been abuse happening, sexual assault perhaps. If Sauter had taken advantage of the fifteen year old, and the girl refused to tell her mom about it, it could have been because Mirabelle didn't want to jeopardize her relationship with Agatha, or cause a fight between the sisters. She also might have blamed herself.

"That's why Wilhelmina confronted her sister," he went on. "Hell, she didn't even know *for sure* what she was accusing her sister of, but she initiated the conversation. She's a good mother," he insisted.

"Were you there?" asked Carter.

"I don't have to be there for every conversation," he shouted, his face twisting up, offended that they didn't believe him, which wasn't the case.

"Okay," Danny intervened to defuse the tension. "Wilhelmina *told* you about all this?"

"Yeah," he said, calming down. "She felt, I don't know how to describe it... On the one hand, Agatha assured her that nothing was going on. She also promised to talk to Sauter about it, which Wilhelmina said wasn't good enough. All she cared about was getting a guarantee that if her sister took Mirabelle, Sauter wouldn't show up. So Agatha promised her that as well. I guess you could say my impression of the situation was that my girlfriend didn't buy it. She kept things on good terms with Agatha, but I could see in her eyes she wasn't going to let Mirabelle go off with her aunt again."

Carter shot Danny a sideways glance. They were thinking the same thing. So he asked Grady, "Mr. Willis, do you know for a fact that Sauter killed your sister-in-law?"

He groaned, glanced at the ceiling, and complained, "Wilhelmina's going to kill me for this. But Mirabelle overheard her mother explain all this to me. Mirabelle ran off that night."

"What night was this?" he asked quickly.

Locking eyes with him, Grady stated, "The 10th. The night Agatha was killed."

Danny knew exactly what needed to be done.

And Grady must have anticipated as much, because he once again began groveling, "I'm not her legal guardian. I can't give you permission to talk to her. But I know what she saw that night. And if you need to arrest Sauter, then you're going to need to talk to Mirabelle. But you can't yank her out of her shoots and all that crap or Wilhelmina is going to kill me."

She felt Carter's eyes on her, and when she met his gaze, the way his square jaw tightened said it all—they might have a witness to the murder.

Rising from her chair, she thanked Grady for taking the time and offered him her business card, which he tucked into the front pocket of his jeans.

"Things are dicey at home," he mentioned, implying that their discretion would be appreciated.

"We can talk to Mirabelle without bringing you up," she assured him. "You've been a big help, really."

"You'll talk to her with Wilhelmina present, right?" he asked, genuinely concerned for the girl.

"We'll see," she told him.

"Sauter's your guy," he insisted.

"That was our feeling all along," she agreed.

As Carter held the door open for them and she walked Grady out of the interview room and through the bullpen, she couldn't help but wonder why Wilhelmina and Grady hadn't brought Mirabelle into the station the second they'd learned she may have witnessed a brutal crime?

When she came to the receptionist's desk just shy of the lobby, however, she got her answer—Wilhelmina, dressed like a damsel in a bad noir film, burst into the precinct, dragging her daughter along by the wrist.

At first, Danny's instinct was to shield Grady, but when Wilhelmina spilled towards her boyfriend and dramatically hugged him, as if performing the final scene of a poorly written play, the scenario struck Danny as too orchestrated to be genuine.

"Ms. Bauer, hello," said Danny. "I wasn't expecting you."

As Wilhelmina peeled herself off Grady, Danny caught sight of Mirabelle.

The girl was mumbling to herself, her gaze fixed on the slick floor like an actor in the throes of last minute line memorization.

"Can we talk?" she asked Wilhelmina, as she led the woman away with her daughter in tow.

Carter hung back with Grady to ask a few more questions.

Sighing melodramatically, Wilhelmina stripped her large sunglasses off her face, revealing smeared mascara, and declared, "Every word of it is true!"

"We can talk in here," she suggested, walking the mother and daughter into the first interview room.

As they piled in, Danny glanced over her shoulder and touched eyes with Grady who was looking on. A strange smirk crept across his face. It gave Danny a bad feeling.

"I understand you didn't have much time to speak yesterday," she said to Wilhelmina, as Carter wrapped it up with Grady and strode through the bullpen to join them.

"I can't apologize enough for that," Wilhelmina said without sounding apologetic. "I guess I was in denial, but I'm here now. Mirabelle is here and we can go over what happened that night, just the three of us." When Carter closed the door, she smiled and revised her point, "Just the *four* of us."

"Can I get you anything? Water? Coffee?" he offered, pulling out one of the chairs for her, though sitting didn't seem to interest her.

"I'm fine, thank you," she said. "I haven't much time, but I want to make a statement so that we can put this whole messy business behind us and go about our lives."

If only it would be so simple, thought Danny, who then pondered why Wilhelmina would assume this meeting wouldn't take long. Hadn't her daughter been molested by an ex-con only to witness the murder of her aunt?

Danny maintained a poker face, however, as Carter urged the distraught woman into a chair.

Mirabelle had been slinking around the perimeter of the room, her chunky boots clapping against the laminate floor. Her light green eyes angled on Danny in a way that unnerved the detective. She was still mumbling to herself. A plotting praying mantis.

Danny asked her if she would like a soda, but when she jumped at the offer, Wilhelmina snapped, "That's too sugary." She barked at her daughter, "Sit down. You're making everyone nervous."

"Actually, why don't you come with me?" Danny suggested, inviting Mirabelle to join her at the door, which caused Wilhelmina to bolt out of her chair and drop the whole act just as quickly.

"You can't speak with her without me in the room," she asserted in a brittle, unsure tone.

Equally surprised as her mother, Mirabelle suddenly looked like a deer in headlights.

Before nearing the woman, Danny shot her partner a sly glance, and he immediately approached the fidgeting girl and began asking her friendly questions about the rainy weather and her favorite flavor of ice cream.

With Mirabelle occupied, Danny was free to corner the mother.

"Ms. Bauer," she began, speaking quietly. "Your boyfriend suggested that Mirabelle might have been assaulted, perhaps on more than one occasion?"

Caught off guard, Wilhelmina hardened.

"I have to take an accusation like that very seriously," she went on. "It would be best if I could speak with your daughter alone."

"Because you think *Agatha* abused her?" she guessed, recollections of their initial meeting at Vital washing over her. "We're not here to talk about that. My daughter wants to tell you what she saw the night of the 10th. She saw that man kill my sister. Lewis Sauter."

"Yes, we'll get her statement regarding that, as well. But I can't overlook any crime," said Danny firmly. "If Sauter assaulted your daughter, then I'll charge him with that as well."

As if to herself, she mumbled, "What the hell did *he* do?" Then to Danny she insisted, "I keep close watch on my daughter."

"I'm sure you do and just because she might have been assaulted doesn't make you responsible. No one blames you."

"I really need to be in the room, you understand?"

"Ms. Bauer-"

"It was my fault," she interjected. "I should've made time for you earlier, and I apologize. I didn't tell you everything I know. That's why I'm here now." She was pleading. "Please. If you could please ask my daughter your questions with me in the room."

Why? Danny wondered. So that Wilhelmina could control the words as they came out of her daughter's mouth, and make sure Mirabelle only said the 'right' things?

In an effort to get through to her, Danny promised, "I've been doing this for a really long time. Girls Mirabelle's age are far more likely to disclose what's happened to them if I interview them one-on-one."

"But really, we don't have much time," she groveled, full of dread.

Unfortunately for Danny, the fact of the matter was that the police couldn't legally interview Mirabelle alone without her mother's permission. But Wilhelmina clearly didn't know that. Hence all the pleading and begging.

That being said, Danny was concerned for Mirabelle's mental health and welfare. She also suspected that Wilhelmina, Grady, and even Mirabelle had cooked up a plot to lie to the police. But for what reason, Danny didn't know.

All she knew was that she planned to get to the bottom of it right now.

"I want you to understand where we're going with this," Danny continued explaining. "We believe Sauter is dangerous. He's our prime suspect at the moment, but this isn't a straightforward case. If Sauter also assaulted your daughter, we might be able to use one crime to prove the other. It would give us probable cause to get into his apartment where we believe we'll find evidence of your sister's murder. Do you see how critical it is that I speak with Mirabelle alone?"

Wilhelmina seemed not only ambivalent but also terrified, so Danny offered her a reassuring smile. "Help me put the man who killed your sister behind bars. Mirabelle is a big girl," she added. "She models like an adult, she can handle a one-on-one conversation."

"I should've never let her go off with my sister," she groaned.

Wilhelmina seemed dedicated to maintaining her image—mother of the year?—but from where Danny was standing it was a performance that left much to be desired.

"You can't watch her all the time," Danny reminded her.

Visibly nervous, Wilhelmina finally agreed.

"I won't be with her long, I promise," Danny said. "Mirabelle? Why don't you come with me?"

The girl's eyes were glued to her mother, and a look of confusion came over her.

Her mother told her daughter to go ahead with the detective.

Mirabelle slinked towards Danny, who then led her out of the interview room, while Carter spoke with Wilhelmina.

Together, Danny and Mirabelle walked slowly beside one another, crossing through the narrow corridor and rounding into a fully furnished conference room.

Rain ticked against the glass panes. In one corner, a vending machine hummed. There was a children's play area occupying the far end of the room.

Timidly, Mirabelle edged towards the table, as Danny closed the door for privacy, but neither sat. Instead, Mirabelle leaned against it, jutting her hip out and hugging her slender waist, as she crossed one chunky heel over the other.

The girl looked nervous.

"What's it like having your mother work as your manager?" she asked to warm the girl up.

"Fine," she said, as she noticed the vending machine.

"Are you hungry?"

"Yes!"

Danny fished a few quarters out of the back pocket of her jeans and fed them into the vending machine slot, while Mirabelle figured out what she wanted—M&M's, peanut butter cups, chocolate covered pretzels, and the like.

The girl smiled at every option.

Danny suggested, "Skittles?"

"You won't tell my mom, will you?"

"Our secret," she said with a wink.

The girl smiled a huge, toothy grin. When she had made up her mind, she pressed her finger against the glass and said, "Skittles, Ring Dings, and M&M's."

"My favorites," Danny mentioned before pushing the corresponding buttons and waiting for the plastic packets to fall from their metal rings.

When they did, Mirabelle snatched the candies from the compartment and wasted no time breaking the wrappers open. She devoured one candy after the next, stuffing them into her mouth.

"Let's have a seat," said Danny, inviting her to the table.

They sat beside one another, the girl plopping down a little too close for comfort.

It gave Danny a strange feeling and made Mirabelle seem a lot younger than fifteen.

"Can you tell me about Agatha?" she began.

"She came here from Germany a year ago," she said, which corroborated Grady's statement.

Before Danny could ask another question, Mirabelle set her candy aside on the table and glanced at Danny with a look in her eye that was far from innocent.

It was odd.

Danny let out a little laugh, feeling awkward. "You okay?"

She laced her fingers with Danny's, which caused the detective to stiffen uncomfortably. "You're really pretty except for that bruise on your chin."

Danny slipped her hand out of Mirabelle's and touched her face. She had forgotten about the blow Sauter had given her.

Danny clasped her hands together and rested them on the table, as she said, "I appreciate that, but let's talk about your aunt."

Disinterested, Mirabelle began fiddling with a plastic wrapper.

Did the girl feel rejected?

Strange.

"Did you like spending time with your aunt?" she coaxed.

Mirabelle nodded and shrugged.

"What did you two do together?"

"Went for walks," she said unenthusiastically.

"That sounds nice," she replied. "Did Agatha introduce you to any of her friends?"

When she didn't respond, Danny asked, "Did you ever meet a man named Lewis Sauter?"

Her eyes widened with recognition and every muscle in her frail body seemed to tense up. In the next moment, she clenched her jaw as if some part of her didn't want to admit it.

"A few times," she said in a small voice.

"What did the three of you do together?"

"Just went for walks like I said," she replied in a smoky voice.

Danny let some time pass before gently pressing her with, "Where?"

Mirabelle tilted her head and began chewing her bottom lip. "Prospect Park. We rented a boat once."

This added significance to the lake, she thought before asking, "Ever go to his place?"

"No, just the park," she said in a hollow tone.

"What about friends?"

"I don't have any friends," she sheepishly admitted.

"I mean, did you ever spend time with friends of your aunt's besides Sauter?"

As the girl shook her head, all Danny took from this miniscule crumb of information was that Mirabelle moved in extremely isolated circles, a tidbit that she had suspected anyway.

Discontinuing that line of friendly conversation, she turned to the darker accusation at hand.

"Did you ever spend time with Sauter alone?"

The girl murmured, *No.*

"Mirabelle," she said in a soft voice, inviting the girl to meet her gaze. When eventually she did, Danny asked, "Was Lewis ever inappropriate with you?"

A bewildered look came over the girl's face. Her brows knit together and her fidgeting intensified—crumpling the plastic wrapper and chewing her lip.

Danny rephrased the question.

"Did he ever touch you inappropriately?"

"I don't feel well," she groaned.

"Can I get you some water?"

Mirabelle winced and clutched her stomach.

Danny couldn't help but wonder if the girl was faking to get out of the interview.

Or perhaps Sauter had molested her, and because of it, talking about him was making her sick.

If Danny gave her a break, however, she would lose momentum so instead she forged ahead, but kept a close eye on Mirabelle's mental state.

"Did Lewis take advantage of you in some way? You did nothing wrong," she reminded her. "You can tell me." When that failed to get her talking, she posed a direct question. "Did Sauter ever touch you?"

Mirabelle angled her pale eyes at Danny, but this time they looked glassy.

"Yes," she breathed, but the admission sounded more like a question as if she was unsure about giving a straight answer.

"Where did he touch you?" she whispered. "This is very important."

Frowning as though a bad taste had filled her mouth, she moaned, "All over."

"Was it over your clothes or under them?"

After a rocky hesitation, she disclosed, "Both."

"Can you remember any dates?"

She shook her head and again said, "I don't feel good."

"Okay," said Danny, drawing in a deep breath. "I just have a few more questions."

"What's going to happen to him?" she asked, her glassy eyes widening with what appeared to be concern.

"We'll have to write up your statement," she began explaining. "Then the district attorney will speak with you to go over what happened. Lewis will be held in jail so he can't hurt you or anyone else. Then eventually there will be a trial."

She cringed, clutching her stomach all over again, and Danny wasn't sure if the idea of a trial had caused the pain, or if the candy she had inhaled wasn't agreeing with her.

"I know it sounds like a lot and it is, but you're doing great." Danny touched her hand reassuringly and finally asked, "Did you go to your aunt's house this past Sunday night?"

After a moment, she said, "I can't remember" in a small voice.

"But your step-dad-"

"He's not my step-dad," she snapped.

"Right," said Danny, starting over. "Grady... he mentioned that you took off the night of the 10th. Did you go to your aunt's house that night?"

Danny was so close she could taste it, but the girl was shutting down.

"If you went to Agatha's that night, it's very important that you tell me. Listen," she said, leaning towards the girl in a secretive hunch. "I can tell there are things you aren't telling me. I can see that you're scared. I've been doing this a long time, and I promise you, if you tell me what you know, no one is going to hurt you." She let that hang for a beat then asked, "Did you go to Agatha's house that night?"

"I feel sick," she groaned, keeling over. Her forehead touched the table.

When she lifted her face, her demeanor had darkened. Beads of sweat had formed across her hairline and upper lip as though she had sprung a sudden fever. She looked dazed.

Danny reached for her forehead, asking, "May I?" and when Mirabelle didn't object, she pressed her inner wrist to the girl's slick brow. She felt hot and clammy.

"You're burning up."

"I feel sick," she repeated impatiently.

"Wait here," she said. "I'll get your mom."

As she rose from the table, the girl grabbed her arm, her wide and desperate eyes locking on her, and said, "You have to make this go away."

Not understanding, she asked, "Make what go away?"

"I have shoots and runway shows all month. Fashion week is around the corner. She'll kill me."

"Who will kill you?"

"This whole thing needs to go away," she insisted. "That's why we're here... so that you won't come by again. Do you have what you need? Did I say the right thing?"

Taken aback, Danny stared at her.

"Mirabelle," she said with authority. "Are you telling me the truth or are you telling me what you think I want to hear?"

"The truth," she blurted out in a panic, clutching the detective's arm even tighter.

From where Danny was standing it sure didn't sound like it, and yet the miserable look on Mirabelle's face gave her pause.

"He assaulted me, like you said. He killed my aunt. All those things. Whatever it takes. Please. You can't come by anymore."

"Lewis Sauter raped you?" she asked.

"Yes," she insisted.

Danny wasn't convinced.

The longer she studied the girl, the murkier her instincts became. She couldn't make heads or tails of any of this. Was Mirabelle lying? Or had her admission only seemed desperate because she was suddenly delirious with a fever?

Testing her, Danny asked, "Can you describe Lewis Sauter?"

"What do you mean?"

"What does he look like?"

Stammering incomprehensibly, she rattled off some nonsense so Danny clarified, "His height, eye color, race? Any distinguishing marks?"

"He's white," she guessed quickly then began racking her brain. "Um... average height, I think, average looks."

Working with her though it seemed doing so would amount to a pointless exercise, Danny sat and asked, "Anything else?"

"Like what?"

She thought for a moment then suggested, "How old would you say he is?"

"Ah, Aunt Agatha's age?"

"Okay," she said, keeping her expression neutral. "How did he dress?"

"Normal, I guess."

"Can you tell me what his hair looks like?"

"Brown, average," she supplied, consistently avoiding any kind of specific description.

Again, she asked, "Any distinguishing marks?"

But the girl only blinked, at a loss for words.

Sauter's scar was unforgettable.

Danny rose from the table and told the girl, "I'll get your mother now."

Danny was skeptical. Had Mirabelle ever seen the gift shop janitor before in her life? She doubted the girl had been molested by him.

Which meant that the entire morning had been a colossal waste of time.

It also meant that Wilhelmina Bauer was up to something far more sinister than so-called saving her daughter's modeling career from a scandal.

"You mentioned you've never been to your aunt's house," she said off-handedly as she neared the door. "But you saw the murder, so where was she killed?"

She stared at Danny, trapped.

"Mirabelle, what's going on?" she asked, hoping the girl would level with her. "Why are you here?"

"I don't feel well!" she yelled, getting emotional.

"I'll get your mom," she said and excused herself.

On the way out, Danny closed the conference room door behind her, and rounded through the bullpen, nearing the interview room where Carter had been speaking with the model's mother.

She gave a quick knock then let herself in, all the while her gut was telling her that just because Wilhelmina had pressured her daughter into conveniently scapegoating the one man who Danny had indicated might have been involved, didn't necessarily mean that Lewis Sauter was innocent.

Not that it sat right with her, but Danny was prepared to use whatever she could to advance the investigation. She needed to get inside Sauter's apartment.

As soon as she touched eyes with her partner, he paused the interview.

Wilhelmina lifted her gaze from one of the photographs on the table—a face shot of the four year-old boy—and finished her thought, "A beautiful child. He could've modeled."

"Mirabelle's not feeling well," Danny told her and the woman immediately rose from the table.

"How did she do?" she asked.

Danny touched eyes with Carter, who also seemed curious.

"Good," she said.

"Was she...?" she began to say but couldn't find the right words at first. "Did that man... touch my baby?"

"I'm still looking into it-"

"Looking into it?" she blurted out, appalled. "Did he attack my daughter or not?"

"I'd like to speak with Mirabelle again when she's feeling better."

Outraged, she yelled, "That man violated my daughter and killed my sister. There's nothing to talk about. I want him arrested." Tearing through the room, she bypassed Danny and turned on her heel when she reached the door. "My daughter's life will not be ruined by this. She's a good girl and she told the truth. You have everything you need."

With that she marched around the corner and disappeared into the bullpen in search of her daughter.

As the dust settled, Danny neared Carter, who seemed wound up if not offended as he vacated his chair. Perhaps Wilhelmina had exhibited those feminine wiles of hers in a scattered attempt to pull the wool over his eyes.

She asked, "What's your take on this?"

"She told me what I wanted to hear. I can't use any of it."

"Something's off with them," she agreed, the hum of the precinct spilling through the open doorway.

"What did the daughter say?"

She sighed, pinching the bridge of her nose as if she'd rather not admit how badly it had gone. "Well, she did *disclose*," she said, delivering good news before sharing the disturbing truth of the matter.

"Sauter was sexually abusing her?" he asked, highly skeptical.

Danny plowed all ten fingers through her mop of hair, stating, "That's what she said."

"Come on, you don't buy that."

"Honestly, Carter, I don't know. Her initial reaction when I said Lewis Sauter's name looked to me like genuine horror. Like she knows him and doesn't like him. Like there's history. If she was faking it, then she's a better actress than Meryl Streep. But when we came to the easy part, and all she had to do was describe him physically, she couldn't. Or she wouldn't. All I know right now is that I want to use whatever I can to get into Sauter's apartment."

"I'm on the same page."

Though nothing had been decided, they left the interview room and hooked through the bullpen to report to their lieutenant. But Franco was otherwise busy with Wilhelmina in front of the receptionist's desk.

Wilhelmina looked irate and Franco seemed to be in the throes of calming her down.

She demanded, "Where is she?"

"Lower your voice, Ma'am," he insisted.

Wilhelmina tried to shove Franco, as she demanded, "Where is my daughter?"

Franco caught her wrists, gently wrangled her, and urged her back, as he said, "Did anyone see that teenager leave?"

Rushing over, Danny asked, "What's going on?"

Franco pulled Wilhelmina aside so that a stream of police officers entering the precinct wouldn't tramble them.

"You!" she blurted out, jerking free from the lieutenant and pointing her manicured finger at Danny. "You left her by herself and now she's gone!"

"Ms. Bauer!" Franco yelled over her. When she piped down, eyes flaring—*what!*—he explained, "I'll send officers out to find her. Could you try calling her?"

"My daughter doesn't have a cell phone," she snapped as though the lieutenant was some kind of moron.

Carter wasted no time waving over every available uniformed officer. He took them aside, got them up to speed, and dividing them into groups of three, he sent them out to search for Mirabelle in every direction.

"She couldn't have gone far," Danny assured the mother, which did nothing to calm her down.

"Unbelievable," she hissed and paced away.

Danny wished she could chalk this up to another one of Wilhelmina's performances, but the woman's panicked reaction seemed more than genuine. Mirabelle running off wasn't part of the plan.

"How could you let this happen?" Wilhelmina asked, blaming Franco.

The lieutenant looked far from sympathetic.

"I'm not going anywhere until you find her," she went on. "Do you understand?"

"No one's asking you to leave, Ms. Bauer," he said dryly.

She snorted in disgust then parked herself on a chair beside one of the detective's desks. She held her head high and folded her arms, refusing to engage further.

The detective whose workstation she had invaded seemed more than slightly put off to have some crazy woman seated kitty-corner from him.

She warned, "If anything happens to her..."

The partial threat was meant for Danny since the girl had vanished during their interview. Mirabelle hadn't struck her as the rebellious type, though. Danny doubted that Mirabelle had ever ventured into Kensington alone. If anything happened to her, *indeed...*

She pulled Franco aside and spoke quietly so that the woman wouldn't overhear. "Based on Mirabelle's statement we have enough to get a search warrant for Sauter's place."

"I'll see what I can do," he said, glancing at Wilhelmina.

"I'm not surprised the girl ran off the first chance she got," she said quietly, as she eyed the woman. "Her mother's a real piece of work."

Franco agreed. "I don't trust her. If you ask me, she should be your prime suspect if Sauter doesn't pan out."

They silently observed Wilhelmina, then Danny suggested, "Let me hunt around for her daughter."

"Fine."

Danny collected her raincoat from the back of her chair when she reached her desk. As she pulled her coat on, she approached Wilhelmina and asked, "Any place she might have gone?"

Glaring up at her, she seethed, "If I had any idea where my daughter goes when she runs off, I'd find her myself."

It gave her pause. Had Mirabelle taken off like this before, disappeared into the city? Wilhelmina had seemed to imply as much, but questioning her along those lines would only waste time.

Leaving the woman, Danny started through the station house and set off into the rainy afternoon.

Two grueling hours later, as chilly winds constantly bit into her, threatening to snap her umbrella inside out, Danny had searched for the girl in every coffee shop and bookstore. She had hoofed it down every slick street and avenue, and had checked every crowded subway platform and bus stop throughout Kensington and its bordering neighborhoods.

But she'd had no luck finding the girl.

Instead, Danny found herself on Ocean Parkway, one block from home.

The row houses lining the street were bathed in shadows, the sky overhead darkened with swollen clouds.

As she walked north along the sidewalk through the drizzling rain that bounced off the canopy of her flimsy umbrella, she noticed her mother's Volvo parked along the curb. Nora was home.

Last night, her mother had called asking to come over, but because Nora tended to overstay her welcome, Danny had made excuses—*I'm exhausted from work, turning in early, catch you tomorrow?* She had thought having a night to herself would be enough time to sort through the myriad reasons for why her mother had confronted Tommy. It was as though she needed to arrive at her own conclusion before she confronted Nora, and yet speculating had gotten her nowhere. There was no way to guess her mother's reasoning.

The more she obsessed, in fact, the worse her mind whirled with fears that Nora had done the unthinkable—told Tommy that his son had died—and it was that very fear that compelled her to bypass her own stoop and trek up her mother's.

She looked at the second floor windows before reaching the landing. The lights were on inside, causing an amber glow to shaft out into the gloomy haze. Coming to the entrance door, she rang the buzzer and began folding her wet umbrella.

"Hello?" said Nora through the speaker-box.

She spoke up over the stiff wind, saying, "It's Danny. Do you have a minute?"

"Danny!" she exclaimed. "Come on up!"

Her mother sounded cheerful, which would only make this conversation more difficult.

The door blared, buzzing and dislodging, so she pushed into the lobby, which looked identical to the one in her own building.

After crossing into the dimly lit stairwell and climbing up to the second floor, she walked, sneakers squeaking over tiles, to the very end of the corridor where a tattered welcome mat rested on the floor in front of her mother's apartment.

Danny propped her umbrella against the wall, wiped her soggy sneakers on the mat, and then gave the steel door a little knock.

Immediately, the door popped inward. Nora was beaming on the other side. When she noticed the fading bruise on Danny's chin, however, her smile dropped.

"My God," she breathed.

"It's nothing, Ma. Really, I'm fine," she insisted, urging her mother aside, as she edged into the shallow foyer that was overwrought with stacks of what appeared to be recycling—newspapers and catalogs and old magazines.

As they trailed into the living room, embarrassment came over Nora. "You'll have to excuse the mess. How are you? I didn't expect you to swing by. Is everything alright?"

Absently, Danny said, "Yeah, Ma, everything's alright," as she took in the sight of the cramped quarters.

It wasn't simply a mess. It was packed to the gills with haphazardly stacked boxes, pillars of old magazines, and shoeboxes interspersed with crushed cans. It appeared Nora had never thrown anything out in her life.

Had she turned into a hoarder?

Danny was reminded of how long it had been since she'd set foot in this place. Years. Nora always came to her apartment, not the other way around, and Danny was beginning to understand why. The living room was a labyrinth of clutter.

"I was just about to clean," she said sheepishly, as she grimaced at her living conditions.

It was heartbreaking and almost shook Danny's resolve.

Almost.

"I just wanted to ask you about something."

"Oh?"

Danny scanned the sea of boxes for a place to sit, but the couch and chairs weren't immediately obvious. Each was buried under heaps of clothes, she soon realized. So, she decided to come out with it from where she stood between a bone-dry Christmas tree donning dusty ornaments and an old mini fridge teetering on top of what appeared to be a fort of cracked VHS cassettes.

Easing into the topic at hand, she mentioned, "I noticed you were in O'Toole's the other day."

"You weren't stopping by, were you?" Nora carefully asked. "Because I'm serious about this, Danny, that man should not be in your life."

"He isn't," she assured her in the vain hope that if Nora felt relieved, then she would be straight with Danny. But if she attacked her mother, then Nora would only shut down. "Why were you there?"

She sighed and touched her hair, collecting her thoughts. "Well, you know how I feel about him."

Danny let some time pass before pointing out, "That doesn't answer the question. What were you talking to him about?"

Ambivalent, Nora muttered something about how Tommy was no good, which only made her daughter stiffen with impatience.

"It's not your place to tell him about Gregory," she asserted, staring her mother down as she waited for a reply. "You didn't tell him, did you?"

Why wasn't she answering?

"Did you?" she pressed, her tone wavering badly. Her heart punched up her throat harder and harder with every passing second that her mother didn't respond.

"No," she bristled and the tension that had seized Danny rushed out of her. "I don't like being interrogated."

"Why were you there?"

When Nora didn't answer but instead slumped remorsefully, Danny told her, "I saw you. You were arguing with Tommy, and I want to know what it was about."

"Honey, I don't want to upset you-"

"Stop stalling," she insisted.

"I should've told you," she apologized in a flimsy voice. "But I know how sensitive you are when it comes to him."

"Just tell me!" she snapped. Sick of this already, she wanted straight answers. She'd had enough lies for one day thanks to the Bauers. "Tell me, please," she finally begged.

Indignantly, Nora composed herself, touching her hair again and smoothing her hands down the mauve cardigan she wore before admitting, "He stopped by the other day when you were at work." She paused to read her daughter's reaction, which meant that Danny must have looked as shocked as she felt. "I was very polite to him," she assured her. "*Very* polite."

"He came by my apartment?"

"Now, why would he do that?" she challenged, implying that Tommy must have been plotting to rip Danny's heart out of her chest a second time. "Listen, sweetheart..." she trailed off in an effort to choose her words carefully. "He doesn't deserve another chance."

"Why did he come by?"

"He had some presents for the baby," she said, as though Tommy's gesture had been too little and far too late. Then she quickly offered, "I didn't tell him about Gregory. I know it's your place and not mine. You might write him a letter-"

"So, you were polite," she interrupted, wrapping her head around the chain of events, "took the gifts, sent him away, and then what? You stopped by the bar to chew him out?"

"As a matter of fact, yes," she admitted. "It took a few days for it to sink in, and when it did, I felt angry. How dare he?"

"Please stay away from him," she said, exhaustion having edged into her tone.

"I have every intention of staying away from him, really." Holding Danny's gaze, she feigned a trustworthy smile, then bluntly commented, "You look tired."

"Where are they?"

"What?"

Danny glanced around the room. It was safe to assume her mother hadn't thrown them out so she clarified, "The gifts?"

"It'll only upset you," she warned as if her daughter's foolishness caused Nora almost physical pangs of regret.

"Stop worrying about what might upset me!" she snapped.

Nora let out a little huff then hopped through the maze of junk before disappearing into her bedroom to fetch the presents Tommy had brought for the baby.

A moment later she returned with a Babies R Us bag and two saggy helium balloons, their yellow strings loosely anchored to the handle. But Nora didn't seem eager to hand it over.

"Stop worrying about me," said Danny, taking the bag.

Cautiously optimistic, she asked, "Would you like something to eat?"

"I have to get going," she said distractedly as she peeked inside the large bag at what appeared to be a generous stack of wrapped gifts.

When she turned for the door, Nora tried to stop her by saying, "I don't want him destroying you."

As she left her mother's apartment, Danny said under her breath, "I'm already destroyed."

After leaving Nora's building, she didn't head straight back to the precinct, but went to her own apartment.

She set Tommy's bag of gifts down on the floor of the baby's room and collapsed, haunted by multiplying anxieties.

Did he want her back? What if she fell for it and got crushed?

What was he going to think of her when he finds out she had failed to keep their son alive?

Gaining control of her emotions though her vision blurred with tears, she began opening the first present. It was a yellow sippy-cup with a fluffy lion decal on its side.

It was then that she knew why Tommy had walked out of her life, and it had nothing to do with his fears of becoming a father.

Chapter Thirteen

SHEETS OF RAIN slapping the bedroom windows woke Carter from a long night of fitful sleep. The air was cool and damp, the room dim with haze where sunlight should've been.

He rolled over and stretched his arms across his wife's side of the bed, but Kathy wasn't there.

From downstairs, his son's muffled laughter competed with his daughter's hot tirade, both of which billowed up through the floorboards.

Kathy shouted over them—*Matty, don't fling your eggs at your sister! Amanda, you're not wearing that skirt to school! Christopher, Chris? Christ! Where the hell is your brother?*

As Carter listened to his family, he smiled. Loving bickering. He didn't like missing out on their morning shenanigans. But if he didn't hustle into the shower and get dressed, he would be late.

He tossed the covers back and lumbered out of bed.

The window was cracked open by about five inches, he realized as he crossed the room, which explained the draft. Kathy loved falling asleep to the sound of rain. It was one of her many quirks he had fallen madly in love with.

After pushing the windowpane down to the sill, he rubbed his eyes and made his way to the bathroom, as Kathy jogged up the stairs.

She had probably heard him walk across the floor, he thought, as he squeezed toothpaste onto his brush and eyed his tired reflection in the medicine cabinet mirror. Beneath his ribs was a bullet wound scar that had healed badly, as well as the faded marks of a lonely childhood that continued to haunt him—cigarette burns, whip switch scars, and other evidence of what he had survived.

He spat toothpaste into the sink and rinsed his mouth, as Kathy filled the doorway, looking like the vision of beauty that he'd first laid eyes on fifteen years ago.

She had always reminded him of Botticelli's The Birth of Venus. Her long, blonde hair spilled over her shoulders. Her rosy cheeks and alabaster skin were as angelic as her piercing blue eyes.

Though her expression at the moment held animosity. The tightness of her mouth implied she had no intention of censoring whatever was on her mind.

Beautiful and unforgiving in a casual pair of jeans and pink sweater that hugged her full figure, she remarked, "You slept late."

"You got up early," he countered. If they were two ships passing in the night, it was both their faults.

Carter could smell an argument.

"You've been distant," she mentioned, folding her arms.

He took hold of her waist, drawing her close, and explained, "I'm still getting used to the department."

"Is that all it is?"

"Of course," he said softly before silencing her with a kiss, which she barely reciprocated.

She urged him back, pressing her hands against the firm wall of his chest. But he held her hips against his. She wasn't going anywhere.

"I don't think this case is good for you."

"Kathy," he warned.

"This *particular* case is going to affect you, Carter."

"Don't make me regret telling you about it."

He released her. He really didn't want an argument.

"I don't have the luxury of picking and choosing my SVU cases based on my wife's opinions, you know that."

"You sound condescending," she said hotly.

"I'm not being condescending," he assured her before pointing out, "how would it have looked if I refused my first case?"

After staring at him for a moment, she crossed into the bedroom and jerked open the top drawer of the dresser. As she proceeded to pick out his tie and socks, she complained, "Things are supposed to be *better* now that you're not gone for weeks on end, working undercover."

"They are," he insisted, as he watched her from the doorway.

She angrily busied herself, playing the role of the doting wife and resenting every second of it, as she assembled his outfit for the day.

"You're still gone all the time."

"I come home every night," he reminded her.

"But I don't *have you*," she shot back, locking eyes with him. "Your body comes home, but your mind is elsewhere, and your partner is a woman."

He should've seen it coming, his wife's distrust.

She lived in a constant state of suspicion that Carter would slip up with another infidelity.

They suspended hostilities when their fourteen year old daughter, Amanda, traipsed into the room.

Amanda's eyes were rolled so far up in their sockets that it seemed they might get stuck. She presented the outfit she'd changed into—tight jeans and a sensible sweater, *happy?*—as though there was no greater insult than being told what *not* to wear.

"Was that so hard?" Kathy asked her, and their daughter scrunched up her round face, and rolled her eyes again. "Don't hurt yourself."

Amanda tossed her hair and sang, "You can take the girl out of the skirt, but you can't take the skirt out of the girl!"

As she swayed her way out of the bedroom, Carter shouted, "What does that mean?" He asked his wife, "What does she mean by that? Is she seeing a boy? Amanda! You're too young to date!"

"Leave her alone," said Kathy, returning to the topic at hand. "You mention that woman a lot, your new partner. She's ruining what little time we have together."

"Nothing is going on," he promised.

Kathy shook her head, but Carter knew at this point she was only exasperated with herself. She was the one who had chosen to stick with him after the infidelity. "I told myself not to worry, but..."

"Then don't worry," he said, though it seemed to fall on deaf ears. "I listened to you. I transferred. I'm not in a dark place anymore. I'm with you every night."

"And with another woman every day," she added sorely.

Carter thought it would be in poor taste to remind her that the woman he had mistakenly slept with hadn't been his partner, so he went with, "I love you."

"I have to get the kids to school."

When she turned for the hallway, he stopped her by saying, "I'm never going to do that to you again."

"I want to believe you," she said, sounding defeated. "But we're not going to get through this if you keep canceling."

"Can't we meet with the counselor in the evening? There's no way I can time my lunch break for marriage counseling, not when I'm working a case like this."

"I can ask," she compromised. It was something. "You have to deal with what happened to you. You have to talk it through and come to terms with your bad childhood. Or else you're never going to escape this pattern of running off and trying to fix yourself by fixing the world. Don't you see that?"

"I will never cheat on you again," he promised. "Never."

"Okay," she said to end the conversation. "Please watch what you say to me about that woman."

"Danny?"

"I don't want to hear her name." She pinched her eyes shut, all five feet three inches of her cringing. "It's *very* triggering."

"Okay," he agreed.

The horse was dead, but Kathy kept beating it. "Dr. Valdmanis said it's one of my triggers so if you could *please* not talk about other *women*."

"She's not *other women*," he argued. "She's my partner."

"Do you want this to work?" she fired back.

"Yes."

"Then don't talk to me about other women."

With that she marched down the hallway, leaving him to stew in the sludge of his deepest regret.

Up until his transgression, their marriage had been built on a mutual understanding, though neither of them had ever stated it outright. Carter was the grateful, blue-collar cop who had married a gorgeous woman who was obviously too good for him. He was supposed to do anything for her. That was his end of the deal.

Kathy's job was to be a supportive wife who never complained about the long hours that kept her husband from coming home. He was the bread-winner. She was the housewife.

They had both known this going in.

He had trusted Kathy, which was why, a few years into their marriage, he had opened up to her about his difficult upbringing and the abuse he had survived.

But doing so had been unwise.

Kathy had lost respect for her husband once she'd learned he had been sexually abused. She'd never looked at him the same after that.

Carter had *needed* a woman to *look at him* and *see a man*.

And *that* had been the real cause of his infidelity.

A woman had come along. She had looked at him the way he wanted to be seen, the way his wife *used to* look at him, and he couldn't say, no. He had cheated on Kathy. He hadn't been able to live with himself, so he told his wife.

That's when all of his demons had emerged.

He had been working like a dog to conceal those demons ever since. He wanted his marriage to heal. But he wasn't keen on marriage counseling.

Besides, Carter hadn't even engaged in a full-blown affair, not in the traditional sense. His involvement with another woman had been a means to an end. While working a long stint undercover, he'd gotten close with his target. He shouldn't have slept with her, but in a superficial sense, he had been motivated by the goal of closing the case. And it had worked. She'd spilled every last detail about trafficking children, exploiting them in the most horrendous ways, and though Carter had succeeded in bringing her down, he couldn't live with what he'd done. But confessing the infidelity to Kathy had been an even bigger mistake.

As he showered quickly and dressed, the haunting memory was soon replaced with a yearning feeling. He *did* want to heal their marriage. He wanted his wife's support.

He would've liked to talk to Kathy about Mirabelle Bauer, about the fact that she had run off and that no one at the precinct had managed to find her. He wanted to share with his wife the concern he felt for their own daughter. What if Amanda ran off and caused them the same grief? But these days, Carter couldn't discuss anything with his wife unless their marriage counselor was present to moderate every concern, comment, and question.

By the time he reached the kitchen downstairs his kids were gone. There was enough coffee in the pot to fill a mug, however.

After splashing some cream into his coffee, he returned the carton to the fridge, and his cell phone began vibrating in the front pocket of his slacks.

Danny's name and number flashed across the LCD screen so he swiped it, accepting the call, "Yeah?"

"The warrant came through for Sauter's place."

Outside, a car horn bleated.

"That's me," she added.

"Tell me you have coffee," he said, setting his mug in the sink before hustling into the foyer where his parka was hanging next to Kathy's on a coat rack.

"You're in luck," she told him.

He threw on his coat and sneakers, and jogged down the stoop. The rain was relentless, so he kept his head down as he ran to the car that was idling along the curbside.

Danny had a thing about driving, namely she had been avoiding it, so when she hopped out of the vehicle and jogged around to the passenger side door, he wasn't surprised.

He settled behind the steering wheel and adjusted the driver's seat and mirrors.

Rain pelted the roof and hood of the car.

Once she had buckled up in the passenger seat, she mentioned, "Head over to Ditmas," and he eased out into the street.

As they drove through Kensington, windshield wipers flapping and the sedan crawling with the congested flow of traffic, he realized that the silence between them felt comfortable, a striking contrast to what it was like to be around his wife these days.

When he slowed to a stop for a traffic light, he glanced at her, comments about the case forming on the tip of his tongue, but became distracted by her slightly puffy eyes.

"You okay?"

It took her a moment to understand what he was referring to, and when she did, she brushed over the question. "Never sleep on your face after eating a bowl of pasta."

From where Carter was sitting, it was obviously more than that—it looked as though she'd been up all night crying—which only meant he shouldn't have pried in the first place.

"Working undercover you have no one to talk to," he mentioned, easing his foot on the accelerator, as they drove. He quickly glimpsed her from the corner of his eye to gauge her reaction, not that she had one. Her emotions were bottled tight as a drum. "It's a nice change of pace having a partner."

"I'm not going to tell you my deepest, darkest secrets, Dobbs."

Companionably, he teased, "Oh you will. I have that effect on people."

She smiled, but nothing else was said until they came to the middle of Ditmas Avenue where a line of brick buildings towered over the bodegas and bars that spanned the block.

"That's it," she said, leaning over the dashboard so she could look up at the sixth floor windows of the largest building.

"Looks like we're the first ones here," he commented, as he pulled the sedan along the curb.

Climbing out of the vehicle, she asked, "You think we'll find something?"

He chugged his coffee then joined her on the sidewalk where the rain was pissing down. "Don't tell me you're having doubts."

Debating, she eyed the traffic streaming down the avenue for a beat and admitted, "I've been going back and forth. He's creepy. I'll give him that."

"We'll find something," he assured her.

"I begged Franco to release him."

It landed like a fist to his gut, knocking the wind out of him and stopping him dead in his tracks. "You what?"

"He's still in his cell," she told him. "But yeah, I asked."

"I know guys like Sauter," he warned her, but stopped himself from saying anything else.

He had to kill the impulse to reveal why, though. As cold memories leached out from the darkest corners of his mind, nagging him to open up, he kept his mouth shut.

They walked through the rain to the building entrance, thrust the door open, and began crossing through the dimly lit lobby towards the elevator.

"Listen," she said, keeping at his heels. They ducked into the elevator, its pre-war double-doors having momentarily confused him. As the car jimmied up the shaft, she went on, "I'm coming a little undone, too. Four days into this investigation and we've got nothing on Sauter. I know what it means."

"We're about to get something on Sauter," he promised, feeling oddly betrayed by her doubt. "This case isn't going to go cold and wind up in the basement of the 66th."

"I hope not," she said, unencouraged. "I'm just saying we have to remind ourselves to see what's there, and not what we want to see."

"Releasing Sauter isn't the answer."

"Look, I don't think he's innocent," she argued, as the elevator door jutted aside. They stepped out into the dingy corridor, and she added, "But that doesn't mean he's guilty. I think he knows something. I think he's dying to get in the middle of our investigation, and I think if we follow him, we'll get a jump on this thing."

"We've already gotten a jump," he said, referring to the search warrant that they were now acting on. As they neared Sauter's apartment, he added, "Everything we need to know is on the other side of this door."

But it wasn't.

After waiting for the super to let them into the apartment unit, after finding Sauter's bizarre shrine to Agatha Bauer, his alcohol stash, and a horrifying amount of roaches—both dead and scurrying—the detectives were no closer to solving the case than they had been four days ago when they'd stared down at their victim on the muddy shore of a lake in Prospect Park.

There hadn't been one computer in Sauter's apartment. Nor had there been one printer to tie the slippery man to the photos of the young boy that had been found with the dead body.

And because of it, Carter was ready to drive his clenched fist through a wall.

Forensic investigators were combing through the place, collecting fingerprints and waving UV lights over every surface in search of blood.

Carter excused himself into the corridor to get some air.

He hated second-guessing his instincts, but he had to ask himself, *had* Sauter killed the German immigrant? Seriously, *had* he?

Was Sauter a master at covering his tracks? Or was the family with whom Agatha had reconnected far less innocent than they appeared?

Grady Willis was a real piece of work, and Wilhelmina Bauer was no better—that brazen performance meant to fool the police had been an act of pure insanity as far as Carter was concerned.

At this point, as much as it infuriated him, he would have to assume that anyone could have killed Agatha Bauer. Everyone was a suspect, including the willowy model. All three of them had pointed a finger at the one person the police had been investigating in the first place—Sauter. Maybe Danny and him should investigate Wilhelmina, Grady, and Mirabelle…

He gave up ruminating when Danny peeked her head out into the corridor. Her cell phone was pressed to her ear. She told whoever was on the other end, "Yeah, he's here." Covering the mouthpiece, she told Carter, "Franco's releasing Sauter."

"Great," he grumbled.

"It might be," she said optimistically before slipping back into Sauter's apartment.

He paced down the corridor and came to a window. Looking out at the dreary street—cars whipping by in the rain, pedestrians hunched under umbrellas as they hurried down the sidewalk, traffic lights changing colors one blink at a time—he thought about the men who had stolen his childhood.

The basement, that chamber—the ritualistic torture of those dark years surged to the forefront of Carter's mind, and he was filled with a deep and unshakable hunch.

What if the boy from those printed photographs was somewhere out there, alive? What if he was close, perhaps hidden somewhere in Kensington?

His intuition came at a very high price. It made Lewis Sauter right. The man had insisted that abused children grow up to become psychic. Carter felt his sixth sense piqued at the moment. He started to feel *certain* that the boy was alive...

Franco had ordered them not to waste time investigating the boy.

But right then and there, Carter made the decision not to follow the order.

He knew he had to dig deeper now more than ever, and get to the finishing line, even if it meant running the race on his own.

As he stared at the miserable weather, he vowed to learn everything he could about the Bauers.

There would be no other way to find the boy.

Chapter Fourteen

THE CORRIDOR LIGHT was flickering overhead, as Lewis Sauter scraped his key into the lock on his apartment door, his skin zinging with anticipation, his mind reeling with excitement, fantasies of the alluring detective arousing his every inch.

She had stiffened in response to him, scared yet surrendering, when he had brushed up against her, pinning her to the jail cell bars. Her big eyes had flared, that pretty little slanted mouth of hers drifting open. She'd smelled of chamomile and gun grease and unwashed skin—natural oils.

Had she left some trace of herself behind in his apartment, he wondered? Would he find her intoxicating scent clinging to the otherwise stale air in his home?

He wasn't concerned the police might have trashed the place, only curious about what Danny had thought of it. Had he crept into her mind as she had hunted through his belongings? Had the titillating memory of his hard body pressing against hers swept through her thoughts as she had discovered his little shrine to Agatha? Had she gradually realized his capacity to worship a deserving woman? Did it make her jealous of Agatha? Did she now wish for Lewis to worship her? Perhaps she'd yearned to be alone in his apartment, away from the other cops, so she could lie on his bed and feel close to him…

Thunder cracked outside, bringing with it a sudden downpour. Rain pounded on the roof and jarred him from contemplation.

He finally entered his apartment, stepping inside and closing the door. First, he inhaled deeply, but the air smelled only of mildew and expensive cologne—probably the football player's, he surmised with a frown.

Next, he studied the space, the shadows that glided across the floor and walls thanks to the flow of traffic outside. His sagging mattress was propped against the far wall. All the cabinets in the kitchen were open. The tin cup meant to catch drips from the leaking ceiling was on its side. A fat drop plunked against it and he grimaced before flipping on the lights. He quickly turned the can upright. It was then that he noticed his desk. It was bare.

They'd taken his photos of Agatha, his sketchpad, *damn,* even his bottle of whiskey, he realized, standing over the child-sized chair. Nice of them to empty his trash bin, he thought, peering down at it.

After nearing the mattress, he muscled it to the floor—*thud!*—then proceeded to shove it to where it belonged beneath the window, which he opened to neutralize the thick cologne smell that had been irritating his throat.

A gust of rainy wind slapped in, clearing the stale air. He used a wooden dowel that he found wedged against the molding to prevent the pane from sliding down to the sill.

He should've bought whiskey on his way home, or a sketchpad.

Staring out at the glistening street, the twinkling buildings across the way, their curtained windows where figures in silhouette went about their lives behind closed doors, he welcomed a fresh wave of fantasies that centered on the detective with the slanted mouth.

What if she lived beyond one of those windows? His luck wasn't nearly so good, but then again anything was possible. This was New York City after all, the land of big dreams.

It was also a playground of illusions where people could embody statuses they didn't actually possess and flaunt personas that didn't begin to capture their true personalities, everyone faking it until they made it except that no one ever did. Dark intentions behind the bright eyes of every passerby. An inviting grin was often a hint of sinister motives. Women could be sirens and lure men out to sea, where they would only end up drowning.

But Agatha hadn't drowned him. He'd been too smart and too quick. His intuition had been his shield, guiding his hand.

At first, she had fooled him. She had played the part of the tender and grateful immigrant. She had fulfilled his every lustful wish. Agatha had satisfied his *needs* during their boat rides across the lake at Prospect Park, she had been quite adventurous!

She had been his muse. He had loved her and had spent late nights sketching her likeness on high-quality paper.

But Agatha's facade had only been smoke and mirrors.

It hadn't lasted.

When he had seen her for who she really was—the real Agatha had been a waking nightmare that would have never let him go—he had wanted her dead.

But she shouldn't have been killed.

He missed her now. And missing her was far worse than the turmoil of emotions she had caused him.

The fact was that Lewis had discovered that Agatha had known his mother.

The information had been too much.

Agatha had been his *special friend*, and his mother had been his worst enemy. How could they have *known* each other? *Liked* each other?

What about Danny? he suddenly wondered. Would *she* like his mother if they ever met?

Fears cloyed at him, liquefying his bowels, as he considered Danny's true nature.

What if she was planning on tricking him as well?

Would she meet the same fate as Agatha?

As if he could escape the haunting image of the woman who had deceived him, he bolted into the kitchen area and began smacking the cabinets closed. But it didn't rid those images from his mind.

Someone urgently pounding on his door did.

Perhaps Danny was here to apologize...

He stiffened in his jeans at the thought, as he pressed his eye to the peephole.

Through the peephole he saw big eyes—muted green yet screaming—staring back at him.

Mirabelle!

He unlocked the deadbolt, threw the door open, and pulled her inside.

She looked like a sewer rat on the brink of death.

Wet, blonde hair hung in stringy strands over her shoulders, and the girl's pale mouth was open, her chest heaving.

She was shivering badly, her teeth chattered. She took a few shaky steps. There was a look of remorse in her eyes.

"What happened?" he breathed.

She threw her soaking arms around him—*I've missed you!*

He urged her off and ushered her deeper into the apartment.

"I did something stupid," she blurted out, flying into a panic as she began pacing and shaking the nervousness out of her hands. She kept her head down, her gaze fixed on the wooden floor. Without warning, she demanded, "Where were you? I was waiting in the alley for hours. What were the cops doing here?"

"Searching for clues," he told her. She turned on her chunky heel and started pacing again. "What stupid thing did you do?"

"Did they find anything?" she asked over him.

"What would they find?"

She locked eyes with him. Panic was written all over her pretty face. "What would they find? I don't know. Maybe something they planted? They're gunning for you, don't you get that?"

"I can handle it," he said, enjoying how Danny was once again seeping into the forefront of his mind. "Tell me what you did."

"We have to get out of here," she said in a thin, smoky voice. His question hadn't reached her. She scanned the room, taking inventory of the belongings he would need to pack. "We have to run away."

"I can't run away. I'm on parole."

"I can't model anymore," she snapped. "I hate it. I hate her, *them*. I hate all of it."

"I know," he said sympathetically as he took hold of her sopping shoulders so she wouldn't start flitting across the floor again. "Maybe you should warm up in the shower?"

"I'm fine."

"You're trembling."

"I *told* them," she confessed.

Intrigued, he cocked his head, wondering what his little friend was referring to.

"The police asked my mom about you," she explained, her husky voice turning shrill as she detailed the horrors that had occurred without him. "My mom made me say all this crap." No longer on the brink of tears, they were spilling down the sharp angles of her cheeks, she added, "I tried to take it back, you know? I tried to make it seem like I don't know you. I can't please them all!"

Muffled TV chatter rose through the walls, his neighbor having heard enough drama from Lewis' apartment for one evening.

"Shhh," he said.

"And now I can never see you?" she raged on. "Agatha's gone, so we can never be together!"

Brushing her wet hair off her damp cheeks and holding her face, he whispered, "You're seeing me now."

"I told them you raped me."

Now that was interesting…

"That's okay," he assured her, just another web to untangle.

"It's not okay," she cried, jerking free of his strong grasp. "They think you killed my aunt."

When he didn't react, her eyes shifted with sudden suspicion. "Did you?"

"You can't think that," he warned.

She apologized and forced herself to breathe. Doing so only released a fraction of the anxiety that had wound up inside of her. Then she began pacing again, her chunky boots clomping across the floor. But it wasn't enough, so she plopped down on the bare mattress instead.

"They're going to arrest you," she worried. "They're going to take you away from me, and I can't live like that."

Joining her on the mattress, he wrapped his arm around her. She felt damp and smelled of flowers.

"Did you write up a statement? Sign it?"

Hesitating, the ragged edges of her nervous energy smoothed out, and dim hope flashed across her features.

"No," she breathed.

"Did you speak with the district attorney? Did you answer to a grand jury?"

"No," she said, sounding stronger.

He offered her a friendly smile, pleased with himself that he had put his little friend's fear to rest.

"So they won't arrest you for killing Agatha," she gradually understood.

"See? Everything's fine."

Lewis began reminiscing. "Remember when we first met?"

"At the park," she remembered in a whisper. "When Aunt Agatha and I were standing on the shore and feeding the swans."

"And I walked up."

"And I asked her who you were," she added.

"And our eyes locked."

"You saw the real me," she whispered, smiling. "You *knew*."

"And I see the real you now," he said, looking at her fondly.

She couldn't stay here, though, not forever like she most wanted.

"I know how strong you are," he went on.

Her mouth twisted and she groaned, "They're killing me."

"You're not going to let them kill you," he firmly told her.

She didn't look encouraged.

"You don't know what it's like," she complained.

"I do know what it's like, that's how I know you can handle it. Come on," he said, trying to get off the mattress, but she clung to him.

"I can't go back there," she begged in a tone he'd never heard come out of her before. "Why can't I live with you?"

He studied her face for a long moment, observing the anguish that hardened her delicate features.

"What?" she asked.

"I might need you to do something for me."

Curiosity mixed with apprehension slowly spread across her skeletal face, and she nodded, "Okay, on one condition."

"That you don't have to live there anymore?" he guessed easily.

The look on her face was confirmation enough.

He didn't want to lie to the girl—as a registered sex offender, there would be no way he could take her in, he shouldn't even be spending time with her—but he agreed anyway, with one caveat. "It's not going to happen overnight."

"That's okay," she said quickly, every inch of her ready to hear the plan.

"I'd like you to do it tonight," he added, as he held Danny's image in his mind.

Mirabelle smiled, but he didn't notice. All he could see was the detective in his imagination.

But then Danny's pretty face interchanged with his mother's.

The jagged scar across his forehead suddenly burned, as a dark premonition came over him.

Danielle Foster was more than just the object of his current obsession.

He decided…

She would be *the one*.

Chapter Fifteen

SHAKING RAIN OUT of her hair, Danny entered 24 Hour Dine, a diner in the heart of Kensington. The place was packed.

As she neared the hostess stand, she noted that almost every table was occupied, the stools lining the counter as well. Adjusting to the noisy hum of the place and the thick scent of pancakes and fried food in the air, she scanned the many customers and determined she was the first in her party to arrive.

"Dinner for one?" asked the hostess. Her syrup-stained uniform implied this wasn't her night.

"Two," she said, as she gave the restaurant and its countless faces another scan to be certain she hadn't overlooked the emaciated model. "A booth if you've got it."

The hostess plucked two laminated menus from the stand and led her down a row of occupied booths lining the windows. Rain ticked faintly against the glass.

When she came to a vacant booth, which was still dirty from the previous customers—crumpled napkins, dirty plates, a tumbler on its side—the hostess cursed under her breath then shouted for a busboy to—*clean this up!*

"We'll have this cleared in a sec," she apologized, glaring in the direction of a frazzled teenager who was hurrying over with an already-full bus tray. He clanked his bin on the table and began stacking the scattered plates on top of one another with the efficiency of a blackjack dealer collecting chips.

For Danny, the long night had taken an interesting turn. While she had been staking out

Lewis Sauter's apartment building, the suspect having been released from custody, she'd spied *Mirabelle* of all people creeping along Ditmas Avenue in the pouring rain.

At first Danny had thought it had been an incredible coincidence that after running off, evading the police, and hiding out God knows where, Mirabelle had suddenly appeared near the one address that the detective had been staking out. But then the girl had gone inside the building.

Not an hour later, Mirabelle had emerged, clomped down the sidewalk in her chunky heels, and ducked into a bodega where she must have somehow charmed a stranger into letting her use their cell phone. She'd called the precinct and asked to meet with Danny and no one else.

Danny had gotten the call from the precinct while she had watched the girl do all this.

The girl was up to something and Danny feared to imagine what.

As the busboy finished up wiping the tabletop, Danny glanced out the window for Mirabelle, but was met with her own reflection.

"There you are," said the hostess, as she set the menus down on the table. The busboy shuffled off with his mountainous bin towards the kitchen, and she asked, "Coffee?"

"Please," Danny said, sliding into the far side of the vinyl booth so that she could watch the entrance.

Her raincoat was bulky so she made quick work of wriggling it off and balled it beside her just as Mirabelle—wet and tattered—cautiously approached the empty hostess stand, having slipped inside the restaurant.

She looked ghostly, standing in the stark light—her skin pale, her hair scraggly, the hollows of her cheeks shadowy. Skin and bones masked in skittish apprehension.

Danny stood, getting her attention with an inviting wave.

Trailing up the aisle, she used long strides, her chunky heels clomping over the checkered floor. Almost all of the customers took notice of her.

"Hey," she said breathlessly when she reached the table.

After she settled into the booth, Danny mentioned, "Your mom's really worried about you."

The girl's subtle reaction didn't come with a response. She gazed out the window next, and Danny got the feeling that Mirabelle was rejecting the entire concept that Wilhelmina would be concerned.

"I'm glad you got in touch," she said, just as their waitress swooped in with a steaming mug of black coffee for Danny. "Would you like something to eat?"

"Yes," said Mirabelle eagerly before diving into her menu to skim the options. "I'll have pancakes and hash browns and sausage and eggs."

"Midnight breakfast?" the waitress asked brightly, clarifying the particular dish the girl had ordered.

"Yeah, and chocolate milk?"

"You got it," she said with a wink, as she noted the beverage on her pad then turned.

"No wait," said Mirabelle, catching her. "A chocolate milkshake. Yeah, that's what I want."

The waitress made a note then off-handedly mentioned that it might be awhile—*we're getting slammed!* She sauntered off towards the kitchen.

Though Danny was tempted to compliment the girl for having ordered so much food, she sensed doing so would have a detrimental effect, since, for Mirabelle, eating seemed to come with a side of guilt. So she held her tongue and studied the girl, who was staring out the window and perhaps working up the nerve to explain why she had insisted on meeting Danny at the diner and not the precinct.

Giving her time to collect her thoughts, though she had to assume the girl's explanation could be laced with lies, she poured half-and-half into her mug then selected a sugar packet from the cluster of condiments on the table. She stirred the sweetener into her coffee with a spoon.

But Mirabelle didn't seem close to coming out with it. In fact, she looked increasingly lost the longer she sat staring silently out the window.

Easing into the issue at hand, Danny asked, "Why did you leave the precinct without your mom?"

Finally, the girl angled her pale green eyes across the table, but her gaze didn't exactly land on Danny. She just looked vacant, scared perhaps.

She looked slightly ashamed as she said, "I lied to you before at the station. I said some things that weren't true."

Maybe her explanation *wouldn't* include another tangled web of lies, thought Danny optimistically.

"Go on, I'm listening," she encouraged.

"I thought if I told you the truth, you'd tell my mom and I'd get in trouble." Her dainty eyebrows drifted up her forehead with apprehension as she added, "I couldn't deal with it."

"Why would you be in trouble with your mom for telling the truth?"

She uttered, "Because..." in a small voice before groaning at whatever had come to mind. "If I told you the truth, then I'd have to tell you where I go and what I do when I'm alone. My mom doesn't know that I sometimes go off on my own..."

Recalling Wilhelmina's prior comment—*if I knew where my daughter goes when she runs off, I'd be there now*—Danny was certain the woman wasn't entirely in the dark, but that didn't mean the girl's fear of punishment wasn't justified.

Cleaning the slate, Danny suggested, "Don't worry about what you told me before, just tell the truth now, okay?" The girl let out a rocky breath in agreement, which prompted Danny to quietly ask, "Did Lewis Sauter sexually abuse you?"

"No," she emphatically whispered before insisting, "I just... I could tell that's what everyone thought so I went with it."

"Okay," she said easily, though Sauter's prior arrest for statutory rape sprung to mind. "Are you involved in a consensual, sexual relationship with him?"

"God, no!" she blurted out, repeating *God! What? No!* as though the entire concept was yucky. "If you knew me," she added with an amused laugh, "there's just no way."

When she challenged the girl's point, she kept her tone friendly and conversational, careful not to push too hard yet keen to hear anything she could about Sauter that might give her leads as far as his associations or habits. "Why not? He's a good looking guy."

Mirabelle screwed her face up, staring at the detective in abject horror, then said, "I'm into girls. How is that not obvious?"

It certainly explained her attempt at holding Danny's hand in the precinct conference room and that misplaced compliment—*you're really pretty*. Danny straightened her spine, absorbing the information, and blew on her coffee before taking a sip.

"I didn't want to be presumptuous and *assume*," Danny said offhandedly.

"But you could tell, right?" There was a mischievous glint in her eyes and she perked up, perhaps enjoying a brief reprieve from disclosing whatever it was that she was here to talk about. She placed her hand on the table, but was too timid to touch Danny's. Instead, she asked, "Do you have a boyfriend?"

"I do not," said Danny, unsure about indulging the girl's curiosity.

"I didn't think so," she said knowingly. "What about... a... girlfriend?"

"I'm single," she said in a neutral tone, as she mentally composed how to get this conversation back on track.

"But you're into girls, right?" she guessed. "The short hair, no makeup, the way you dress."

"Well, no, as a matter of fact. I just had a baby, so... definitely wouldn't have gotten that far if I didn't like men."

She wasn't sure why she had said it—mentioned Gregory. Mentioning him at all implied that her son wasn't dead. In a way it felt good to time-hop and see someone's face light up in response.

Mirabelle congratulated her, though she didn't seem as thrilled to hear the news as others had been. Regardless, for a split second Danny got lost in imagining Gregory at home in his crib, alive and happy.

But the moment was fleeting. As reality crept in, her heart sank, and because of it, she plowed all ten fingers through her short mop of hair to get her focus back.

"Why am I here, Mirabelle?"

"You asked me if I went to my aunt's house that night, Sunday right?"

"Did you?"

"That's why I'm here," she said, pressing her palms to the table as she again worked up the nerve. "My mom just wants this to go away. You should arrest her," she complained.

Danny knew she was stalling.

"And why's that?"

"Because she lied to you," Mirabelle shot back as though it was obvious. "Because she made me lie to you. Will you arrest her?"

Danny was getting the feeling that the girl was interested in getting her mother out of her life first and foremost, so she offered, "I can pass it along, but no I won't personally arrest her. My job is to investigate the homicide."

She huffed out of frustration, folding her arms.

"Did you see something Sunday night?" she gently prodded.

Leaning into the edge of the table in a secretive hunch, the girl took a moment to formulate her response, her gaze drifting as though she was replaying events in her head.

"Lewis wasn't the only friend of Agatha's I met." She let that hang for a moment. "See, my mom can't know that I was spending time with all these other people, okay?"

"I won't breathe a word of it to anyone," she promised, though the girl's concern seemed convoluted.

"I wanted to hang out with Lewis so I went to his place, but he wasn't there. Then I went to a few other spots where I sometimes meet him-"

"Like where?" she interrupted.

"I don't know," she said, annoyed that it would matter. "The park, the lake, around? But I couldn't find him so I went to my aunt's house, because he's there sometimes."

Walking through the timeline, Danny summarized, "So you were home, overheard your mother tell Grady that she wasn't going to let you see your aunt anymore, then you ran off to find Sauter?"

"Basically," she said, but it sounded like she was guessing. "Lewis is basically my best friend. We meet up all the time."

"I know this seems frustrating, but I need all the facts. Grady mentioned something had upset you and you ran off that night," she explained.

"Grady wasn't there," she said. "He was at the bar."

She hesitated only because what Mirabelle was saying regarding this one detail didn't match up with

Grady's statement. According to him, he had been consoling Wilhelmina over her prior argument with her sister. Mirabelle had overheard and slipped out.

Playing it off as though there was no discrepancy, she asked, "So it was just you and your mother at home?"

"Um, well, I don't know where Mom was. Why does it matter?"

Danny smiled at her, backing off, then supplied, "So you jogged over to your aunt's house when you couldn't find Sauter in the usual places."

"Yeah," she said as if put off that they were covering the same ground she had literally just explained.

"You didn't take the bus or a cab?"

"No, I was on foot."

Danny needed to determine that every word out of the girl's mouth was true so she asked, "You arrived at Agatha's house, where is that?"

"112 Cortelyou Road," she recited.

"Okay."

"It was raining and the lights were on. I came to the door and peeked through the small window, because I heard a man and I thought it was Lewis, but it wasn't. It was another friend of Agatha's and they were arguing."

"Do you know his name?" she interjected, fishing her notepad out of her raincoat pocket so she could record every detail.

"Randy something."

"And what time was this?" When she found a pen as well, she flipped to a fresh page in her notepad and began quickly scribbling.

"Like seven or eight or something," she said before complaining, "you're acting like I'm the one who did something wrong."

"It's my job to ask questions," she kindly reminded her. She set her pen on the table and clasped her hands together. Then she leveled with the girl. "You lied to me at the station so I'm questioning everything you say. I'm not trying to offend you. It's just how this works. Got it?"

Mirabelle stared at her, dumbfounded, then slumped back in the booth, accepting the rules.

"I got there at seven or eight," she repeated. "Randy was arguing with Agatha."

"Where?"

"In the living room."

"So you were able to *see* them?" she questioned, picking up the pen, poised to record every detail in her notepad.

"Yeah, I saw them. I saw Randy kill my aunt."

Danny's attention locked on the girl. Mirabelle had essentially conveyed the exact same story at the precinct, except at the precinct she had incriminated Lewis Sauter. If Mirabelle's objective was to assist her mother in making this whole thing go away, then she could've easily mentioned Randy during her interview. Why would Wilhelmina push for Sauter's arrest when arresting Randy—the real perp—would've done the trick in terms of making the scandal go away to protect her daughter's modeling career? And why would knowing Randy put the girl in worse trouble with her mother? It didn't make sense.

Bearing in mind that Mirabelle's admission was coming hot off the heels of her hour-long encounter with Sauter, Danny had no choice but to dig for exact details, no matter how graphic, to test whether or not the girl was spouting more lies.

"Could you describe what you saw?"

"Yeah, okay," she said, tucking her long, blonde hair behind her ears and composing herself. "They were arguing and facing each other."

"Can you remember if it was in the middle of the living room, or behind the couch, more in the kitchen area? Or where specifically?"

"Ah, in front of the couch."

Danny recalled there had been a coffee table directly in front of the couch, so she asked, "In the middle of the living room? In front of the coffee table?"

"Yeah, I guess," she said, screwing her face up as if to say, *why would that matter?* "And then he killed her."

"Again, I'm sorry, but-"

"He hit her in the head," she clarified.

"But if he was facing her..."

"It happened so fast, I don't know. She turned around, like to sit..." she stammered. "Like she was done with him, you know? So she moved to the couch and sat. That's when he hit her from behind, and he didn't stop hitting her even after she was on the floor."

"What did he hit her with?"

"A sculpture thing," she explained. "I don't know what it was a sculpture of exactly. It was, like, an abstract piece of art, maybe marble? It's always on the kitchen counter next to the coffeemaker."

"And then what?"

"Then, I don't know, I ran off," she said, glancing nervously at Danny. "Don't ask me why I ran off, but I couldn't help her, you know? I couldn't fight a *man*."

"Why didn't you call the police?"

"I don't have a cell phone."

"You could've asked to borrow someone's cell phone-"

"In Kensington?" she sarcastically challenged. "As if people are *that* friendly here. Yeah right."

"You could've told your mother," she pointed out.

Mirabelle shook her head, gazing out the window as though no one in the world had ever understood her. "I can't tell that woman anything," she hissed.

"How did Agatha know Randy?"

"I have no idea."

"She never mentioned it?"

"No."

The details of the murder corroborated Jill Andover's account of how the crime had gone down that night, but Mirabelle's motivation for revealing this now instead of days ago when she'd first had the chance, and the fact that she was throwing a brand new suspect into the mix wasn't sitting right with Danny.

Something was off.

At the risk of causing the girl to shut down, she had to ask, "Mirabelle, did Sauter put you up to this?"

"What?"

"Did he feed you this information and instruct you to lie to me?" she said, looking her square in the eye.

"No!"

"I saw you go into his apartment building an hour ago-"

"Because we're friends!"

"--then you came out and called the precinct to invite me here," she stated point blank.

"How do you *know* all that?"

"This is what I'm hearing from you," she said, breaking it down for the girl. "You couldn't find Sauter that night, which means you don't know for sure that he didn't kill your aunt."

"Randy did," she insisted, filled with anger. "I saw him."

Danny talked over her, "He could've told you the details, roped you into lying to the police for the second time." When she didn't respond, Danny questioned, "How would he know what to tell you if he didn't kill her himself?"

Doubt gradually clouded her expression and she seemed to shrink with dark revelations. But a moment later, she straightened her spine and declared, "I know what I saw."

Danny had no choice but to put the strange conversation on hold when their waitress approached carrying a steaming plate of stacked pancakes and greasy hash browns, which she plonked in front of Mirabelle along with a chocolate milkshake.

"How're we doing?" she asked Danny. "Can I get you anything else?"

"A refill?" she said, sliding her mug of lukewarm coffee over.

The waitress scanned the busy diner then waved over another waitress, who had been slowly stalking up the aisles with a carafe of coffee to refill mugs.

As she padded over and refreshed Danny's coffee, the detective watched Mirabelle stare at her meal as if daunted.

Choosing her words carefully once they were alone, she asked, "Is your mother putting too much pressure on you?"

The girl snorted something like a laugh, but didn't otherwise respond, as she unrolled her bundled utensils, fisted the fork, and began shoveling eggs and hash browns into her mouth.

They sat in silence, the hum of the restaurant softening all around them as customers gradually slapped cash on their tables and shuffled out.

Ten minutes passed—the girl scarfing down pancakes like a feral cat and Danny sipping coffee as she considered whether or not 'Randy' was valid.

Did he even exist?

When it seemed Mirabelle had finished—she pushed her plate aside and leaned back in the booth, draping her bony hands over her stomach—Danny asked, "How are things at home?"

"Terrible," she said bluntly, as she glanced through the rain-spattered window, narrowing her eyes. Her gaze softened as if a disturbing memory was taking hold. When she returned her attention to Danny, her eyes were brimming with tears. She swallowed hard, perhaps choking down emotions she couldn't begin to explain, and told her, "You get that guy Randy, and I'll be fine. I know it."

"You spent time with Sauter so you didn't have to be home?" she speculated, studying the girl's wilting posture, the apprehension clouding her expression—she didn't want to go back to her mother.

"Stop calling him that," she halfheartedly snapped.

"What? Sauter?"

"His name is Lewis, and yeah, I'd rather hang out with him than be home. When I was with Aunt Agatha and Lewis, I could pretend they were my real mom and dad. They were so great to one another. He loved her. He loves me. And Aunt Agatha made me feel good about modeling. She was really into beauty, you know?"

The countless self-portraits in the woman's house came to mind.

"Agatha modeled in her day. Her dad made her. She was like a slave, I think. She didn't like to talk about it, but you could just tell it had killed her. She got me, you know? She could relate."

"So, you opened up to her about what it's really like?" asked Danny, leaning forward. "What is it really like?"

A queasy look came over her. "The last person I told was killed, so no, I'm not going to tell you," she snapped and silence fell between them until Danny was struck by sudden thought.

"I need to ask you something," she said, as she turned her raincoat over and unsnapped the breast pocket where she'd been keeping a photograph of the four-year old boy. It was a long shot and she was all too aware of Franco's order not to pursue any crimes related to the small child, but she'd rather leave no stone unturned.

She set the photo on the table, the boy's scared face filling the 5x8 print.

"Do you know who this boy is?"

Mirabelle froze, a glimmer of what appeared to be recognition flashing behind her eyes, as she stared at the child.

The girl's reaction reminded Danny of Sauter, that look in his eye when she had asked about his mother. Her gut told her that she was striking the same nerve with Mirabelle, so she pushed, "Do you know who he is?"

Her mouth drifted open, but no words came out, and as she picked up the photo for closer examination, her brows knit together.

"Have you seen him before?" she repeated. "Or even just photos of him somewhere? Perhaps in your aunt's house?"

"Not in my aunt's house," she said in a far away voice.

"In Randy's possession possibly?"

No response.

"But you've seen him?"

Snapping out of it, she set down the photo and said, "No, I haven't seen him."

Danny frowned. "Are you sure?"

"I haven't."

"You sure you don't recognize him?" she pressed, sensing the girl was withholding.

The waitress appeared, stealing their attention as she dropped their check onto the table.

After thanking her, Danny found her wallet, pinched out a few bills, and reviewed the check before handing both over.

"You're taking me back, aren't you?" asked Mirabelle.

"My car's outside," she said, confirming as the girl groaned.

Pulling her raincoat with her, she slid out of the booth with the 5x8 in hand and followed Mirabelle through the diner.

She paused briefly at the glass door to bundle up, while the girl exited into the drizzling rain, and this dark, never-ending night. She didn't hang her head or hunch her shoulders. Rather she seemed to welcome the uncomfortable weather just like Danny had the night of her son's passing—reveling in her alone time, finally free since her mother wasn't with her, yet blissfully unaware that Gregory was leaving this world at that very moment.

In some small way, she knew exactly how Mirabelle felt—*enjoy what you have, because things could always get worse*—though the girl's secrets and lies, as hazy as the night itself, prevented Danny from feeling a true kinship.

Danny pointed to the brown sedan parked down the block, as she briskly passed the girl and they hurried through the rain.

When they reached the vehicle, she unlocked and opened the passenger side door for Mirabelle, who folded herself neatly inside.

After shutting her door, she was quick to hop off the curb and round to the driver side where she slid in behind the steering wheel, slammed the door closed, and fastened her seatbelt.

"You were sick the other day," she commented, glancing at the girl who was mimicking her—pulling her safety belt on and adjusting the back of the seat. "Are you feeling better?"

"It comes in waves, feeling sick," she mentioned nonchalantly, as Danny turned the engine and pulled out into the street. "I feel fine now, though."

"Where to?"

"Anywhere," she said breezily, resting her head against the seat.

"I mean what's your address?"

"I was afraid of that," she said in an almost humorous tone.

Danny had to admit the girl was growing on her, but until this Randy character checked out, she couldn't afford to lower her guard.

"I live on Coney Island Ave," she said before mentioning the cross street.

As they drove, Danny explained how she would interview Randy and pass her findings along to the district attorney who would likely need to speak with Mirabelle.

The girl digested the news relatively well, but as they came to her building, she asked, "How are you going to find him?"

"We have ways," she said, throwing the gear shifter into Park and killing the engine.

"You're coming up?"

"I'd like to speak with your mother."

"Not about Randy," she said, suddenly anxious.

"I'd like to make sure she doesn't flip out at you."

"Oh," she breathed, popping her door open.

As Danny lumbered out of the sedan and into the drizzling rain, she noted that the Bauers lived in a rundown brick building, which didn't at all represent Wilhelmina's slick image.

Like so many residential buildings in Kensington, the lobby was small and dingy with cracked tiles and buzzing fluorescent lights. Its redeeming quality, however, was that it had an elevator, though Mirabelle seemed in no rush to reach it.

In fact, it seemed that from Mirabelle's point of view being landlocked at home was no different than being incarcerated at Alcatraz—rationed meals, limited time in direct sunlight, and always at the mercy of her warden-like mother.

Dragging her chunky heels and taking long, sloppy strides, she trailed behind the detective, who pushed the call button the second she had reached the elevator.

When the elevator door slid open with a ding, they stepped inside where the girl pressed the third floor button before leaning against the wall.

Her mood darkened as the car ascended, and when the door opened, she didn't move a muscle to get out.

Holding the door and coaxing her into the corridor—Mirabelle was groaning, tilting her head back, her shoulders slumped, dreading what punishment might come—she said optimistically, "It won't be that bad. Your mother is going to be relieved if anything. She cares about you."

"She cares about herself," she complained. "And the way she loves me..." she trailed off cringing, then straightened her spine and reminded herself, "I won't be here forever."

After following Mirabelle down the corridor—the girl crawled, dragging her feet to prolong the inevitable—Danny knocked loudly on the last apartment where TV chatter from some sporting event was billowing through the wall. The volume lowered, replaced with the sounds of scattered footfall and muffled voices, Wilhelmina and Grady perhaps discussing who might be here at this hour.

Finally, the door drew inward and Danny almost didn't recognize the stately yet sallow-faced woman on the other side—pale lips and washed-out eyes, her hair in curlers trapped under a mesh net, the freckles that peppered her nose and cheeks evident on her alabaster skin.

Wilhelmina was wearing baggy sweatpants and a faded flannel shirt, looking more vagabond than Versace and twice her age.

"Detective!" she said, so alarmed at the unannounced visit and so intent on Danny not peering into her apartment that at first she didn't notice her daughter skulking around the corner.

"I have Mirabelle," she said, her tone implying that she'd like to come inside.

Wilhelmina's eyes narrowed on her daughter. Her mouth pressed into a furious line, which soon lifted into an appreciative smile.

"Thank God!" she exclaimed in delayed reaction, spilling into the corridor where she pulled her daughter into a grandiose hug, giving Danny a chance to spy her apartment—messy yet homey quarters that smelled faintly of beer and microwave popcorn.

When the woman realized her daughter wasn't reciprocating, she released her and didn't seem pleased to find Danny nosing into the doorway.

"Can I come in for a minute?" she asked.

"That's really not necessary," she said, declining as she urged Mirabelle inside.

"I think it would be best if we discussed a few things," she mentioned before discretely adding, "so she doesn't run off again."

Though she clearly didn't want to, Wilhelmina widened the door for her to enter.

It wasn't merely messy, she realized, but resembled her own mother's home. Dusty boxes and magazines were stacked against the foyer walls. The kitchen counters, which Danny glimpsed as she followed Wilhelmina, edging deeper into the apartment, were covered in nests of coupons and miscellaneous items—cleaning products, junk mail, potted succulent plants that appeared dying if not dead. The living room wasn't as haphazard, she noted, but it was far from tidy, though framed photos of Mirabelle lining the walls enlivened the otherwise dismal décor.

Wearing a stained wife-beater, Grady was reclined in a squashy sofa-chair, clutching a canned beer in his right hand, the remote control in his left, the top button his jeans undone as though he'd just gorged himself, eyes glued to the television—Knicks versus Lakers, the NBA playoffs in full swing. He wasn't so much unaware of Danny as he seemed to be ignoring her outright, even after she'd said, *hello.*

A tense moment later, Mirabelle realized based on her parents' mood that there would be no immediate consequences for having disappeared for days. She traipsed off down a narrow hallway and ducked into what Danny assumed was her bedroom.

"I'm concerned Mirabelle might be under way too much pressure," she began, directing her unease at Wilhelmina since the boyfriend was otherwise disposed.

"I'm concerned there is a rapist-murderer out there who you haven't done a damn thing to arrest," she bristled hotly.

"She ran off for a reason," Danny said, maintaining her composure. "She's fifteen. Maybe she needs more time with her friends. She might like to enroll in some after school programs. She needs an outlet so she doesn't act out."

"She doesn't need any of that," Wilhelmina snapped before making a concerted effort to control her emotions. Using a friendly tone, she explained, "I home school my daughter and she has plenty of social activities. I assure you this won't happen again."

She let her point hang, but it only made Danny more curious. Mirabelle wasn't in school? Her entire life revolved around modeling? No wonder she clung to Lewis Sauter. She probably felt smothered by her mother.

As if to conclude the visit, Wilhelmina mustered a smile that seemed to pain her and began ushering Danny towards the door, saying, "Thank you so much for finding her. You take care."

Mirabelle bounded through the living room, singing, "Danny!" Excitedly, she grabbed hold of the detective's arm and told her mother, "I just want to show her something."

"You'll show her nothing!" she asserted. "She's on her way out!"

Danny allowed the girl to pull her through the living room and down the hallway where they turned into her bedroom—having a poke around could prove fruitful, though she wasn't sure what she expected to find.

Mirabelle plopped down onto the bed beside her modeling book, which was laying open, and immediately began pulling out one of the photos—a close-up shot of her brooding face, those sharp eyes of hers gleaming directly at Danny from the glossy print.

"I want you to have this," she whispered, every inch of her having come alive. "And this," she added with the scattered exuberance of a child. She offered Danny a postcard featuring a clothing designer whose name sounded vaguely familiar—Bruce Tilden. "It's my fashion show tomorrow night. You have to come."

"Ah," she stammered, pocketing the postcard and taking the girl's modeling photo as well.

"Really," she insisted, her mood turning sullen. "Aunt Agatha was going to come, but now..."

"I think I can make it," she said to cheer the girl up, as she carefully rolled the print and tucked it into her raincoat pocket. She didn't want it getting wet outside.

"You know what you need?" she said abruptly, leaping off the bed and clutching Danny's hand.

She bounded out of the bedroom and slipped into the bathroom where she shut the door like a giddy schoolgirl who'd just ditched class with her best friend.

Bubbling, she flipped open the medicine cabinet and began searching through a wealth of cosmetics that were lining its plastic shelves.

As Mirabelle selected eyeliner and shadow, filling her hands with makeup, Danny awkwardly scanned the cramped bathroom, which hadn't undergone a renovation in at least three decades.

"I think a little black shadow will do the trick," she decided, pulling Danny's attention back to the cluttered shelves. "You have something to wear, right? A dress?"

"Ah, yeah," she said absently, her attention now fixed on a little glass vial of clear liquid on the bottom shelf. There was a syringe needle tucked beside it.

At first it occurred to her that Grady Willis might have an addiction far worse than alcohol, but the prescription label didn't say methadone.

Premarin.

Danny hadn't heard of it.

From the other side of the door, Wilhelmina shouted, "Pardon me, Detective, but I really am going to have to ask you to leave." She pounded on the door, causing her daughter to startle and laugh and shove the makeup she'd collected against Danny's chest.

Once Danny had pocketed the items, Mirabelle giggling all the while, she opened the door and immediately apologized.

But the woman was already advancing on her daughter and scolding her. "You think I don't know what you're doing in here? You think I can't hear you? Do you have any idea how expensive makeup is? What in the hell has gotten into you?"

"We were just leaving," said the girl indignantly, as she veered around her mother and sashayed into the living room.

Wilhelmina kept at her heels and Danny followed after at a respectful distance.

"Thank you so much for bringing her home," she reiterated with a profound lack of gratitude.

Her daughter opened the apartment door, mooning fondly at the detective.

The woman's malevolent glare was enough to send Danny into the corridor.

"Goodnight," said Danny.

As she started for the elevator, she could feel Wilhelmina's cruel eyes burning into the back of her head until their apartment door clicked shut behind her.

Glancing over her shoulder, she waited for the sounds of an argument to billow out from the apartment.

But none came.

As she waited for the elevator, Danny wondered about the syringe needle, Premarin, and what the prescription might be for.

Chapter Sixteen

BRACING THE KITCHEN counter where a nest of coupons was threatening to spill onto the floor, Wilhelmina mentally replayed the ordeal—greeting the detective, embracing her daughter, combating Foster's insulting advice, those backhanded suggestions meant to improve her daughter's welfare. Attempting to convince herself that her reactions and overall attitude had been reasonable made her hands shake and her chest tighten. What if the detective *knew*?

Her anxiety dovetailed into a frightening array of paranoid presumptions.

What had Mirabelle told the police? Had Grady come up during her interview, the twisted dynamic of this faltering family? What if the police were now investigating a whole new crime?

Wilhelmina shouldn't have been proactive about trying to make this whole thing go away.

Her mounting regrets solidified in her stomach, and she thought she might be sick.

Horrified, she forced some air into her lungs, straightening her spine and releasing the countertop, which caused coupons to flutter down to the linoleum tiles.

Ignoring the mess, she told herself that the only thing to do at this point was nothing at all. But her treacherous subconscious wasn't done with her yet.

Agatha had found out, which meant the detectives could as well.

The freight train was barreling down the tracks and Grady wasn't the only one tied to the rails.

When she touched her head with an unsteady hand and felt her hairnet, the lumpy curlers beneath, she grumbled. She looked terrible in her saggy sweatpants, the tattered flannel that had permanently molded to her every curve.

Her apartment was no better. It screamed poverty, lower class, a slum. And the impression all of it had made on the detective would surely work against her. Only the rich and powerful got off scot-free, and in Foster's eyes Wilhelmina no longer resembled a woman above the law. This disturbing realization set Wilhelmina's teeth on edge.

One glance at Grady swigging beer—his slicked-back ducktail mullet and trailer-trash undershirt practically bragging he was some kind of loitering, schoolyard pervert—filled her with an exhausted sense of misgiving. She should've never asked him for help.

She was itching for a fight, so she strode into the living room with her hands on her hips, her brow furrowed and eyes fiery, and stared daggers at him.

He hardly noticed. His eyelids were heavy and his jaw was slack. The dopey expression on his otherwise handsome face indicated he was perhaps one beer away from passing out. Rather than provoke a blowout—he hadn't even glanced up at her—she gave up and paced away, as a tidal wave of memories crashed over her.

She had watched Grady grow from a boy into a man, from skinny to muscular, and from timid to bold over the years. She had organized his photoshoots, coordinated his schedule, and had made sure he was always paid on time. Wilhelmina had been working as his agent's underpaid yet passionate assistant.

In those days, Grady had been a smooth-chested American heartthrob. He'd had those *eyes*. It had been obvious he would become a star. He had walked with swagger. Vanity Fair had described him as 'panty-melting' at one point.

Wilhelmina and Grady had been so attracted to one another that they had gotten swept up in a thrilling, secretive romance. A lifestyle had developed between them of sneaking off to kiss and fondle one another, any opportunity, every excuse, and best of all Grady hadn't cared that she had a kid.

But now, more than a decade later, he was barely recognizable, the stressful years of being an icon having detrimentally eroded his once-sexy looks. The years had unraveled his effervescent spirit and chipped away at his personality. Though he'd fought the downfall, his method of invigorating his ambition had also destroyed him—trading one addiction for another. His new love had stolen his charm, as well as his youthful glow, and worst of all, it had damaged his love for Wilhelmina.

Alcohol.

Grady was still kind and clever, funny at times, committed to follow her lead and doing as he was told. But only in the morning and always before he got the itch to have his first drink. He was a zombie otherwise, a mere apparition of his former lively and sharp self.

She considered confronting him about the precinct and possibly revamping the plan since the one she'd devised had obviously backfired. Steering the cops towards the man they were after anyway, giving them the statement they were looking for, telling them what they wanted to hear should have resulted in the police leaving them alone once and for all.

But it hadn't, and if she initiated a discussion with Grady now while he was floating in a bog of inebriation, he wouldn't have the wherewithal to brainstorm alternative plans, soothe her anxiety, or assure her that he would never let her wind up in prison. His own horrendous vice—alcohol—had technically *caused* the crime she feared the cops would discover. It would be nice if Grady would take responsibility for that, at least by setting her mind at ease now, but comforting her hadn't been his priority in years.

She had the impulse to smack him sober, but it wouldn't do any good. Besides, she still had a soft spot in her heart for him, for better or worse.

Groaning himself awake, Grady rattled his can of beer, sloshing the warm dregs around inside, then knocked it back.

"Don't get bent out of shape," he told her before crushing the can and flinging it in the general direction of an overflowing laundry hamper that he often mistook for the trash.

"Grady, the plan we discussed was cut and dry!" she hissed. "But you had to go and insinuate my daughter's being molested? That complicated everything!"

Her complaint landed on deaf ears, so she reminded him, "Mirabelle was only supposed to tell the police that she witnessed Sauter killing Agatha. That's all! Then the cops would've arrested him, case closed. But you couldn't stick to the script, could you?"

"I *improvised*," he slurred, angling his dry, bloodshot eyes up at her. He squinted as though the room was too bright. "I got creative. You made Plan A, and I thought fast on my feet, coming up with Plan B, so what?"

"We didn't need a Plan B!" she shouted to wake him up. "You gave those cops something *else* to investigate, namely *us*. You think that helps?"

"Like I said," he replied. "Don't get bent out of shape."

"How can you be so calm about this?" she shot back, glancing over her shoulder at her daughter's closed bedroom door. "We don't know what Mirabelle told them."

He was in no condition to come up with solutions, so Wilhelmina muttered a silent prayer under her breath that the worms Grady had released would slither back into their can.

And it must have worked, because he asked, "You want to do it or should I?"

"That's your answer for everything," she grumbled, heading for the hallway.

In a sudden burst of aggression, he sprang to his feet, but his balance was no good. A few staggering steps later and his hand met with the arm of the recliner, saving him from a spill across the floor, but also derailing his train of thought. He was probably seeing double.

Advancing on him, she hissed, "She's getting harder and harder to control you know, and where are you? You haven't helped in years."

"Agatha wasn't helping," he loosely sneered, pointing an unsteady finger in her face as he wobbled with the sway of the spinning room. "Your sister was pushing. I told you she wouldn't back off."

"Enough," she barked, cutting him off. She couldn't bear to hear him finish his point, though it was already shafting through her brain.

But he wouldn't quit. "You think anyone's going to understand us? This family? How we operate?"

"I never said people would understand."

"You act like they will," he countered in a brief moment of sobriety as he miraculously came into himself. "You acted like Agatha would accept us, accept you because 'we're family.' She was never your family."

"And she's dead," she reminded him, as she marched towards her daughter's room. She didn't need to hear another *I told you so* from her drunk boyfriend, that was for damn sure.

When Grady called after her, "You going to do it?" she ignored him in favor of knocking on Mirabelle's door. "Fine, then I'll do it," he mumbled, shuffling off into the bathroom.

She gave her daughter one more warning knock and said, "I'm coming in," before pushing the bedroom door open.

The amber glow of her daughter's bedside lamp illuminated Mirabelle. The girl was stretched out on her stomach, on the bed, with her feet in the air. Her blonde hair cascaded over her shoulders and onto a magazine she was flipping.

But when Wilhelmina edged into the room, the girl took one look at her and could smell it coming.

She bolted upright, scurrying to the headboard and pulling her knees up to her chin to protect herself.

"Why did you run off like that?"

"I did everything you said," she insisted.

"Where did you go?"

"I felt sick. I went to the clinic."

Wilhelmina knew when she was being lied to. Not to mention that Mirabelle wasn't very good at it.

"You were gone overnight and you obviously didn't sleep at the clinic."

"I didn't sleep at all," she groveled, perhaps aiming to appeal to her mother's maternal side. The thing was, Wilhelmina didn't have one. "I feel better," she added with a pathetic attempt at a smile.

Wilhelmina sighed, drinking in the sight of her troubled daughter, and tried not to recall the detective's advice.

"I know it seems like a lot," she began. She used a soft, measured tone, which Mirabelle tended to respond to. "But you're on the cusp of greatness. No one looks like you." As her daughter loosened her grip on her spindly legs, Wilhelmina sat on the edge of the bed, vaguely aware that Grady was banging around in the bathroom, cosmetics clattering to the tiles, as he drunkenly searched for the girl's medicine in the cabinet.

"Do you understand that you're going to be a millionaire? You'll be able to travel the world. You'll be set for life, but that's not going to happen if you miss your photoshoots, runway shows, and other commitments."

Her daughter's gaze went vacant as though she was rejecting the entire concept of becoming a supermodel.

"It's very important that we persevere," she explained.

As she reached out to comfort Mirabelle, the girl recoiled, shifting away on the bed.

Heavy footfall lumbered up the hallway and soon Grady filled the doorway. He clamped a syringe needle between his thick fingers like a cigarette.

Cringing at the needle, Mirabelle whined, "The medicine makes me sick."

"It makes you *beautiful*," she corrected.

"No, please," she begged in a small, defeated voice, as Grady slowly stalked towards her.

Liquid beaded at the tip of the needle.

Wilhelmina rolling her eyes at Grady. He was obviously too drunk to administer the shot.

Wilhelmina stood and held her palm out. When he didn't hand the syringe over, he was shuffling to maintain his precarious balance instead, she grabbed the thing out of his limp grasp and said, "Off with you."

"You got this?" he asked.

"Go lie down, for God's sake," she told him.

Grady steered himself out of the bedroom and up the hallway.

Facing her daughter, she eyed the syringe to check there were no air bubbles within the liquid.

Dreading this, Mirabelle leapt off the bed and defensively balled her fists.

"I'll have Grady hold you down if you resist," she warned. "You need this."

Mirabelle faced the inevitable.

She clenched her teeth, breathed heavily through her nose, and worked up the resolve to get through this. Next she jerked her jeans open and yanked the waistband down her right hip, presenting her bare buttocks to her mother.

As Wilhelmina jabbed the needle into her daughter's ass and squeezed the plunger, Premarin—thick and icy— seeped into the girl's system.

Wilhelmina reminded her, "You're going to be a star."

Chapter Seventeen

STARTING A BRAND new day after only three hours of bad sleep on the couch wasn't boding well for Carter. The marriage counseling session he had participated in last night had incited argument after argument with his wife, both in Dr. Valdmanis's office and at home.

The unfortunate result of which was that Carter had been exiled to the living room, Kathy having claimed the bedroom because, in her words, she needed time and space to rinse off his emotional diarrhea.

He had made the most of it, however, booting up his laptop and searching through the national police database. He'd also scoured the internet for anything he could find on the Bauers, Grady Willis, and Lewis Sauter. Persistently, he had examined each and every tidbit he came across, considering it through the lens of how it might relate to the four-year old boy who the Cyber Crimes Unit had presumed dead.

One of them had to be a pedophile, he'd told himself, and though Carter prided himself on his ability to sniff out a predator—often all it took was looking a perp in the eye—after several hours of pouring over Wilhelmina's spotty accomplishments, Mirabelle's scantily-clad modeling jobs, Grady's prolonged demise from burgeoning icon to rundown alcoholic, and Sauter's barren Facebook page, he hadn't managed to draw any conclusions.

Complicating matters was his own tumultuous upbringing, which had haunted him with every click of the mouse.

Initially, as a rescued child, Carter hadn't remembered a thing due to trauma-induced amnesia, a startling phenomenon that survivors often experienced. He had been rescued from his captors at the age of twelve. While living with an emotionally unequipped yet financially stable foster family in the months that followed, it had gradually dawned on him that he had literally and profoundly forgotten the sexual torture he had endured in those cages, in that basement chamber where his abusers had hidden him in plain sight on Seton Place.

After he had been rescued, his mind had almost instantly repressed everything about Seton Place. It wasn't until Carter had graduated from the police academy and began working as a beat cop that he started recalling the abuse. The memories had been coming in grim flashes ever since.

Carter wondered if the boy from the photos was alive, out there somewhere, but completely unaware of the sexual torture he had survived?

Would he be all the harder to find because of it?

Did he not know that he still needed to be saved, that he wouldn't be safe so long as the man behind the camera was left to roam freely?

Carter thought about all of this as he arrived at the Kings County Hospital.

The morgue door swung open and Jill Andover found him.

"You need a personal invitation?" she teased. "Danny's already inside."

He choked down the dregs of his lukewarm coffee, tossed the cup into the trash receptacle beside the door, and accompanied the medical examiner into the sterile room.

Danny was nursing her own cup of coffee and standing beside a computer where Jill had enlarged a few images on the screen that neither detective recognized.

His partner seemed well-rested, which was baffling considering her encounter with Mirabelle Bauer the night prior. Danny had briefed Carter by sending him a series of text messages earlier that morning.

"It took longer than expected," said Jill, as she settled on a chair in front of the computer. "But I was able to identify the synthetic fibers we found on Bauer." She scrolled the cursor over a magnified image, and Carter was finally able to make sense of what he saw—a thread composed of slick, black fibers woven around thinner brown ones.

"It's luggage," she said, impressed with herself. Blowing up the next image—a soft-sided suitcase—she mentioned, "I won't tell you what a headache this was, but I was able to trace the actual fabric to three textile vendors, all in China. The Chinese vendors make this fabric and sell it to manufacturing companies in the U.S. who produce the actual luggage."

None of this sounded promising to Carter until she elaborated.

"I'll spare you the details, but I was able to narrow down the manufacturers who use this exact material. There are only a handful."

"But the luggage could have been sold anywhere," Carter pointed out.

"What are you suggesting, Jill?" asked Danny, ignoring his pessimism. "That the killer transported Agatha in a suitcase?"

"That's exactly what I'm suggesting," she confirmed with a smile.

"There were black scuff marks on the living room floor," Danny remembered out loud. "Behind the couch."

"Which the wheels could've left," Jill supplied before swiveling on her chair and pulling a sheet from the printer beneath her desk. "You put that much pressure on plastic wheels, a body inside a suitcase, it's bound to leave marks. I have a list of brands for you."

After the medical examiner handed her the sheet, Danny skimmed the list until her gaze reached the middle of the page at which point her eyes brightened. She told Carter, "Nolan & Weissman manufacture in the Brooklyn Navy Yard."

Eagerly, he took the sheet and carefully read each brand. He looked over Nolan & Weissman's information, committing the address to memory. "Looks like Nolan & Weissman sell their products locally," he added, handing the sheet back to his partner. "The others are distributed to the west coast, but that doesn't narrow it down for us. There are three million people in this city. Anyone could've bought a suitcase."

"The fibers I found," Jill went on, "were *cut*."

He cocked his head, not quite grasping her point. "Meaning?"

"There's a chance the suitcase was cut in some way, damaged," she allowed. "But you see here how both ends of the thread are cut cleanly?" she asked, magnifying another image on the monitor.

"I don't follow," said Danny, closely examining the screen.

"This Nolan & Weissman suitcase has a black nylon interior lining. The cut fibers we found are from the exterior. So why would cleanly cut exterior fibers be on our Vic if she was placed inside the suitcase?" She paused for dramatic effect then answered her own question. "I don't think the killer bought the luggage. I think he stole a reject that wasn't finished."

"You think he *works* at the manufacturing company?" asked Carter, astonished. "That's quite a leap, Jill."

"You have your hunches," she replied. "And I have mine."

Danny backed away and pulled her cell phone from the breast pocket of her raincoat.

"What are you thinking?" he asked his partner, joining her.

"Mirabelle mentioned a man named Randy," she said, sending a call through to the precinct. "If someone by that name works at the manufacturer in Brooklyn..."

"Then we just blew this case wide open," he supplied, his heart rate elevating.

Danny turned her shoulder, focusing on the phone call. As she updated the lieutenant, Carter wandered off towards a bare steel table to think.

Though it irked him to put himself in the killer's shoes, he couldn't help but travel down that road. Agatha had known her attacker. She'd agreed to meet him. Anticipating the emotional aftermath of the conversation had compelled her to call Bill Muller, the manager of the gift shop, to get Monday off. According to Wilhelmina, she hadn't seen her sister that night but rather a week prior. According to Grady, however, she had. Wilhelmina had argued with Agatha then returned home to vent at her boyfriend. Mirabelle had yet another account of that night, claiming that neither her mother nor Grady had been home at all. Each of them had lied, contradicting one another and thus leaving a gaping hole in the timeline. Regardless, Mirabelle had gone to her aunt's house and witnessed a man bludgeon Agatha to death, but she ran off and didn't see what had transpired afterwards.

The attacker had then wrapped Agatha's head in a garbage bag, carried her up the stairs and proceeded to violate her with a wooden object, after which he stuffed her in a suitcase, one that he had brought along? He somehow got her to Prospect Park and dumped her on the shore of the lake with the pornographic photographs of a little boy.

Sloppy. Unfocused. Emotional.

Or had it all been planned?

The method of rape seemed oddly meaningful, as did the particular location at the lake. Sauter had gravitated to the dumpsite. Mirabelle had indicated its significance as well. She'd often spent time with her aunt there, and she'd also met Sauter on the shore after sneaking away from her mother's tyrannical custody.

But what did it all mean in terms of this Randy character?

Though an obvious theory didn't leap out at Carter, the boy from the photos crossed his mind.

Were Randy and the four-year old boy one and the same?

As soon as he posed the question, a darker one sliced through his brain.

If given the chance, would Carter ever hunt down his own abusers and murder them?

He wrestled with the thought then buried it in the back of his mind. Perhaps one day he might revisit it along with the rest of his haunting past.

But for now, it was too disturbing.

"Ready?" Danny called out from the doorway, having thanked Jill, who was rolling a dead body out of an industrial refrigeration unit in the wall, on to the next homicide.

If he was ready, it was only because he was harboring a secret hope that the boy from the photographs had exacted his revenge against his abuser, seizing an opportunity that Carter had never had growing up.

If Randy was now assembling luggage in a factory across town, the detectives were about to find out.

The Brooklyn Navy Yard still resembled the industrial shipyard it had once been following the American Revolution when it had been used to build merchant vessels. Spanning two hundred acres along the waterfront that stretched from the neighborhoods of Williamsburg and Vinegar Hill, the Navy Yard was currently the home of countless manufacturing companies as well as small businesses. But the Navy Yard wasn't public. A twelve-foot steel wall separated the Yard from the public, wrapping the full perimeter.

As fat raindrops plopped down, all of Brooklyn was covered in a thick blanket of fog. Carter steered the sedan through the dreary atmosphere, turned off Flushing Avenue, and squeezed the brakes as they came to a security booth at the Navy Yard.

After rolling his window down, he flashed his badge at the guard, who leaned out of the booth, the hood of his blue poncho catching the rain.

"Nolan & Weissman is in Building 3?" asked Carter, as the man eyed his ID and scribbled a note on his clipboard.

"You can park at the loading dock!" he shouted over the wet wind. He punched a button on the console beside him. The security bar in front of the sedan jutted upwards. The guard added, "Fourth building on your right!"

They drove through, veering around idling trucks as well as men at work. Carter scanned the brick warehouses, none of which were numbered.

Danny had been quiet in the passenger seat, thoughtfully flipping through two palm-sized notepads and reviewing the various clues she had recorded since the onset of their investigation.

Stealing a few sidelong glances at her didn't garner her attention so he asked, "You trust her?"

"Mirabelle?" she asked, turning the question over in her mind, as Carter concentrated on driving to the back of the fourth building and keeping an eye out for the loading dock. The landmark didn't come into view until he had circled clear around to the street-side of the facility.

"No," she said frankly then quickly revised her answer. "I don't know. I think she's a puppet. And I think the only real choice she has in life has to do with deciding *who* gets to pull the strings, if that makes sense."

"She insisted Sauter was innocent," he pointed out, reminding her of the most peculiar aspect she'd relayed within those early morning text messages.

"You used the word 'emphatic' to describe her certainty."

"Which tells me that she *could* be telling the truth. Sometimes witnesses, especially teens, grapple with the truth for a long time before they finally come out with it. Or…"

When the implication struck him, he didn't like it. "Or Sauter was the one who witnessed Randy kill Agatha and he didn't want to get involved since he's on parole. So he told the girl to relay the story."

Carter pulled into a parking spot in front of the loading dock where men were rolling dollies packed to the gills with crated paint cans and hollering at one another. A cube truck beeped loudly at the far end of the platform, backing up until its rear-end slammed into cement.

"Let's hope Randy didn't skip town."

He killed the engine and watched the windshield wipers die on the glass, rain pooling along their rubber blades.

"Hey," she said, bringing him back into himself.

Sighing, he admitted, "I'm going through all this crap with Kathy."

"Oh?" she said, interested though slightly apprehensive. When she asked, "Want to tell me about it?" he knew she was only being polite, but he still felt tempted to get dark emotions off his chest so that he could go into the factory with a clear head.

If he opened the floodgates, however, there would be no way to get the water back in the dam later. Disclosing the muck and mire that this case was churning up inside of him and explaining how it was affecting his marriage in the worst way simply wasn't an option.

"I do," he admitted. "But now's not the time."

She held his gaze and said, "Sometimes it's easier to solve a case than it is to solve a problem at home."

"Ain't that the truth." He opened the driver's side door and mentioned, "I'll take the lead on this," then climbed out into the spotty rain.

At the far side of the loading dock was a set of steps, which he padded up, shouldering around a line of workers who were carrying boxes into the parking area. Twin doors stood at the middle of the platform, and as soon as he entered with Danny at his heels, he came to a bay of freight elevators.

"Should be on the sixth floor," she told him, pressing the call button.

When the elevator banked, he was impressed with Danny's aptitude as she pulled a nylon strap, separating the horizontal doors and stepping into the metal car of the freight elevator. With the same precision, she hoisted the doors closed, and soon they were riding up to the top floor.

As they did, Carter wrestled with the sense of urgency that was burning in his chest. It had been eating him alive all week. Sauter's head games had been tormenting him. The red herrings Danny and he had been chasing had chipped away at his confidence. The perpetual dead-ends had landed like a fist to his nose every time.

Carter felt suffocated with fear that the killer was celebrating the likelihood that he would get away with it all.

He refused to give Randy the chance. A small voice in the back of his mind warned him not to make assumptions. Randy was innocent until proven guilty. But as the freight doors rattled open and he barreled into the concrete corridor with Danny, Carter was filled with determination. The killer was as good as caught.

The door to Suite 602, which had Nolan & Weissman's name and logo stenciled across it, stood ajar. Inside the factory, the dirty thuds and punches of assembly machines roared—hydraulic presses drilling bolts and sewing needles zipping through fabric.

Nothing about the place implied they ought to politely knock before entering so they edged into the factory where shabby-looking workers manned a grid of industrial machines. To Carter's trained eye, they all appeared to be Mexican.

One man wasn't, however. Among the workers was a middle-aged White man with a high forehead, thinning hair, and a look of authority on his face. He wore earplugs and prowled up one of the aisles, watching the workers like a hawk. Pausing beside one of the female workers seated at the sewing machines, he leaned into her ear and shouted something in Spanish, criticizing her work it seemed.

When he stood, perhaps feeling eyes on him, he noticed the detectives and immediately strode over, pulling out his earplugs.

Carter made introductions, shouting over the machinery racket, "Detectives Dobbs and Foster."

"Please," said the man, gesturing to an office. "I can't hear a thing."

After inviting them into an airless room that was outfitted with two desks and numerous filing cabinets, he closed the door and the deafening wall of machinery noises was instantly muffled.

A mousy-looking young woman was hunched at one of the desks, typing. She lifted her nose, sensing more than seeing that there had been a disturbance.

"Rose," said the man, regarding his secretary with dreamy fondness that she didn't appear to appreciate. "Why don't you take a break?"

She screwed her face up in response and Carter could almost read her thoughts—*where am I supposed to go?* Regardless, she huffed out of her chair, fluffed her skirt, and made quick work of slinging her purse over her shoulder. She scurried past the detectives, taking the long way around to avoid brushing up against her boss. She had the good manners to shut the office door on her way out.

Carter wasted no time diving into the issue at hand. "You have an employee named Randy working here?"

"Whittaker, yes," he said, turning a bit flush as he unbuttoned the top of his shirt—the brief interaction with Rose had him hot and bothered. "What is this about?"

"Can you tell us if he was working Sunday night?" he asked.

"No one works Sunday night," he bristled. He seemed to brace himself for the worst as he asked, "What did he do?"

"We'd rather address that with him if he's working today," Carter explained, but the floor manager wasn't having it, not immediately anyway.

Shaking his head, he vented, "The wrong kind of cheap labor."

Danny was the one who asked, "How's that?"

"I'm in good standing with the labor commission," he assured them as though dispelling any suspicions was of the utmost importance. Using a *just between us* tone, he said, "I like Mexicans. They're hard working. They don't complain. They don't ask for raises too often. I *prefer* them." After a disgruntled beat, he mentioned, "But when the parole board calls asking to send me ex-cons, I *have* to take them on..." but trailed off with a little shrug. "Technically, ex-cons are cheap labor, too, but then what do I have to deal with? Surprise visits from the police!"

Carter asked, "What did Randy do to get locked up?"

"That's what I'd like to know," he blurted out.

"You don't know what he was incarcerated for?" he questioned.

"*You* don't know?" asked the man.

Keeping his tone even, Carter admitted, "We didn't know his last name until you mentioned it."

"He's on the registry," he said as though Randy Whittaker's sex-offender conviction reflected badly on him. "Honestly, I didn't want to learn more. I hired him at a minimum wage rate and he hasn't caused me any *major* problems... until now."

Danny had tucked herself into the corner of the room to take a phone call, presumably with Franco.

"Could you bring Randy in here?" asked Carter. "I'd like to speak with him."

As the floor manager slipped out of the office, Danny pocketed her cell and said, "Franco's pulling up Whittaker's record. He'll get back to us in a sec."

"We've got a sex offender who makes luggage who wasn't here Sunday night, and we've got a witness who puts him in Agatha's house the night of the murder," he summarized as though arresting Randy Whittaker was a foregone conclusion.

"It's something," she agreed.

She was downplaying it, so he promised, "He's good for this."

The way she began studying him told Carter that he wanted this too badly. His partner didn't think he was seeing straight and a terrible conflict flared hot in his chest because of it. She was right, but it didn't mean that he was wrong about Whittaker.

The door creaked open, revealing a factory worker who could hardly be described as a man. Tall and sinewy with a head of bedraggled, blonde hair and milky green eyes, Randy carried himself with the sadness of a beaten dog. He looked terrified in his oversized tee shirt and baggy jeans.

Unless Carter's eyes were playing tricks on him, the kid was a dead-ringer for their four-year old boy.

"Boss said you wanted to see me?" he asked in a timid, nasal voice as he glanced apprehensively from Danny to Carter.

Noise spilled in from the factory floor behind him until he closed the door.

Cordially, Danny invited him to have a seat.

He preferred to stand.

"I'm Detective Dobbs," Carter said, sailing through formalities so that he wouldn't feel for the kid—he had that look about him, misery that could move a man to tears. "This is my partner, Detective Foster."

Randy quickly glanced over his shoulder at Danny then defensively folded his arms. He fixed his worried attention on Carter.

"Your boss tells me you weren't working here Sunday night."

The kid, who couldn't have been a day over twenty-three, let out a strange laugh. "Let me guess, some kiddie got molested and you think I did it?"

The longer Carter stared him down, the more the kid shrank. "I wasn't aware that *that* was what you were convicted for."

Randy's expression drooped as badly as his posture—*oops*.

Danny scrolled her thumb over the LCD screen of her cell phone and began reading, "Served five years for molesting a young boy."

Randy started stammering, "That was- It wasn't- Some kid points to a doll's crotch and I get sentenced to five years in Attica?"

"The jury believed him," she shot back then told her partner, "ask him about his cellmate."

Carter's brows shot up his forehead. "Not Lewis Sauter…?"

When Danny nodded, Carter grinned. Their prime suspect and Randy were co-members of some perverse child-molesting brotherhood in prison? He asked Randy, "You bunked with a guy named Lewis Sauter?"

"Sure," he said, his tone brittle with nerves, though he attempted to play it off as though the coincidence meant nothing. "Why? What do you think I did?"

"Let's start with where you were Sunday night," he suggested.

"At home. I'm under house arrest." He lifted the hem of his pants, showing an ankle monitor. "I live with my mom."

"What's the address?" he asked.

Randy insisted, "Ask my parole officer if you want to know where I go and at what times."

"I will," he said before repeating, "what's the address?"

"Cortelyou at McDonald, alright?"

"In Kensington," Danny supplied.

"That's right," he confirmed in a small voice. "And my mom can tell you I was home all night."

"See now," said Carter, making a performance of disingenuously sympathizing with the kid. "A mother for an alibi doesn't hold as much weight as you might think."

"What does Sauter have to do with this?"

"It's not important," he said, angling in on the kid, who seemed on the brink of tears. Carter couldn't ignore the fact that he had a soft spot for the guy so he didn't lean on him too hard, only looked him up and down.

Black threads clung to the kid's jeans and the loose-fitting tee shirt he wore.

Carter gently pinched a cluster of threads off his shirt, ignoring Randy's objections, and placed the fibers in the plastic bag that Danny had offered, ready on the quick.

After tucking the sealed evidence bag into the pocket of his parka, he said, "Tell me about Agatha Bauer."

"Who?"

"The woman you killed," he softly prodded.

"Whoa, hey!" he cried, feet shuffling as he backed away from the detectives. "I didn't kill anyone. Fondling kids in the park? Yes. Taking someone's life? Hell no!"

"Turn around please," said Carter.

"What? No! Why?"

"We're bringing you in."

"Why?" he demanded in a frail tone.

"Those cross streets you mentioned puts you at the intersection where Agatha Bauer was murdered," he said, strangely regretful that this arrest didn't feel like it should.

He was gentle with Randy, as he secured his wrists together, gingerly cuffing him. Danny recited his Miranda rights.

When she was finished, Carter explained, "We have an eyewitness who saw the whole thing go down. You can call your mother from the station, okay?"

Though Randy was swearing, spit flying through his teeth, he was smart enough not to resist, which only made Carter feel for him even more.

As he gently ushered Randy through the factory, his stomach bottomed out and his heart sank. He had the urge to whisper something to the kid, confide in him that they were the same, and also berate him like a father because in his mind Randy could've handled his anger in a different way. The wounds that might never heal didn't have to get infected, so-to-speak. Carter's broken life was evidence of that.

But Carter revealed none of this as he escorted Randy Whittaker across the loading dock where drizzling rain pissed over concrete steps.

He would wait until the two of them were alone.

If he was equipped to get a confession out of anyone, it was the kid whose life Carter could have been living.

Chapter Eighteen

THE INTERROGATION had gone badly. Whittaker had maintained his innocence, his increasingly stunned confusion causing his timid responses to turn angry.

Carter had insisted that Danny leave the room—*he'll level with me but not if you're here*—as though time with the kid was of vital importance.

He'd flipped off the audio recorder. Afraid that any hint of the lieutenant would send Whittaker careening into comatose refusal to the detriment of the case.

He had asked Franco to shut the blinds and not watch through the one-way mirror. The lieutenant had granted him leeway despite Danny's quiet skepticism.

Carter had been acting more and more strangely, in Danny's estimation. The intensity with which he was functioning at every stage of this investigation seemed to be treading into the territory of desperate.

But after Carter had worked the kid for only twenty minutes, Whittaker said the magic word—*lawyer*—and that was that.

Danny gave herself the once over. The lighting in the bathroom of her apartment was flattering, yet her reflection in the medicine cabinet mirror looked too pale, *austere*, the asymmetry of her mouth grotesque. She tried to fix it with lipstick, but followed the lines too carefully, which only accentuated the problem. Giving up, she eyed her dress—a thin and slinky black number that didn't hide her protruding stomach.

The memory of her encounter with Carter after he'd slammed the interview room door, shutting Whittaker inside, seeped into the forefront of her mind.

She had asked him why he'd needed privacy and if the perp had let anything slip, anything they might be able to go on. But he hadn't responded, only stalked off into the bullpen, grabbed his parka from the back of his chair, and continued on, avoiding Franco in favor of getting the hell out of the precinct.

When Danny had previously taken her shot at Sauter, the two of them alone in a jail cell, she had disclosed something she shouldn't have—how she really felt about her overbearing mother. She had done this as a means to get Sauter talking.

It made her wonder...

What desperate measure had her partner taken? What secret had he revealed to Randy Whitaker to get the kid to talk?

She checked her cell phone, which was resting on the sink counter, but there weren't any new text messages or missed calls.

It had crossed her mind to reach out, shoot Carter a text message or place a quick phone call to make sure he was alright. But she had decided against it. He would cool off in his own way and in his own time.

She flipped the medicine cabinet open and selected a bottle of perfume. After spritzing her neck and inner wrists, she returned it, slapped the mirror closed, and had second thoughts about the black dress she was wearing. It hugged her too tightly. She didn't have the stomach for it, both literally and figuratively. Turning to the side, she sucked in. Better, she thought, but not practical.

If she chose the right jacket, however, she could get away with it, she told herself as she emerged from the bathroom, high heels clicking over hardwood floors.

She entered her bedroom and began hunting through her jewelry box in search of earrings.

In the kitchen, Nora was banging around, scrubbing a glass pan by the sounds of it with the faucet running full blast.

After fastening gold hoops through her ears, she began rummaging through her closet for a coat, found a gray leather jacket she thought would do, and threw it on as she neared the foot of the bed where Mirabelle's modeling photo along with the fashion show invitation were resting on the duvet.

When Danny was fifteen, she'd had a mouth full of metal braces and huge red-framed glasses that had dominated her face. Her friends had been similar, geeks and dorks, obsessed with straight A's and high marks, ambitious to get into the best universities even though they were years away from applying.

As a teenager, she had never felt as beautiful as the girl staring up at her from the glossy print, and it made her wonder. Did Mirabelle ever have fun? Did she know what it meant to be a kid? Did she have friends, a crush?

Considering the short leash Wilhelmina kept her on, Danny doubted it, though the notion that the girl was a slave of sorts gave a whole new meaning to Lewis Sauter. He was certainly an odd friend to have, but she could see why Mirabelle cherished him. He provided an escape, much like the one Danny had indulged in with Tommy O'Toole.

Opening the nightstand drawer, she paused before tucking the glossy print inside. Sauter's penciled portrait of her stared up at her. Had giving her the sketch been a peace offering of sorts, or a passive way to reveal an obsession?

She set the print of Mirabelle over Sauter's drawing, tucked the fashion show invitation into her jacket pocket, and closed the drawer. Then she started up the hallway.

"Don't you look stunning," said her mother, angling a pan into the drying rack on the counter, as Danny rounded into the kitchen. Nora's tone had been tight, her compliment weighted with concern. She turned the faucet off and pulled yellow dish gloves from her hands, adding, "I almost didn't recognize you."

"Thanks," she said cautiously, trying and failing not to think about her ex. "I feel pretty good."

An unsettled look came over Nora's smile as she asked, "Are you going to be out late?"

"I don't think so," she replied, collecting her purse from the living room couch and avoiding her mother's searching eyes. Things had smoothed over since she'd confronted Nora about the bar, but Danny didn't trust it—the eye of a hurricane could be deceivingly calm. "The fashion show shouldn't take longer than twenty minutes."

"And this is the girl who witnessed that murder?" she asked, worried.

"The suspect line-up is tomorrow," she mentioned, implying that her arduous SVU case was as good as closed. A second later, having riffled through the contents of her purse, she realized she'd left her cell phone in the bathroom.

As Danny strode up the hallway, testing whether or not her hips could still sway—she hadn't felt like a woman in months—her mother asked, "Do you think it's wise to get personally involved?"

"I'm not getting personally involved!" she called out over her shoulder, trying not to sound defensive, as she grabbed her cell from the bathroom sink and slipped it into her purse. She returned to the living room where Nora was wringing her hands. "I could use a night out."

"But it won't be a *big* night out, right?"

Danny sensed where this was going.

Fears that her daughter would swing by O'Toole's were washing over Nora.

"Like I said, the fashion show shouldn't be longer than twenty minutes."

"And you'll come straight home?" When Danny responded with a sigh, turning for the apartment door, Nora added, "It's just that you've been so strong. You don't need those kinds of complications in your life, not when you're doing so well, Danny!"

"What I do in my free time is my business," she firmly reminded her mother.

"I only want what's best for you," she pushed.

Danny let out an uncomfortable laugh, knowing she was about to lash out. She sounded exhausted as she told her mother, "It's too much. I need space from time to time."

"I give you space," she objected. "You're on your own for twelve, sometimes fourteen hours a day."

"For work," she allowed, not that the implication was registering with her mother. Nora only blinked.

"Sometimes I need to decompress by myself," she explained, their perverse dynamic rearing its ugly head. Oftentimes Nora seemed more like a nagging wife than a mother, and it turned Danny's stomach. "I don't know when I'll be home," she said, having run out of steam. "Thanks for dinner. I'll see you later."

With that she yanked the door open, leaving Nora to stew.

Danny had forgotten her umbrella.

It was misting out. The block was blanketed in semi-darkness until she reached Caton Avenue where a street lamp illuminated the intersection in an eerie glow.

She turned the corner, heading west towards the F train, which would take her into Manhattan. The stillness of the night was strangely ominous. Though the occasional car growled up the street, the neighborhood seemed unusually sleepy. Pedestrians were few and far between, the bodegas quiet.

Where rock music usually billowed out from O'Toole's there was only the sound of damp wind whipping past the corner. The bar should've been packed and rowdy on a Friday night.

Maybe it was the quietude or perhaps the fact that she hadn't felt this pretty in ages. Maybe it was her mother's incessant concern putting Danny on edge, but when Danny slowed, nearing the bar, she wasn't just fantasizing about going in. She was debating.

She owed Tommy a conversation, an explanation—he was completely in the dark about their child's tragic death. She had thought his interest in her hadn't been stronger than lust; that realizing their weak bond had compelled him to run off scared, that he'd known raising a child together would've been too real for him.

She'd spent months resenting him for walking away without so much as a word. Though they'd argued, though she'd confronted him and fought and begged him not to do this, not to coward out of his child's life, his responses had been cold and monosyllabic—*I can't.*

But the gifts for Gregory had been an indication. He'd changed his mind, and though she was terrified, she needed to know why.

If there was even a sliver of a chance she could have him in her life again...

It seemed impossible. Things had gotten ugly towards the end. The months apart had fueled her anger, hardening resentments into heavy resignation. Could two people ever recover from something like that?

She wondered what would've happened if she'd been home the night Tommy had stopped by with the gifts. Would she have screamed, cried, or sunken into speechlessness, unable to tell him the truth about their son?

Maybe she could simply thank him for the gifts, she thought, test the waters that way.

After glimpsing the bar patrons through the misty windows—there were a handful scattered throughout the tables, a lone cop hunched over a cold lager at the bar—she heaved the wooden door open and stepped inside.

The scent of the place brought her back—bitter hops commingling with the faint smell of dish detergent and stale cigarettes.

She was instantly reminded of those nights when she used to press through customers, making her way towards the far end of the bar where she'd have a better shot at catching Tommy's attention. His sexy mouth would lift with a crooked smile after their eyes had met, both of them wanting, *needing,* what would surely follow the second after he locked up—their secret.

Nervously, her heart racing to dizzying levels, Danny edged deeper into the place, self-conscious all the while. No one was manning the bar, however. She glanced around, looking for an employee, but only saw patrons.

This was nerve-wracking. She touched her short mop of hair, mentally cursing that she hadn't let her mother's gossipy friend, Nance, give her a trim. Then she smoothed her hands down the front of her dress, feeling horribly awkward.

There was an *Employees Only* door at the back of the bar, and when it swung open, Tommy shouldering through with a case of beer in his flexed arms, she felt her heart punch hard in her chest.

Their eyes locked and he froze, the backdoor swinging in and out behind him until it gradually stilled.

She tried to smile but it felt stiff. She hoped she didn't look as scared as she felt.

"Hi," she managed, though her voice was thin.

The glint behind his slate-gray eyes was just welcoming enough—was he glad to see her?—so she drifted cautiously over.

But Tommy didn't immediately respond.

He slid the case of beer onto the counter, cracked the cardboard open, and began stuffing bottles into an ice bin under the bar, glancing at her here and there as if to apologize, *just need to get this squared away.*

She tucked herself near the end of the bar, having felt awkward about standing in the middle of the room. Resting her hands on the counter, she reminded herself to breathe as she watched him, though she was sure not to stare.

The meaty bump on the bridge of his nose where it had healed badly after a brawl, the slick yet rippling skin running down the side of his neck where he'd been scalded while fighting a fire, every inch of him brought her back to those long, lustful nights that she often wished, deep down, had never ended.

When he had emptied the case, he set the cardboard box on the floor and edged around the side of the bar, giving her his full attention in a way that made it hard for her to think.

She cleared her throat, suddenly dazed he was standing so close.

"Thank you for the gifts," she said, but it sounded too formal. She was having a hard time looking at him. "It was very thoughtful."

When she dared to glance at him again, he looked away, his brows knitting together as he struggled for the right words. He soon gave up and offered her a shy smile instead, mentioning, "I stuck with yellow. Wasn't sure if you had a boy or girl."

"A boy," she said softly, hoping she wouldn't break down in tears. "Gregory."

"Gregory," he echoed, smiling, as he turned his son's name over in his mind. "Any pictures?"

"Ah, yeah," she said, fumbling for her purse.

Her cell phone was lodged in the bottom, and as soon as she had it in hand, she began scrolling through her photos until she found the ones she had taken of Gregory.

Angling the screen towards him, she brushed through a few shots—their baby swaddled and sleeping soundly in his crib, then one of him dopey-eyed with a bottle in his mouth.

Tommy was leaning in close so she offered him her cell then watched him brighten as he eyed each photo, though there weren't many.

After getting his fill, scrolling back and forth, he handed her the phone and his expression turned serious.

He let some time pass before asking, "What made you decide to come?"

She had the urge to answer his question with one of her own—*what made you change your mind?*—but instead she simply replied, "The gifts."

"Listen," he began, as he plowed his fingers through his salt-and-pepper hair. "I know things got bad between us."

Her heart rate spiked.

"I got cold feet," he admitted quietly. "It was like we went from zero to sixty in the blink of an eye and..." He drew in a deep breath, absently scanning the room, then returned his attention to her. "I wasn't prepared, and I acted like an idiot, but..." Again he trailed off, searching for the right words. "Man, I thought you would give me a chance."

She studied him, somewhat confused. "What do you mean? After our blow out I didn't hear from you."

"I knew how you felt, Danny," he said, not that it lined up with her recollection of things at all. "I kept trying and trying, and believe me, I regret what I did. It was immature of me to use our fight as an excuse to shut you out. I should've just moved into your place. It shouldn't have even been a fight. I don't know why it struck a nerve when you suggested moving in together. We shouldn't have fought that night, and I shouldn't have broken up with you just to end the conversation. I regret doing that. But when I came around, when I came to my senses... I don't know. You should've let me in."

"What are you talking about?"

He became a bit frustrated, as he said, "Look, I'm just going to say it. I think it's total bullcrap that you hide behind your mother. We had something real, and real things come with bumps in the road. I shouldn't have pushed you away. Fine. But when I realized I'd made a mistake and that I wanted you, and that I wanted to be a family with you and the baby, you couldn't even face me? You sent your mother to talk to me for you?"

She remembered the encounter between Nora and Tommy the other day.

"You mean when she came to the bar the other day? I didn't send her."

"I'm not talking about two days ago," he challenged. "I'm talking about months ago. I'm talking about," he stopped abruptly so that the freight train of his anger wouldn't bash through her. "You and I fought. Then I snapped out of it a week later. I've been trying to get in touch for months. I showed up at your place again and again, and Nora was like the damn dragon guarding a castle."

Astonishment washed over her.

"Then she went from defense to offense, coming to my apartment, the bar. God, it was like I was being harassed by this crazed messenger warning me, threatening me to stay away from you. Every time I went to your place, she's there."

He cooled off, staring at her for answers, but none came. She was stunned.

He went on, "Part of me always thought it wasn't you making those threats. That's why I kept trying, but then I had to ask myself, do I really want to fight for this? You're a package deal, Danny, and your mother is nuts."

Mortified, overwhelmed with shock, she couldn't think straight, her mind was reeling with sudden and abject horror. Anguish riled through her that her own mother would sabotage the only relationship that had truly mattered to Danny. Tommy had been fighting for her the whole time? She couldn't control the surge of emotions rising in her chest.

She muttered incomprehensibly about her cell and email—why hadn't he contacted her?—but then remembered that when things had gotten particularly painful between them during those gut-wrenching weeks of silence, she had blocked him on all fronts, afraid that if she didn't, he would float back into her life and break her heart all over again.

"I don't know," he said in a small voice. "I don't know if I can handle Nora breathing down my neck every time I show up to see my kid. I don't know if I want to live like that."

He let the notion hang for a terrifying moment, and Danny's stomach bottomed out because of it, then he insisted, "But deep down, I *do* know. I can handle it. Maybe you don't want me in the same way anymore, but I have a right to raise my son. And for the record," he went on, his stern tone softening as he closed the gap between them and placed his hand on hers. "I've missed you."

How was she supposed to tell him about their son with him looking at her like that, with hope in his eyes, their affection for one another rekindling?

"Hey," he breathed, searching her eyes, which was how she knew she was crying. "Hey, I'm just venting. I don't care about the past. I want to start fresh."

Confessing that Gregory had passed away was on the tip of her tongue, but she felt too emotional to come out with it. She wiped her eyes, vaguely irked that mascara was probably running down her face.

"He's, um... Gregory," she managed, having stolen a few deep breaths. "He, uh," she tried again.

"Can I see him sometime?"

She swallowed hard, desperate to control her emotions, and forced herself to look at him. He must have sensed something was very wrong, because the twinkle behind his eyes darkened.

"A few weeks ago," she began, pinching her eyes shut and riding a swell of sudden grief. If Tommy knew, would he walk away for good? Finally, she steadied her voice and said, "He died."

The silence that followed was brutal.

Tommy slumped and a faraway look of confusion came over him.

"It was Sudden Infant Death Syndrome," she said in a small voice.

But she wasn't sure he had heard her. He was slipping away. Dazed, he took a step backwards then another. It was more than she could bear.

She whispered, "I'm sorry."

The next thing Danny knew, she was tearing through the bar. Her palms slapped against the door and she spilled out into the damp night, but the misty air didn't reach her lungs. It felt like her mind was splitting apart.

She began walking without any concept of where she was headed, high-heels clicking over asphalt and wet wind biting into her.

The magnitude of realizing that she could've had him this whole time if Nora hadn't harassed him into staying away was crippling. He could've held his son, could've looked into his eyes and cared for him, loved him, but Nora had robbed Tommy of the chance. There was no forgiving it.

In a fog, her thoughts scattered, she was so furious, all she knew was that she had just lost Tommy for good. He wouldn't want anything to do with her now, and she couldn't blame him.

Drained, having trudged for hours through Kensington, trailing down commercial avenues and hooking up residential blocks, her legs numb and damp, barely seeing her surroundings, her mind blank, consumed with grief at the level of her soul, she came to the north end of Ocean Parkway and suddenly craved her warm bed. She felt as though she could sleep for a thousand years.

When she reached her building, she lumbered up the stoop. After keying into the dimly lit lobby where Camil was tirelessly mopping the floor, she slinked, head down, towards the stairwell. He commented something about how nice she looked, but it didn't register. She was bogged too deeply in despair.

Heaving open her apartment door, having trekked up to the second floor, she peeled off her damp jacket and tossed it. She locked up next.

As she trailed into the living room and kicked her heels off, her ears pricked up at the sounds of humming, footfall, and other faint noises that were all coming from the baby's room.

The moment she rounded into Gregory's bedroom, she was stunned.

It was empty.

The crib was gone.

There was a paint cloth lining the floor, the green walls were covered with white patches.

Her mother held a paintbrush, headphones covering her ears, as she worked happily to rid all traces of Danny's son from the apartment.

Enraged, Danny's heart pumping madly and her blood boiling, she closed the distance between them, jerked the headphones off Nora's ears, and yelled, "What have you done?"

"Sweetheart!" she startled, her eyes filled with maternal sympathy that didn't last. "It might seem extreme, but I've been reading a book about grieving, and you really have to move on if-"

"Shut up!" Her hands balled into fists, but she was shaking too badly to use them. "You have no right!"

"I'm your mother," she shot back. "I have every right."

Her tone had changed, deepened authoritatively as though Danny wasn't a grown woman but merely a child who wouldn't know what was good for her if it bit her in the ass.

"You don't want to hear it," Nora went on, "but everything happens for a reason. You didn't want a baby, you didn't plan for it." She tried to smile, but she looked irritated to have to be the only one who was facing the cold, hard truth. "The last thing you needed was a filthy, little boy."

"*What?*" Danny breathed.

Nora stood her ground.

"How can you say that?"

Suddenly, Nora started talking over her, raising her voice and asserting, "I was a single mother! I wouldn't wish that kind of hell on my worst enemy. You don't need to take care of someone, Danny. You need to be taken care of. It's time to forget Gregory!"

"Get out!"

Danny grabbed her mother by the arm and began dragging her out of the baby's room. As she brought her mother through the apartment, Nora was indignant, voicing her opinion.

"It's for your own good! You need to move on! You're best on your own without a man, without a screaming baby, just us!"

When Danny got her into the foyer, Nora turned on her heel and began pleading, "You're my whole world! I'm sorry, I shouldn't have done this, but the book I read made some very good points! Consider this an intervention. You must be forced to let go! I just want you to move on and be happy. Just you and me!"

But Danny wasn't buying it. In fact, every word out of Nora's mouth disgusted her. She threw the door open, shoved her mother into the hallway, and slammed the door in her face.

Chapter Nineteen

"THANKS FOR COMING," said Danny, as she leaned heavily against the doorframe of her apartment, looking haggard in a ratty sweatshirt and faded jeans. Her eyes were puffy and smeared with makeup.

Assuring her it was no problem, though nothing could have been further from the truth—excusing himself from bed to go to Danny's apartment in the middle of the night had caused Kathy to blow a gasket—Carter offered her an understanding smile.

When she widened the doorway, stepping clumsily aside and inviting him in, he kept his guard up and entered, unsure about the professional boundaries that were now blurring between them.

She had been drinking, that much was obvious, judging her Merlot-stained lips and unsteady gait.

She shut the door and lumbered slowly towards the couch.

Given the late hour and his partner's dejected mood, and considering how his wife had balked when he'd taken Danny's call hot on the heels of yet another argument, it didn't take a fortune teller to foresee that this visit would complicate the already debilitating strain on his marriage.

But he wasn't about to leave Danny in the lurch.

She plopped onto the couch, folded her legs, and proceeded to top off her wine glass, The bottle was half-empty.

Carter didn't join her on the couch. Instead, he took a lap around the living room, taking in the surroundings—modest furnishings and bare walls except for three NYPD Medals of Honor and one Medal of Valor. The scent of potpie lingered in the air.

He glimpsed the living room window where rain clattered over the fire escape outside, its hum emanating, though muffled, through the apartment.

"How'd it go with Whittaker?" she asked sluggishly, having gulped more wine. "Did you take another run at him?"

He removed his damp parka, draped it over the arm of the couch, and said, "Is that why you asked me over?"

"No," she admitted in a far away voice, the heavy rainfall beyond the window stealing her attention for a moment. "Just curious."

Whatever was eating her had to do with something other than their case. But realizing this only made Carter hesitant. He wasn't about to sit down next to her, but he settled on the armchair.

A morose silence ensued, Danny staring despondently out the window, Carter ineptly racking his brain for ways to jumpstart the conversation.

If she hadn't asked him over to discuss the investigation, then he was at a loss.

"I'm having my doubts," he commented. "Whittaker's mother is adamant that he was home all evening on the tenth. His ankle monitor shows no activity, and if you ask me, he's too disorganized. I don't see him killing Agatha, violating her, having the wherewithal to stuff her in a suitcase, and bring her to the park." Gauging her reaction, he allowed, "Sauter could've set him up." But he'd misread her expression.

"Then why didn't we find the suitcase in his apartment when we searched?" she challenged in a lucid swell of sobriety.

"Because this case is impossible?" he offered, but his humor landed badly. "Maybe Sauter has other properties."

"Other properties? He can barely afford rent."

"I've got to tell you," he said, cutting her off and conceding, "I don't think he's our guy, and Whittaker isn't either. Murdering and raping a fifty-somthing German woman isn't exactly Whittaker's M.O. Plus, he would've been a teenager himself at the time of the boy's abuse according to Tenenbaum in the Cyber Crimes Unit and how he had dated the photos."

"Whittaker's not the boy from the photos?" she asked, thrown. She tapped her forefinger against her wine glass, while mulling over the setback.

"I'll be the first to admit, I thought he was, but there's no way. The kid from those photos was off the grid. Whittaker was in school at the time. He has a good mother."

As Danny began sipping her wine, once again slipping off to a far away place that Carter sensed had more to do with personal turmoil than their dead-end investigation, he felt his uneasiness grow.

"Bottom line," he went on to ensure the conversation remained productive. "Whittaker's mother gave me a childhood photo of him, one where he's about four years old. I ran it over to forensics. It wasn't a match for our boy. Bone structure is all wrong."

"What did you talk to him about?" she asked. "All that privacy you needed… Did you get anything at all?"

"Didn't pan out."

"Like when I spoke to Lewis," she commented, relating to him.

"What can I do for you, Danny?" he asked, frankly. "Why am I here?"

Staring out the window at the clattering rain and the dark starless sky, she said, "I'm having a really bad night."

In the time it took for her to work up the nerve to elaborate, it occurred to Carter that his partner wasn't wallowing, or being self-indulgent. She was punishing herself for some reason. Carter recognized that behavior. He could all too easily identify with her—how many nights had he used his own vices to unburden his heavy conscience? Countless.

"I messed up," she confessed darkly, looking him dead in the eye. "We're trained to notice every detail, but at the end of the day, I'm blind."

Relating, though he couldn't be sure what she was specifically referring to, he offered, "We shouldn't have to be hyper vigilant in our personal lives."

Uncrossing her legs and leaning forward, she set the empty wine glass on the coffee table then rubbed her eyes, digging her knuckles into the sockets. When she lifted her face again, she looked like hell.

"What's going on?" he said, gently inviting her to open up.

"My mom..." she murmured, as she refilled her wine glass. It was a clumsy pour. Merlot trickled down the outside of the glass and left a ring on the wooden coffee table, but she hardly noticed. "She threw a wrench into this *thing* I was having."

Carter recalled her mentioning a bartender, the father of her deceased baby.

"I didn't see it," she said as if only to herself. The wine was making her introspective yet talkative. Words were tumbling out of her now.

"The whole time, I didn't see that she was keeping him at bay. I never sensed it. I never questioned why he hadn't come around, and..."

Again she fell silent, this time to drain her glass. She immediately poured more and the bottle clanked against glass, the wine spilling freely.

"And damn it," she hissed, pinching her eyes shut and shaking her head before meeting his gaze. "I came home, and my mom was clearing out Gregory's room. I lost it."

It took a few seconds for Carter to recall that Gregory was Danny's late son, and the individual who her mother had kept at bay would have to be the bartender—the ex.

"I'm sorry," he said, feeling genuine anger on her behalf.

"It might seem abstract," she went on, looking spent. Unburdening was taking it out of her. She wasn't even holding her wine glass firmly, so he quietly took it from her loose grip, and set it on the coffee table.

"This case..." she sent on. "The way Wilhelmina coddles her daughter yet poses the biggest threat to her... It's like, I keep seeing my own mother in

Wilhelmina. I don't know if I'm driving myself crazy, or if there's something to it."

"Like what?" he asked, as he mentally rewired his brain in terms of all he had previously theorized.

"I really don't know," she moaned, groping for the glass. "The *'mother knows best'* attitude. That aspect. The suffocation, the smothering, what it does to a person. Can one person's *selfishness* kill another?"

She had stopped making sense. Her words were garbled, and yet she wasn't entirely at sea. The boy from the photographs had also stirred in Carter a world of torment that had dredged up his past.

"Why haven't we ever looked at Mirabelle?" she wondered, again rubbing her eyes roughly with her knuckles.

Carter could almost see her distorted logic, the faulty parallels it implied. Danny had been betrayed by her own mother so, using one dilemma to explain the other, she was finding reasons for why Mirabelle might have sought revenge. But Wilhelmina wasn't the Vic, her sister was.

However, that didn't mean Agatha hadn't betrayed her niece in some irreparable way.

Every piece, each character in the tapestry of this warped motif was connected to the crime at hand.

"You think we should take a harder look at Mirabelle?" he asked after giving it some thought. "I have to be honest with you. I don't see her hauling a dead body up a flight of stairs or stuffing one into a suitcase. She's barely a hundred pounds."

"I know," she agreed. "But Wilhelmina is certainly abusing her on some level. Why isn't she the Vic? It doesn't add up. I thought Mirabelle was protecting Sauter, but we combed through every inch of his place. He didn't do it. I can't stand this," she said quietly, falling into deep, brain-addling contemplation.

After a moment of Danny staring at the rainy window and Carter thinking about the few facts they actually knew, she offhandedly mentioned, "I found a drug called Premarin in their bathroom."

"The Bauers' bathroom?"

She nodded then added, "When I brought Mirabelle home. Ever heard of it?"

"No," he said before guessing, "pills?"

"You inject it," she explained, as she sluggishly patted the front of her jeans, looking for what he could only assume was her cell phone.

She'd had way too much to drink so when she tipped off the couch, aiming to stand, he sprang to his feet and caught her then gently urged her back down.

"Who are we calling?" he said, pulling his own cell from his slacks.

She stared up at him and said, "Jill."

"It's almost midnight," he told her.

Jill was literally the last person Carter wanted to call in the middle of the night. That being said, he knew that she would pick up his call.

He found her contact number, sent the call through, and pressed his cell phone to his ear. As it rang, he settled onto the couch.

Jill's voice—husky with sleep—came through the line.

"Dobbs?"

"Hey, sorry to wake you," he apologized, as she let out a dreamy sigh.

"It's okay," she said softly. He could hear bed sheets rustling through the line. "What can I do for you, Carter?"

"Have you heard of a drug called Premarin?"

After pausing briefly to think, she said, "Sure."

From the sidelines, Danny urgently reminded him, "You inject it!"

Holding his hand up, he relayed that detail to Jill then asked, "What's it for?"

"You're not at the precinct, are you?" she asked distractedly, having heard his partner in the background.

"What is it used for, Jill?" he repeated.

"Hormone replacement therapy," she said. "It's estrogen."

Chapter Twenty

SHE SHOULDN'T HAVE polished off that bottle of wine last night. Ordinarily, Danny wasn't one to overdo it by drinking until her vision blurred.

But the emotional rollercoaster she had undergone—facing a man she'd once loved and finding her mother erasing all traces of Gregory, *the last thing you needed was a filthy little boy*—had rendered her miserable.

Shutting her brain off to protect her mind from splitting apart had been a necessary evil.

But her brain hadn't exactly turned back on by the time she arrived at the 66th.

She draped her raincoat over the back of her chair, booted up her computer, and discretely tucked the glossy print of Mirabelle into a random file in the lap drawer of her desk. Accomplishing each was a labored effort.

Her temples were pounding, and it didn't help that the station house was filling up. Detectives and police officers alike stomped through and complained about the rain. Phones blared, and civilians—some worried, others shrill—demanded answers at the front desk.

Suffering, she dragged herself into the break room where a fresh pot of coffee was brewing. After pouring a mug, doctoring it with cream and sugar, and hoping like hell that flooding her system with caffeine would whip her into shape, she returned to her desk where Carter was on his knees, examining the pump beneath the seat that was responsible for lifting his chair higher. He failed to figure out the mechanics, however.

Gulping creamy dark roast and trying not to move her head for fear her migraine would swell, she sat gingerly then asked, "You get home okay?"

"Eventually," he said, as he got to his feet and dusted off his slacks, having given up on the height of the seat. He sat and offhandedly mentioned, "I swung by Wilhelmina's."

"Did you?" she asked, interested. She stole a few more sips of coffee, impatient that it hadn't yet snuffed out her headache, and set the mug on her desk.

He ran his meaty hand down his face, expressing that his effort had been a waste of time. "I watched her building. No one came or went. I spent an hour at Sauter's pursuing the same hunch."

"You thought Mirabelle would turn up?"

"She went to his place before," he reminded her with a resigned shrug. "They're in cahoots."

"To cover up the murder?" she questioned skeptically.

"They're up to *something*," he maintained, planting his elbows on his desk, his attention now locked on his computer.

She happened to agree, but her gut told her that the odd couple's objective was to free Mirabelle from her mother's custody. Murdering Agatha Bauer would have been pointless. Not to mention that Danny believed Mirabelle's love of her aunt, which the girl had conveyed time and again, had been genuine. Likewise, she agreed with Mirabelle's impression of how Sauter felt towards the German immigrant. They didn't want Agatha dead. They wanted to be a family, just the three of them.

It had been Wilhelmina Bauer who had implied that Agatha hadn't been a blameless victim—*if you suspect Agatha of something, well then… I suppose my instinct to protect my daughter was justified.*

What was she hiding?

The syringe needle came to mind.

"Jill said Premarin is estrogen for hormone replacement therapy."

Carter gave her the same screwy look of unabashed leeriness that he had last night. "That's not a lead, Danny," he said frankly, his mountainous shoulders rising, every inch of his body language implying, *this is ridiculous.* "Wilhelmina's going through menopause, case closed. I don't know why you're acting like Premarin is some kind of smoking gun."

"But Wilhelmina is, what? Forty-five? She's too young to be going through menopause," she argued.

"You don't know that."

"Oh, you know women better than me?"

"Is that the hangover talking?" he shot back before breaking it down for her with more sarcasm than she appreciated. "There's *evidence*, and then there's *not* evidence. Estrogen is not evidence."

As Carter scrolled through emails, Danny spent a thoughtful moment downing her coffee. She proposed, "What if Wilhelmina isn't the one taking it?"

"You think Mirabelle's going through teenage menopause?" he challenged.

"I didn't say that, but let's think this through. She's underweight. She doesn't eat. What if she isn't menstruating?"

"So her mother shoots her up with estrogen so that aunt flow can get back in the swing of coming to town?" he questioned, highly skeptical if not annoyed with the brainstorm. "Or maybe the girl shoots herself up with estrogen to grow her boobs without otherwise gaining weight."

"High fashion models don't want boobs," she countered, slipping into deep thought, her instincts telling her there had to be something to it. But every theory that came to mind fell short.

"Look, if you want to grill Mirabelle about it when she comes in for the line-up today, then knock yourself out."

Danny was about to comment on his acrimonious mood when an out of breath woman stormed into the station. She looked infuriated. Her blonde hair was sopping. Her tight blue eyes scanned the bullpen. Her mouth pinched into a jealous snub the second she laid eyes on Danny.

Marching over, she clipped shoulders with a passing police officer and glared hotly as though it had been his fault, then redirected her fury at Danny.

When she reached their adjoined desks, she angled over Carter, planted her fists on her plump hips, and stared daggers at him. "Can I talk to you?"

"Kathy," he said, dumbfounded. After a stammering beat, he managed, "This is my partner, Danny-"

"Now!" she demanded.

Ashen with shock, Carter rose to his feet, as Danny awkwardly looked on. His wife shifted her extreme suspicion back and forth between the detectives.

Like a gentleman, Carter placed his hand on the small of her back and began steering her towards the break room, but she wasn't having it. Furious that he would have the audacity to touch her, she jerked free, turned on her heel, and immediately launched into a confrontation for everyone to hear. "You didn't come home last night."

"I came home," he insisted, his voice falling into a hard whisper as he struggled to stay cordial. "I didn't want to wake you so I slept on the couch."

"What were you doing at her place all night?"

"Nothing," he said, glimpsing Franco who was breezing around the front desk, entering the precinct. "Let's talk over here."

But she didn't budge. "You slept with her, didn't you?"

"No!"

Snorting a disgusted laugh, she looked away as though the sight of him turned her stomach.

Danny buried her head in the Bauer case file on her desk and tried not to eavesdrop, which was more than she could say for the rest of the cops in the bullpen, Franco included.

"Come on," Carter groveled. "Can we not do this here?"

The lieutenant seemed miffed from where he stood, his dark eyes narrowing on his newest detective whose wife was making a very public display of raking him over the coals. So Danny, with the aim of distracting him, hopped to her feet despite her throbbing temples, and started through the bullpen, approaching Franco.

"Hey," she said, acutely aware of the mounting argument between her partner and his wife. They were getting loud.

The lieutenant jutted his chin in Carter's direction, asking, "Trouble in paradise?"

But before Danny could answer, Kathy's shrill voice cut through the air:

"It's Saturday! You should be home with your kids!"

By the looks of it, Carter had had enough. Gripping his wife's upper arm, he escorted her into the break room and out of view where they continued their argument, hissing accusations at one another.

Franco commented, "I take it now's not the time to introduce myself to the missus?"

"He just needs a minute," she said, hoping the excuse was accurate.

"The DA will be here in an hour," he reminded her. "Where are we with Mirabelle?"

"We're about to head over and bring her in for the line-up," she explained, as Kathy's sharp voice cut through the precinct:

"You think I'm an idiot? I'm not doing this with you anymore!"

Livid, Carter ordered, "Lower your voice!"

Franco's eyebrows shot up to his hairline hearing that and he groaned, "Christ," as Danny smiled uncomfortably, knowing full well her partner wouldn't live this down anytime soon. "Go without him. Something tells me Carter's going to need a personal day."

"He's not going to like it," she told him.

"He's not going to have a choice."

Having overheard enough discord—all of SVU was getting an earful—Franco decisively strode towards the break room, but Danny stepped in front of him once again, anything to save her partner from the embarrassment of their lieutenant mediating his marital problems.

"You know Whittaker's not good for this, right?" she disputed point blank.

"We've got an eyewitness," he shot back, amazed that she would double-down when the cards she had been dealt were clearly in her favor. "If she IDs him, we'll get a warrant to search his mom's place. We don't need a confession. The DA has enough to run with."

Thrown by his resolve, she said, "Lieutenant," but couldn't follow through with her objection. Though she was aching for a conviction, she would rather let the case go cold than send the wrong man to prison. And yet, she couldn't seem to articulate the argument. Damn hangover.

"You followed the evidence," he reminded her, as he delivered a congratulatory jab to her shoulder, which sent searing pain through her skull. "And the evidence points to Whittaker."

"Based on the statement of a confused teenager," she contended.

"Whom you vetted," he reminded her, annoyed at her sudden lack of confidence. "The DA will question her. Other than picking up Mirabelle to drive her here, this is out of your hands, Foster."

Knowing that if Franco used her last name, he wasn't interested in her opinion, she pressed her mouth into a dissatisfied line and uttered not one word.

At least the argument coming from the break room had quieted during their brief debate, relieving Franco of any reason to enter. He barreled into his office, leaving Danny to ponder the fragments of their deteriorating case.

When Kathy emerged, her dejected husband filling the doorway behind her, she glared at Danny, slowing her step as she passed before continuing on through the bullpen.

For a man whose build resembled a linebacker's, Carter looked like a flogged schoolboy.

"Hey," she said, as she approached him despite Kathy's suddenly watchful eye. "The lieutenant says you can take the day to be with your family."

His expression went long. Waves of embarrassment crashed over him. To Carter, this wasn't good news but rather a sign that Franco finally had the reason he had been looking for to 'can' him. Kathy on the other hand seemed happy as she drifted towards them.

Before he could argue, which would only get him into more hot water with his wife, Danny told him, "Go. I'll keep you posted on the line-up. Franco says this thing is out of our hands now anyway."

Screwing his face up, he asked, "I thought the line-up was a formality. We're on the same page, right? Whittaker didn't do it."

"And Franco will come to realize that soon enough," she assured him. "I'll lean on Mirabelle like we talked about."

Kathy snorted another disgusted laugh as though she'd just overheard Danny sexually proposition her husband.

Ignoring the interruption, she explained, "If I get anything out of her, you'll be the first to know. Okay?"

Snidely, Kathy asked, "Can I have my husband now?"

Danny let the hostile remark roll off her back and offered the jealous woman her hand. "I'm Danielle Foster, by the way."

"I know who you are," she snapped as she took hold of Carter's thick arm, claiming her territory instead of shaking Danny's hand. "The next time you need a man in the middle of the night, don't call my husband."

When Carter met his partner's stoic gaze, the look on his face was apologetic. In a silent response, Danny gave him an *'it's fine'* smile, which of course Kathy misconstrued. She immediately strutted off in an insulted huff, dragging her husband along.

"Keep your phone on," she called out good-naturedly, as her partner rounded into the lobby with his bitter wife, shuffling off like a football hero who'd just gotten benched.

After throwing on her raincoat, she downed the rest of her coffee, ignoring that it was cold, slapped the mug on her desk, and scrolled through the contacts on her cell phone in search of Wilhelmina's number.

She wasn't at all surprised when at first the woman refused to tell her where her daughter was, bristling and sputtering something about a critical Jean Pierre Johansan photoshoot. Danny held the phone away from her ear so that Wilhelmina's piercing tone wouldn't rattle her brain.

"Bottom line," she sharply interrupted. "Mirabelle needs to ID the guy she saw at your sister's house that night."

"And then what?"

"Don't you want this to be over?"

A long sigh came through the receiver and finally the contentious woman recited the address—a gallery in Chelsea—which Danny scribbled onto her notepad.

"She won't wrap up for another hour," she warned. "You can't drag her off in the middle of her photoshoot."

"Ms. Bauer," she said sternly. "The moment I get there I'm taking Mirabelle, with or without you."

There was a click and then a dial tone blared in Danny's ear.

After a painstaking drive into Manhattan—gridlocked on the BQE, inching over the Brooklyn Bridge, navigating through streets and avenues in horn-bleating bumper-to-bumper traffic as a torrential downpour beat against the windshield, its deafening hum filling the sedan—Danny pulled along the curb in front of a gallery called Reingold Fine Arts where Mirabelle was presumably in the throes of a photoshoot.

When she entered the gallery—a cavernous warehouse with oil paintings curated artfully on the white walls—there wasn't a soul in sight. But she heard music, muffled yet distinct, playing faintly from beyond the far wall.

Shaking rainwater from her hair, her soggy sneakers squeaking over buffed floors, she crossed through the oblong gallery and neared a white divider where a giant portrait of an androgynous youth was mounted.

Bare-chested, wearing suspenders and crisp slacks, a cigarette dripping from his cherubic lips, eyes fixed with a determined squint while he straddled a motorcycle—the boy in the painting captivated Danny.

Tearing herself away, she walked around the dividing wall and saw a door standing ajar. As she slipped into the back studio, she discovered a similar scene as the one she had interrupted at Vital not a week prior. Except now Wilhelmina was smack-dab in the middle of it.

Wilhelmenia seemed to be pleading with Jean Pierre, while all of the production assistants conversed. It was safe to assume Wilhelmina had broken the news to the photographer about her daughter's obligation to the 66th.

No one had taken notice of Danny and she'd like to keep it that way, so she crept along the perimeter, staying in the shadows, and came to a curtained area—a makeshift changing room. From within the changing room came the sounds of rustling and groaning.

She wasn't sure how to knock, but tapped on the thick curtain anyway and whispered, "Mirabelle?"

"Yeah?" the girl groaned.

"It's Detective Foster. Can I come in?"

Feebly, Mirabelle muscled the heavy curtain aside. Her free arm covered her bare chest. She wore a tulle ballet skirt. The garment hung loosely off her pointy hips as though it was two sizes too big.

"Oh!" said Danny, surprised the girl wasn't dressed. "I can wait if you're not ready."

"I don't care," she said apathetically as she staggered off, dragging her bare feet and nearing a clothing rack where designer ensembles were tightly lined. She began sorting through the glitzy garments until she found a pink cotton tee shirt. Pulling it from the rack, she complained, "You didn't come to my runway show last night."

Her nude back was long, dewy skin stretched over ribs. Her narrow waist appeared unnaturally slender. The girl's bony spine was slick with perspiration.

The girl's emaciated figure distracted Danny, and she felt the urge to force feed Mirabelle complex-carbohydrates.

"I had every intention of making it to your fashion show," she explained. "But something came up."

"You're here to apologize?" she challenged, glaring at Danny over her bony shoulder. Her furious eyes narrowed as she fiddled with her tee shirt, in no rush to actually put it on. But her wounded attitude didn't concern Danny as much as her flushed cheeks and sweaty arms did. She looked as though she had broken out into a cold sweat.

"I really am sorry," she promised. "I'm also here to drive you to the precinct. We need you to ID the man who killed your aunt."

Shaking out her tee shirt, she faced Danny with no sense of modesty that she was naked from the waist up.

Danny turned her back to the girl—just because Mirabelle seemed fine without privacy didn't mean Danny should encourage her.

But Danny had already glimpsed the shape of the girl's chest. It had been unavoidable, and the image was burning into the forefront of her mind now—two puffed plateaus that hadn't looked quite right.

"I feel sick," Mirabelle moaned, slumping her shoulders forward with a heaving sigh.

"We can get some food on the way."

"Food is the last thing I need," she murmured, as she plopped onto a stool.

Danny rushed to her, but the girl still had her faculties enough not to fall over. She sat hunched with her elbows on her knees. Breathing itself was a labored effort. The tee shirt slipped from her fingers.

"Why do you feel sick all the time?" she asked from a crouched position as she held the girl's slick shoulders, all too aware that Wilhelmina could burst in at any moment and misunderstand the situation.

Mirabelle didn't respond. She only stared through her eyebrows at Danny, so she asked in a low whisper, "Are you injecting estrogen? Is that why you're ill all the time?"

"Can't you see what I am?" she said, her eyes lolling in their sockets as though she might faint. Her left elbow slipped off her knee and she would've tumbled to the ground had Danny not caught her.

"No, what are you?" she asked, but Mirabelle was seeping into another stratosphere, her smoky voice thin as a thread as she insisted:

"I didn't see anything that night. I'm sick of this."

"You didn't see Randy Whittaker at your aunt's house?" she asked, unsurprised—lying seemed to be the girl's consistent mode of operation.

"You have to leave me alone. She's killing me."

"With the injections?" she pressed.

"Aunt Agatha tried to stop her," she breathed in a chilling effort to stay conscious.

"Stop who?" she asked. "Your mother?"

But Mirabelle was too far gone to answer.

Without warning, she spilled forward.

Danny tried to muscle her back onto the stool, but she spilled through her arms like wet noodles.

When she hit the floor, taking the detective with her, her ballet skirt slipped down her thin thighs and Danny was confronted with the answer she'd been seeking.

And it jarred her to the core.

Surrounded by the finest dusting of pubic hair was a penis.

Mirabelle was a boy.

Chapter Twenty-One

HAVING CALLED AN ambulance while cradling Mirabelle in her arms, Danny experienced an eternity pass before medics charged through the gallery.

As first responders swarmed the unconscious girl, packing into the changing area and pushing Danny aside, Wilhelmina was hysterical. She kept at their heels and demanded they unhand her daughter. When they ignored her and focused on resuscitating Mirabelle, Wilhelmina blamed the detective.

Five minutes later, the medics had strapped the girl to a gurney, administered an IV, and brought her back to life with smelling salts. They rolled the gurney, rushing her towards the gallery exit, as Wilhelmina jogged after them.

Danny looked on from the sidelines, her elevated heart rate gradually subsiding with relief.

But the feeling didn't last.

She drove like a bat out of hell through the pouring rain, windshield wipers thwacking, the cherry siren atop the sedan wailing, until she came to a screeching stop in front of the 66th Precinct.

She wasted no time racing to her desk, as horrifying revelations sprung to mind.

She jerked off her raincoat and rummaged through her desk drawers. The drawers were overwrought with case files, expense reports, and crime scene photos.

She hunted through the contents of her lap drawer next until she found a photograph of John

Unknown. She slapped the close-up onto her desk, the little boy's scared face filled the photo.

Remembering that she had tucked Mirabelle's modeling photo into a random filing folder on her desk, she thumbed through each and every one, and when she finally located the glossy print, she lowered onto her chair and studied the two images.

John Unknown and Mirabelle Bauer, side-by-side.

She examined Mirabelle's eyes first—pale green yet gleaming—then shifted her attention to the boy's. The iris of his eyes might be the same shade but she didn't feel confident, so she moved on to analyze their overall shape, noting the arch at the outer corners, the distance between the eyes.

The model's were similar.

She studied their jaws next. Both had wide and crisp jawlines, their razor-sharp cheekbones cut along the same angle in each photo.

Mirabelle's nose was unique—a dainty point, flared nostrils, the bridge straight as a pin—and John Unknown appeared to share the same one. The noses looked identical.

She didn't realize she had dialed the forensics department until she felt her desk phone against her ear.

Adrenaline pounded through her system so hard that her hangover was essentially obliterated.

"Yeah, hi," she stammered to jumpstart her frenzied brain. "I need a facial comparison analysis. I've got photos of two individuals here. I need to know if they're the same person."

"Scan 'em in! Email 'em up!" said the chipper man on the other end.

"Great," she said, as she dropped the phone and scrambled to collect the photos.

She leapt to her feet with the photos in hand.

She didn't want to get ahead of herself, but she could feel that she was right. Mirabelle Bauer and the four-year old boy were the same person.

Her mind raced with similarities and connections, as she hurried towards the corner of the bullpen where an industrial printer stood in front of a set of rain-beaten windows.

The thunder outside underscored her urgency.

She pressed Mirabelle's modeling photo face down onto the printer glass and hit scan without lowering the lid. After punching the console to email the image to forensics, she used the same whiplash speed to scan and send the face shot of John Unknown.

She returned to her desk with the photos, mentally reeling from the discovery she had made.

Wilhelmina was deranged. She had raised her son in a vacuum, isolating him from the world and abusing him frequently and severely. She had shared the pornographic images of her son, using the internet.

At what point had Wilhelmina stopped sexually abusing her son and started altering his sex? What had caused her to decide one day that her son would be her daughter? She had stripped him of all identity, groomed him to be a girl, and injected him with estrogen, as an added measure to ensure the transformation.

Then she had shoved him into the limelight to model as a girl.

It was sick.

But could it have motivated Agatha Bauer's murder?

Had the older sister discovered the secret, sought to intervene, and been shut down in the most gruesome and fatal way?

Mirabelle's murmured admission shafted through Danny's mind—*Agatha tried to stop her.*

Her train of thought was interrupted when an email popped into her inbox. She wasted no time opening the attachment that had come with it, an image of Mirabelle's face overlaying a computer generated composite of John Unknown as a fifteen-year old. The layered faces were highlighted with transparent green markings meant to illustrate select facial features that perfectly matched. The brow bone, cheekbones, jawline, and shape and size of the nose were all glowing green. In the upper right corner she saw: *98%*

"Holy crap," she breathed, as she grabbed her desk phone.

Clamping the phone between her ear and shoulder, she punched Carter's cell number into the keypad.

He picked up after the first ring.

"Danny?" he answered over the sounds of his children cackling in the background. Not a split second later, his wife objected—*are you kidding me?* Carter immediately covered the mouthpiece, but Danny was still able to hear him bark, "Can you please lay off it?"

"Carter," she began as soon as he'd returned. "Mirabelle is the boy."

Shock cut through him and the line went quiet. Then he said, "You serious?"

She heard him pace away from his rambunctious children, Kathy chewing him out all the while. Next came the sound of a door slamming shut, Carter having locked himself in a quiet room.

"I was with Mirabelle and she fainted," she quickly explained. "As she fell, her skirt came down. Carter, she has a penis." There was only stunned silence on the other end so she elaborated, "I had forensics run a comparison using two photos, because I didn't trust my own eyes. It came back as a 98% match. Mirabelle and John Unknown are the same person."

When finally the dark implications surrounding the discovery hit him, Carter asked, "Where is she now?"

"At the hospital with her mother."

"You have to let me talk to her," he insisted, as the boisterous sounds of his kids swelled through the receiver, an indication he was moving swiftly through the house.

"Carter," she said before stopping herself.

Before, when he had tried to talk to Whittaker, Carter's efforts had been wasted. And Danny hadn't had better luck with Sauter. This time, they would need to confer with Franco and meticulously plan their moves. They couldn't afford to act fast without focus.

"Just get over here," she told him. "I'll brief the lieutenant in the meantime."

"She might not remember the abuse," he stated, apprehensive.

"Which is why we need to talk to Franco," she cautioned.

Though his kids had fallen silent in fear of their angry mother, Carter wasn't so easily intimidated. Ignoring Kathy's shrill objections, he stepped out into the blustering rain.

"Everything okay over there?" asked Danny.

"I'm on my way," he told her before shouting: "It's work, Kathy!" A slammed door came next, and as he jogged to his car, he yelled, "Wilhelmina's out of her damn mind."

Deafening rain clattered through the receiver like static, making it hard for Danny to hear him.

She asked, "Should we bring a psycho-analyst in on this?"

"No," he shouted over the wind, as he slammed his car door shut. "You know if a therapist is present when a victim discloses, the defense will claim the vic was coached, and tear apart the whole case at trial. I'm not going to let that woman get off. If I hear the term *false memory*, I'll punch a wall."

"She has to remember, Carter, or else-"

"I know," he barked, then took a breath to cool off, exhaling loudly into the receiver. "Which is why I need to talk to her."

The sounds of the engine firing up came through the line, as she asked, "You think Wilhelmina's good for Bauer's murder?"

"You don't want to know what I think," he told her, anger percolating in his deep tone, but Danny was thinking the same thing.

They now had a decent working theory—Agatha had learned of the abuse, discovered the child pornography, and confronted her sister, and Wilhelmina had killed her to keep the past a secret.

But that was the problem. It was a *theory*, one in which they would have to prove with evidence.

She told him to drive safely and returned the phone to its cradle, as the grisly details of Agatha's murder surged to the forefront of her mind.

The bludgeoning. Wrapping a garbage bag over the woman's head. Hauling the body upstairs. The post-mortem rape with a wooden object. Stuffing the body into a suitcase. Dumping her in the park. Planting child pornography—those bone-chilling images of her own son that *she* had taken with a camera no less—on the mud in the dead of night, as rain thundered all the while.

Only a lunatic...

Was Wilhelmina Bauer so depraved? Was she capable of that kind of maniacal criminality? And if so, what had turned her into a monster?

Chapter Twenty-Two

WILHELMINA'S MUSCLES were still trembling, having heaved her daughter down into the subway after the ER and up the stairs again once they had reached Kensington.

She hoisted the girl through the lobby of their building and down the hallway. She caught her breath in the elevator.

Wilhelmina was already worried about the hospital bill that they had no way of paying. Another goddamn burden she couldn't deal with.

It wasn't easy getting her half-dead daughter into her bedroom in the apartment, but she did her best.

She flung Mirabelle onto the bed and took a step back, desperate to catch her breath.

As she stood in the open doorway of her daughter's bedroom, glaring at the girl as soft lamplight kissing her dainty yet listless figure, she realized that Mirabelle was the bane of her existence.

The girl looked half dead from where she was sprawled on her bed—lying face up on her back, one skinny arm draped over her eyes, her blonde hair spilling wildly across the pillow, gangly legs bent together. She was out cold.

Wilhelmina had saved her daughter, and what was the thanks she got? The girl constantly complained, resisted, and fought tooth and nail, as though the little boy inside of Mirabelle refused to die.

Mirabelle had been born Matthew Bauer some fifteen years ago in the dead of one wintry night. During the long labor, Wilhelmina's fingernails had broken where she'd gripped the edge of her bathtub.

Seated on the freezing porcelain, pushing with all her might, face flexing and guttural groans cloying up her throat, she'd been determined to give birth at home so that there wouldn't be a daunting hospital bill and insurmountable debt. It had been the only conceivable way for a newly single woman to begin motherhood. When finally, after eight grueling and tortuous hours writhing on the bathroom floor, her son had emerged—slippery and shrieking—from her body, Wilhelmina realized there would also be no birth certificate, social security number, nor any documentation linking her child to herself or the world.

A happy accident.

Nursing him had been hell. Tending to his constant, insufferable needs had grated on her spirit.

Clawing at her sore nipples, demanding of her things she didn't want to give, screaming bloody murder when she refused, he had been a filthy little brat. As he'd grown from an infant into a toddler and from a toddler into a raucous two-year old, the funnel of her misery had narrowed even more. His incessant neediness had caused Wilhelmina to despise her son.

She had fantasized about drowning him in the bathtub, smothering him with a pillow, and putting an end to the relentless depression of a motherhood she hadn't asked for.

But she hadn't needed to succumb to her darkest dream.

A better idea had soon come to mind, one that centered on the talent agency she'd been hired at, and its brand-new model—Grady Willis.

When Grady had entered her world like a knight in shining Armani, he had immediately sensed her anguish. And when she'd finally welcomed him into her home, he took firm charge of fathering her sniveling son, always behind closed doors and always to her deepest satisfaction. The shrill wailing that had sliced through her eardrums and rattled her brain miraculously ceased thanks to Grady.

Years had passed and she had never questioned his *methods*, never knocked on the bathroom door or discovered the special brand of *discipline* he was using to get control over her son…

… until one day she came across a handful of photos.

She had been horrified.

Yet, she knew that if she confronted him, he would leave.

She hadn't been prepared to lose Grady for any reason.

She'd hid the photos, confiscating them for safekeeping without his knowledge, and never broached the subject for any reason.

But she had needed to do *something* to stop the abuse.

Her solution? She began the long and arduous task of turning her son into a daughter, a bright and burgeoning star, the model Wilhelmina herself had never been, and her boyfriend's sexual interest in her child gradually ebbed away.

Grady had tamed him and Wilhelmina had transformed him.

Theirs was a perfect partnership.

But Mirabelle was entirely ungrateful.

In truth, she hadn't thought much of her child until he'd become a beautiful young girl. She felt badly about it, but time mended all wounds. Peace had found its way into their home...

Until Agatha had returned, swooping in on her high horse and discovering it all.

Wilhelmina realized her jaw was clenched so she made a concerted effort to breathe deeply, releasing the tension that had gripped her, and eased her daughter's bedroom door closed before starting through the living room where Grady was glaring, bleary-eyed, at the television while sucking on a can of Coors.

Observing him, she tried to make sense of her low mood. While she regretted having fallen in love with a monster, she had been looking forward to spending time with him. Clearly, he wouldn't be capable of giving her attention tonight, not in his current state.

She didn't have the energy to wrangle him back to planet Earth, much less tell him about the trip to the hospital and the overwhelming medical bill that had resulted. One ride in an ambulance had cost thousands!

Mirabelle was expensive enough without an unexpected visit to the ER.

Wilhelmina's every penny had been spent on estrogen if not modeling composite cards, test shoots, professional prints, fashionable outfits—her modeling binder alone had been over three hundred dollars. She considered it an investment, but the fees were never ending. Her daughter's modeling income didn't compare with the financial hemorrhaging that came with it.

Grady grunted something about dinner, having sensed she was near, so she padded into the kitchen and began poking through the freezer, recalling microwavable lasagnas she'd stocked up on a month back.

As she stripped away the packaging and stuffed the frozen dinner into the microwave, Wilhelmina's insides began to crawl with panic.

She should've never allowed Mirabelle to speak with that detective lady alone. The girl must have botched her statement, giving Foster more reasons to hunt instead of steering her away from the family, and it didn't help that her daughter hadn't stuck to accusing Lewis Sauter. Who the hell was Randy Whittaker anyhow?

The look that had come over Foster's smug face when Wilhelmina had charged into the changing area tightly behind those first responders…

Wilhelmina shuddered to remember, pinching her eyes shut. Her daughter had barely been dressed, just a flimsy skirt separating her *boyish secret* from prying eyes…

The detective might very well know now…

Terror-stricken, Wilhelmina turned her attention to the lasagna rotating inside the droning microwave.

This was all Agatha's fault, and realizing this transported her back to a time that made her ache to have a beautiful life once again.

Her childhood home in Germany had been gargantuan—an *estate*, in fact. Positioned on the Unter den Linden where cherry blossoms undulated in the warm breeze every spring, their chateaux had been regal. Maman had passed away during childbirth, a tragedy, which the family did not speak of—Wilhelmina felt responsible even though it had really been the fault of those terrible doctors. Papa had raised the girls with the help of twelve servants. He had been a kind man of few words, incredibly prosperous, and had *doted* on the eldest of his two daughters, Agatha, a fact that secretly pained both girls, though Wilhelmina had never discovered the source of her sister's discomfort.

Wilhelmina often wondered about who she might have become, what her life might have looked like, if her sister hadn't smuggled her out of Germany weeks after Wilhelmina's eighth birthday. Might she have married a wealthy German aristocrat? Would she be dining in Berlin right now, associating with high society types, and humbly accepting compliments for a bountiful modeling career that she would have certainly had experienced if her sister hadn't deposited her in the U.S.?

Instead of living the high life, Wilhelmina was trapped in Kensington, Brooklyn, with a lowlife who she hated herself for loving. Every minute of her existence was spent scrounging for cash to pour into her daughter's career. She lived her life in a constant state of holding her breath for her daughter's 'big break,' but she couldn't be certain it would ever come.

Papa won't know you're here, Agatha had told her, as they'd meandered through Prospect Park, Brooklyn—Wilhelmina, a young girl in her petticoat and tights, Agatha towering over her with the face of a severe woman and the spirit of a skittish child. *I'll come back for you, I promise!*

Her sister's grand, sweeping gesture to save Wilhelmina—*from what?*—had been anything but a salvation.

Selfish.

A lie at best.

Wilhelmina had been teased and taunted at her new American school. Crass boys had flipped up her skirt, ambushing her from all sides. Her teachers had been blissfully unaware though they'd stood off to the wayside, her torture unfolding in plain view.

It had gradually dawned on her—her sister's egomaniacal plan. Agatha had wanted Papa all to herself. She'd wanted to be the star of the family, never to be outshined by her younger sister. She had begged Papa to fund her modeling career and after years of basking in his undivided attention—those long mentoring sessions deep inside his bedroom chamber, while Wilhelmina had always been excluded—Papa had granted Agatha's modeling wish.

But doing so had only fueled Agatha's narcissism, her obsession with her own handsome looks. All the while she'd ushered Wilhelmina into the next room every time Papa came around.

As far as Wilhelmina was concerned, her sister snatching her in the middle of the night and flying her over to America had all been a giant ploy to rob Wilhelmina of an abundant life. And when finally, decades later, Agatha had returned and spoke of a hard life with Papa...

Wilhelmina's blood had boiled over.

She should've never welcomed Agatha into the fold. She should've never trusted her by leaving her alone with her daughter.

When Wilhelmina had come home one afternoon to find her sister chuckling with Mirabelle in the living room even though she'd warned her daughter never to allow the woman into their apartment, her stomach had bottomed out with a dreadful kick.

Later that night, as Grady had slept in his squashy recliner, she'd hunted for the photographs—her failsafe to prevent her boyfriend from ever walking out, *if Grady ever tried to leave her, she would blackmail him with the child pornography he had made while abusing her son!*

But that night, she had discovered that the photographs were gone.

Agatha had taken them.

The next thing she knew, her sister was calling her, demanding that they speak privately at once…

Bad blood, Agatha had said, accusing Wilhelmina of having become like their papa despite the measures she'd taken to prevent it. *You've got the same sickness in you.*

But she hadn't. It was Grady, and his habit had long since passed. It wouldn't have been fair if the terrible truth came out…

Everything Wilhelmina had done was to *protect* her family, both Grady and Mirabelle!

The microwave beeped and she was yanked out of the time warp.

She made sloppy work of setting the lasagna on a tray and carrying it over to her boyfriend, who was bogged in an alcohol-induced haze.

She pulled a folding table in front of him that lived beside his recliner and slapped the steaming tray down, ripped off the plastic cover, and reminded him not to drink his dinner.

Thoughts of Lewis Sauter nettled her from the back of her worried mind.

Sauter should've been arrested, shackled, and shipped off to prison where he wouldn't be able to spill the dark truth about Mirabelle's unusual upbringing and the gender transformation that had followed.

Wilhelmina didn't know for certain that Satuer had learned of the family secret, but erring on the side of caution, she had to assume he had. Why wouldn't Agatha have confided in her lover?

Dangling loose ends made her sick.

"We have to find out what she told the police," she said, as Grady inspected his meal, steam wafting up around his face.

"Now?"

"I want you to get it out of her," she told him sternly, her stomach twisting with knots. "Whatever it takes."

In a bold attempt at defiance, he pushed back in his recliner, leering up at her with bleary eyes.

"It's not over," she reminded him before glancing at her daughter's bedroom door, which caused a rush of anxiety to zing through her veins. "*Discipline* her if you have to."

"Like *old times*?" he sneered with an aroused grin.

He heaved to his feet and the TV tray spilled sideways, lasagna tumbling across the floor.

As he staggered towards Mirabelle's room, muttering incomprehensibly, Wilhelmina kept at his shuffling heels.

Shouldering open the bedroom door, he fumbled with the fly of his jeans.

Her daughter woke up. Mirabelle was groggy, vaguely aware there was a disturbance. When he grabbed her by the hair, jerking her to life, Wilhelmina only smiled.

"What did you tell the police?" he demanded.

Mirabelle thrashed wildly underneath him as though the last five peaceful years hadn't occurred. She whined and scrambled to get away, but didn't answer as he held her down, annoyed that she was squirming too much to properly punish.

"What did you tell them, huh?"

Bad blood, and Wilhelmina liked it, strangely paralyzed with arousal as she looked on.

"Get the needle!" he ordered.

Intoxicated at the sight of Grady on top of her daughter, Wilhelmina stood motionless in a trance. Every time he screamed for the needle, his palm open and jutting towards her as he held her daughter down, she flinched but couldn't rush off into the bathroom to fulfill his demand. She felt hypnotized, anticipating what would come next.

In her mind, she heard her sister bellow, *you've got the same sickness! What have you done to her? What have you done?*

She remembered her own reply, *you don't know what it's like being a mother!*

Cruelly, Agatha had slapped her across the face, livening her senses and stinging her cheek. Rage had flared hot across her skin, as she'd paced into the kitchen while her callous sister had sat on the couch.

Snapping back into herself—her daughter's pathetic whining filling her ears—she warned

Mirabelle, "This won't end until you tell me the truth!"

But it did end.

Thud—the front door bashed in.

Stomping footfall filled the apartment, and a woman yelled, "Police!"

Wilhelmina whipped around to find a gun barrel in her face, Detective Foster on the other end of the weapon.

The African-American all-star spilled into the bedroom. He pulled Grady off her daughter and decked him square in the jaw.

When her boyfriend was slammed against the wall and fell, the detective violently yanked him up again and delivered another powerful blow.

The next thing she knew, she was on the ground with her arms twisted behind her back, as cold metal clamped around her wrists, Foster having overpowered her.

The detective began reciting some legal mumbo-jumbo, as she thrust Wilhelmina to her feet.

Bad blood, she thought, as she was hauled through the apartment.

Her daughter watched, white-faced and shaken, from the bed.

Unexpectedly, relief suddenly washed over Wilhelmina.

She had been arrested.

There would be no more bad blood.

Chapter Twenty-Three

"THE RAPE KIT came back negative for Touch DNA," Franco informed them from where he was leaning against his desk with his arms folded. He wasn't pleased.

Rain ticked against the office windows to his right. "I'm not going to stand here and tell you that you should've let him rape her, but at least then we'd *have* something."

Danny could almost hear the thoughts unfolding in her lieutenant's fast-working mind—his brightest detective had spent hours with Mirabelle Bauer in the hospital using every trick in the book to jog the girl's recollection of the childhood abuse, and it had gone badly.

Mirabelle didn't have a single cohesive memory prior to turning twelve when her mother had begun injecting her with estrogen and coaching her on how to conceal her gender.

Amnesia was common. Oftentimes, the worse the abuse that a child survived, the harder it was for that person to remember any of it later on in life.

A nurse had eventually ushered Danny out of the room, giving the detective no choice but to return to the precinct, empty-handed.

Looking past Carter who was standing with his back to the one-way mirror, the lieutenant glimpsed the glass where, on the other side, Wilhelmina Bauer was examining her reflection.

She fluffed her curls and frowned at the rumpled pantsuit and scuffed heels she wore. The woman had no clue it wasn't a real mirror, and that the detectives were watching her. Her attorney had yet to arrive.

"Come on, we don't need Touch DNA," Carter suggested, as he joined Danny to form a physical alliance. "We caught the guy in the act."

"You broke into their apartment without a warrant! There's no evidence of Willis sexually assaulting her. Their lawyer is going to have a field day with the fact that you had zero probable cause to enter."

"We know what we saw," he insisted, gaping at the man as though the lieutenant had been against them from the start. "You've got two eyewitnesses right here," he added, indicating his partner and himself.

"I've been doing this a long time," Franco asserted. "I've seen it all."

"And I've testified more times than I can count," Danny evenly reminded him. "No attorney is going to be able to dismantle the word of two cops who saw the exact same attack."

"Can we just be real for a second?" interrupted Carter as he returned to the one-way mirror and pressed his thick index finger against the glass where Wilhelmina was now checking the corners of her mouth for lipstick smears. "The minute we search her dump we're going to find the murder weapon, the suitcase, the wooden object she used on her sister, the printer and pornography. This case is airtight."

"This case won't be closed until it's closed!" he countered, raising his voice. "And it's far from airtight."

Danny was just as thrown as her partner, and she had to wonder if it was Franco who couldn't see the forest for the trees.

"This is where we're at," he continued. "We *might* be able to charge Grady Willis with attempted rape in the first degree. We *might* be able to charge Wilhelmina Bauer with aiding and abetting. But it'll amount to what any defense attorney will argue was an isolated incident, *and* the defense will highlight that my detectives discovered the isolated incident through illegal means. You broke down a door without probable cause or a warrant! What the hell were you thinking?"

Franco composed himself and went on, "The defense will be able to argue that the scene the police mistook for assault was actually two loving parents disciplining their child. A jury will buy it, trust me."

"You've got to be kidding me!" yelled Carter, who looked like he was ready to drive his fist through a wall.

Franco held his ground. Danny knew the look on her lieutenant's face. If Carter didn't cool down, it wouldn't end well for him—*you want me to write you up for insubordination?*

"This is coming straight from the district attorney," he stated when Carter gained control of himself. "You've got nothing that proves Bauer had been habitually abusing her daughter, and from the standpoint of a trial even the facial comparison of John Unknown and Mirabelle that forensics ran for you is thin."

Carter opened his mouth to object, but Franco held his hand up as though he'd heard enough. "An isolated disciplinary incident doesn't prove Bauer killed her sister."

"Bull," he snorted, pacing away.

"There's no evidence, Dobbs! There's no-"

"The photos!" he shot back, turning on his heel.

"Which could be any child!" he yelled louder than Carter, causing Danny to jump. "The photographic match was only ninety-eight percent. Their attorney will focus on that two percent," he informed them. "They've got reasonable doubt right there."

Even though she didn't want to believe it, Danny asked, "You think they might walk?"

"If no one talks, then yes," he confirmed, staring dead at her. "Not to mention that the DA hasn't been in love with our investigative methods so far. She issued a search warrant for Sauter's place. We found nothing. She issued an arrest warrant for Whittaker. He wasn't our guy. I've had to answer to her at every turn, and quite frankly I'm sick of apologizing for your sloppy police work."

Carter pressed his thick lips into a furious line to keep from exploding.

Danny took a thoughtful lap around the office.

"I'm working on getting you a search warrant for Bauer's apartment," Franco went on, which caused her partner to blow a gasket for an entirely different reason.

"Christ, next time lead with that, would you?"

Ignoring Carter's astonishment, Franco explained, "The DA won't charge 'attempted rape,' not without evidence. But I think I can convince her to issue a search warrant to look for child porn, and by extension you've got a shot at finding the murder weapon."

Carter did not look reassured, but the lieutenant continued anyway:

"I have to tell you, if Bauer didn't do it, or if she was smart enough to get rid of the evidence, then we've got nada. They won't see the inside of a jail cell, much less go to prison. They won't even see the inside of our holding cells down in the basement of this precinct."

Danny was reading him loud and clear. They needed a confession. Period. And given the fact that the seedy couple had lawyered up, the detectives were facing an uphill battle to say the least.

She neared the one-way mirror and observed as Wilhelmina turned on her designer-heel the moment a defense attorney in a three-dollar suit entered the room. The attorney slapped his briefcase onto the table and shot her a thousand watt smile.

Danny didn't like the guy's confidence.

As the attorney invited Wilhelmina to take a seat beside him, Danny turned to her partner and said, "It's go time," and threw open the office door.

"Get a confession," Franco ordered before nearing the one-way mirror to study the woman who had started it all.

The interview room door stood closed, and as Carter took hold of the handle, he said, "She doesn't know what Mirabelle told us."

"For all she knows, Grady Willis just threw her under the bus," she agreed, though she sounded insecure.

Deep down she was roiling with apprehension and by the looks of him so was her partner.

The case would either live or die based on Wilhelmina's confession.

Carter whipped open the interview room door for Danny and followed her inside.

As she came to the table, Wilhelmina didn't acknowledge her, but straightened her spine and directed her attention to her 1-800 attorney, whose sharp eyes, slicked-back hair, and aggressive pen tapping implied he'd already formulated a solid strategy to keep his client out of prison.

"Detective Foster," Danny said, making introductions as they settled onto the chairs opposite the attorney and client. "And this is Dobbs."

"Feinstein," he replied, as he skimmed his handwritten notes. He proposed, "Ms. Bauer would like to cut a deal."

"Would she now?" asked Danny, as surprise commingling with outrage flared hot in her chest. She touched eyes with Carter, who looked insulted. "From where we're sitting, we've got her on a decades worth of felonious sexual assault of a child in the first degree. That's a Class B felony."

"Yes, that *would be* a Class B felony," he condescended. "But I doubt you have that. At best you pressured a troubled transgendered teenager who has a history of mental illness and eating disorders to generate *false memories* in order to incriminate my client. Come on, detectives, you know Mirabelle Bauer's statement will never hold up in court. Let's not waste time. My client was a victim in all of this, after all."

Refusing to admit to herself that Feinstein had just single-handedly slaughtered her resolve, Danny challenged, "Oh, she was a *victim*?"

Carter sat, silently fuming that the attorney had used the ultimate weapon against them—implying that Mirabelle suffered from 'false memory syndrome.'

"How was she a victim?" Danny pushed.

"It's nice of you to ask," he said with a smile. He set his pen down and thoughtfully clasped his hands together. "My client was terrorized, a prisoner in her own home, powerless under Grady Willis's control-"

"Who she was financially supporting," Danny pointed out. Next she rattled off a long list of examples that illustrated Wilhelmina's freedom. "She was held captive by a man who she left on a daily basis? Who had no physical control over her? Who had no way of preventing her from going to the police to report the abuse that was being inflicted on her daughter?"

Danny laughed. "Pardon me," she went on. "I meant to say 'inflicting on Wilhelmnina's *son'* who she was injecting with prescription-grade estrogen despite the serious risks it posed to his health! She did all of this so that she could have the pretty little girl she'd always wanted? Yeah," she scoffed, "your client's a walking billboard for victimization."

Recuperating from a state of intense fragility, Wilhelmina told Danny, "What do you know about it? Are you even a mother?"

The question landed like a fist to Danny's chest, but the detective refused to react.

"You abused your daughter in concert with Grady Willis," Danny said unemotionally.

Vexed, Wilhelmina pointed her finger at Danny and blurted out, "You have no idea what a filthy little brat he was!"

Feinstein wrangled his client back onto her chair.

Caught off guard, the phrase *filthy little brat* bounced around Danny's brain, but she shook it off, vaguely aware that Feinstein was in the midst of explaining:

"Ms. Bauer is willing to tell you what she knows about the abuse, and everything Grady did, which she had no part of."

Wilhelmina tapped him on the shoulder and when he leaned in, she whispered something in his ear. He nodded his head as if her suggestion was good.

"She'll give a statement in exchange for full immunity," he offered.

Outlandish!

Danny leaned across the table and sneered, "You're out of your mind."

"You have to understand," Wilhelmina pleaded, as a pained grimace came over her face that wasn't at all convincing. "I love her. I never meant for anything bad to happen to Mirabelle."

Carter fired back, "What about when she was your son? Ever mean for anything bad to happen to her then?"

"You don't know what it was like," she insisted, ignoring her attorney's attempts to silence her. "I was going to kill my baby boy." She sucked in a quick, quavering breath, Feinstein begging her—*don't say another word*—but Wilhelmina's woes were already tumbling out of her. "It was exhausting trying to stop myself. I don't know if it was postpartum

335

depression. I couldn't stand him, I just couldn't!" she sputtered as though the memory of nursing her baby left a bad taste in her mouth. "Allowing my boyfriend-"

"She didn't 'allow'," corrected Feinstein. "You have to stop talking!"

But she ignored him in favor of being understood.

"Allowing Grady to discipline my son was all I could do not to hold a pillow over his face! He cried constantly. He destroyed my body and my life. I don't condone what Grady did, but how is it worse than me killing my son? Mirabelle is alive and well-"

"She's far from well," Carter informed her.

"Grady should be locked up, I fully agree," she went on. "But I am a victim in all of this! You don't know what it's like to be a mother! It cuts you off from the world! It cuts you off from your *dreams*, and it eats you alive! Oh, and the crying! All those shrill cries," she choked, disgusted, cringing. "I could've killed that little boy, but Grady intervened!"

Feinstein pinched the bridge of his nose, defeated.

Wilhelmina was just getting started.

As Carter began asking questions about the night of the murder, Wilhelmina was more than willing to explain as much as she could.

But when he started really pushing—*you bashed in her skull, raped her post-mortem, stuffed her in a suitcase!* Wilhelmina's shocked reactions appeared genuine to Danny. Her shouted replies sounded authentic—*that's what happened? I didn't do that! My God!*—as she spoke over her attorney and his half-hearted attempts to shut her up.

Danny was suddenly consumed with all that Wilhelmina had said about being a mother. It disturbed her.

Wilhelmina had been disgusted with her son's incessant shrieking, the way in which he'd shattered her otherwise independent life. She could have smothered him and restored her sanity.

She could have killed him.

Filthy.

Jarred, the word echoed through Danny's mind, but the voice attached to it wasn't Wilhelmina's.

The last thing you needed was a filthy, little boy.

Danny shook her head, willing herself to focus on the interrogation at hand.

Everything happens for a reason.

Nora's tone slithered through her brain, jerking her off balance.

Everything happens for a reason.

A reason?

Why had her mother said that?

What was the reason Gregory had died?

You don't need anyone except me.

Her mouth went dry. Carter was staring at her expectantly, but she couldn't place where they were in their line of questioning. "Ah," she muttered. "Mirabelle..."

"Told us about the abuse," he supplied, sensing something was off with her. He kept glancing at her but she couldn't connect with him. He said, "She also told us her aunt had figured it out."

Abruptly, Danny bolted to her feet, she had to get out of there. Her mother's snide comment cut through her mind again—*the last thing you needed was a filthy little boy.*

"You okay?" asked Carter.

"Water," she said confusedly.

It made enough sense to Carter, so he resumed asking Wilhelmina question after question, as he angled across the table.

She slipped out of the interview room and leaned against the door as soon as she'd closed it.

It felt like her brain was splitting apart. She told herself she must be losing it, that she needed to get a grip. Yet dark thoughts kept swelling inside her, causing her mind to reel with disturbing possibilities—Gregory had cried almost constantly just like Wilhelmina's son, the woman would've killed Mirabelle had Grady not intervened, but Danny had never wanted to kill her son...

Danny hadn't been home the night he died, though...

Nora had been watching the baby...

"No!" she insisted out loud as soon as the connection had formed.

She walked briskly into the break room, fumbled for a plastic cup beside the water bubbler, and with shaking hands, held the lever down, begging herself to forget, as ice-cold water streamed from the spout.

As she drank, water dribbling down her chin, she mentally wrestled with flashes of the aftermath of Gregory's death—going to the hospital, falling apart, her mother calmly consoling her, *you don't need anyone except me.*

Nora had driven Tommy away.

She had stripped all traces of Gregory from the baby's room.

There was no one in Danny's life other than Nora.

You don't need anyone except me.

What if...?

Smothering... Danny had said it herself when she'd disclosed to Sauter in that jail cell, freely admitting how truly suffocating her mother could be.

There hadn't been an autopsy. There was no need.

"Gregory died of SIDS," she reminded herself, trying desperately to abandon all suspicion.

Absently, she felt for her cell phone and the next thing she knew she was dialing a familiar number.

Jill Andover picked up on the third ring.

"Hey, kid," said the medical examiner in a friendly manner.

"I need a favor," she said in a hollow voice that sounded strange to her own ear. She didn't feel like she was attached to her own body anymore, but floating above it. "Can I get an autopsy on an infant?"

Jill let out a breathy laugh, reminding her, "That would be my job, wouldn't it?"

"It's not for a case," she said, elaborating only to add, "the infant will need to be exhumed. I'll fax over the paperwork."

Lowering the phone in a daze as Jill's voice came clipped through the receiver—*you okay? You don't sound like yourself*—she turned to leave the break room, but Carter and Franco were approaching.

They needed to organize their plan of attack against Grady Willis, who the detectives would interrogate next.

As hard as she tried, she couldn't grasp what they were saying.

Every part of her psyche was shutting down.

Chapter Twenty-Four

THE INVESTIGATION accelerated at full speed after Grady Willis and Wilhelmina Bauer had turned on one another from where they sat in separate interview rooms.

Danny worked the alcoholic as he nervously plowed his fingers through his slicked-back ducktail mullet, trying to jumpstart his wet brain into firing on all cylinders.

In the next interview room, Carter played good cop with the model's mother, who had sent her attorney home in favor of selling her boyfriend down the river.

Grady began timidly, a crass comment here—*the boy had always looked girly*—a perverse justification there—*teaching the boy his place*. Something in his tone made her proceed warily. At first, he didn't so much confess as *confide*, doling out tidbits of his depraved escapades as if the detective might share his degenerate morals.

Formal interrogation techniques told her to remain silent, and after a minute or so of giving the pedophile her full attention—keeping her expression neutral, replying evenly when appropriate—the techniques paid off. Grady barreled headlong into a confession though it was glib, saturated in smug comments, and came with, worst of all, intermittent leers for approval. He had an attorney present, but the guy was a public defender and secretly rooting for Danny to lock his client up and throw away the key.

As she listened, her stomach churned and bile stung the back of her throat, his descriptions were so disturbing.

Then she had a sudden epiphany relevant to Grady's initial visit to the precinct. He had insinuated that Lewis Sauter had seduced Agatha as a means to get to the girl and molest her. At the time, it had struck Danny as plausible, but the greasy deadbeat hadn't been speculating about Sauter, she now realized. Casting a smokescreen, Grady had in fact been talking about himself, projecting what he'd done to Mirabelle onto the gift shop janitor.

Danny glared at the despicable son-of-a-bitch with disdain, as his attorney explained to him the benefits of pleading guilty.

When all was said and done during the two simultaneous interrogations, however, neither suspect had copped to the murder. But there was a silver lining.

Grady had insisted his girlfriend had gone to Agatha's house on the night in question. At the same time, he had provided an alibi that exonerated him from the murder, leaving his girlfriend guilty of the crime.

The district attorney had been watching the interrogation unfold from the other side of the one-way mirror, and soon she was eager to issue a search warrant. She wanted to help in any way she could to get Wilhelmina Bauer off the street.

Silver linings were sweet. They got their warrant.

Before sending the detectives to the Bauer's apartment on the other side of Kensington, Franco briefed Danny and Carter on the importance of locating the murder weapon, suitcase, and wooden object.

"We've got them on child sexual abuse. That's it. We know Wilhelmina murdered her sister, but unless we can prove as much, this case will go cold. Remember, she didn't confess."

With the full force of SVU's forensic team behind them, both Danny and Carter were itching to bag and tag every last fiber.

The detectives stormed into Wilhelmina's cramped apartment and began searching all crevices and hidey-holes, scavenging through haphazardly stacked boxes and miscellaneous relics throughout Bauer's home.

At the onset, Danny challenged herself to operate like a machine—unemotionally, single-mindedly, pushing all concern for her son and the circumstances surrounding his death from her worried mind. It was all she could do to keep from shattering.

But as the night wore on, doubts and fears gradually crept in. She was acutely aware that at this very moment across town Jill Andover was dissecting her son's remains in the bowels of Kings County Hospital.

Standing in front of the bedroom closet while forensic investigators combed through the living room, Danny handled an outrageous amount of disturbing photographs she'd found amidst Grady's possessions—Matthew Bauer at countless ages, in various states of undress, suffering unimaginable harm.

She recalled that dreary morning at the lake when she'd skimmed through the muddy 5x8's of John

Unknown and a strange calm had washed over her realizing that her own son would never be exploited, would never cower or cry at the hand of an abuser, never feel terrorized or powerless.

But in his final moments Gregory *had* been terrified and powerless…

Riveted, she pushed the horrifying thought from her head and reminded herself not to jump to conclusions.

From the living room, one of the investigators shouted, "We've got a printer here! Epson PictureMate!" while his peer celebrated—*scanned the laptop hard drive, we've got years-worth of child exploitation!*

But Carter snapped in a furious reply, "Where's the murder weapon? Where the hell is it?" He stampeded through the apartment and appeared in the bedroom doorway where he scowled, "It's not here!"

Startling, Danny faced him and confirmed, "I haven't found anything either except for more child porn."

He kicked a shoebox that was blocking his entry then circled it, fuming, his square jaw tightening. "There should be something here. Blood, a Nolan & Weisman suitcase, the murder weapon, *something*." When he realized his partner had sat on the edge of the bed, he asked, "What's with you?"

She snapped out of it again, focusing on his frustration, the defeat in his intense eyes, the rage rolling off him. He could explode at any moment, though his pacing seemed to keep the impulse at bay.

She's going to get away with it, thought Danny, but out of respect for Carter who looked tormented with grief, she did not voice her prediction.

"They're going to be locked up for life," she assured him.

"Wilhelmina did it," he insisted, convinced, as he took another lap around the room, walking it off. "We've got a motive. We've got Willis placing her in her sister's house. How are we supposed to convict her without evidence?"

"Carter," she said, rising to her feet but keeping at a respectful distance. "She's going to prison."

Calming himself, he ran both hands over his shaved head as though it was all he could do not to come apart at the seams.

"Something else happened that night," he ruminated, his hands now on his hips, gaze fixed on the bedroom window where sheets of rain were slapping the glass pane. "Wilhelmina's deranged, but I don't see her violating her sister's corpse... something else went down that night... something else..."

She was about to comment when her cell phone began vibrating in the back pocket of her jeans. Distracted, she checked the LCD screen and her heart lurched up her throat as she registered who the caller was—Jill Andover.

"Excuse me," she said, as she drifted towards the open doorway.

Carter's face said it all. He was fed-up, so she rounded into the hallway, pressing her cell to her left ear.

"Jill?"

The medical examiner's voice came low and serious through the receiver. "I don't want to do this over the phone."

Her stomach bottomed out, and as she keeled forward, she steadied her balance by bracing the wall. She began inching towards the living room, taking one rocky step after the next. Her shoulders hunched and her head hung, every cell in her body nervous to hear the truth.

"Danny?"

"Yeah," she found herself saying, so overwhelmed that she'd lost all concept of her surroundings. The living room whirled all around her.

"Can you come by my office?"

She padded into the kitchen area where forensic investigators were no longer rifling through clutter. "I'm in the thick of it."

"I really don't want to do this over the phone," she repeated, remorseful in her low tone.

"Just tell me, Jill."

"How did you find Gregory that night?"

"What do you mean?"

Briefly hesitating, Jill closed her office door, the sounds of which came faintly through the receiver. Optimistically, she suggested, "The cause of death could have been *positional* asphyxia-"

"Speak English, Jill!" she snapped.

"Did you find Gregory on his stomach, perhaps with a blanket near his nose, something blocking his airways?"

"No, he was on his back. What does it mean?"

Again, she fell silent for a heavy moment. "If he was on his back and there were no signs of positional asphyxia that's why his death was thought to be caused by Sudden Infant Death Syndrome."

Relieved, Danny let out a stuttering breath.

"But SIDS babies are generally between two and five months old," she went on. "They typically die during winter. These two criteria don't factor into your son's death."

Reeling with dread, she demanded, "What are you telling me, Jill?"

Danny knew Jill didn't want to have to say it. But she came out with the truth, sounding more like a pained friend in this moment than an expert.

"When a baby dies of SIDS, an autopsy won't uncover signs of trauma like rupturing of the blood vessels in the lung walls or inflammation in the respiratory system... Or any symptoms that result from smothering and suffocation."

Danny's knees buckled, but she caught the kitchen counter.

"I found clear signs that Gregory was struggling to breathe," she said, deeply regretful. "If I had examined your son after his death, I would've ruled it as infanticide. Danny, your son was killed."

A lump rose in her throat and tears were suddenly pouring down her face.

Carter took immediate notice, having joined the investigators in the living room.

"Hey," he said, approaching her.

She bolted to the apartment door and groped for the doorknob, her vision blurring, Jill expressing her deepest condolences in her ear—*I'm so sorry, Danny, I'm so sorry, who was with him?*

Spilling into the corridor and whipping the door shut behind her, she did not want Carter or any of them to come after her, to voice concern or console her. She didn't want to talk or explain, but to simply snatch a breath of privacy and release the emotions she had bottled up.

Danny thought she could pull herself together and fake her way through this harrowing, nightlong search for evidence. But Danny was wrong.

There would be no way to overcome what was now crashing over her—unbridled horror.

The truth of that night—her mother had killed her baby—scrambled her mind and sliced through her heart, sucking the air out of her lungs.

As she barreled towards the elevator, she didn't realize she'd let her cell phone slip through her hand, that it had shattered against the hard laminate floor. She didn't hear Carter step out into the corridor and call after her, as she ducked inside the elevator car.

The next thing she knew she was crossing through the lobby, stumbling and shuffling, every part of her shutting down as the horrifying truth swallowed her.

When she burst out onto the sidewalk, sheets of chilly rain bit into her.

Traffic swooshed past in either direction, the night sky pressing in.

Without warning, she began walking faster and faster, her legs moving as if on their own.

She saw nothing but felt everything—she was anguish personified—as Kensington pulsed all around her, sleepy and surreal, a waking nightmare masquerading as a familiar cityscape… one in which she knew she wouldn't survive.

Chapter Twenty-Five

LEWIS SAUTER STOOD in the pouring rain—his denim jacket soaking, his jeans stiff and uncomfortable—and eyed a familiar brown sedan that was parked across the street from his little friend's apartment building.

Crown Victoria, 2007, license plate number XVF9878, empty except for a lifeless cherry siren resting on the floor in front of the passenger seat, the vehicle belonged to the object of his obsession, the detective with the slanted mouth who he had been admiring from a distance ever since he'd been released from the precinct jail.

Touching the slick hood of the sedan as rain bounced off it, he mentally conjured the woman's impish smirk he'd sketched over and over again, those sad puppy dog eyes, the dimple that had puckered her left cheek when she'd gotten sassy with her partner, the way her shoulders had slumped whenever she'd lingered outside of that bar, spying a man who would never love her like Lewis.

But his addicting reverie was soon shattered when the memory of Agatha's vehement eyes came to mind. His German lover had fallen silent, halting in her living room, and those soul-murdering photographs had slipped from her long fingers. Lewis had screamed at her, *she deserves to die for this, let me do it!* Agatha had replied with compassion, *you'll do nothing, I'll talk to her.* It disgusted Lewis.

Why had she defended her monstrous sister?

Why couldn't she feel as outraged as Lewis that her niece had been sexually tortured as a child?

In that moment, confrontation swelling dangerously between them, her severe expression had mutated before his very eyes. The woman he loved had morphed into his mother, his mind playing tricks on him. His cruel mother had made a game of tormenting Lewis his entire childhood…

And Agatha had suddenly reminded him of her.

There had been no way to distinguish between the two of them.

Agatha and his mother were one in the same.

That's when he had known she'd deceived him all along. She wasn't the sweet, generous, regal woman he had fallen in love with, but rather the worst kind of coward.

Realizing this had filled him with hatred so black and vile that he'd quaked with hallucinations of strangling Agatha, squeezing the life out of her, bashing in her skull or drowning her, anything to end his rage.

Looking back, he now understood that the flashing vision hadn't been a fantasy but a premonition.

When he had lurked outside her front door and spied through the window—having returned some forty minutes after slamming the door in her face and walling her out of his life because she had refused to plot her sister's murder, refused to vindicate his precious little friend—the premonition came true.

Agatha had been much too soft on her sister who should've been executed without mercy. And it had cost the German immigrant her life.

When the wind changed directions, chilly rain biting into him sideways, he surged back into his skin.

He sensed the object of his obsession was near even before lightning cracked overhead, brightening the heavy sky and illuminating a woman who was shuffling in the opposite direction along the sidewalk, across the street and half a block away.

Tall, long legs, her signature mop of hair matted from the downpour—Danny.

An omen.

Sticking to his side of the street, he began creeping through the relentless rain, following and slowly gaining on her, glancing over his shoulder every so often to be sure her quarterback partner hadn't emerged from the building with the aim of calling her back to the investigation at hand.

When he came to an intersection, as light traffic whooshed through the orange signal, he jogged to her side of the street and realized she was without her raincoat, the thin sweater she wore sodden and clinging to her hourglass shape, her holstered weapon jostling on her perfect hip.

It was then that he knew she had come undone. He could feel her dark mood. She exuded misery from her lumbering gait, as she walked in a daze. Her head was hung as though nothing in her surroundings was of importance or consequence. There would be no better time for Lewis to act on the incredible connection that he knew tightly bound their twin souls.

Detective Danielle Foster was there for the taking.

Rushing up behind her in the whipping rain, he locked his sights on her gun. He reached out, acutely aware they were alone on a desolate street, and snatched the GLOCK, jerking it from her holster. He thrust the barrel to her spine.

She didn't gasp or flee. She didn't spin around or blindside him with some police academy maneuver meant to overpower an assailant. She merely stopped walking and in a flat, hopeless voice told him:

"Go ahead. Kill me."

There was something beautiful about her brokenness.

Keeping the gun pressed against her body and closing the gap between them, he rounded her, coming face-to-face with Danny, as he pushed the barrel into her stomach.

He gazed into her empty eyes, rain dripping from both their noses.

Lewis wanted nothing more than to bring her to his secret place and never let her go.

"I have a better idea," he said as an aroused grin spread across his face. "Let me share your pain."

Chapter Twenty-Six

THERE'S A FINE line between willingness and resignation, and as Danny entered the German immigrant's stripped-bare bedroom, her own gun digging into her back at the hand of a dangerous man, she realized she had been functioning with neither. Rather, she felt an obscure sense of reckless abandon as though she had divorced from her mind, her body, and the emotions that had threatened to pull her into an endless abyss so deep and dark that if swallowed, she would have forever remained tumbling and desperately clawing with no concept of which way was up.

She had failed to protect her son.

The impulse to destroy her mother had been powerful yet crippling. It had consumed and warped her. She didn't recognize her own thoughts. Her beating heart seemed strange and out of place. Whatever life she was living seemed to have nothing to do with her.

And though the softest, weakest part of her whitewashed mind was silently screaming at her to whip around, jut her elbow hard into his face, wrestle the gun away, and save her skin, the defeated feeling that had taken over her spirit oddly welcomed whatever might happen to her now.

When Lewis nudged her, she stumbled heavy-footed towards the four-poster bed where a mattress, as naked as the walls surrounding it, lay crookedly in its frame.

He shrugged off his soaking jacket as he juggled the gun from one hand to the next without taking his dark eyes off of her then let the garment plop onto the floor.

Folded and resting on the dresser was a laundered bath towel, which he tossed at her. There were other signs as well that he'd returned to his dead lover's house since the police-search almost a week ago—a few empty Coke cans crushed and lying on their sides in a corner of the room, the smell of sour whiskey in the air. A drawing had been thumb-tacked to one of the walls, it was of Danny standing beneath the O'Toole's sign.

When she did nothing but clutch the towel, stunned at the sight of her likeness, the exceptional realism of her saddened expression that his drawing had captured, he told her, "Dry off."

Had he been stalking her?

As she blotted her damp face, she said, "I know you didn't kill her."

"Sit on the bed." He motioned the gun towards the crooked mattress then turned his back in favor of opening the top dresser drawer.

A sudden urge swept through her to lunge, strangle her arms around his throat from behind, and choke him to the ground. But just as adrenaline zinged through her veins at the thought, he faced her once again, holding a sketchpad and pencil in his hand.

Perturbed that she hadn't obeyed, his eyes narrowed under the shadow of his hooded brow, and a split second later he advanced on her with astonishing speed, aiming the gun at her head as a reminder of who was in charge.

When the barrel met her forehead, he used his thumb to release the safety mechanism and with whiplash accuracy cocked the gun, forcing a bullet to scrape into the chamber.

"You aren't going to want to be standing for this," he informed her in a tone that was too considerate to trust. "You'll get tired."

She swallowed hard, her gaze fixed on his resolute expression, and lowered to the bed without making any sudden movements.

"You're going to draw me?"

At his command, she scooted backwards across the mattress until she felt the wall behind her shoulder blades.

He sat on the edge of the bed, facing her and crossing his legs, and rested the gripped gun on his folded knee. He placed his sketchpad on the mattress in front of him.

As he studied her, scratching his pencil over a fresh page and glimpsing his progress here and there, her heart rate gradually subsided and trepidation began churning, thick and queasy, in her gut.

"I want to document the *before* and *after*," he explained.

It sounded like a veiled threat, and because of it she realized she was no longer shivering. She was trembling.

"*Before* what?" she asked in a small voice, mentally calculating their proximity and how she might overpower him now that she was coming back into her right mind.

"Before we do what I have planned," he smoothly mentioned.

"What do you have planned?" When he didn't answer, she said, "Is this how you and Agatha spent your time?"

"Don't!" he snapped—Danny flinching in response. He exerted control over his strained tone, finishing the thought, "Don't say her name."

Danny let some time pass as she assessed his shifting mood, and when it seemed he'd fallen into a relaxed trance, sketching her, she said, "You came over here that night, didn't you? You brought the suitcase."

"The suitcase was a gift from Randy," he said dryly without looking at her. "He gave it to her months ago."

"You found out about Mirabelle," she pushed. "You-"

"Is this what you do?" he challenged, staring dead at her. "Distract yourself to keep your world intact?"

She held her tongue in fear she had angered him.

"You ignore your own dark world by focusing on someone else's."

"Maybe," she said. "I think I know what happened that night."

Ignoring her comment, he told her, "We're both ruled by our obsessions. The only difference between us is that I honor my infatuation and you tell yourself it's true love." He let that hang for a moment and as he did, insult and sickening intrigue washed over her. "I'm going to free you, Danny. I'm going to show you how to channel your compulsions, onto me, so that it isn't wasted on a man who doesn't want you."

Tommy surged to the forefront of her mind, but she restrained the impulse to lash out. Instead, she asked, "You've been following me?"

"I've been protecting you," he corrected.

"I'm not obsessed with him," she said, though much to her horror she immediately questioned whether or not he was right.

She had drifted by the bar as if magnetized to the very idea of Tommy on more occasions than she cared to admit. He had filled her thoughts every waking minute and had seeped into her dreams throughout the night. Envisioning Tommy in her life had the power to uplift her often-cloudy moods.

But they had shared something real. They had a chance for a future together. She couldn't have been obsessed. She had every right to be hopeful.

"It blinds you," he went on, having ignored her objection. "Your obsession distorted your judgment."

The statement, its past tense context, the way his confident tone had sliced through her stomach like a knife—there was no mistaking what he was referring to…

Somehow Lewis knew about the worst night of her life.

"No one could've seen that coming," she whispered, willing herself not to believe him.

"You had to spy him that night, had to get your fix so your addiction wouldn't consume you, and it came at a terrible price."

"How do you know that?" she asked in a shaky voice.

The gun was in her face in the blink of an eye, Lewis having lunged at her, and as she breathed heavily, staring down the barrel, he angled over her.

Adrenaline spiked through her veins, every inch of her was poised to claw his eyes out no matter how many times he pulled the trigger. But she knew that if she acted on impulse she would never make it out of this abandoned bedroom alive.

Whispering, "Don't talk back," Lewis relaxed into a seated position, loosening his white-knuckle grip on the gun as if his command over her had nothing to do with it. "I'm psychic, remember? That's how I know."

A tense moment lapsed, Danny's heart bottoming out as self-hating revelations crashed over her. Could he be right? If she hadn't left her apartment that night just to glimpse Tommy, her son might still be alive today.

A glimmer of arousal brightened behind Lewis's eyes as he drank in the sight of her wilting state, his gaze traveling the length of her—those full breasts that had a habit of lactating at the worst possible times, her protruding stomach that refused to return to its original, flat shape.

Was she obsessed?

Had her infatuation with Tommy blinded her?

Was she, by some terrible twist of fate, responsible for her son's murder?

Losing Gregory had jeopardized any possibility of having Tommy in her life.

Had she brought it all on herself by some circular, self-sabotaging design?

What if the man seated across from her, calmly sketching her likeness as he formulated depraved plans of making her his was somehow her equal, somehow meant for her, her true destiny even if it amounted to her own personal hell?

What then?

Rage blossomed in her chest, her pulse suddenly throbbing in her ears, hands shaking, mind going blank and black, her vision tunneling onto his vulgar face, that repulsive scar across his forehead, and without warning, without thinking she sprang towards him, screaming, "No!"

She tackled him off the bed.

In an instant, her fists were flying.

When they hit the ground, they began thrashing in a nasty tangle, Danny fighting for the gun that Lewis was struggling to angle at her chest.

She shrieked:

"You brought me here to violate me, postmortem, just like you did to Agatha's dead body! You knew she wouldn't stop her sister. You let her get murdered, and then you succumbed to your obsession, having her one last time, you sick piece of garbage! I'm nothing like you! Goddamn you! I'm nothing like you!"

As they wrestled in an ugly struggle for the gun, she knew with every fiber of her being that she would kill him if he didn't kill her first.

BANG.

Chapter Twenty-Seven

"YOU'RE HOME," said Kathy, her voice husky with sleep from where she stood at the foot of the stairs like an Athenian goddess, her blonde hair tousled and spilling over her shoulders, the white nightgown she wore hanging off her every curve, her blue eyes big and dreamy.

Carter had been seated on the living room couch in semidarkness, listening to rain tick against the windows, and brooding for what had felt like hours, his partner's sudden disappearance weighing heavily on his mind.

"I would've come up but I didn't want to wake you," he said absently as he mentally replayed his lieutenant's profound lack of concern for Danny's whereabouts. Carter's urgent, dead of night phone call—*she walked out of the search, I can't reach her, she didn't answer when I rang the buzzer at her apartment, I'm worried*—had been met with Franco's hard-boiled attitude—*so you're telling me Danny was acting like Danny?*

Something happened, he had insisted, resisting every urge to add *I can feel it.*

When Carter didn't elaborate, Kathy glided towards him through the living room.

"Is everything okay?" she asked in a soft tone, as she noticed the shattered cell phone he was holding in his hands.

"You don't want to hear it."

"Carter," she said, as she sat beside him and rested her warm hand on his thigh. "I don't think either of us has been ourselves lately." After falling silent at a loss for words, she told him, "We have to tear down this wall between us, and I know I had a hand in building it, but…"

He glanced at her, hopeful.

"I'm working on giving you the benefit of the doubt and trusting you," she assured him. "The more I know about what's going on with you, the easier that will be, so talk to me."

Running his big hand down his face, he pulled himself together and when their eyes met, he said, "Danny ran off while we were wrapping up our search. I haven't been able to get in touch."

A nervous wave rippled through her expression. Carter could almost see her mustering the resolve it would take to have a conversation about the other woman in her husband's life. She pressed her full lips together a few times, hunting for the right words to say, then offered, "Did you try calling her?"

He indicated the broken cell in his hand before explaining, "This is her phone. I went by her place. I know she isn't there."

For some reason, ever since he had watched his partner duck into the elevator earlier that night, the first day of the investigation had been lurking in the back of his mind. The way the bodega clerk—portly and greasy and stuffing packs of cigarettes into an overhead display—had dodged his questions was troubling him. In his gut, Carter had known the guy was withholding. He'd sensed—intuitively and profoundly—that if he'd taken the clerk downtown, locked him in an interrogation box, and leaned on him hard, then some critical aspect of the truth would've been brought to light.

He couldn't explain why, but he deeply sensed that returning to the bodega across the street from Prospect Park would somehow rectify matters with the case, or perhaps with Danny. There was something to it, but he couldn't fathom what specifically.

Kathy lifted him out of wooly contemplation by rubbing his arm, and asked, "Where did you go just now?"

Stumped, he shook his head, rejecting his hunch.

"If I'm certain about anything," she went on in an encouraging tone. "It's that you're damn good at what you do. So, if you think something's wrong, then it is. And if you have an idea of how to fix it, then that's what you need to do."

He searched her kind eyes for a long moment, his chest swelling with immense and unexpected gratitude that the woman he'd fallen in love with, the mother of his children and light of his life, had returned behind those bright blue eyes.

When his eyes misted over, she whispered, "What?" with a smile.

"I just love you," he said softly, "that's all."

Dawn broke through the balmy streets of Kensington, as Carter drove, windshield wipers pulsing, through the drizzling rain. He was itching to radio the precinct and request backup, but for what, he didn't know. Clenching his jaw to restrain the urge as fire broiled in his gut, he angled the sedan along the curb in front of the bodega that had been consuming his thoughts.

The storefront gate was rolled up, dim lights were on inside, and as Carter climbed out of his parked vehicle into the dreary morning, he noticed the entrance door was propped open by an inch with a rubber stop.

He would have to proceed confidently and with only the subtlest edge of intimidation, exerting the kind of muscle he had failed to use a week ago, if he expected to get the truth, the whole truth, and nothing but the truth out of the man who had eluded him.

After letting out a jutting breath and forcing some air into his lungs, he tempered his unease and whipped the door open, entering the bodega.

Whether or not it would be his lucky day was up for debate but at least the same clerk was manning the counter—a stringy comb-over covering his otherwise bald head, a lit cigarette dangling from his chapped lips, his black and beady eyes scanning the sports section of the morning paper.

In an assured manner, Carter pulled his badge from his waistband and approached the counter.

That's when it hit him. The acute hunch that had centered on his initial suspect—Sauter. That hunch had never left him, and was suddenly shafting through his mind now. There was only one man who could've taken Danny.

"Lewis Sauter," he stated, locking eyes with the clerk who instantly turned pale at the name. "How do you know him?"

Good, thought Carter as he studied the stammering man, *lead him to believe you already know.*

"I don't want no trouble," he said, snubbing his cigarette in an ashtray on the counter and folding the newspaper.

"Then answer me," he pressed, broadening his shoulders and coming into full height as he clipped his badge on his waistband without glancing down.

"What makes you think I know some guy named Lewis Sauter?" he bluffed.

"Did you do time together?" challenged Carter, exercising the first of many guesses that were springing to mind as he recalled the suspect's long rap sheet and prior connection to Randy Whittaker.

"At one point," he admitted. "But it's not like we were friends in Attica."

"Do you know why I'm here?" he asked confidently.

The clerk froze. The only indication he was terrified was his shifting eyes. He was racking his brain for ways to escape.

"Look, I barely know the guy," he conceded, shrugging anxiously and letting out a nervous laugh that implied the opposite. "He stops in from time to time. I'm nice to him based on our history."

"I'll ask you again," Carter said firmly. "Do you know why I'm here?"

Briefly scanning the street outside as if he expected the cavalry to arrive, he ran his hand over his mouth, weighing his profound lack of options.

"I didn't do nothing and I don't want no trouble," he warned in a weak voice.

Carter didn't even blink.

"This ain't about that dead woman they found in the park, is it?"

When the detective narrowed his impatient gaze on the man, the clerk bristled, skimming the clutter of gum and candy bars stacked across the counter as though it would help him strategize.

"It could be much worse than that," Carter finally cautioned. "Sauter might be angling to do it again, and right now I'm dead certain I'm looking at his accomplice."

"Hell no, man!" he said, as he started around the counter. "I'm not going down for this!"

Quickly, he led Carter down an aisle, heading towards the back of the store. He insisted, "I was here that night. People saw me. Then I went straight to my girlfriend's place."

Astonished that any woman in their right mind would willingly go to bed with the guy, he followed the clerk into a walk-in storage closet where items—boxed cereal beside canned beans, diapers next to toilet paper and cleaning products—lined the shelves.

"He asked me for a favor," the man stammered as he began pulling out a brownish-black suitcase that was tucked under a sloppy desk. "I don't know what's in it. I don't know anything about anything."

"Move!" Carter barked, as he dropped to his knees in front of the Nolan & Weisman suitcase, his hand already on his cell phone to call Franco.

Having given the detective some space, the clerk looked on, wringing his hands and murmuring, "I don't even know the guy."

With whiplash speed, Carter laid the luggage on its side, unzipped the large compartment, and was instantly confronted with a marble statue of Lady Liberty—bloody yet majestic—laying beside a toilet plunger and what appeared to be apartment keys.

Immediately, he understood what had happened the night of April 10th after Wilhelmina Bauer had bludgeoned her sister to death.

A sickening feeling rose in his stomach.

If Sauter had Danny…

He choked down the disturbing notion and called his lieutenant, reeling all the while with possibilities of where the deranged culprit might have taken his partner.

In the fifteen minutes it took for Franco and the rest of SVU to pull up outside the bodega, Carter paced anxiously in the storage room. His instincts told him that Sauter was *hiding in plain sight*, but where?

The clerk, dread-stricken, kept bothering him, insisting he couldn't go back to Attica.

"Shut up," he told the guy.

Growing up, Carter had spent years locked in a basement.

The world had gone on without a care, without a clue that a young boy was being held captive inside a quaint house. The white picket fence and quiet suburban block told passersby that this was the home of just another family realizing the American dream.

He had been hidden in plain sight.

What if Danny had been taken to a similar location?

What if she was being held captive somewhere close by, hidden in plain sight?

Carter heard footfall filling the store, SVU investigators had arrived with the lieutenant.

Trusting his burning instincts, Carter grabbed the keys from the suitcase, shoved them deep into the front pocket of his slacks, and walked briskly to meet Franco at the front of the counter.

"I couldn't reach Danny," said the lieutenant whose troubled tone finally matched Carter's concern for his partner.

"The suitcase, murder weapon, all of it is in the storage room. Sauter's guilty of the post-mortem offenses," he quickly mentioned as he threw the entrance door open and stepped into the windy rain.

"Where are you going?" Franco called out.

But Carter refused to waste even one second by pausing to explain.

His partner was somewhere out there, and if he didn't find her as quickly as humanly possible, he knew she wouldn't be alive for long.

As he steered the sedan into the street, he pulled the keys from his pocket and was struck by a sudden revelation.

He maneuvered an ambitious U-turn before hitting the gas, having realized what the keys belonged to, and barreled full force and headlong towards the intersection of Cortelyou and McDonald. The house where Lewis Sauter had reveled in lustful degradation of his once-breathing lover was blazing in the forefront of Carter's mind.

He knew the location where Sauter would have likely returned to, seeking the same twisted pleasure.

The ticky-tacky house, damp and shoddy, was bathed in misty shadows. Morning light cut through spotty clouds overhead, causing a blinding glare to hit the windshield, as Carter came to a quiet stop along the curb.

He killed the engine, and after climbing out, his heart punched up his throat at how safe and cozy the second floor windows appeared.

Cautiously jogging up the steps, he neared the door, every cell in his body poised to hear commotion inside.

But there was none.

Certain not to make any unnecessary noise, he scraped the key into the lock—it fit—and opened the creaking door. He drew his weapon and listened for any signs that his partner might be somewhere within.

As he crept through the foyer, scanning the empty living room and coming to the foot of the stairs, he sensed he would find them on the second floor.

Edging up the staircase and gripping his GLOCK with both hands, elbows locked, eyes wide and alert, he heard the faintest movement coming from the bedroom. He stilled, listening hard and steadying his heavy breathing, and when all was quiet, he stepped onto the landing.

His blood froze in his veins the second he saw Lewis Sauter filling the bedroom doorway at the end of the hall.

Sauter's shirt was stained with blood. He sneered at the detective.

Carter cocked his weapon, fully prepared to blow the guy's head off.

Carter ignored the vision of Danny's lifeless body though it flashed through his terrified mind.

Just as his index finger stiffened on the trigger, he heard moaning—wet and guttural—emanating from the darkened bedroom.

A strained voice filled the air, "Don't shoot!"

"Danny!" he yelled, charging down the hallway.

Sauter vanished into the bedroom.

Carter spilled in after him and found his partner shivering in a bloodstained crouch on the floor, her back against the foot of the bed, the gun in her right hand loosely aimed at Sauter who was now standing in front of the dresser.

Carter realized she was using her other hand to stop the bleeding where she'd been shot in the thigh.

"Don't shoot him," she breathed in an exhausted daze.

As he dropped to his knees, eyes wide and locked on her wound, the blood seeping between her fingers, she told him, "We need him to testify against Bauer."

"Shhh," he told her, fumbling for his cell phone to call 911. "It's over. You're safe."

Relieved that she'd been found, she slipped away, unconscious.

Carter touched eyes with Sauter and knew that waiting for help to arrive would feel like an eternity passing.

Epilogue

BY SOME MIRACLE, the bullet hadn't punctured a major artery, nor had it struck bone.

After two miserable, doped-up days spent yearning to get the hell out of Kings County Hospital, Danny had muscled onto her crutches against the advisement of her doctor and cabbed it home in the middle of what meteorologists were referring to as *Hurricane Nora*, the destruction of which would be nothing compared to its original.

Danny sat on the edge of her bed, as sheets of rain slapped against the window with such force that the glass pane was rattling in its frame. Outside, the skies were so dark and heavy that if she hadn't known better, she would've guessed it was midnight and not half past four in the afternoon.

The nightstand drawer beside her was open, but she couldn't bring herself to pick up the drawing inside. Instead, she absently studied the woman it depicted—sorrowful, standing with her palm pressed against a rainy window, eyes round and staring at a shadowy man within a bar.

In the sketch, she looked sad, blind, pathetically hopeful that dreams could come true despite the nightmarish world she lived in—could this really be her?

Was it an accurate portrayal of her true self?

Those terror-stricken minutes—or had it been hours?—she had endured with Sauter after he had shot her, after she had wrestled the gun out of his weakening grasp, and after firing again and again into the wall to stun him into obeying her orders, every flashing memory of the ordeal seeped into her thoughts.

After all that, their time together had eventually become something she could have never foreseen…

Though she'd had mixed emotions about it then and still did, he had fulfilled his suggestion; the one he had made to her on the street. Instead of killing her, he had shared her pain.

They had bonded.

She didn't want to think about it, so she slowly closed the nightstand drawer, shutting the sketch inside and deciding that there would be no way to ever know if he'd been right about her obsession with Tommy, or wrong. There was no discerning whether or not he had been genuine when he had identified with her anguish over Nora; no telling if he'd been sincere about his self-proclaimed love for her. And there was also no way of telling if the reason Lewis had become obsessed with Danny was because he'd never learned how to truly love; he'd never been taught…

…and, in his words, neither had she.

One thing was certain, however, she no longer thought of him as *Sauter*. In her mind, he had earned a first name.

Lewis had agreed to testify against Wilhelmina Bauer in exchange for an ever-so-slightly-reduced prison sentence, the district attorney having been only marginally in favor of cutting a deal after honing in on his many post-mortem offenses. The D.A. had argued—*is this a guy we really want out on the street in a decade?*

All told, Lewis would have faced five years for necrophilia, three years for improper disposal of a dead human body, and two years for obstruction of justice, but the DA had generously rounded his sentence down to seven years to be served in Sing Sing where, much to his elation and SVU's chagrin, Mirabelle could visit him from time to time.

The lithe model, who would always have a special spot in Sauter's heart, had been placed in the remarkably appropriate foster home of a wealthy Upper East Side married couple. The bubbly wife was a former cover girl, and her husband was some kind of real estate tycoon. Both were enthusiastic about pouring all of their attention and finances into Mirabelle, her soon-to-commence private schooling, her future and aspirations. The world would be Mirabelle's oyster, and she deserved it.

After tucking her crutches under her armpits, Danny hoisted herself off the bed and, swinging in a strange rhythm with thunder cracking high over Kensington, she made her way down the hallway.

She paused in the doorway of the baby's room. With Carter's help, she had managed to recover the crib from Craigslist though she was only partially certain it had been Gregory's. Likewise he'd done her the favor of dropping off a number of paint cans—the color of green ivy—that she'd asked him to pick up from Home Depot. Someday she would say goodbye to her son, but not before she was ready, and not because the woman who had smothered him out of this world thought it best.

She was not looking forward to doing what had to be done.

Moving slowly and carefully, she locked up her apartment with a new set of keys she'd had made, having hired a locksmith to fortify her home against Nora.

As she used her crutches to make her way through the corridor, cautious about the slick floors and babying her bad leg, she tried and failed not to overthink all that she planned on saying to her mother.

After hobbling down the stairwell, she muscled the heavy door open and edged into the lobby where the building super was standing nose-to-glass in front of the entrance door and looking out in awe of the powerful rainstorm, his ordinarily grumpy, grumbling mood momentarily suspended.

When Camil Usov realized she was coming up behind him, he was quick to open the door.

"We have saying in Russia," he told her offhandedly in that thick accent of his. An easy smile came over him.

"Oh yeah?" she said, lingering in the open doorway as rain sprayed across the threshold. "What's that?"

"Беда́ никогда́ не прихо́дит одна́," he sang, chuckling to himself. When she cocked an eyebrow in response, he translated, "When it rains, it pours."

"Clever," she teased, but the idiom implied that trouble has a way of multiplying. Bad omens. And though Camil seemed tickled by his all-too-literal application, Danny's smile dropped as a quaking sense of dread rolled through her.

She touched eyes with him, returning a somber smile, and began swinging her way into the merciless rain.

Consumed with a dark sense of foreboding, she was hardly present as she hobbled up the sidewalk, climbed her mother's stoop step-by-step, and rang the buzzer.

When Nora's voice came through the speaker-box, crackling with static—*who is it?*—Danny announced herself.

The next thing she knew, she was knocking on her mother's apartment door, visions of Gregory and all that she'd lost ebbing away from the forefront of her mind.

When the door drew inward, Nora was immediately aghast to discover her daughter had been injured.

Danny feigned a friendly smile and asked, "Can I come in?"

"My God," she breathed as she eased backwards, allowing Danny into her cramped and cluttered apartment. "I should've called. I should've stopped by," she began rambling. "I knew something was wrong, but I also knew you were upset with me, and I wanted to give you space."

She closed the door and continued lamenting her many maternal mistakes.

"Ma," said Danny to steer her mother towards what would soon become the most difficult conversation of their lives. "I'm fine. It looks worse than it is."

"Does it?" she asked, her face screwing up with empathetic anguish as she eyed her daughter's leg.

"The case is closed," she said.

"Miracle of miracles!" she exclaimed before bursting out with relieved laughter. Her mother's cackling sounded strangely nervous to Danny. Nora clapped a few times, calming herself, then mentioned, "I have baked ziti if you're hungry. You look thin."

"I'm not hungry," she said, her tone dropping under the weight of her conscience.

Though everything that had happened was all she had been thinking about for days—everything she'd learned based on the autopsy, that gut-wrenching call with Jill Andover—she hadn't been able to bring herself to truly accept the consequences.

And it felt like a ten-ton weight was pressing down on her heart because of it.

Starting slowly and choosing her words carefully, she said, "Ma, I wanted to talk to you about something…"

Nora took a few remorseful steps backwards, her way of inviting Danny into the living room, not that there was any easy place to sit. The apartment was still a labyrinth of clutter, a hoarder's paradise.

She began preemptively apologizing, "It wasn't my place to take initiative with the baby's room, and Danny, you have to believe me when I say, I truly am so sorry about that."

"You called him a filthy little-"

"I know," she said, her hands flying up to ward off the ashamed wake of her unintentional callousness. "I was frustrated, oh! Not with you," she quickly clarified, her eyebrows knitting thoughtfully together as she shook her head, horrified at her behavior. "I did all the wrong things. I said all the wrong things. I *will* say that Gregory did cry a lot," she allowed in a charitable effort to forgive herself. "But I let my impatience get the best of me, and I shouldn't have said and done any of the things that I said and did. I'm sorry."

When it seemed her mother had run out of steam, a terrible war of sadness mixed with vindication began brewing inside of Danny. She wanted to believe Nora. She wanted to trust the innocence that her mother's explanation had implied.

But she couldn't.

Speaking in as neutral a tone as she could manage, she evenly stated, "Ma, I ordered an autopsy for Gregory."

Nora's apologetic expression went long, her aged face turning distinctly serious as she asked in an equally emotionless voice, "You exhumed him?"

"He didn't die of SIDS," she said, unable to meet her mother's darkening gaze.

"That's insane," she blurted out, fully registering the implication.

Mustering enough gumption to look her mother in the eye, Danny said, "I know what you did."

"What are we even talking about here?" she asked, mouth gaping as she let out a baffled laugh. "You're telling me that my grandson didn't die of SIDS? What does that mean? What are you saying, Danny?"

"He was smothered."

"And you think I had something to do with it?" she shot back, fully angered now.

Maintaining a calm demeanor, though it came at the expense of her sanity, Danny told her, "I'm not asking if you did it, Ma, because I already know-"

"This is crazy," she snapped, pacing off not that there was anywhere to go within her maze of ad hoc junk.

Seeing Nora in a panicked tizzy, she realized more than anything that her mother was probably terrified of the repercussions—a trial, prison, and worse, admitting to her own daughter, to the most important person in her world, that she had done it, had stolen Gregory from Danny so that no one would stand between them.

Danny softly told her mother, "I can't handle you getting locked up."

"There has to be some kind of mistake," she interrupted, but her tone had finally betrayed her. She sounded flat and soulless. There was no light behind her eyes.

Danny swallowed hard, choking down emotions that were threatening to tear her apart, and concluded, "I'm not going to turn you in, Ma. I'm not going to report what you did."

"I didn't do anything!"

"You killed my son!"

"I'm sorry!" she screamed.

Staring at her, locking onto her mother's apology, she knew it would be the closest thing to a confession that she would ever get.

A brutal moment of silence followed—Danny's stomach bottoming out with a kick, Nora's eyes gradually brightening in hopes that her daughter might find it in her heart to forgive her.

"I'm not going to have anything to do with you," said Danny though on some level declaring as much crushed her as badly as it did Nora.

"No," she breathed, her knees buckling.

"It doesn't matter that we live close by in neighboring apartment buildings," she tried to assert. "You'll never see me again. I think that's punishment enough."

"Please, Danny, don't," she pleaded, her tone cracking as though her spirit was being ripped from her body. "I'll do anything."

"It's too late for that," she said in a small, disappointed voice before whispering, "take care."

It was a very long walk to the lobby.

When she stepped outside into the downpour, she didn't feel the chilly rain pounding over her; didn't care or even realize that she had never bothered to throw on her raincoat or galoshes.

She started down the sidewalk, swinging on her crutches, the soggy sneaker of her good leg splashing through puddles as she went, but she didn't turn up her own stoop.

When she came to the first intersection where, across the street, Tommy's bar stood dark and empty, an eerie sense of hope began replacing the despair that had filled her mind, body, and soul.

He simply had that effect on her. Whether it was good, bad, or ugly, it was true.

As she considered the disturbing possibility that she might in fact be obsessed, the storm let up, receding with almost miraculous speed.

Just then, the sun broke through, dazzlingly bright, and the glory of it felt like an answer to all her doubt.

Suddenly, the wooden door of O'Toole's swung open and Tommy emerged, stepping out onto the sidewalk and examining the fragile sky, awestruck that the hurricane had vanished.

Lowering his gaze, their eyes met then locked.

When he smiled in a way that couldn't be misunderstood, she returned the sentiment and knew, for all her questioning and for all the pitfalls and frustrations of the harrowing case she had survived, that this day, this moment, connecting with Tommy O'Toole from across the street in the blazing sunshine—a simple, beautiful exchange that held a world of promise—marked the beginning of the rest of her life.

It felt like she had just gotten home.

THE END

Please take a moment now and leave a review if you enjoyed this novel!

ALSO BY MIRA GIBSON

Thomas from the Sea

Who Killed Leeanne?

The Kensington Killers: The Complete Series
Lunatic (The Kensington Killers, Book One)
Crank (The Kensington Killers, Book Two)
Maniac (The Kensington Killers, Book Three)

The New Hampshire Mysteries: The Complete Series
Daddy Soda (A New Hampshire Mystery, Book One)
Rock Spider (A New Hampshire Mystery, Book Two)
Tar Heart (A New Hampshire Mystery, Book Three)

ABOUT THE AUTHOR

I write mystery novels, detective novels, sleuth mysteries, and psychological literary fiction! You can find me most days working on my computer in the sunshine of beautiful Long Beach, NY where I dream up small town characters and write dark mysteries that are filled with unsuspecting tenderness.

Find me on Facebook! **/MiraGibsonAuthor**

Visit MysteryRoyalty.com to learn more.

www.ingramcontent.com/pod-product-compliance
Lightning Source LLC
Chambersburg PA
CBHW021338310726
48971CB00001B/184